THE LAST RAE OF HOPE
BOOK I: A HERO RETURNED

by Eura "Euphridia" Abrams

Riverfolk Books

The Last Rae of Hope Book I: A Hero Returned

©2023 Eura "Euphridia" Abrams

Cover Artwork by fuyudust – fuyudust.artstation.com
Map by Lara Zanatti Reis

First published in 2025 by Riverfolk Books.

Riverfolk Books
http://riverfolkbooks.com

DEDICATION

This series is warmly dedicated to all the wonderful characters out there trying to be normal in a world that often feels like it's gone off-script. May your journey be graced with the kind of companions who stand by you through the wildest of storms and the brightest of days, ready to share in both the laughter and tears that abound amid the fantastic and absurd madness we call life.

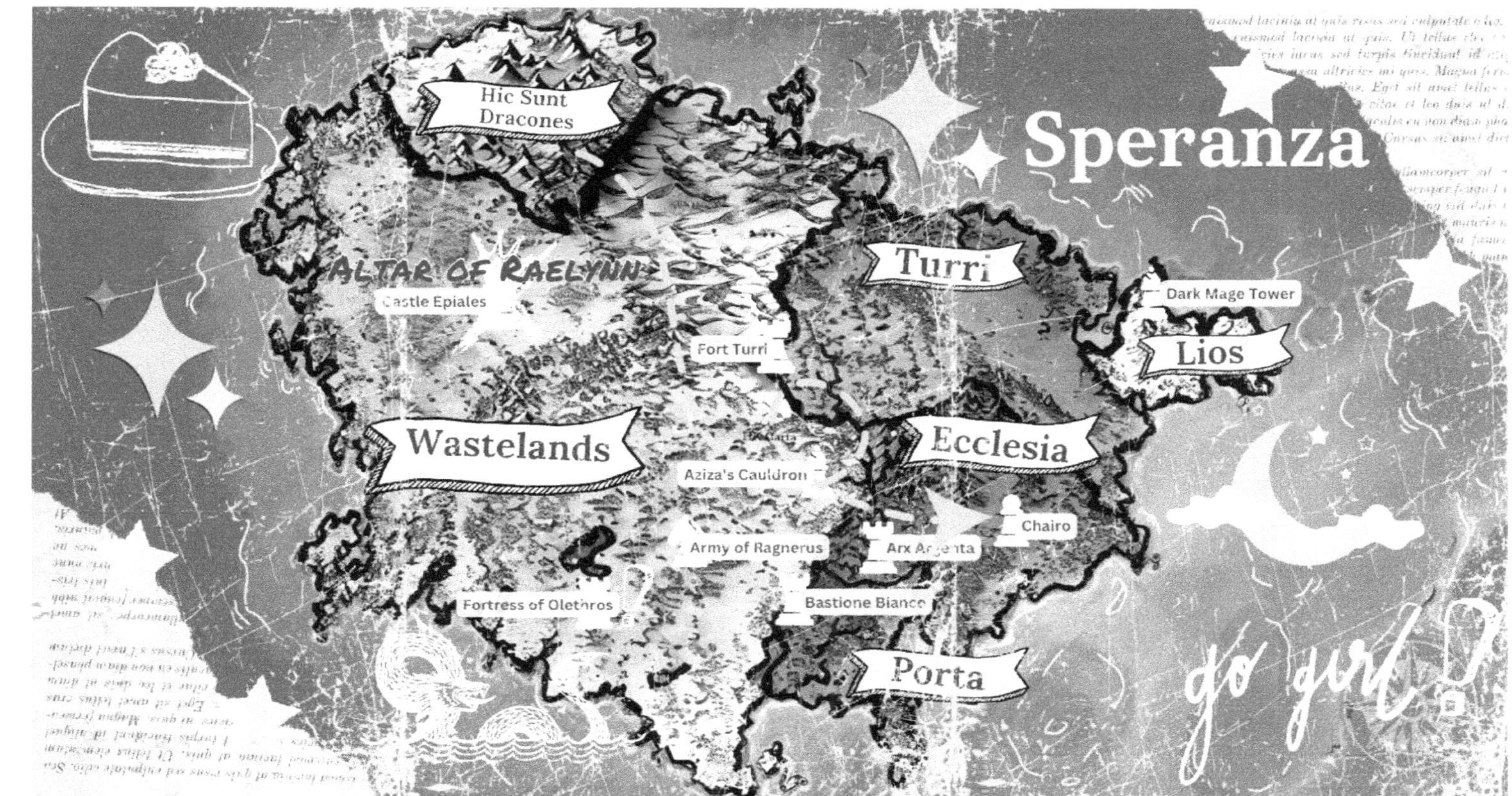

Speranza
Hic Sunt Dracones
ALTAR OF RAELYNN
Castle Epiales
Turri
Dark Mage Tower
Lios
Fort Turri
Wastelands
Ecclesia
Aziza's Cauldron
Army of Ragnerus
Arx Argenta
Chairo
Fortress of Olethros
Bastione Bianco
Porta
go girl!

PROLOGUE: HOW DID I GET HERE?

I wish I could have laughed. Perhaps it was the increasing lack of oxygen to my brain. You'd think being choked to death would be enough to stay my cynical sense of humor, but I found the disparity between my imagined post-high school life and where I was now hilariously at odds.

But you know, I bet almost everyone feels that way when they enter the workforce as a full-fledged adult. Especially when the publishing company you start working for fails to provide the proper training and tools to ensure a safe and comfortable working environment. In fact, I think they've ignored almost every OSHA standard. But I digress.

Shifting focus to my current predicament, I realized the ethereal twilight around us had turned to midnight, blocking out my peripheral vision. The icy hand of encroaching death had already numbed the lower parts of my body, but my head and neck still burned with a sharp, searing pain.

Demon King Olethros, The Dark Serpent, Second of Evil, was living up to his title in earnest, acting like *a giant number two*. Oh, my best friend Nora would have loved that snarky insight, but alas, we had been separated earlier during our epic battle.

I was suspended in midair by his death grip, surrounded by the numerous nightmarish tendrils he commanded from the emblazoned magic circle on the marble floor. The runes of unholy might that formed his power source flared anew as he called upon them, dispersing some of the darkness that had begun to claim me. My sword, the Will of Euphridia, had fallen somewhere into the abyss below, and there was no way I could reach it now.

"I warned you not to come here! I told you to stay away!" he shouted directly into my face as his hand twisted, forcing me to gaze into his evil emerald eyes as inky black animus leaked from their sides. He was right, of course. But that didn't justify *killing* me, did it? I've already died six times, maybe, but just because I've always done it this way doesn't mean I had to do it the same way again.

"You've already lost this fight. Tell me what you know about the Goddess's plans, and I'll make it quick!"

I'd have liked to make a quip about how exactly he expected me to respond while he was crushing my windpipe.

Instead, I spluttered something unintelligible, unable to manage my oral secretions. He relaxed his sharp claws around my throat only slightly, allowing a gasp of air. As the dark haze around us thickened, my thoughts became increasingly morose. *Maybe he was right. Perhaps I was only prolonging my suffering by continuing to breathe.* I had naïvely believed that if I could just have a crucial conversation with him, we could come to a mutual understanding. I mean, I get it. Conflicts at work are inevitable, but they don't have to escalate beyond the point of reason. *Oh, sweet sarcasm, my faithful companion! Thank you for helping me maintain my sanity through my last moments.*

"You're doing this all wrong," Raelana's voice echoed in my mind. *"You know you are well past the point of de-escalation."* Clearly, she, a lingering remnant of a past hero, didn't fully comprehend what I was preparing for.

I know my plan failed. I should just give—

"No. Improvise. Plans are subject to change."

And just what am I—

"Allow me."

My lips parted as Raelana used my voice to shout scornfully, "Your father would have been oh so proud of what you've become, Phorutos!"

Phorutos? That wasn't any name for him that I knew of. But it clearly struck a chord with him.

His face contorted in abject horror and fury. With a bellow, he flung me towards the ground in a fit of unbridled rage. The cold, blood-slick floor welcomed me as lost kin with a hard and muffled thump. The tendrils bound to my hands and legs pulled and retracted back into the magic circle, barring me from standing back up.

You just made him even angrier! What exactly did you call him!?

Raelana Demonslayer let out a spiritual snort of satisfaction. *"His true name means things that mingle in the wind… or more contextually, 'trash.' You will thank me later. Watch."*

"I am nothing like he ever was!" he shrieked, his voice tinged with madness. "How dare you call me that! I will make you suffer for—" His tirade cut off abruptly as a cloud of darkness spewed from his body, plunging him into irrational animus overload. His form began to writhe and convulse behind smoky shadows even as he charged mindlessly towards me. But now that I could breathe properly, away from his dark influence, I could concentrate on the essential things, like focusing my will to break free from the now-weakened shadowy bindings that held me in place.

"Choose, Rachel. How will you end this? With your sword, or…"

The sword, shimmering in the darkness, seemed the safest bet. It was forged by the Goddess Euphridia herself for just this sort of occasion. I didn't have much strength left, either. But I knew he wasn't acting like his *authentic* self, and I would *eventually* regret not taking a chance for a better resolution. If I wanted to make things right and get the *"good ending,"* I would need his help. Either way, I resolved to hold him accountable for his *detestable behavior* later.

I… want to try something different this time.

"Very well. I will continue to help you for as long as I am able."

"…"

What? Another voice? …Which past hero are you now?

"…"

Oh, sorry. Never heard of you.

"…"

You want to know how I got here in the first place? Well… okay, but I'm a bit busy right now, and it'll take a long time to explain. When I have time, we can start by talking about back when I was in high school. All sorts of absurd stories begin there…

CHAPTER 1: HIATUS ANNOUNCEMENT

The cover was whimsical and capricious, with a smiley face here and an inspirational quote there, but on the inside, the note had the panic-inducing words "see me after class" in bold lettering. I was being summoned to the guidance counselor's lair to explain my recent transgressions.

"I don't have time for this," I muttered under my breath as if I were somehow the victim. I hoped the meeting would be quick so I could head to the weight room before the football players overran it. Above all else, I needed to avoid Nora. She'd ask questions, but I wasn't ready to answer them. I crumpled the note in my hand and cautiously surveyed the corridor. Thankfully, it was empty so I could continue to the office with minimal shame.

Upon arrival, I took a deep breath, tugged the long sleeves on my royal blue track jacket to their ultimate length, and opened the door.

The secretary didn't even bother to look up. "Name."

"Rachel," I muttered.

"Which one?"

I admit I had started it, but her demeanor strongly suggested we wouldn't have been friends either way.

"Smith." I let two seconds pass. The secretary scowled. She and I both knew three other Rachel Smiths were attending this school.

"E. Smith," I clarified and waited for a few moments. Another Rachel had that same middle initial, too.

It was about time I put it all together.

"Rachel *Emily* Smith."

Do you know how many people in this world have the same name? Seriously, look it up if you have the chance.

"Why didn't you just say that to begin with?" she demanded with an exasperated sigh. I offered a half-hearted shrug, trying to convey a hint of apology. She pulled up my file on the computer screen and checked me in. "You're late. Dean has been waiting for you."

Dean? Why do guidance counselors insist on first names?

With a curt nod, the secretary pointed towards a door down the hall. Already, I could imagine at least two motivational posters adorning the walls. Maybe the one with a cat on a rope with the caption "Hang in there!"

After walking down the hall and stepping inside, I was sorely disappointed. This must have been the *demotivating* room instead. It didn't help that the vertical blinds cast shadows reminiscent of bars in a prison cell. Mr. "Dean" was nowhere in sight, so I took a seat on a cold metal folding chair, my gaze fixed on the gray cement walls. Wasn't he supposed to be waiting for me? Karma for annoying the secretary, I suppose.

The minutes ticked by from the square metal clock imprisoned on the wall within a steel cage. My eyes eventually drifted over to the shatter-proof mirror at the end of the room, positioned about six inches lower than my natural height with a caption that read "Did you smile today?"

I wandered over to it.

"I was smiling just fine until I was told to come here; thank you very much," I told the defenseless mirror as I bent down to get a good look at myself. My coppery blonde hair was starting to grow out of its choppy bob. The ends were curling this way and that, but I could now pull off a ponytail if I needed to. I sort of liked the way it did whatever it wanted without regret. I took off my thick, rectangular frames and blinked several times. I looked better without them, but unfortunately, contacts were simply not an option. My eyes had a bit more gold than most hazel eyes, which I figured was the universe's way of apologizing for such poor vision. It's too bad it had placed value on form over function.

I tried distracting myself by making several ridiculous faces, but suddenly, I was struck with the idea that maybe this room was also under surveillance like every other part of the school. I quickly sat back in my seat and waited quietly, nervous that someone saw me acting like a goofball.

Get it together, Rachel. You have to act normal.

After an eternity or so, rounded up, a middle-aged man dressed in slacks and the quintessential "dad sweater" entered the room. I glanced at the clock and saw it was already half past four. My workout plans were definitely off the table now.

"Hello, Rachel. My name's Dean. Would you mind if I called you Rachel? Or do you have another preferred name?"

"Rachel's fine."

Get to the point already.

Of course, deep down, I knew I would be annoyed with anything coming from his mouth. I knew I wasn't here for a *good* reason.

"Rachel, you haven't completed your post-high school plan essay. It's required for graduation, so it's quite important."

I know, I know.

He looked at me with a hint of concern. "This isn't like you, Rachel."

Really? You're the guidance counselor for over three hundred students. How could you possibly know what I'm like?

"I just…" Just what? Ah, no, I had some sort of excuse but lost it.

I began scratching nervously at my right wrist. Dean glanced down at my hand, and I quickly pulled it inside my jacket.

"Rachel, I get the sense that something's bothering you."

There he goes, using my first name *again*. Just because I said you could use it doesn't mean it should be in every one of your sentences. Do you think we'll become friends if you say it enough? That's just dollar-store psychology right there, and it's pretty transparent when the other party knows what you're trying to do.

He attempted a reassuring smile. "Why don't you tell me what you're thinking about?" I looked away and said nothing. He waited a while, but I outlasted his patience and made him surrender first. I was adept at the war of awkward silences, and I could be pretty stubborn.

"Rachel, I'll give you a five-day extension, okay? Please take some time to think about what you want to do. You're a bright kid." I think he meant "You haven't committed any known felonies, so there's still hope for you."

"Thanks." I'd be more thankful if you forgot the whole thing, but…

"And since I'm doing you a favor, Rachel, you're going to do a favor for me, too."

Whoa, buddy, what?

Dean still had that unchanging smile plastered over his face. "I'm going to review your essay personally, and then we will look at college applications together based on your writing."

College? Weren't applications already due? What if I don't want to go to college? What if I can't afford college? I felt my chest tighten suddenly, draining the strength in my arms and forcing a bead of sweat down my temple.

"Okay," I replied numbly. What is wrong with me? Why couldn't I tell him off?

Because ordinary people don't make a scene. They just go with the flow.

You don't want to stick out, do you?

"I'll see you again on Tuesday at the same time. Oh, and I'll also be discussing this with your mother."

What the heck? Why on earth would you drag *her* into this?

For a fleeting moment, I almost pitied him. However, he had made several assumptions about me and would have to learn the hard way. I'm pretty sure there was an alert somewhere in my file to never, ever contact my mother unless it truly was the apocalypse, but he must have ignored it. Well, rest in peace, *Dean.*

"Yes, sir," I responded in a sullen tone.

"Call me Dean, Rachel."

Oh, that is not happening.

I slunk out of the office and closed the door behind me. How long was I in there? Who was the president now?

"Huhuhuhuhu…" A creeping, evil laughter echoed down the hallway as Nora's petite frame, crowned with long, curly hair, rounded the corner. Her eyes met mine, and to emphasize her displeasure, she slammed a nearby locker door shut as another student finished putting his books in it. He jumped, startled, but opted for a safe retreat as he scurried down the hall.

With a dramatic flourish, she pointed at me with a crooked index finger. "You've been avoiding me since the last bell! We need to talk! NOW!" She might have been able to pull off the intense look if she didn't have such a mischievously mousey face.

"Whatever do you mean?" I asked innocently as I continued to my locker. Like always, my trusty softball bat was waiting for me, and I found its weight comforting. Together with my athletic ensemble, even most teachers thought I was part of the team, but I was just pretending well enough not to get kicked out of the intramural sport. My walk home was long, and I didn't want to go alone. The bat provided extra security, but on school grounds, I had to make sure not to carry it in a menacing way, so I shoved the business end into my sporty backpack.

Nora chased after me. "The latest chapter posted! What are your thoughts? I have so many questions! What did you think about—"

"No spoilers," I interjected, folding my hands piously as I turned to her with an exaggerated wink.

"What? Seriously!?" She stamped her tiny feet in frustration. "Chapter fifty-seven has been up for over two hours already! You're never gonna be in the top ten comments at this rate! BitterDarkTroll53 is already ranking at number three, you know."

I had no intention of competing for top commenter. That would get me unwanted attention!

"I stopped reading just after the hiatus announcement."

Nora wrinkled her nose. "Not cool! I need Rae's opinion on Rae now!" It's not a coincidence that my nickname is the same as the main character's in the story she wanted to discuss. Nora assigned it to me the day we met, and I can't really get her to stop.

Everyone else around here calls me Rachel. I suppose I'm okay with making an exception just for her.

"It's the hiatus that's not cool!" I grumbled. "That means it probably ends on yet another cliffhanger, and there's no real guarantee the author's coming back soon. I'm not strong enough to go through this again with another story…" I theatrically slammed my back into a set of lockers to make as much noise as possible as she pulled out her phone.

"Tomorrow, my house, three o'clock," Nora commanded. "You will be caught up through chapter fifty-seven, and we will discuss this like the sophisticated adults we will someday actually be. You may bring visual aids if necessary, as long as you don't forget the snacks. We'll need to work on an action plan."

What? It's so bad we need an action plan?

"I don't know if that will be possible," I admitted.

She glowered at me with violet eyes. "Why?"

"Dean's going to call my mother."

"Who the F is Dean?" I wasn't censoring her right there. She actually said the letter *F*.

"The guidance counselor."

"Ah! What's with guidance counselors and first names?"

Thank you!

"He wanted to talk to me because I didn't finish that essay."

She cocked an eyebrow. "*You* failed to turn in an assignment on time?"

"Maybe I'm finally rebelling?" I suggested. While I wasn't a star student in most ways, finishing my work on time was typically a point of pride.

"Doubtful. Try again."

"It's a stupid assignment." I slid down the lockers to sit on the floor.

"Well, yes, but that's not why you didn't do it either."

With a resigned sigh, I said, "I just don't want to talk about it. Let's change the subject."

"Okay, read the chapter now, and we'll discuss it." She gestured towards my backpack.

I crossed my arms, feeling a bit stubborn. Our conversations always circled back to the story when we had nothing else to chat about. Couldn't we find another mutually agreeable topic? What if we have nothing else in common? Since moving here, I had tried so hard to be normal, fit in, and be just like her, my first and only real friend. But what if…

Nora settled down beside me. "You're afraid to check on Schrödinger's cat, aren't you?"

I sighed at being slightly misunderstood but decided it would be easier to just go with the flow. "Even if it's alive in there, it reeks of decaying flesh. A climactic chapter followed by a hiatus announcement is the telltale sign of literary abandonment."

Despite my deeper concerns, I was still curious about what the chapter had to say. "Raelynn won, right? I mean, she always does so…" I paused. "Wait, no, no spoilers! It's just, you know, she's so overpowered. Of course, she has reason to be, but nothing can *really* happen to her. She's the hero!"

I ignored Nora's baleful stare and continued, "Relias is okay, too, right? He's always by Raelynn's side and always seems to know what to say and do to fix the situation. He wouldn't let anything bad happen to her."

Nora hid her face behind her backpack, concealing any hint that may leak through her expression. "You said no spoilers… the audacity of asking me what happened… you…" I might have short-circuited her brain.

"Wait. No. What happened? Something went wrong. No, don't tell me!"

"No. Noooo. I absolutely cannot talk to you about this right now!" Nora stood up and stormed off, leaving the hallway in eerie silence. However, my phone vibrated a few moments later, and messages started popping up one after another.

Nora: *Don't talk to me again until you catch up on your assigned reading!*

Nora: *3 p.m. tomorrow unless you're grounded.*

Nora: *Bring three boxes of strawberry chocolate pretzel sticks.*
Nora: *Wait. One box should be green tea.*
Nora: *After we discuss and plan, I'll help you with your essay.*
Nora: *This doesn't count as talking!*
Nora: *Text back so I know you understand!*
Nora: *Text back!*

I literally texted her the word "back" and put my phone away. Time to go home and talk to… Mother.

CHAPTER 2: CLIFFHANGER

I came through the door to find my mother just finishing a phone call. "Yes, alright." She paused, fixing me with her sharp gaze. "Thank you for letting me know."

Crap.

"Rachel."

"Yes, Mother?" I gave her a sheepish glance as I stowed my bat in the corner behind the front door.

"I spoke with your guidance counselor… Dean." Her nose flared slightly as her dark eyes glittered.

"Oh well, yes, that's what I wanted to talk to you about. You see—"

"You're going to comply with the new deadline?"

"Yes, and—"

"That's fine then." She grabbed her purse.

That's it?

"Wait, where are you going?" I asked.

"Work. I have a new client who prefers meeting during the evening hours. Dinner's on the table. If you don't want it, order takeout."

I gave her a bewildered look. "You're not mad?"

"Should I be?"

"Uh…" Honestly, yes, you should. I mean, I failed to turn in a major assignment. Dean wasn't wrong… it really isn't like me to shut down like this. Shouldn't you be lecturing me? Grounding me? Revoking privileges? At least raise your voice like you do when a stranger irritates you!

Don't just ignore me…

"Oh. About college," Mother added as an afterthought, purse slung over her shoulder and car keys in hand. "If you want to go to college, it's no problem. If you don't, then you don't. It's your choice."

She was way too nonchalant about this. I mean, college fees are expensive! "What about all of the medical bills?" I asked for the millionth time.

She considered the question for less than a second. Actually, that was being generous. She gave it no thought before answering. "They're not your problem to worry about."

Yeah, I get it. I was a minor when it happened, and I'm still a minor for a few months. But that doesn't make the bills magically disappear! Just how much more was there to pay off? If they were no problem, would you be going back to work after dusk? I already told you I'm not interested in going for further scar treatments. Dermatologists ask too many creepy questions about their history!

Mother started walking towards the front door, her long, dark hair swishing in counterpoint with her hips. "If there's something you want to do, you should just do it. Don't let the Deans of the world push you around. Own your choices." She then put on her high heels and stepped outside. My presence felt as inconsequential as the coat rack I stood beside. Though, it wasn't normally her style to say goodbye before leaving.

After the door shut, I continued to stand there, staring at it, consumed by an odd feeling of incompleteness. With a sigh, I walked to the dining room, where I sat at the table and ate dinner in solitary silence. It was slightly bland but palatable, like every other meal she cooked.

After dinner, I entered my room, unlocked my laptop, and stared at the writing prompt. It was almost a habit by now. I knew what it said by heart, but maybe the great prophecy would come if I looked just a *little* harder. The lines of text would unravel like the secret code in a legendary quest, revealing the path I was meant to take.

After a full three minutes, I realized it was futile and looked for something else to do. I loaded chapter fifty-seven of *The Last Rae of Hope*, figuring now was as good a time as any.

> *It was the sulfurous odor of iron and brimstone that brought Rae back to the chaotic scene before her. She lay prone on a rough, cold stone floor, clutching her sword tightly in her right hand. Her shield lay several feet away, battered and misshapen. In front of her, however, was the monstrous corpse of Epiales, Demon King of Nightmare. The golden rays of light that had shielded her from his final attack of toxic dark mist began to fade away.*

She killed him! She actually defeated the demon king! Way to go, Raelynn! The previous chapter had ended with an all-or-nothing clash between the two legendary titans.

> *Rae's eyes took in the sight of Epiales, slathered in thick, ichorous blood that somehow looked even worse than it smelled. For a dreadful few moments, Rae's ears could only register empty silence. She felt, rather than heard, her pounding heart and rapid exhalations as she released her sword from her aching grip. She then attempted to rise to a kneeling position. Her legs faltered, and she took a more side-lying approach to sitting. She opened her mouth slowly and listened for her own voice but could not form any intelligible words.*

Well, I suppose after a rigorous battle, even the best of us would be at least exhausted. It might be too soon to let go of that sword, though.

> *"Raelynn!" Relief swept over her as Relias's voice rang through the air. Her closest companion, the one that had always been at her side, hastily closed the distance between them. The holy sage was murmuring excitedly as he summoned a soft, white glow to his hands.*
> *"Raelynn…" Relias repeated. "You did it! You—" Relias suddenly stopped as the bottom of his white silk vestments caught*

upon a strange rock jutting out from the floor. He canceled his
healing spell and reached to free himself.

Oh, that's not good. No, no, no, don't stop with the healing spell
now! Raelynn needs you! Get in there, man! See, you always heal up as
soon as possible after a fight. Even novices know this! There's a
99.9% chance that the demon king has a second form.

The throne room door burst open with a dull boom. "My, what
an absolutely stunning spectacle!" another familiar voice spoke from
beyond the threshold. "Please, allow me to be the first one to
congratulate you on your victory." Rae pulled her eyes from the
grotesque corpse before her.
"Oliver," Rae quietly acknowledged as she watched the dark
mage stride leisurely, yet confidently, toward her. He had a slightly
jovial expression, with both eyes closed in a crafty, fox-like fashion.
Rae then turned her gaze towards Relias, who was still fighting with
the hem of his robe. It was then that an inky shadow shot out from
the rock, encircling and binding the holy priest in place. Behind him,
the throne room doors slammed shut, sealing the three inside. Rae
rallied once again to sit up, only to fail a second time with a
frustrated grunt.
Oliver chuckled. "Oh, don't worry. I just want our party
members to hold still for a bit. There are probably all sorts of dangers
still lurking in this room. For example, that blood is quite poisonous
to humans. It would be rather humiliating if the 'First of Men' here
killed himself by falling in a puddle, don't you think?" Oliver half-
stepped, half-skipped over a pool of congealing black ooze as if to
make his point.

Toxic mist and poisonous blood were not unheard of in these
fantasy situations. However, Relias was the wise yet ageless great sage
appointed by the Goddess herself. I didn't think a bit of tainted blood
would do him in. As for the whole "First of Men" title… I admit, I
appreciated finally having that called out. Let's not forget the Goddess

created a woman first. Did she go around calling herself the First of Women? The First of Humans? Certainly not!

"Where the hell were you?" Relias demanded as he squirmed against the writhing shadows.

"Tch." Oliver didn't even bother to glance at Relias as he walked past him. "I told you I'd be even less than useless in the fight. Using dark magic against him would be like attacking the Goddess with love, friendship, and lukewarm herbal tea."

Oh, you suspiciously smug sorcerer. What are you up to now?

Oliver stood over Rae, fixing her with a long, inscrutable stare, exposing his rarely seen emerald eyes. Rae returned his gaze defiantly with an angry, challenging glare.

"Raelynn Lightbringer, Knight Captain of the Holy Order of Gold, Chosen One of the Goddess, Seventh Appointed Hero of Legend, and Wielder of the Faith and Will of Euphridia," he intoned in an oddly serious voice. "I officially acknowledge your mortal victory over Epiales, Demon King of Nightmare, Origin of Evil, and Eternally Accursed." He let out a long, suffering sigh, but it cut off abruptly with a shrug. From his temples, shimmering black horns emerged as their essence swirled upward, solidifying into existence before each one ended in a sharp point that appeared to be dipped in gold. Simultaneously, a sinuously long tail formed from his backside, culminating in a spade-like point that hovered just inches above the ground.

I gasped audibly. He was a demon! Not just any demon, but the demon king's second-in-command! I had been telling Nora he was just misunderstood and complicated, you know, like most dark mages. How could he betray me like this!? Oh man, now I owed Nora twenty bucks! Why now, though? Why would a demon lord let Raelynn kill his boss? I thought all demons had to be loyal to their superiors. Then again, I suppose an underhanded betrayal was the only way he could get promoted.

"It's a shame that your continued existence in this world is quite a liability to me." Oliver's voice had returned to its more normal, almost conversational tone. "So with all that in mind… Do you have any last requests?"

Relias struggled desperately, but his efforts were futile; only muffled cries managed to escape as the binding shadows swept across his mouth. Raelynn took a tremulous breath, speaking his true name between gritted teeth. "Demon Lord Olethros…"

The demon smiled. "Soon to be Demon King Olethros," he quipped in a self-congratulatory manner.

Rae wiped the blood from her mouth. "My last request… let Relias and the others leave unharmed." She winced and huffed sharply, adjusting her posture as she forced herself to continue. "By others… I mean…" Her words were cut short as she doubled over in pain, clutching her abdomen. Her hand came away covered in black and red blood. There wasn't much time left before the Goddess Euphridia would call her home once again.

Had Raelynn already given up? She hadn't even made a move for her sword and shield. I could sort of understand she was too injured to start her customary heroic speech, but she needs to at least try to defend herself!

"Yes, yes, the other three waiting outside the doors," Olethros casually responded, listing the members of Raelynn's party on his clawed fingers. "Laverna the Thief, Aleph the Ox-like, and Iron Tiger Tetora." He shook his head, grinning with amusement. "Rather unimaginative and redundant titles all around when you say them out loud. Oh… did I miss anyone?"

Truth be told, I was quite fond of the trio. What a shame they only got name-dropped in this chapter. Laverna, or Vernie, as her closest friends called her, collected other people's valuables and stories in equal amounts but freely shared them, provided you had enough alcohol on hand. Aleph was a calm, collected ox-man who solved his most significant problems with a giant war hammer. Tetora was a hotheaded martial artist with white tiger features who spent his free time trying to pick fights with Aleph. He never succeeded because Aleph was overly tolerant of everything, only responding with a smile and an occasional unruffled chuckle. The chapters dealing with their somewhat comedic exploits were entertaining. Maybe the author felt their antics would be out of place in such a decisive battle?

I looked at the slider on the right side of the webpage. There wasn't much more left to read, so things were most likely coming to a head. This was usually the part where it seemed like you should despair, but something inevitably happened, and a new juggernaut of might and right saved the day. A new companion, perhaps? Raelynn gets a new power? Or maybe Relias finally unleashes his holy fury while finally declaring his obvious but unspoken feelings for Raelynn? I took a deep breath and braced myself. Oh, Olethros, you're going to get *exactly* what you deserve!

> *"No. Just get on with it," Rae spat as she curled into a trembling ball on the floor.*
>
> *"Ah, but I can't rush this, you know. If I simply kill you, you'll just spring up again in a few hundred years like the plague. Instead, I'm going to do something a little more… permanent. I'm just not interested in repeating this cycle anymore." Olethros held out his left arm and summoned a giant, gleaming black scythe to his hand. He then slammed the blunt end to the floor, shattering the stone tile beneath it. A dark purple magic circle burned into the floor to form a perimeter around Rae, ensnaring her in a barrier of translucent midnight.*
>
> *"I reward your efforts by sending you directly on to the next world! May our paths never, ever cross again!" He then put his right hand to the glowing scythe, infusing the entire area with demonic animus. The binding around Holy Sage Relias faded as the demon lord focused on Rae, allowing the priest to rush forward again.*
>
> *"Stop! I won't let you do this! You can't!" Relias screamed in abject horror as he flung himself between them, but it was too late.*

Rae's form vanished, leaving only her dented, blood-spattered armor behind. Relias scrambled to stand, whirling to face Olethros.

"Oh my... I think I'm going to miss her." Lord Olethros frowned and made a curt gesture at Relias, barring him from coming closer with a veil of dark, pulsing animus. He then sauntered over to Rae's sword, plucked it off the ground, and hid it within the deep folds of his cloak.

"A souvenir to commemorate our parting will ease my thoughts, I suppose." Lord Olethros then glanced at Relias one last time, taking in the looks of rage and horror battling for dominance across his face. He then smiled a little too widely and teleported away, leaving a ghostly laugh behind.

Relias shivered, finding himself completely alone with the corpse of the fallen demon king. He pulled his arms to his chest, fell to his knees, and fervently prayed. But a divine shriek abruptly interrupted him, reverberating through all of creation.

"Holy Sage Relias! I can't find Rae! What happened to Rae!?" The voice of Euphridia, the Goddess of Everything, was filled with hysteria. At that moment, the world's light flickered and dimmed as if mirroring her despair. Even more dreadful, perhaps, was when the Goddess's wails cut off suddenly, plunging the entire world into an icy, dark panic.

I reread the last several paragraphs over and over. Was Raelynn... dead-dead? What did he mean by the next world? Is that a euphemism for the Void? Why can't Euphridia find her? What happened to her body? Her soul? All the world's light went out? Why did Euphridia's wails cut off? Did Olethros do something to her, too?

I tore my gaze away from the screen. Tears spilled from my eyes, and my whole body shook uncontrollably. Why was I so upset about this? It was just a story... but... my chest tightened for the second time today, harder this time. Sweat poured down from my temples into my eyes, blurring my vision. A wave of fear and nausea hit me, and I put my head down on my desk, shutting out the harsh glare of the computer screen before me.

"It's just a story, it's just a story!" I tried to reason with myself, but it felt too real. I felt like I had lost something priceless. I was known to get overly invested in fiction, but this was ridiculous!

Do what the nurse taught you, Rachel. It's just one of those again. I held my breath and slowly counted from one to five before exhaling with the same count and cadence. I repeated this until I could eventually open my eyes and lift my head. Pushing the laptop away, I grabbed a pen and paper, doodling complete and utter nonsense as I let the last waves of anxiety sweep over and through me. By the end of the attack, I was overcome with exhaustion, and the only thing I could do was slink from my chair to my bed. I pulled my blanket over my head and hid from the world for as long as possible.

CHAPTER 3: CONFRONTING THE VILLAIN

I stood in the middle of a large, circular office. Or maybe it was some kind of arcane library with the checkout counter improperly placed at the far end? Its curved walls held row after row of books and scrolls over every inch. The floor was a single expanse of polished black marble, flecked with gold and gray, and a magic circle inscribed with gold runes sat at the exact center. I turned my attention to the desk; it was huge and littered with stacks of papers just waiting to spill over into chaos. Then my gaze locked on who was sitting at the desk—the source of all things wrong in the world.

He appeared to be absorbed in a scroll, which he held open before himself, but his eyes were closed. A few strands of long, silvery purple hair fell past his brow in slight disarray, just begging to be fixed. The gold tips of his horns sparkled as they caught the surrounding violet torchlight. He suddenly flinched, turned his face towards me, and dropped the scroll with a clatter. His faintly reptilian irises flashed into view for a brief moment before he regained his composure.

"You're not supposed to be here, you know." Demon Lord Olethros, or now Demon *King* Olethros, I presumed, picked up the scroll he had dropped and rolled it up.

"How could you do that to her!?" I demanded with a screech, advancing on him and his desk.

"Ah… you'll need to be more specific if you want an actual answer." He smoothly brushed the stray hair from his face and tucked it carefully behind his right horn.

"Raelynn Lightbringer, Knight Captain of the Holy Order of Gold, Chosen One of the—"

"The name is sufficient. Multiple titles are tedious." He sighed. "Now, just what do you mean by *that?*"

"You killed her! Murderer! You sent her straight to the next world!"

I really should have brought my bat.

He tilted his head. "The next world?"

"That's what it says in the web novel, right here!" I shoved my phone at him.

He frowned thoughtfully at the screen but made no motion to take it from me. "Are the spiders… inside that box?"

"Spiders? What spiders!?" The terrible thought jarred me, and I almost dropped the phone. I can't stand spiders! They're born of nightmares, you know.

"Surely there would be spiders to maintain this web of which you speak?"

"It's not that kind of web!"

He looked slightly disappointed with the answer. "Oh. But it's a novel?"

"Huh?"

"Novel," he repeated the word patiently. "Is a web novel a type of novel? Novel being derived from the word novella and not to be confused with novel, as in new."

"Uh, well, yes… novella, novel, book, whatever!" He was being intentionally tiresome. "But I don't see what that has to do with our conversation."

"Just a moment." He stood up and floated over to one of the many bookshelves behind him. He summoned a sizeable green book down from the shelves and quickly turned to a specific page as if he knew exactly where to look.

"Novel. Noun. A *fictitious* prose narrative longer than a short story, which depicts one or more *characters* engaging in actions to tell a series of related events." He snapped the book shut and raised an eyebrow at me as if to ask "Are we on the same page now?"

I hesitated. "You're a character in it, too, but you don't look fictitious to me. See, it's right here!" I thrust the phone at him a second time. "It even says what you're doing, spelling it out in black and white to the reader. Evidence!"

He took the phone from me, glanced at it disinterestedly, and said, "There are only a few words here, and none have anything to do with what you're talking about."

I yanked the phone out of his hand ungraciously. "You need to scroll down. Like this." I pulled my finger up and down the side of the phone's screen to demonstrate. "Understand?"

"Paperless scrolling. How convenient." He held out his hand, and I slammed the phone back into his grasp, being sure to step back before he could grab me. Unconcerned, he sat back at his desk and tilted the phone this way and that while scrolling.

"Who writes prose like this?" He swiped faster and faster until he hit the bottom. At first, I thought he was just pretending to read, but I noticed his gracefully curved eyelashes twitching. How could he read with his eyes closed like that?

"Ah, the author's on hiatus. Hopefully it's for a literary sabbatical." He wrinkled his nose in distaste.

"Well!?" I wasn't in the mood for his unnecessarily critical observations.

"Well, what?"

"Did you murder Raelynn Lightbringer?"

"Of course not." He shrugged and offered my phone back to me, which I took cautiously, then reestablished my distance.

I stood there, dumbfounded. He wasn't a liar. Don't get me wrong; he wasn't someone you trusted. He just had his overblown sense of pride and drew the line at bold-faced lying. He preferred using subtler ways of delivering misinformation. Would that mean that Raelynn is actually alive, then? In the next world? Where was that, exactly? I was about to hit him with a barrage of follow-up questions, but he preempted me.

"It's very apparent that you're quite upset over this story, but... I'm not sure you understand what's going on here." He gestured vaguely to the office surrounding us.

"I'm *here* to get justice for Raelynn! That's what's going on!" I put my hands on my hips defiantly. Murder or worldly banishment— they're both at least felonies, right? Is worldly banishment even a thing? I supposed there might not be a precedent.

"How did you get here?"

Wait, how *did* I get here? One moment, I'm in my warm blanket, and... now, things are getting a little harder to see. I touched my face. Maybe it's because I didn't bring my glasses?

"I want you to take a moment to look at yourself."

"Self-reflection?" I wondered aloud. It was hard to keep a focus on what was going on.

He sighed again. "No, I meant it literally."

I glanced down at myself and gasped. Suddenly, I was completely transparent. I swiped, unsuccessfully, at a stack of papers on his desk. My hand went through the entire stack and out the other side. What happened to the phone in my hand? I remembered it seemed solid just moments ago, but now it was nowhere to be found! What in the world was going on?

"Now I'll ask again, where do you think you are?"

"I'm dreaming... aren't I? I was in my bed and..." I trailed off.

"And who do you think I am?"

"A... figment of my subconscious?" It was the best I could come up with.

"Are you asking me or telling me?"

"Oh. Oh dear." How stupid could I be? I'm asleep in bed, and this is all a silly dream.

"You seem much calmer now," he said approvingly as he relaxed back into his seat.

"Sorry... um... what should I call you?"

He shrugged. "Anything you want."

"I'm still going to call you Olethros. I mean, you look exactly like him." Or how I had imagined him, anyway. The author hadn't included him in any cover art, so it wasn't easy to tell.

"Hmm, Olethros, meaning destruction and change? That is acceptable to me." Is that what his name meant? "What should I call you?" His left eye opened slightly.

An idiot, really, but I didn't say that. "Rachel."

"It's a pleasure to meet you, Ms. Rachel. I'd shake your hand in customary greeting, but it seems that isn't possible. Pity."

"Um…"

He leaned forward and clasped his hands together, placing them on the desk. "I don't believe this… *web novel*' was the only thing upsetting you. If I am a figment of your subconscious, as you say, then that would mean I'm a part of you, right?"

"Uh, sure."

"Then it would be in my best interest to help you with what is causing you such distress, right? I mean, meeting like this is a little…"

"Weird?"

"Agreed. So tell me, what's upsetting you so much that you'd come here like this?"

I renewed my focus and mulled his question, closing my eyes so I wouldn't mentally wander because of the… *scenery* before me. It couldn't hurt to speak my mind to my imaginary friend, er, enemy? Frenemy? No, those weren't right, either. A figment of my subconscious it is, then.

I inhaled. "Everything… everything's changing, and nothing's the same anymore. I don't know what I want to do next. Nothing feels right, and… the future frightens me."

"How so?"

"I'm… Okay, so there's this essay I'm supposed to write. It's about what I see myself doing in five years. I don't even know what I want to eat for lunch tomorrow, and I'm being pressured to make all kinds of life choices. I wish someone would tell me who I'm supposed to be and what I'm supposed to do."

"You want someone to *tell you* what you're supposed to do?" He looked taken aback.

"I'm afraid I'll get it all wrong and mess everything up," I confessed.

"Oh, it's because you're growing up," he concluded, almost to himself.

"What?"

"You're finally able to make your own choices, and you're realizing those choices have consequences. I'm told that's all part of growing up. Feeling anxious about it is natural because you've never done it before."

"Why me, though? Nora's not upset. She's excited! Right down to the day she retires, she has everything planned out." Nora had even accounted for three different projected inflation rates in her life plan.

"Who's Nora?"

"My best friend."

"Ah… she's not from another web novel, is she?"

"No, she's real, I swear!" This wasn't the first time I said that particular line about her. Most people don't believe my descriptions of Nora, but once you've met her face-to-face…

"Have you told Nora how you're feeling?"

"No… not really. I don't want her to think I'm…"

"Scared?"

"Yeah." I'm supposed to be the tough one.

"Ms. Rachel. If Nora is your best friend, as you say, she probably already knows you're struggling with this. You don't have the right face to hide your feelings. I expect she is waiting for you to open up to her."

"Maybe… She had offered to help with my essay. Maybe I can talk to her about my feelings then, you know, subtly." So subtly, I don't seem crazy. You know, like a normal person who doesn't have dreams like this.

"You truly have *no idea* what you want to do?" His tone was faintly disbelieving.

"Not really." Maybe I had some selfish motivations deep down, but nothing was bubbling to the surface.

"Is this essay somehow legally binding? Will your instructor hold you accountable in five years if you are not doing what you said you wanted to do?"

"No…"

"Then make it up. Lie. Write what you think they want to hear."

"You mean fake it until I make it?"

"Exactly. The essay itself isn't the problem, so why waste time on it? Meet the minimum requirements for completion and move on. You're putting an extraordinary amount of energy into avoiding it, but that won't amount to anything. You also realize, of course, that what you want to do in the future will always change depending on your present circumstances? Therefore, locking yourself into your life's *culminating purpose* is futile."

Everything he was saying sounded perfectly reasonable. I looked around for a chair to sit in, but it was apparent this was not a room meant for casual consultation. Even if there were another chair, I'd probably phase through it. "You're right, of course…" I trailed off as things around me got cloudier. Was this office from the web novel, or did I make it up? I couldn't recall such a place before. A familiar melody began to play, but I couldn't pinpoint its source.

"Ms. Rachel." I blinked and looked at him. Was I not paying attention? "I think our time is up, but before you go, I want to encourage you to forget about this web novel you've been reading. There's a plethora of good literature out there with better stories to tell."

"Okay."

"You promise?" He cocked his head to the side questioningly.

"Yeah. After tomorrow, that is."

"What's tomorrow?"

"Mmm… I promised to talk about the last chapter with Nora. You know, closure and all."

"I can respect closure. Okay then, you promise you'll let this story go after midnight tomorrow?"

"Yeah."

"You won't go back and reread it?"

"Uh-huh."

"You'll finish your essay and move on with your life?"

"Mmhmm." Everything was turning dark.

"Wonderful. Don't forget your promise to me."

I couldn't reply, because the next moment I awoke to the sound of my phone ringing.

CHAPTER 4: CLOSURE?

My phone continued to vibrate against my nightstand, pulling me awake. Nora's name was flashing on the screen. I accepted the call because I knew the consequences would be dire if I didn't.

"Are you grounded?" Nora asked breathlessly. Was she running and talking on the phone again? Or just excited?

"No." I put her on speaker, sat up, and rubbed my face sleepily.

"Are you just waking up?"

"Yeah… why? What time is it?" I rubbed my arm, realizing my skin felt clammy and I was covered in cold sweat.

"Half past noon."

"That's not late for a Saturday," I said with a yawn as I stretched, noticing I was still in my blue track jacket from yesterday.

"Don't be late, okay?"

"Yeah, I just need to shower." I really, *really* needed it.

"Then you read the—"

"Yes, and I had the strangest—" I cringed. Oh no, there was no way I was telling her about the dream. "I mean, I'm prepared for our discussion."

"Three o'clock."

"I'll be there with the snacks."

"Over and out." Nora ended the call without another word.

After a rejuvenating hot shower, I stocked some bags with the requested snacks and headed to Nora's house. It was a short walk, and a pleasant breeze tempered the summer heat. Before entering Nora's inner sanctum, I had to navigate the kitchen, overseen by the stout but formidable Mama Perez. I stepped inside the open screen door and was blocked by the chef herself.

"Taste!" It was more a command than an offer. Held out from her hand was a forkful of cheesecake.

I cleaned the fork as she watched me expectantly. "It's delicious! Cotton-style cheesecake?"

Mama shouted up the stairs. "She got it! One try!" It seemed this was a test, which I had just passed with flying colors. She handed me two plates, each topped with a slice of cheesecake and a generous serving of fruit. "Dinner at six, save room!"

"Thank you," I said as I carefully balanced the plates and bags and went upstairs. Upon entering Nora's room, I flopped down on my favorite bean bag chair.

"Cheesecake?" I offered her a plate.

"Nah." Nora waved her hand. Mama would be heartbroken if she knew! I had no choice but to make the ultimate sacrifice and finish both slices before dinner. To pay for her silence, I tossed her half a dozen boxes of chocolate-covered pretzel sticks in assorted flavors.

"It's really good," I told Nora after finishing the first slice. "A little tart but also sweet, and it melts in your mouth. Might want to recommend whipping the egg whites for just a little longer next time, though."

"Got it," she said distractedly. Nora had a one-track mind when she was focused on something. She grabbed a pile of papers and sat across from me in the other bean bag chair. "I hereby call this meeting to discuss *The Last Rae of Hope* to order. We'll begin with a discussion of the latest chapter. Rae, you may now present your thoughts."

"It's absolute garbage," I declared, folding my arms across my chest. I usually just gave the author compliments, but not this time.

"Go on." Nora's eyebrows raised in mild surprise.

"Why did she write it like that? Relias does practically nothing, Raelynn gives up, and *Oliver...*" I scrunched my face tight.

"Yeah?"

"Well, he said what he was doing, but it doesn't make any sense! I mean, I get it, but I don't like it." Let's leave it at that. No need to say I was so mad I dreamt him up to accuse him of murder.

Nora proffered a hand. "We're not supposed to get it."

"Huh?"

"We're not supposed to understand because the author doesn't understand!" She abruptly jumped up from her chair. Clearly, she had been eagerly awaiting the chance to deliver this speech. "The author focuses on Rae, right? What she's doing, what she's thinking, what she's feeling. Sure, she pulls in some insight about the others here and there, but it's obvious Rae is her favorite. That's why the chapter is so jarring! Rae is practically dying, so she's not thinking or feeling much except weariness and pain. Then poof, she's gone! For real, gone. The author is stunned! Completely blindsided!"

"Uh, doesn't the author control their characters?"

Nora shrugged. "Characters can take on a life of their own. Happens all the time in my fanfics."

"Nora… I'm being serious."

"Okay, okay." She waved her arms. "Think, though! It's obvious the author is having trouble. You're right about Relias, too. He doesn't seem like he knows what to expect."

"No one's ever defeated the demon king before, so I kind of get that." I was already pulling back on my own criticisms, getting ready to end everything on a more serene note.

"But how can a great sage not know just to heal up their wounded party member? That's basically their only job as a resident squishy."

I frowned and scratched my right wrist. Suddenly, I remembered something. "Oh, I owe you twenty bucks. You know, about *Oliver*." I pulled out some cash I had been trying to get Mother to take.

"Nope. I can't accept it." Nora waved off the money.

"Why not?"

"I said he was a demon in disguise who was supposed to stop the party from reaching the demon king's castle, but I had the timing and motivation wrong. Happens even to the best of us." She paused, opened a box of white chocolate pretzel sticks, and selected a single stick to admire before devouring it. "Back to the author, though."

"What about the author?"

"It's obvious she's written herself into a thorny corner, so that's where we come in."

"I beg your pardon?" What crazy scheme was she concocting this time?

"Look, if we don't do anything, we're looking at more than just a hiatus. We need to save Rae, Rae!"

"Nora…" She did that on purpose. As if I could be a *hero like her*…

"I'm thinking we start with leading comments, you know? Baited hooks to help the author. Stimulating situations. We'll disguise our intentions in the form of 'what if!' Like, *What if Rae isn't dead but… trapped between dimensions? In hyper-sleep?'* Except we can't use that term, or it's going to go sci-fi."

"Nora," I tried again.

"We can gather other fans in on it too. Launch a whole social media campaign!"

"Nora!"

"What?"

"I don't…" I was getting upset again. My head started throbbing, and tears welled up in my eyes. I pulled off my glasses and applied pressure to both sides of my nose. "I don't want to do anything like that. I'm just going to let it go."

Surprisingly, Nora didn't argue. She said "Okay" in a softer tone that contrasted with her impassioned speech.

A long interval of silence passed as I tried to pull myself together.

"I'm sorry," I sniffled.

"Are you… crying?" She hopped from her bean bag to mine. "You are! Actual tears! You've never cried in front of me before. Even when you took that soccer ball to the face!"

"We won't have anything in common now!" As I curled into a ball, I started bawling, putting my arms over my head. All of my worries spewed out of me at once. "I promised myself after midnight I'd distance myself from this story. But it brought us together! Now you're gonna abandon me just like the author did this story and just like I'm doing now, and I probably deserve it!"

Nora patted my head. "So that's what's been eating you? You big dummy. We're going to be friends forever." I was slightly surprised she understood my convoluted thought process on the first try.

"Promise?" I asked hopefully.

"Who else will put up with me?"

"Your insanely rich and ruggedly handsome future husband?" I suggested between sniffles.

"Yeah, but I won't meet him for at least six years yet, and even then, he's going to be busy with his interstellar travels, so you know, I'm going to have a lot of free time on my hands."

"You're not going to go with him?" I knew she was being silly to distract me, but it worked.

"Nuh-uh. I get car sick. Could you imagine cleaning up something like that in zero gravity?" She pulled my arm off my head. "Feeling better now?"

"A little."

"Oh. About the soccer ball thing. I was aiming for the goal, so…"

"I believe you. Even if you had tried, I don't think you could have done that on purpose."

Nora abruptly rose, her movement swift and decisive as she reached for her laptop. "Are you up for a Viking funeral?" she proposed, her eyes glinting with a hint of mischief.

"Raelynn's not dead! She's not!" I almost shouted it.

She's… healing or something. Taking a break?

"I don't mean for Rae. I mean, for the story itself." She spoke as if the solution were the most natural thing in the world while completely ignoring my unhinged outburst. I guess that's why we got along, though.

"How do you have a Viking funeral for a web novel? We have nothing to set fire to, let alone a sea to set it adrift in."

Nora's eyes sparkled. "Simple, we'll do the next best thing. Let's comment-bomb the chapter with an alt account!"

Oh, that really was an evil idea. Yet, I couldn't help a conspiratorial grin from pulling at the corner of my mouth.

"What would the account name be?"

"NoWayNoRae?"

I blinked, then giggled a little too much at that. "Let's do it," I agreed.

Would you believe NoWayNoRae was already taken? But NoRaeNoWay was still available, at least. For the next several hours, wrapped up in our silly teenage thoughts, we crafted a commentary masterpiece of vitriol. We did, however, sprinkle in some suggestions here and there as opportunities for improvement. The only break we took was for dinner because Mama Perez insisted. No one ever got hungry in her house.

It was very late when we had made our final edits. I reread the declaration of criticisms and makeshift action plan we had forged one more time, and then I paused. "I can't post this."

"You just click 'Post Comment.'" Nora pointed. "We'll break it up if we're past the character limit."

"Okay, technically, I *can* do it, but I won't."

"What?"

"It's too mean, especially in the beginning. I can't. If this story didn't exist…"

Nora sighed. "Yeah, I know what you mean."

"I still can't believe you caught me reading it on my phone from that height. You were at least five rows up in the stadium!"

"I have my ways of finding kindred spirits." She tapped her fingers together in front of her face, trying to look mysterious.

"Perfect eyesight?"

"That would be one of them, yes. The other is the uncanny ability to not pay attention during school assemblies."

"I think everyone has that one." I handed her the laptop. "Look, I won't blame you if you want to post it, but—"

Click.

Nora posted it, and I suddenly got a chill down my spine.

"How could you do that!?" I was such a liar; I was definitely blaming her.

She shrugged. "It needed to be said."

"But we were… we were *really* mean!" Even as I gestured at the laptop, a little heart emoji popped up in response to our post from BitterDarkTroll53. "Look, even the old hag agrees! She never likes anything unless it's full of spite!"

Nora smiled impishly. "My goodness, what are you so worried about?"

"Karma!"

"We didn't use any obscenities or anything. We just said what we found upsetting and offered pointers. Besides, we used an alt account. What could possibly happen?"

"It's like you're begging the universe to prove you wrong! You're not actually supposed to say 'what could possibly happen' out loud, either! You know this whole thing is—"

An alarm went off on her phone. "Time's up!"

"What?"

"It's Sunday now. You said you were done with this story after midnight, right?"

"I-I did… but…"

"So, let's start on your essay."

I opened my mouth to complain, but no words came to me. Besides, Nora could be quite stubborn, especially when she had the luxury of using your own words against you.

"Ugh, fine!"

We didn't know it then, but it turns out that the universe takes its sweet time to settle karmic debts.

✳✳✳

Post-Chapter Omake

Nora: *You know, there's no solid evidence outside of myth that Viking funerals were held on water. However, many involved human sacrifice!*

Rae: *What! Then why did you suggest such a thing?*

Nora: *I knew you didn't know that.*

Rae: *Stop destroying my childhood fantasies!*

Nora: *You fantasized about having a Viking funeral at sea?*

CHAPTER 5: TIME [SKIP] TO GET A JOB

After years of hard work, Mama Perez finally expanded her café. It was a busy, cheerful place just as you came into town, as well as the exclusive spot where Nora and I held our weekly catchups. We had been quite involved in its development during our college years, going so far as to co-author our joint capstone project about the trials and tribulations of owning and maintaining a restaurant. At first, I had simply been going through the motions, majoring in business just like Nora did so we could stick together. However, I had come to enjoy the work that went into the café, especially all the process improvements we made along the way. It had grown bigger and bigger over the years as a result of our efforts, taking over not one but two other retail units.

Mama Perez, grateful for our assistance, always made sure to set aside two slices of her now-famous cotton cheesecake for the occasion. I had just started on my slice when Nora walked into our private alcove dedicated just to us.

"You're late, you know." I watched Nora take the chair across from me.

"Fashionably so," she agreed cheerfully, calling attention to her new watch. I gave her a thumbs-up for her tasteful choice. Only Nora could pull off an accessory covered in both hearts and dragons.

"Since I got here first, I get to share my news first, right?" It was all I could do to contain myself. For once, I had something positive to say.

"Enlighten me. I'm all ears," Nora smiled.

I took a deep breath. "So, after applying to forty-seven different entry-level college graduate positions, I finally have my first face-to-face interview tomorrow!" My struggle toward financial independence would finally pay off. Well, maybe I would start to pay off my college degree, at any rate. Regardless of what Mother said, I felt it was important not to leave her with any of my debts.

"Same!" Nora chimed.

"What?"

"Not the forty-seven part, but I, too, have an interview tomorrow!" She smirked.

"When?" I asked curiously.

"Noon."

"Me too! Where?"

"Cooperative Universal Publishing."

The smile I had been sporting slowly slid off my face. "Project coordinator, special projects division?"

"Yeah, wait, how did you know? Did Mama spill the beans?"

"No—"

She gasped and half-jumped from her seat. "We're interviewing for the same position! Oh yeah, we're *rivals*! This is going to be awesome!"

"What are you talking about? This is bad! We'll be in direct competition!"

"No way. Now, we're twice as likely that one of us will get the job! When that happens, we just open the door for the other!" She gestured as if opening a door like a trained butler might, complete with a sitting yet somehow respectful bow. Trust Nora to see the positives.

I took another bite of cheesecake. "I wonder why we're scheduled for the same time, though. Don't they usually stagger these things?"

"I heard some places do group interviews."

While she was probably right, my skepticism grew. "Aren't those usually multi-level marketing scams?"

Nora shook her head confidently. "I'm sure this isn't the case with CUP."

"CUP?"

"Cooperative Universal Publishing. CUP. Honestly, Rae, I'm a little surprised you applied there."

"What do you mean? I've been applying everywhere!"

"Yeah," Nora agreed. "But you know, your promise to yourself?"

"What promise?"

Nora blinked several times. "You have absolutely no idea, do you?"

"Obviously I don't...?"

She sighed, shaking her head with a humorous smile. "Honestly, you should at least do basic research before going into an interview. Bring up DivinitEpub."

The web novel app? Curious about what she was getting at, I unlocked my phone and launched it.

"Look at the bottom of the homepage."

The words "Cooperative Universal Publishing" were printed in the tiniest font at the bottom. "Ah. It sounded familiar, but it's such a generic name. But what's this promise you're talking about?"

"You didn't see the second splash banner yet, I guess. CUP recently bought the rights to..." Nora stopped and gave me an anticipatory smile. "Maybe you shouldn't swipe right."

So, of course, I swiped right and read the banner aloud. "Coming soon to DivinitEpub, over three hundred of your favorite stories previously only available on WebNovela." Wait, WebNovela? The defunct platform that had hosted *The Last Rae of Hope* back when we were in high school?

"What a coincidence," I said with as much unruffled calm as I could muster.

She twirled her hair around her finger several times, her classic nervous habit. "That's all you have to say?"

"Yeah. I'm over it, for real."

"You sure?"

"Yep." I truly believed I was. For half a decade, I had avoided all conversations, posts, fanfics, and "whatever happened to" web articles. This wasn't to say it had a viral following, but there were a few dedicated fans who held virtual candlelight vigils. Even

BitterDarkTroll53 would post something passive-aggressive on the anniversary of its hiatus, if for no other reason than to perhaps bait the author into revealing herself once more.

Nora glanced at my phone, spotting my reading history and thus pulling us off track, probably intentionally. "You're reading *I Fell in Love with a Vampire Cowboy?*"

"Look, the premise isn't all that bad. I mean, cattle are pretty big, right? So they have a lot of blood, and it would just be a waste if—"

"Too many abs," she criticized as she scrutinized the cover photo. "Says *you.*"

"No, someone literally drew too many abs on those vampire cowboys. What is that, a sixteen-pack? Ridiculous. The guy would be sixty percent stomach. It's not anatomically correct."

"Technically, it takes place on another planet, so they're *alien* vampires."

"Oh, that makes perfect sense, then. Props to the artist," Nora said, taking my phone and swiping through the image gallery.

"I'm telling you, I'm in it for the story, not the eye candy." Maybe she would have believed me if I had used a phrase better than "eye candy." Nora raised an eyebrow at me.

I coughed delicately. "Anyway, back to our interviews."

"Sure." Her tone indicated I had not heard the last about my latest guilty pleasure.

"What do you think the job entails?" I asked. The posting had been pretty generic.

"Who cares? We'll be working for CUP! Do you realize half of my disposable income goes to them as it stands? If we end up working for them, we'll probably be able to read our favorite stories for free!"

This world is not so free with its material goods. "We might get an employee discount, but even that only happens if one of us actually gets the job."

"Between the two of us, we have it in the bag." Nora took an aggressively large bite of cheesecake. "They'd be crazy not to hire professional fans of the genre."

"I thought you didn't like cheesecake," I remarked.

"I don't, but Mama's watching." I looked over at Mama Perez. She was waiting for feedback, like always. Her desserts were never less than perfect, and today was no exception. I smiled and showed her my empty plate. She seemed satisfied and went back into the kitchen.

"So how funny would it be if we ended up on a project to bring *it* back from hiatus?" Nora asked with her mouth still full.

"No way." I shook my head. "CUP publishes thousands of titles monthly. Never mind the fact that DivinitEpub is just one tiny part of them. They also publish books, videos, art prints… I mean, what are the odds?"

"Big enough that I'm going to reread the series tonight before bed. What about you?"

"Me?" I didn't have plans. "Uh, I'm gonna look up more information about CUP to prepare."

"Smart move! I'll send you a list of websites." Nora opened her phone and began texting me.

"Hey, Nora. If we're competing for a single opening…"

"Don't you dare. You better do your best."

"I didn't even say anything yet!" I protested.

"I know you. Don't you dare tank the interview for my sake! I'll never forgive you!"

"I don't know what you're talking about… I was just going to say good luck to you." I folded my arms and pretended to be wounded by her observations. Truth be told, she had been absolutely right, but I couldn't admit to it after being called out.

"Good luck to you too, then."

"Friends forever?" I asked for reassurance.

"Friends forever."

I spent the rest of the day pretending I was educating myself about CUP while puttering around my room. I was still living with Mother, who continued to work odd hours, and yet again, she wasn't home.

We had another household resident keeping me company, an awkwardly adolescent American shorthair named Chester. Chester had a silver tabby coat that darkened down his back to his solid black tail.

He always had one of his eyebrows half-cocked, like he was just a little confused about everything. He was a sociable cat, and he put up with my affectionate hugs as best as he could whenever I came and went from the house. Chester never failed to endure it, and I never failed to give him a treat. It was like we had a mutual understanding.

"Nora and I are interviewing for the same job at CUP." I placed him in my lap and spoke to him as if he understood everything, acronyms and all.

"Mrow?" he questioned.

"I know, right? She brought up that story again, too."

Chester nudged my hand, and I responded by scratching behind his ear.

"I mean, there's no way, right? Even if I get the job, it's like a one-in-a-thousand chance. It's just magical thinking."

Chester stared at me momentarily, then put his paw in my hand. "Right. The treats." I put him down and gave him a few morsels.

"If I get the job, I'll be able to afford you those top-shelf treats you've been seeing on TV. I heard they even use real meat in them. So wish me luck, okay?" Chester didn't answer. He almost never did. I got up out of my chair and got ready for bed.

***

Post-Chapter Omake

Nora: *You went with a time skip this early in the story?*

Rae: *I was just going to college classes, working retail, and studying. Boring. No one wants to read a whole chapter about that.*

Nora: *What about our spring break in Vegas?*

Rae: *What happens in Vegas stays in Vegas!*

Nora: *…Absolutely nothing happened in Vegas. You could barely handle walking through Madame Tussauds!*

Rae: *Uncanny valley!*

Nora: *You also said the same thing about the Blue Man Group!*

Rae: *To be clear, it's the eyes, not the blue skin. It's* always *the eyes.*

43

Rae: *To be clear, it's the eyes, not the blue skin. It's* always *the eyes.*

CHAPTER 6: NO BACKSIES

I was again back in the demon king's executive office, but the scene had drastically changed. Last time, there was an air of organized chaos, with scrolls and books neatly arranged on the elegantly curved bookshelves. This time, however, the room was a picture of disarray. Papers of various sizes and shapes littered the floor in haphazard piles, and the desk was so cluttered it was completely unfit for any kind of work to be done.

Gone was the imposing figure who once commanded respect from behind his desk. Now, King Olethros lounged languidly on the marble floor, propped uncomfortably against an empty bookshelf with his arms resting at his sides. His eyes were closed, and it was impossible to tell whether he was aware of my presence.

"Hey!" I greeted him casually. I mean, he was a king, but I wasn't one of his subjects. Besides, this was my dream. So, didn't that make me slightly higher on the chain of command? Either way, he didn't look very kingly at the moment.

He winked a single eye open, peering at me through the disheveled locks of his silvery purple hair that I felt an insatiable need to fix. "Still popping up in places you aren't supposed to be, I see. What happened this time?" He made no effort to sit up. He had a pale complexion, as if he had been shut inside for far too long.

"Nothing, really. I just wanted to talk."

"Again?"

"It's been five years," I reminded him.

"That explains why you've aged, I suppose." There were *nicer* ways he could have said that.

"You don't look so great yourself, you know." I plopped down across from him on the floor. "You look like you haven't slept in a week."

"I don't sleep."

"Maybe you should start."

"It wouldn't change anything even if I did." He waved an arm dismissively.

"Do you want to talk about it?" I offered.

"Not really. Just say whatever it is you came here to say." His tone sounded irritated, like I was too much to deal with. I thought we had left on an amicable note last time, but now I was a bit confused. This wasn't going the way I expected, but dreams never really do, do they?

"Ah, fine. Something has come up, but it's not a big deal."

He let out an exasperated sigh. "What has come up?"

"I have an interview for a job tomorrow."

"So?"

Wow, not even a single congrats? I could see he wasn't exactly at his best, but isn't that common courtesy?

"It turns out it's at a publishing company that bought the rights to that web novel I—"

"Do NOT go to that interview!" He jumped up angrily. Startled, I scrambled backward, crab style. I would have taken out half a dozen stacks of papers if I had been solid during my retreat.

"What the heck do you think you're doing, coming at me like that!?" I jumped up and waved my arms defensively.

"You broke your promise!" Although his tone was still angry, he stopped moving towards me. He was floating off the floor somewhat, and I noticed I could see glimmers of torchlight through the simple black cloak wrapped around him. What had happened to all his fancy accouterments? Even the tips of his horns had lost their golden sheen.

"It was an accident!" I shouted. "I didn't know about the buyout until Nora told me!"

"Again, with this Nora person… How suspicious…" He paced back and forth in midair.

"Whoa, I was the one who applied for the job. It's just a coincidence that—"

"*This is not a coincidence!*" He exhaled, obviously trying to calm himself. "Ms. Rachel, just don't go tomorrow. Please." Oh, now we're back to using pleasantries?

"No." I folded my arms.

"What do you mean, no? Do you have any idea what you're getting us into?"

"Tell me why I shouldn't go."

Would you believe he actually hissed at me? Like a snake! So much for those cheap pleasantries.

"Oh, now I get it," I huffed angrily. "You're the part of me that's afraid I won't get the job. You're acting like this because you think I will melt down again. I'm older now, though, and I can handle my emotions better. I don't have any great expectations, but I'll be damned if I won't do my best. If I don't get the job, that's just too bad, but I'd at least know I tried."

"You stubborn—" He clutched his chest, releasing a pained breath before gesticulating dramatically with his arms. "You are in danger, and even worse, you're putting *me* in danger!"

"I don't believe you. In fact, thinking you were anything more than just a dream was stupid. Thanks for your help earlier, but I think I've outgrown you." As the words left my lips, the world around me began breaking apart. The walls cracked and buckled, toppling the shelves and spilling their contents into swirling clouds of debris. It all disintegrated into clouds of dust as the marble floor beneath me fractured, its pieces dissolving as everything disappeared into an abyss of black.

Amidst the chaos, only Olethros himself remained, floating in the darkness with his black cloak blowing in the wind. He was trembling, but I couldn't decide if it was with anger or fear.

"You're going to regret this, you know. Don't say I didn't warn you!" Suddenly, he flickered out of view, abandoning me altogether.

My alarm went off, and I woke up with my jaw clenched painfully shut. What a way to start the day.

***

Post-Chapter Omake

Euphridia: *Attention! We need to incorporate an additional review before we post a chapter, no matter how short it is.*

Rae: *Why? What happened?*

Euphridia: *We received this letter.*

Rae: *"You are hereby notified to cease and desist any and all further unlawful defamation, slander, and libel with regards to your statements as referenced in the latest chapter release."*

Nora: *Is he mad about the entire chapter?*

Euphridia: *No, just the line that reads, "Would you believe he actually hissed at me? As a snake!"*

Rae: *Oh, typo. Like a snake, not as a snake. I guess the grammar checker couldn't catch that one. I better fix that one quickly!*

Nora: *The funny thing is, both are equally possible for him! All the more reason for him to get upset!*

Rae: *…Are you his lawyer?*

Nora: *You know he's the type to self-represent.*

CHAPTER 7: THE INTERVIEW

Nestled on the twentieth floor of a towering skyscraper in New York City, the North American headquarters of Cooperative Universal Publishing awaited us. Nora and I had split a rideshare where I spent most of the hour-long trip doing everything possible to keep her from throwing up. When we finally arrived, we spent a good twenty minutes waiting for the color to return to her face. How was she going to handle the daily commute at this rate? I was reticent to leave our serene suburbs, but the stark reality of necessary relocation was already rearing its ugly head.

"Ready to go inside?" I asked cautiously.

"I was born ready, then I waited too long, but then I grew up, and now I'm ready again!"

Yeah, she was back to her baseline self now. We entered the giant turnstile door and crossed the threshold together. I was worried we would have trouble finding the right office, but it turned out CUP had taken over the entire floor. The elevator door slid open to reveal a young woman with shoulder-length brown hair and stylish glasses awaiting our arrival.

"You must be Rachel and Nora," she said with an acknowledging nod to each of us, which indicated she even knew who was who.

"Yes ma'am," I said. "We're here for an interview."

"It's a pleasure to meet you both. My name is Clare, and I'll be escorting you through the process today." With that, she offered us a smile, then turned on her heel and led us to a conference room. The first thing that struck me as we entered was the glass wall, giving a covert view of the New York City skyline. The table itself spanned most of the room, with at least a dozen chairs stationed around it.

"Before I introduce you to the president, I have some paperwork I'll need you to complete. Please, have a seat." She set down a non-disclosure agreement in front of our respective chairs and then took a seat across from us. I frowned as I tried to understand what it was saying. I got the gist that we could be both a receiving party and a disclosing party of confidential information from this point forward until the end of time, so… basically, whatever happens here stays here? The definition of confidential information consumed the bulk of the agreement, so after a few paragraphs, I just skipped to the end and signed it. Were we going to be told insider information in a preliminary interview?

Next was a paper asking for our emergency contact information. I filled it in with Mother's information and handed it to Clare. Nora followed suit.

"You're interviewing today for the Project Coordinator role in our Special Projects division. This role is a contract-to-hire position. If you're offered the job today, when can you start?" She looked back and forth between the two of us.

Nora answered promptly. "Immediately!"

I hesitated. "Next week." I needed time to prepare before just jumping in.

"Are you willing to travel?" Again, she directed the question at both of us.

"Yes," we both answered in unison.

"Wonderful! Do you have any questions for me?"

I raised my hand slightly as if I were in class. "How many positions are open currently?" I couldn't tell if we were actually competing or not.

"It will depend on the outcome of today's interviews," Clare answered evasively. I tried to exchange a questioning glance with Nora, but she wasn't looking in my direction.

Clare offered no more information either. Instead, she stood up and promptly headed for the door. "President Abrams will be with you shortly. It was wonderful to meet you!"

We waited a few moments in silence, but I couldn't keep it up. I cleared my throat, then leaned toward Nora and said with a hushed tone, "This is a weird interview, right? Why did we have to sign a non-disclosure agreement?"

"I'm sure it's all standard." Nora's gaze remained fixed on the door.

"Why didn't she ask us any other questions?"

"She already has the answers from our resumes."

I tried again. "Why is the president meeting with us?"

"Because he wants to?"

"Isn't he a little busy just to meet two potential peons?" Something was fishy. It wasn't even a guaranteed long-term position.

"Maybe he enjoys meeting people." Nora had a quick dismissive comeback for every question I asked.

"Shouldn't they validate who we are? We could be imposters. Shouldn't they have checked our identification or something?"

Nora waved me off. "Rae, you worry too much."

"You don't worry enough," I muttered back.

If there was one thing I would say about Nora, it would be that although she planned things out in advance, once she was in the thick of it, she just kept moving forward, not necessarily taking a moment to pause and reevaluate the situation. Sometimes, you have to course correct.

The door to the conference room swung open, revealing an older man in a navy pinstripe suit. He had a tan complexion, and his long, contrastingly white hair was pulled back into a slim, low-set ponytail. He also harbored a short and neatly trimmed beard of the same color. His eyes were a deep blue and held a slightly mischievous twinkle.

"Welcome to Cooperative Universal Publishing!" His booming, overly dramatic voice filled the conference room, causing me to jump slightly.

He suddenly pointed at Nora, and she stood up militantly, even offering a sharp salute. "Connecting your world to ours!" Oh, the motto. I remembered it from the webpage.

Then he pointed at me with an anticipatory smile.

"Uh…" Was I supposed to do something?

President Abrams's smile turned to an awkward frown. "We'll have to work on that, I see. Anyway! Let's talk about the Special Projects division." He sat down at the table with us. "Special Projects is exactly what it sounds like. Special. As in extraordinary. And I'm staffing it with extraordinary people. Are you extraordinary?"

"Absolutely!" Nora slammed her fist down on the table to emphasize her point.

"How about you, Rachel?"

"I mean…" I struggled to answer, knowing it was all I could do just to be ordinary.

The president turned to Nora. "Is she?"

"She is. She doesn't like to talk about herself like that." Wait, what was that just now?

"Do you two… know each other or something?" I asked President Abrams suspiciously.

"Ho, ho, ho! I know everyone!"

I wasn't hearing a no.

I glared at Nora, and she eventually flinched under my gaze. I momentarily forgot we were in the middle of an interview that affected our financial futures. "Just what's going on here, Nora? What did you do this time?"

"Ah, as the current president of *The Last Rae of Hope* fan club…"

My eyes widened. "Is this why we could only meet up on Sundays? You've been running a fan club behind my back? Wait… are *you* the only reason I have this interview?"

"You applied for the job, so of course that's not true." Nora tried her best to sound innocent and indignant at the same time. Come to think of it, wasn't Nora the one who had sent me a link to the position? If I recalled correctly, she had texted something like *You remembered to apply to this one too, right?* I can only remember things if I knew about them in the first place! You fiend!

Then I remembered King Olethros's warning. "He *was* right! This isn't a coincidence at all!" I shouted angrily.

"Who is 'he?'" Nora eyed me, and I suddenly clammed up. Oops.

"Yeah, who is he?" The president wore the same curious expression that Nora had. *Seriously, are you two related?*

"Never mind him! What do you two want from me? What is this all about?"

The president bowed his head at the table. "This is about making amends."

"Amends?" I blinked.

"Ah, when I was a little younger, I was a little too free with poor advice, and I didn't know all of 'The Rules.' The Special Projects division allows me to make up for that. Here, we reach out to past content creators and help them reconnect to their worlds while connecting them to ours."

"I don't understand... what does this have to do with us?"

Then, both Nora and President Abrams responded in unison. *"NoRaeNoWay and the 33 Opportunities for Improvement!"*

Was that what people were calling our old diatribe? Did it have some cult following?

I shook my head, still processing my disbelief of this entire situation. "Oh, but Nora and I wrote those comments long ago. We weren't even out of high school yet. I can't even recall everything I said."

Nora indirectly confessed a little more. "Um, Rae... Those *comments*, as you call them, are the reasons we *have this interview.* The author wants to work with us."

Impossible.

She doesn't like working with *anyone.* But maybe, after so many years... maybe she's come around to asking for help?

"So when you asked me about those odds yesterday..." I felt my jaw clenching shut again.

"Heh... yeah, I knew they were 100%." She hung her head.

Shame. Shame on you!

I stared at her for a few moments before I gave in with a sigh. "You want to do this, don't you?"

She lifted her head and nodded, her eyes like an eager puppy.

For the life of me, I didn't know why I felt so apprehensive about what was to come. I wanted to bail, to tell Nora this was a bad idea, but I knew how much the story meant to her. Taking over as the president of the fan club? After all these years?

Oh. It was probably just that stupid dream getting to me. Fear of failure. Except… it's already in the bag now, isn't it? At least for Nora, anyway…

"Why be all sneaky about it? You could have just been upfront with the whole thing."

"You wouldn't have agreed to it otherwise. The author, I mean, content creator, said I had to get you on board or no deal."

Right. CUP doesn't use the word author as it isn't inclusive enough.

"You've met the content creator?" I asked in an astonished voice. "Euphridia" had never, ever responded to any comments from any of her fans.

"No, I've only written to her… weekly. For the past year or so. I spoke with her over the phone too, once or twice."

Aha! It must have been killing her that she couldn't tell me about it for all this time.

"What's her real name?" I glanced at the president, who was being way too silent now.

Nora answered for him. "Eura. Eura Abrams."

"Your daughter?" I narrowed my eyes at President Abrams.

"Mmm… One of my granddaughters, actually! I'm a lot older than I look! Ho, ho, ho!"

I wasn't trying to compliment him, but I guess it worked out that way.

I tapped my finger on the table, mentally piecing it all together. "So basically, we're here to help your granddaughter get her story going again? Put it back on track so it has a happy ending for the good guys?"

"That's a great way to think about it!"

This didn't sound like a normal job in the least. Project Coordinator? Was it more of a creative role? I could rule out being a line editor; my grasp of the English language was a slapdash mix of high fantasy and modern slang, which would just taint any prose it encountered. If I could possibly steer the plot for the better, though… maybe Rae would get a second chance at a happy ending.

I frowned, trying to bring myself back to reality. "This seems like a lot of effort to go through just to help your granddaughter with her writer's block…"

"Yes, but I think the two of you can handle it. I owe it to my Eura to give it a shot!"

I pressed for more. "Then the job is for both of us? You're going to pay all this money to help? I mean, neither of us even went to school for literature or anything." We were more like avid consumers of the medium than professional creators.

"No experience as a writer is necessary! The jobs are yours if you agree to immerse yourself in the project and work together as partners throughout the contract period. There is just one thing."

"Only one?" I asked.

"Only one that's important enough to mention."

"And that is…?"

"My granddaughter… hmm. She means well, but… she has a lot to learn yet. So I hope you can eventually forgive her for all her… mistakes."

"Written or otherwise?" Nora asked.

"Yes!"

"Ha, I'm fine with that!" Nora turned to me expectantly.

"Well, we all make mistakes, so…" I distractedly shrugged off his worries. I was concentrating more on the idea that Nora had manipulated me into getting a job… that paid a decent wage *and* aligned so well with our shared hobbies. Should I be mad or happy? I settled on both.

"I knew you'd understand!" President Abrams clapped his hands with a sense of finality. "So, you're willing to meet with my Eura?"

She's… here?

Another impossibility! At best, she'd just meet us virtually. She probably wouldn't even turn on her camera. At least then, I'd have an excuse not to turn on mine.

I looked at Nora and her wide puppy dog eyes. "Okay, okay! I agree, so stop giving me that look! But we will have a very, *very* long and uncomfortable talk about the ends versus the means later. Do you understand me?"

"Yes! Yeeeeesssss!" She started jumping up and down. How unprofessional.

Suddenly, there was a loud pounding at the conference room door, followed by an exasperated shout. "Let me in now, old man! I can't wait any longer!"

How… how could she possibly be *here*!?

*****

Post-Chapter Omake

Nora: *Hold up! Self-insertion in a story is definitely a rule-breaker!*

Euphridia: *What? I play a vital role!*

Nora: *You still broke a rule.*

Euphridia: *What do you want from me now?*

Nora: *Accountability.*

Euphridia: *You're relentless.*

CHAPTER 8: EURA "EUPHRIDIA" ABRAMS

Eura Abrams was a tall, honey-haired, middle-aged woman wearing oversized tortoiseshell sunglasses, black high heels, and an outdated, bright red power suit. Unzipped and carelessly slung over one shoulder, her luxury handbag seemed on the verge of spilling its contents with every movement as she crossed the conference room.

She looked a lot older than I thought she would be. I guess I imagined web novel authors to be around my age, just trying to get their writing out there and make a few cents to supplement their day job. Eura, however, was the granddaughter of a corporate mogul, so I guess this was more of a labor of love than anything else.

"Out." She made a flippant gesture to chase her grandfather from the room.

"Isn't she adorable?" He laughed as he took his leave. As soon as the door closed behind him, she ran and jumped into the seat directly across the table from us with a squeal.

"You have no idea how long I've been waiting to meet you!" She thrust out a hand towards me. I awkwardly offered my hand, returning the handshake.

How can she be *here* sitting in front of me?

"Actually, ma'am, my name is Rachel. The person you've been corresponding with is Nora."

"I know that." She was still clasping my hand, shaking long enough to be uncomfortable.

"Ma'am—" I started.

"Eura."

"Sorry, Eura. You know, Nora's the one who's been a big fan of your work." I tried to get her to shake Nora's hand by leading her arm over, but she remained fixated on me.

"As I understand it, you're responsible for number three, number eleven, and my favorite, number twenty-four. Too bad it's against The Rules."

"Huh?"

"Number twenty-four is the suggestion that Euphridia rewinds time to before Oliver infiltrates the party and tells Relias what will happen," Nora clarified. Oh yeah, *NoRaeNoWay and the 33 Opportunities for Improvement.*

"Against the rules?" I asked Eura as I finally pulled my hand away from her.

"Yeah. Rewinding time has all sorts of consequences I can't account for."

"You have a certain set of rules for the story?"

"Of course. All content creators have to follow The Rules now." She sighed.

"Isn't it your story?"

"The president has rules for all of us now, no exceptions. Not even for me." Eura shook Nora's hand but dropped it after just a minimal two shakes. "So I'm thinking, number nine, the second half of number fifteen, and a bit of number twenty-nine are the most realistic."

Nora thought about it for a moment. "Seventeen?"

Eura didn't bother to look at her. "No transmigration without mutual acceptance by the transmigrators. Also, there's the whole body-soul compatibility coefficient to consider. The likelihood of finding a positive match is infinitesimally small."

"Oh, of course, of course," Nora agreed. Did she understand any of this? Because I certainly didn't.

I looked between them, got a piece of paper, and started numbering down the side, crossing off the numbers they mentioned were bad and circling the numbers they agreed on.

"Whatever are you doing?" Eura looked at me.

"Oh. I won't remember any of this, so it's best if I take notes." I continued by drawing a line through number seventeen to show it was no good. Then I stopped. "This is still an interview, right?"

"Interview?" Eura looked at Nora for the first time.

Nora shrugged. "He didn't have us sign the contracts yet."

"Old man!" she shouted towards the ceiling.

"Yes, dear?" He was already coming in with papers.

"Oh. It's about time. We don't have all day, you know."

He handed a contract to each of us. Nora simply went to the last page and signed it.

"Ah… You're going to have to initial each page here to attest that you read it in its entirety," he murmured as he pointed out a small line on the bottom right of the page.

"Yeah, okay." She went back and signed them, though I couldn't imagine she saw any words with how fast she moved. I, on the other hand, at least *tried* to do my due diligence and actually read it. Occupational hazards listed everything from paper cuts to dismemberment and, rarely, sudden death. Routine job tasks were equally thorough, including everything from sedentary actions through repetitive movements to strenuous exercise.

"Did you just take every job description there is and put it all together?" I wrinkled my nose.

"Project Coordinator is an extensive role with many other duties as assigned, so we like to ensure we cover all possibilities!"

"Uh-huh." I sighed and gave up. I initialed all the pages and signed the contract, knowing that there was no way it was legally enforceable and that I could walk away at any time. It must have been fun to craft such a work of fiction. I handed my contract to President Abrams after he took Nora's. Eura went to intercept the papers, but he moved them out of her range.

"Eura honey, they're my contracted employees, not yours. So I'm the one who holds onto these." He made his way to the door and left once again, whistling a rather jaunty tune. Eura glared at him, saying nothing until he was gone. Then, she turned to us. "Anyway. We'll start tomorrow and—"

"Next week," I interjected.

"That's too long to wait!" She was obviously used to getting things her way.

"No. I have arrangements to make. I need to talk to Mother."

"Mother?" Eura blinked.

"I think she's going to notice if I'm not around. Maybe not right away, but eventually."

"You... live with your mother?" She seemed pretty surprised.

"Yes, some of us adults can't afford not to." I turned to Nora. "Commuting is going to be hard on the both of us. We should probably look for places to stay nearby, or at least close enough to take the train." Is train-sick a thing?

"Oh, no, you're not going to work *here*!" Eura suddenly laughed.

"Where are we going to work, then?" I asked.

"My place!"

"And where's that, exactly?"

She retrieved her phone from her purse, spilling other objects on the table. "Let's share contact information first, and I'll text you the address where we'll meet up."

After doing precisely that, I got a text with an address. I looked it up online.

"North Catskill Winery and Renaissance Faire?" Maybe she made a typo.

"My place is just a little beyond it, but you can't find a route to it from the map. We can just meet up there. We can even go to the faire first! It's an excellent source of inspiration for me!"

I wasn't ready to answer her just yet. "Nora, this is even farther than I imagined. Do you think I should bring Chester with me? I don't know if I'll be able to come home every weekend."

"Chester?" Eura asked before Nora could reply.

"My cat."

"Oh! Oh. Can I see a picture of him?"

I showed her my gallery of Chester pics.

"Oh, he's just adorable," she said in a flat tone, suggesting it was merely a pleasantry that she couldn't invest in. "It's just too bad that my place isn't exactly catproof… otherwise, I would have said it's okay to keep him with us. He can stay with your mother and keep her company, though. I'm sure she's going to miss you."

Who was she to talk to me like that? I get to choose what I do, not you! I looked at Nora for silent support, but she just shrugged nonchalantly. "No, I meant when Nora and I find a place to stay—"

Eura interrupted me with a wag of her finger. "You're staying at my place for the duration of the contract."

"W-wait, I didn't agree to—"

"Actually, you just did! It was in the papers you signed—snuck it in myself. Don't worry though, I'll arrange everything! Trust me, you'll never want to leave!"

Snuck it in!?

As Eura's words sank in, I looked at Nora for support. I thought even Nora would have a problem with all of this, but the excited look in her eyes showed anything but. I returned my gaze to Eura, who was enthusiastically outlining her plans for our stay, and wondered just what I had gotten myself into.

Well, if it becomes too much for me to handle, *I'll just quit.*

***

Post-Chapter Omake

Nora: *You named the entire chapter after yourself!?*

Euphridia: *No rule against it!*

Nora: …*There is now.*

Euphridia: *Euphridia's Rule? No, you'll have to come up with another name. That one's already been used.*

CHAPTER 9: REN FAIRE

After the interview ended and we were walking out of the building, I rounded on Nora. "Why weren't you saying anything in there?"

Nora smiled brightly. "I didn't see any real problems with what she was asking of us. We need to build some rapport with her before we can push back on the important things later!"

"Push back? She's already too pushy! If we're not careful, we'll end up on the ground," I grumbled, feeling the tension from the interview still lingering as we made our way onto the bustling New York City street.

"She's probably just lonely. From writing to her, I got the sense that she doesn't have anyone to talk to."

"You don't make friends by controlling them!" I huffed.

"Do you think your boss is your friend?" Nora asked, tilting her head as she pulled out her phone to order our rideshare back home.

"W-well…" Isn't she technically our client? Is there a difference?

"I'm not saying we shouldn't try to get along or anything. I'm so proud of you for standing up for yourself and setting boundaries with others!"

I looked at her with a scowl. "You're next, you know."

"Nah. You'll need a lot more practice before you can take me on."

"Why did she practically ignore you?" I asked. "You're her biggest fan."

"That's probably exactly why."

"I don't understand."

"I'm her biggest fan, but that's it. I have nothing else in common with her, so what else is there to discuss? Better to keep quiet and observe." I counted myself very lucky Nora didn't feel that way about me.

"And what's your analysis?" I asked curiously.

"Mmm. We have our work cut out for us. She's very stubborn. She really likes you, though, so we can leverage that."

"I really don't know what she sees in me," I admitted.

Nora hesitated, managing even to look a bit concerned. "I wonder if she figured out your real reader handle…"

I shivered. "That's kind of creepy, isn't it?"

Nora frowned, tilting her head back and forth as if trying to justify Eura's actions. "Well… you did comment on everything, and you only ever said nice things. She probably internalized that and built a whole ideal person around them. Content creators have big, hungry egos, you know, and you gave her an all-you-can-eat buffet."

"I was just rooting for Rae…"

"Don't worry about it," Nora continued, waving her hand. "We'll wrap this contract up quickly and secure us some permanent, full-time work with CUP as a reward."

"Like normal adults?"

"Like normal adults," Nora confirmed, slipping her phone back into her pocket. "Ride will be here in ten."

***

Mother was sitting on the loveseat in the living room with Chester in her lap. They both glanced at me as soon as I came inside.

"You had an eventful day, I take it," she remarked, probably noticing the defeated slouch in my posture.

"You could say that," I murmured, still trying to figure out how to tell her about everything.

"Did you accept the job?"

"How did you know I had an interview?"

Rather than answer me directly for once, she picked up a plate from the end table and took a bite of Mama Perez's signature cotton cheesecake.

"Oh." Sure, you'll talk to Nora's mom over me.

"Well?" She waited for my answer.

"Yes, I accepted the job."

"Nora, too?" For the first time in my life, I noted she looked anxious. Chester perked his ears forward as if he were anticipating my answer. Why was she so worried about what Nora was doing? Didn't she trust me to make crucial decisions on my own?

"Yeah. We both signed a contract."

She leaned back into her chair, and Chester relaxed luxuriously across her lap. "As long as Nora is going with you, I think it will be okay. When do you start?"

***

The week flew by, punctuated here and there by a flurry of texts from Eura and Nora about logistics for our upcoming first day of employment. By Monday morning, Nora and I found ourselves at the gates of the North Catskill Winery and Renaissance Faire. The wrought-iron fence was open, but it was eerily quiet inside.

We walked down a cobblestone path to the main ticket booth, where the attendant waved us through without so much as a glance. We found Eura waiting in the center of a small grove, wearing an ivory dress that blurred the line between an off-shoulder toga and a floor-length ball gown. A gold sash encircled her midriff. Her usual sunglasses were absent, and I could see her eyes were the same merry blue as her grandfather's. Her handbag looked out of place, but at least she had it zippered shut this time.

We exchanged pleasantries, being sure to comment positively on her gown. It was much better than the red skirt suit she wore during our interview.

"Let's go, let's go!" She turned and sprinted down the path. As she ran, I could see she had donned gold sandals that laced up to her knees. We both followed her as she made her way to the marketplace.

As we followed, I couldn't help but notice that there was literally nobody else around. I figured we were just a bit early, but I didn't even see any workers getting things ready. "Where's everyone else?" I wondered aloud, feeling a bit uneasy once again.

"Oh, the faire is closed to the public. I rented it out for the day," Eura explained as if that were totally normal.

"Isn't that expensive?"

"I don't think so?" She shrugged and entered a nearby clothing shop, obviously expecting me to follow.

I was starting to wonder just how rich they were. Was her grandfather involved in other businesses than just web novels? I got that he owned a pretty big platform, but I didn't think there was *that* much money in it.

"Here." My thoughts were interrupted as she handed me a blue tunic adorned with gold clasps and white pants. "Try these! They'll go great with your complexion!"

A single glance told me there was no way I was putting that on. "I need long sleeves. Absolutely no short sleeves." I fussed, handing the tunic back.

"Are you… mad at me?" she asked with a pout, and I cringed. *It was way too early for a full confrontation.*

"Well, no, but look. I just don't like showing my forearms, okay? Or my midriff so…"

"I had no idea you're so modest! It's so cute!" She took the tunic up to the attendant at the counter.

Didn't I *just say* I wasn't going to wear that? I took a deep breath; I didn't want an argument, but it was time to draw a line.

As I followed her to the counter to interrupt the sale, I heard Eura ask the attendant, "I want this, but I need you to add long sleeves, okay?"

Oh, so she was just asking for alterations. I may have jumped to conclusions a *little* bit… but still!

"Of course, my lady." The attendant bowed.

"Oh, and she's going to need a white cloak. With a hood. And lots of hidden pockets. Gold trim. Tasteful. And leather boots." Eura turned to me. "What size?"

"Uh, twelve." My feet were big, sure, but they were in reasonable proportion to my overall height. Otherwise, I'd fall over a lot more.

"Oh! White gloves to match, too. Large, right?"

I nodded lamely in reply. She was hard to keep up with.

"It will be my pleasure to fulfill your request." The attendant bowed again before going into the back of the shop. Eura then squinted at Nora. "You're going to need an outfit too."

"Dark mage," Nora answered immediately.

"What?" Eura blinked several times. "I was thinking… like, a pirate or something." That "or something" made me think she hadn't thought about her at all.

Nora winked and snapped. "Fifth Circle dark mage!"

"Fifth Circle!?" Eura folded her arms. "You might as well just ask to be the next head of the Dark Mage Tower!"

I watched the exchange, dumbfounded, once again feeling slightly out of the loop. "Wait, are we just dressing up like characters from the story?" I blinked.

Nora seemed surprised as she asked, "What else should we be doing?"

"Uh, okay then, who am I dressing up as?"

"Why, Rae, of course!" Eura interjected happily.

"Why does Nora get to choose who she dresses up as, and I don't?" It's because of my nickname, isn't it? Raelynn's great and all, but I could have wanted to be someone else, you know.

"Who do you *want* to dress up as, then?" Eura asked with a tinge of amusement in her voice. Somehow, it felt like a challenge.

"Laverna!" I answered thoughtlessly. Oh, wait…

"Did you forget about her halter top?" Nora reminded me.

"Grah! Fine!" I supposed Raelynn did make the most sense for me after all. I at least knew when to pick my battles.

"Too bad the armor pieces are only cheap replicas, so we'll skip them," Eura said. "You're dressing up as Rae did when she met with the chief of the tiger clan."

I looked at Nora. "Remind me what happened?"

"Rae wasn't allowed to bring her weapons or armor into the sacred bamboo forest when she sought Iron Tiger Tetora's help, as it would signify suspicion and distrust. It seemed a little unfair to me because that rule didn't apply to the tiger clan themselves."

"Got it. Well, at least let me pick the cloth headband."

"Hachimaki," Nora and Eura clarified in unison.

Only a blue one was available, so I didn't get to choose after all. Although I could tie it around my head without help, I had trouble keeping it in place with the knot behind my ear. I finally gave up and put the knot down in the back.

"That's not how Raelynn wears it," Eura commented disapprovingly.

"It keeps popping off."

"You'd look better with longer hair," Eura opined. "Short hair doesn't suit you."

I glanced at Nora, hoping she'd stick up for me, but she nodded in agreement with Eura. I silently marked her as a traitor. "I'll consider it." That was my usual way of saying no.

"The glasses won't work with your ensemble either," Eura noted.

"Unfortunately, I need them to see, so they stay on my face."

"I thought they were just a fashion statement!"

I blinked. "Whatever gave you that idea?"

"Uh. Couldn't you just… No, that wouldn't work. I don't know, get surgery or something to fix them?"

I was so perplexed by her suggestion that I couldn't even get mad at the audacity. Maybe I was just getting used to it. "Surgery can't fix them, as far as I know."

"How tragic…"

Welcome to the real world, princess.

Nora and Eura spent much time arguing over which dark mage robes Nora should wear. Nora preferred darker colors, while Eura kept steering her to lighter fabrics. I had to agree with Nora. Who ever heard of a dark mage wearing white unless they were the villain in disguise? Eventually, I got bored with their bickering over color schemes and ended up looking at other sundries. Ultimately, Eura and Nora settled on a fancy, dark silver cloak embroidered with runes. I wasn't sure what Nora was wearing underneath the cloak, but knowing her, it would be outrageous, and she was waiting for the right time to debut it.

However, my eye caught the polished wooden staff they had selected. It was a fantastic work of art. It was as tall as I was, culminating in a twisted wooden cage enclosing a purple glass orb bigger than my fist.

"Can I see it?" I asked curiously.

"Sure." Nora tossed me the staff, and I took a few practice swings with it.

"It's not one of your softball bats! Hold it aloft!"

I held it up high and shouted "Haa!" I waited for a moment, but nothing happened.

"It's defective." I tossed it back to Nora.

"You always say that. How many times do I have to tell you it's not the magic weapon, it's you!"

Eura watched our playful exchange somewhat wistfully but did not comment. Then, the clothing attendant flagged me down. "My lady, your garments are ready." He handed me the ensemble and then pointed me to a stall where I could get changed.

Once inside, I got to work, changing into everything Eura had picked out for me. Amazingly, it all fit perfectly. Even the pants, which had been blessed with full-sized pockets, were long enough! I took a moment to admire the outfit in the mirror, thinking that despite Eura's eccentricities, she certainly did have an eye for this kind of thing.

Stepping out of the stall, I presented myself to Eura and Nora. "Well? What do you think?"

"Oh, my!" Eura had tears in her eyes.

"You look amazing!" Nora cheered.

I chuckled, feeling embarrassed, but I had to admit this was kind of fun. I figured maybe I should just go with the flow a little more. It's okay to be my real self sometimes, right?

Then, my stomach growled loudly, interrupting our fashion show. It was time to eat.

CHAPTER 10: INSPIRATION

Since so much of my costume was white, I was a little preoccupied with ensuring I didn't spill lunch on myself. My smoked turkey leg was less than half finished before the other two were already on to chatting animatedly about the story. We tried to summarize our brainstorming kickoff session, but Eura kept dancing around the preliminary plot points we needed to solidify.

"So you're going with a time skip, instead?" Nora asked Eura. After checking my notes, I circled number four on the list of suggestions.

"Yes… There is no other way around it at this point," Eura confirmed. "It's been seven and a half years since the events of chapter fifty-seven."

"Not five?" I asked around a mouthful of turkey.

"It's been five years since I published the last chapter, but seven and a half years have passed for the world of Speranza."

Nora pondered this. "A lot can happen in that timeframe. Rae would be… over twenty-two years old by now." She glanced meaningfully at me, but I furrowed my brow and shook my head, trying my darndest to convey my objections mentally.

Don't you dare tell her my age. It's a coincidence. I'm her target audience, remember?

Nora blinked but then cleared her throat. "Um, so what's Euphridia up to?"

"She's about to bring Rae back," Eura replied with a smug smile.

I perked up. "Euphridia herself found her in the next world?" Interesting. That wasn't anywhere on our list.

"Uh-huh." Eura seemed reticent, or maybe she was just bored. Whatever the case, she refused to further elaborate on the details.

"What's Raelynn like now?" I asked.

"Mmm...older...?"

What a basic answer.

"Did she recover?"

"Physically, she's mostly fine, but... she doesn't remember anything from before."

Nora sniffed. "Memory loss trope, huh? Risky business, but we can work with that. Will you have her use forbidden, otherworldly knowledge from the next world to break her current level cap?" She then glanced back down to the list of questions she had written in her leather journal and took a few notes.

"No... given the circumstances, she didn't hone any skills," Eura replied. I was secretly relieved to hear that she wasn't coming back overpowered. Too many stories already focus on the main character becoming, by happenstance alone, an expert on the next plot device that solves all the world's problems.

"So, it was like she was just on vacation?" Nora pursed her lips. "She didn't do anything heroic?"

"Nothing to make note of, anyway."

"Hey!" I interjected. "She deserves a break once in a while! And it's not her fault if she doesn't remember!"

Nora looked concerned. "Surely she did *something important* in the next world during those seven years! Your audience isn't going to be too happy with a sudden time skip with no explanation and no payoff."

"The next world is *boring*. It's not worth writing about!" Eura caught the frown I was making. "Oh! But, even if she can't remember, even if she's older, she's still the same Rae, and that's all that matters! As soon as she returns to where she belongs, everyone will be much happier."

"Ah..." Nora looked a bit defeated. "What about Relias? What's he been doing?"

"Oh!" Eura laughed nervously. "Uh, I'm sure he's fine! Euphridia told him to do whatever was necessary in the interim. He's very capable, so… yeah."

"I'm sure that's true," Nora agreed. "However, I think we need something more solid to work with."

She ignored the request and instead turned her intense gaze towards me. "He's handsome too, right?"

I shrugged noncommittally, but it wasn't enough. It took me a moment to realize she would not continue until I gave her my opinion. "I mean, I guess? The cover art would suggest it anyway…" He had long blonde hair and aquamarine eyes like many male protagonists of the fantasy genre. To me, though, he was Raelynn's one-and-only, so he was off-limits.

"I did my best with Relias, you know."

"Wait, you illustrated your own story, too? You're talented!"

She burst into laughter, though I wasn't sure what was so funny about what I said.

"So, Relias is still around?" Nora asked for further clarification once her laughter died down.

"Definitely… most likely."

Why wouldn't she just say yes?

Even Nora finally looked like she was getting a bit frustrated. "What about the rest of the party?" she asked.

"Mmm… unclear."

I set down my turkey leg and wiped my hands on a cloth napkin. "They're not together?"

"Doubtful. Losing Rae… I don't think they'd stick together without her."

I glanced at Nora's notes, which were full of cross-outs and question marks, then voiced some of my thoughts so far. "So, seven years pass, the party disbands with their whereabouts unknown, there's a new demon king, and the world is without the Goddess…" I tilted my head. "Wait. Was Euphridia gone the entire time!?"

Eura looked a little guilty. "W-well… she was looking for Rae, so…"

"We're looking at a lot of variables here!" Nora mused. "We can take this in all sorts of directions!"

Eura shook her head. "No! One direction. Euphridia is going to send Rae straight to the holy capital. It's likely Relias is in Chairo's main temple, still praying for Rae's return."

I imagined their fateful reunion. "Euphridia should let Holy Sage Relias know that Raelynn's on her way!" Would their meeting jog her memory? Would he *finally* confess? That's how true love works in these types of stories, right? It fixes everything!

Eura's face filled with consternation. "Uh, Euphridia normally *would* send word of her impending arrival, but she's having trouble connecting with Relias."

My thoughts fizzled. "So he might not be okay?" Come on! I can't build the ship if you don't give me the raw materials!

"N-no, I'm sure he's fine. Probably."

A cold thought gripped me. "Wait. Did Olethros… No, he promised to let him go! Even if he's a demon, *he promised!*" He wouldn't *dare* go back on his word.

Eura slammed her fists on the table at the mention of his name. "That bastard! That dirty, rotten bastard! He's why Euphridia can't get in touch with Relias!"

I flinched back at her sudden outburst. You'd think we were talking about real people and not a story. I glanced at Nora for some confirmation that she was being a bit over the top, but Nora barely reacted at all.

"Plausible." Nora inspected her turkey leg for any last vestiges of meat. "Though I think he'd rather just listen in on those kinds of conversations rather than cut them off entirely. I bet they'd be full of important information he couldn't get otherwise." Bold move there, telling Eura she's wrong about her own story.

"Ah, you don't think he'd just put up a barrier to keep Euphridia out completely?" I asked Nora quickly while Eura gritted her teeth, obviously holding back an angry rebuttal. "If I were him, I wouldn't want either of them returning."

"I doubt he has that much power. Remember, he'd have to maintain it, and it's not like he has anyone to help him."

"Uh, what about the other demon lords?" I struggled to recall their names while hastily trying to move through the topic. I could only picture a giant beast of a warmonger and a scantily clad sorceress with enormous bat wings.

"You mean General Ragnerus and Dark Mistress Aziza?"

"Right. They could be in cahoots with him," I offered.

"Cahoots?" Nora laughed at my word choice. "With the signing of this dark pact, we are now in cahoots together for eternity! Calamity to the varmints opposing us!"

"All joking aside, it's possible!" I said defensively.

"They never worked together before." Nora continued to scribble notes even as she turned again to Eura, utterly unconcerned by the fact that her eyes were still blazing with anger. "So you've settled on Demon King Olethros being the new villain, then?"

"He's always been a villain!" Eura yelled. "Even more so now!"

Nora tapped her pencil on her notebook. "You're saying he's even worse than his peccant progenitor?"

I got confused with that one. "Peccant… progenitor?" It sounded a little dirty!

"Evil daddy," Nora substituted.

"Oh." I still wasn't sure if she was being lewd or not.

"He's not bound to the Wastelands like his progenitor was." Eura sneered. "He can destroy anything he wants now that Epiales is gone."

I couldn't help but think about the Olethros of my dreams—oh, you *know* what I mean! "Maybe… he's not interested in following in his footsteps? I mean, he doesn't have to follow his orders anymore."

Eura shook her head. "The only purpose a demon has is to destroy the things Euphridia loves the most! They care about nothing else."

That sounded too one-dimensional. "Wouldn't it be more interesting to examine other possible reasons for—"

"No!" Eura shouted. "He *banished* Rae while she was on the verge of death! All demons are *absolutely irredeemable*. Don't ever, ever question that!"

I flinched at her tone, feeling like she was chastising me for a major transgression. What's wrong with having a complicated antagonist this time around? I kept my head down as I mulled over what she said in sullen silence.

Nora let the awkwardness between us linger for a few minutes as she looked over some notes. "What about Rae's sword? Does Olethros still have it?"

Eura exhaled with a huff. "Most likely."

"With Rae's sword under Olethros's control, it will be hard for her to confront him. He didn't destroy it, did he?"

"No," Eura said firmly. "Euphridia forged the Will and the Faith, especially for Rae. Olethros will never, ever be able to destroy either of them. He might hide the sword somewhere, though." It made sense, considering it was probably the only thing that could kill him now that his father was gone.

"They're a set, right?" Nora pondered. "Are they magically linked?"

Eura *finally* gave Nora something to work with. "The shield and sword were forged from the same star."

"From cosmic metal? That's so cool!" Nora marveled, and I came very close to calling her a suck up before realizing that was precisely the tactic she needed to employ.

"Thanks," Eura preened. I felt her eyes on me again. Did you think I was going to sing your praises, too? I renewed my will not to look at her. Nora could play the good cop.

"Since they're linked," Nora pressed onward, "could Rae use the shield Relias has to find the sword?"

"Oh, yes, she could!"

"So then..." Nora started making a to-do list. "Rae reunites with Relias, gets her shield back, gathers the rest of the party, and goes out searching for her sword and King Olethros?"

"Why would she need to find the rest of the party?" Eura asked.

Recently reprimanded or not, I wouldn't let that one go. "Because they're her stalwart companions!" I shouted.

"All she needs is Relias." Eura waved her hand.

"Vernie, Aleph, and Tetora are just as important!"

"I'm not sure that's really…"

"They have to be in the story! They just have to be!" I stood up and pounded my fists on the table this time, earning a startled look from Eura.

"Just *go* with it," Nora whispered to her. "They don't have to do much, but you should give her this little win. You have *no idea* how long she can hold a grudge for."

"But… it might be hard to find them…" Eura hedged. "For all I know, they could already be—"

"No! They're alive. I just know it!" I folded my arms angrily. *He promised* to let them go, too. Otherwise, Raelynn would have never surrendered like that!

Eura waved her hands. "Alright, alright. She can look for them, too."

I huffed and sat back down, surly about the whole idea of ignoring half the protagonists. Introducing epic characters only to dump them off as fodder a little while later is infuriating!

Eura watched my face for a few moments before laughing nervously. "It'll all work out for the best in the end. I promise!"

"I'm holding you accountable." If anything happened to those three…

"Um… maybe you're just thirsty?" she asked, and I realized she was right. After I conceded with a nod, she reached inside her handbag and pulled out a bottle of red wine with a fancy label.

"What's that?"

"Look!" She turned cheerful again almost instantly.

I read the calligraphic label aloud. "Inspiration." I thought I was thirsty for water, but maybe wine was a better choice. It would probably help me relax and go with the flow. Why hadn't she started our discussion with something like this?

"Seems appropriate," Nora said with a nod, shoving her journal and pen inside her cloak. Eura pulled out two wine glasses and poured one for each of us.

"What about you?" I asked.

"Oh, I don't drink. I wanted to celebrate our collaboration, though."

"What should we toast to?" I asked.

"To happy endings?" Eura suggested.

"To happy endings!" Nora and I responded, clinking our glasses against the wine bottle in Eura's hands.

I remembered drinking a single glass of very tasty wine. Then… nothing for a while. Suddenly, we were walking away from the faire, that much I was sure of. However, I couldn't decide exactly why we were doing so. We were heading towards a nearby mountain peak. I glanced at Nora occasionally, but for the life of me, I didn't know what to ask her.

Why can't I seem to gather my thoughts? Something's going on, but…

A small voice in the back of my head was trying to get me to… do something, but I couldn't understand it. Instead, I just settled on watching my feet march up the side of the mountain, pleasantly surprised with how easy it was. Usually, such a steep grade would have tired me, but I felt like I could do this all day. Nora was matching me step for step, which had me bemused since it meant her stride was comically exaggerated. Eura was in front of us, her gold sash fluttering behind her.

This isn't right, is it?

The peak was covered in dense pines, though here and there, the rocky terrain became exposed to sunlight that streamed in from above. Nestled in a small grove was an ancient stone archway bathed in a broad sunbeam. We headed toward the archway at a synchronous pace. The small voice in my head was becoming more shrill with each step. I still couldn't distinguish any intelligible words, so I ignored it.

"My place is just through here," Eura said brightly, gesturing at the archway. Something was strange about that statement, but I wasn't sure what.

Everything here… it's a little too colorful, too bright.

Eura held out her hands. "Let me take your bags." Nora and I wordlessly handed her the backpacks we had brought for our day trip. Eura took them and set them aside. Then she looked me up and down one last time. "The hair will eventually fix itself, but I don't like those glasses. You'll be better off without them." She reached up and took hold of them at my temples. Her warm fingers briefly brushed the sides of my face as she pulled them off.

"Much better!" she remarked. I looked at her questioningly but again said nothing.

I think… I need those… don't I?

She then turned to Nora. "I guess you'll be useful too, seeing as how you memorized the whole thing. I hate to admit it, but the old man was right." She momentarily pressed her right index finger to the center of Nora's forehead.

"Understand now?" Eura asked her. Nora simply nodded, getting a better grip on her staff that had flickered to life.

Huh, I didn't know it was electric…

"Oh, you two should probably hold hands," Eura continued. "You might get separated if you don't." Nora held out her hand, and I took it. We exchanged glances with one another. I wanted to say something, but I couldn't even formulate a simple thought of my own.

"I wish I could come with you, but it seems I will have to wait until things get back on track. See if you can do something about all the animus in the air. I'm sure it's all *his fault.*" Eura paused for a moment, a brief frown crossing her features. She then shook her head in resolution and locked eyes with me. *"Just… do whatever you need to do to make things right, okay?"*

All I could do was nod back.

Nora and I turned and headed towards the gate. The small voice in my head screamed, and I halted instinctively. Eura, however, was right behind us.

"Sometimes taking the first step is the hardest, so I'll give you a little push." I felt Eura's hand on my back as she hurled me forward through the archway with incredible force.

She called after us, "Remember, don't let go!"

CHAPTER 11: ARRIVAL

You know that feeling, that singular moment when you find yourself flailing about, and the next, you're on the floor, utterly clueless about the space in between? Well, that second moment did not come to me for a dreadfully long time. Instead, I was shocked sober with the nauseating feeling of free falling. I gripped Nora's limp hand and tried to scream, but no sound came out.

We fell through darkness into a clear blue sky, skydiving without a parachute. Below us, blurry land masses grew more prominent with every passing second. A translucent gold light formed a bubble around us, cutting us off from the icy cold air whipping at our bodies and slowing our descent. We piled on top of one another at the bottom of the bubble as awkwardly as two people trying to share a revolving hammock.

"No. Not there. Over there." I could finally understand the eerily familiar voice inside my head.

"What?" I mumbled, peeling my suction-cupped face off the bottom of the floating bubble.

"The Wastelands. Head for the Wastelands."

To the far west, I saw a large, brownish-yellow area devoid of anything resembling vegetation, unlike the eastern portion of the strange-looking continent. It did not strike me as particularly welcoming. "Why should I listen to you?"

There was no response. However, something seized control of me, and I bashed my body into the bubble, turning its course towards the west as we descended.

"Wait, stop!" Again and again, I hurled myself into the bubble's side. I tried to get Nora's attention, but from a side glance, she appeared to be unconscious.

"We need to get a better sense of what's happening out there."

After a few more bashings, the possessing voice let me go just in time for me to collapse.

***

The next thing I knew, I was lying face-up in a pile of sandy rubble. I felt dirty and disoriented. My right hip was particularly angry, so I rolled onto my left side. I think I forgot to mention I was feeling nauseated as well. Never in my life had I ever been so drunk before. What the heck was in that wine?

There was no way I fell from the sky! I probably just tripped over something with my clumsy feet when Eura pushed me.

"Nora, are you alive?" I saw her form sprawled out on the uneven stone tiles around us.

Not like her to trip, though. I probably bashed into her.

"I think so. Are you?"

"I feel awful, so I'm going to say yes." I sat up with effort, brushing rocky dust from my face.

Nora grunted as she used her staff to help her stand.

"My glasses! I can't find my glasses!" I suddenly panicked as I realized they weren't on my face.

"You can't see a thing without your glasses," Nora agreed as she started looking for them.

"Yeah, wait… everything's crystal clear!" I marveled, temporarily forgetting my bruised hip and other complaints.

"Maybe you're still drunk?"

"Maybe." I looked around. The roof of the makeshift amphitheater we found ourselves in was mostly gone, with only a few pillars standing high enough to arc over us. Rubble was piled around all the edges. "I think there are several building code violations going on here. Which part of the faire are we in?"

"Who knows? Eura has the map. Where do you think she went?"

"Not sure, but when she comes back, I'm going to tell her off for pushing us." I stood up, stretching and verifying that the rest of my body was quite sore. I examined my clothing, seeing it was stained with dirt. Worst of all was around my hip, where I think I landed the hardest. "It's all ruined."

"What?"

"My costume. Wearing white is just asking for trouble," I sighed. "Do you think this will come out of my pay?"

"Rae… I think we have bigger things to discuss." She pointed to a giant stone altar in the exact center of the amphitheater.

Within the throne room of the King of Nightmare

Raelynn Lightbringer

Knight Captain of the Holy Order of Gold

Chosen One of the Goddess

Seventh Appointed Hero of Legend

Wielding the Faith and Will of Euphridia

Felled Epiales

Origin of Evil

Eternally Accursed

May Euphridia's light return you to us

I stared at the ridiculously sized altar. "Just how much money does Eura have?"

"You have to admit, it looks pretty realistic." Nora put her hands on the altar, scratching at its surface with a fingernail. "I think it's stone, or at least plated in stone."

"It looks like she went through a lot of trouble for us. I'm all for inspiration, but I feel like we've tumbled into the uncanny valley."

Two masculine voices abruptly echoed in from the surroundings, cutting off our conversation. In a panic, Nora and I nodded at each other, silently agreeing we didn't want to have to explain to strangers why we were rolling around in the dirt, so we swiftly ducked behind the altar. As they approached our hiding spot, I prayed fervently that Eura had gone to get us a wardrobe change.

"I'm telling you, if another pilgrim brings red camellias, I will slice them clear in two! She didn't die!" the first voice declared indignantly.

"No, you won't," the other voice disagreed gently. "You'll just keep complaining about it to me, but that's alright. You'll feel better once you've overcome your excess anger."

"Oh, I mean it this time! Blood spatter everywhere! Screams of agony and—"

"Hush now, we're here." They stopped talking, but I could hear at least one approaching the altar with heavy footsteps. Please don't peek back here!

"It's us again," the deep but gentle-voiced man murmured.

The other voice sighed at first, then took a more aggressive tone. "What's taking you so long to come back? I'm going to give you such a scolding, you know! Three times as much if you haven't been practicing your fighting forms! I—" he halted abruptly and let out a frightening growl. I only thought wild animals could make such a noise!

"What's this?" The gentle one's voice suddenly turned hard. I heard a loud thud and saw the floor tiles surrounding me rattle. Then, a whirlwind of white and gray descended on me, knocking me onto my back. The back of my head hit the stone floor, and I only saw white for a moment. Then I heard a loud sniffing.

As my vision cleared, a gasp caught in my throat. There, before me, was someone who seemed to have stepped out of a wild fantasy. "Raelynn!" He was shaking my shoulders roughly. The initial shock had rendered me speechless. His appearance was almost human but with undeniable tiger-like nuances.

His eyes gleamed with a distinctive golden hue. He had cat-like ears positioned at the top of his head, and his hair was primarily white with black stripes like a tiger's. A set of whiskers, delicate and almost imperceptible, sprouted from his cheeks.

"Where have you been!? Uh, I wasn't worried, of course, but you upset Aleph! How could you do that to him?"

Aleph? As in Aleph and Tetora? But that couldn't be right; they're not real! Real or not, he then crushed me with a fierce hug.

"Tetora, I think she's in shock. That dark mage might have done something to her." I turned slightly and saw a towering man with flowing chestnut hair and dull gray ox horns holding a giant hammer threateningly over Nora. She was frozen stiff, with her hands up as if under arrest. The tile in front of her was utterly pulverized. Had the ox giant done that as a warning?

I tried to gather my wits. "N-Nora wouldn't do anything to hurt me! It's you two that I'm afraid of!"

Tetora and Aleph exchanged a glance.

"On second thought, she doesn't seem like she's possessed," Aleph noted, rubbing at his cropped brown beard.

"But since when is she afraid of anything?" Tetora complained. "What happened to my fierce little dragon?"

"Nora…" I squeaked out loud, but she failed to respond. Swallowing nervously, I tried my best to glare threateningly at Aleph. "Don't you dare hurt my friend Nora!" The ox giant momentarily looked deep into my eyes as if searching for something. "I-I mean it!" I reiterated.

"Yes, I can see I was mistaken about your friend." Aleph stepped back from Nora to give her room. Tetora, however, kept his grip on me. I saw his tail lash back and forth as he picked me up.

"Put… put me down!" I struggled.

"You've gotten weak! Can't even break my hold. Time to train." He carried me out of the ruined amphitheater over his shoulder like a sack of potatoes.

"I'm not who you think I am!" I shouted. I freed my right arm and began pounding on his back as hard as possible. "You're making a huge mistake!" If I had been in my right mind, I would have realized that I was the one making a big mistake. I was trying to beat up an anthropomorphic martial artist with muscles decorating his muscles.

"To the left. I have a knot back there behind my shoulder blade. Maybe your mosquito bite punches will fix it!" He laughed happily and tossed me a few times in the air in what I could only imagine was misplaced exultation.

"Nora!" I screeched, extending my now-free arms out towards her. This time, she took a big breath, and I could see her brain resetting. Her eyes suddenly sparkled. No, Nora, this isn't what you think! Don't fall for it!

"You're Aleph, aren't you? Oh, I've read so much about you!" She was squealing now, her high-pitched voice hitting whole registers above what the average human ear could decipher.

Aleph nodded with a slow smile as he offered Nora a hand and pulled her to her feet. He then returned her staff and allowed her to use his arm for balance. Nora took it and followed behind me with a staggering gait, which became more sure of itself with every step.

"Where are you taking us!?" I demanded shrilly.

Tetora shifted me slightly. "To the village. We have much to celebrate!"

"Stop jostling me, or I'll throw up all over you."

"What, you're feeling sick? When did you become so delicate?" He stopped walking but didn't let me down while Aleph and Nora caught up to us. He must have taken the threat to heart, though, because he stopped tossing me.

"We need to keep moving," Aleph advised. "It isn't safe here."

Tetora started down the dirt path again, and I let myself hang limply over his shoulder, arms splayed down his back. I had no idea what was going on here, but I figured I was stuck along for the ride. We were heading into a dark, sickly forest populated with petrified trunks devoid of branches and leaves.

"Ms. Nora, may I carry you on my back for the rest of our sojourn?" Aleph asked politely. "The forest floor is rather rough and somewhat difficult to traverse."

"Permission granted." She scrambled up his back with glee, clearly taking this much better than I was. "Can I—"

"I would prefer that you didn't," Aleph cut her off. I saw she was staring intently at his horns. "Please put your arms around my neck instead."

"Why don't you do that for me?" I asked Tetora. "Then this wouldn't feel so much like kidnapping, you know."

"You always pull my whiskers when we do that. I'm not stupid." Although he sounded indignant, I noticed he was hugging me tightly again. I knew he would explode when he realized I wasn't actually Raelynn.

Wait, why was I thinking like that? This wasn't real, after all. They were just actors Eura had hired. They were doing an impressive job, but I felt her eccentric nature and apparently limitless funds were taking things a step too far now.

About ten minutes later, Tetora suddenly dropped me on my feet and extended his claws. Aleph also set Nora down, although much more gently, and stepped in front of her protectively.

"How many this time?" Aleph asked.

"Three—no, four. The last one's injured and moving strangely."

I could see three giant, gray, ape-like beasts skulking between tree trunks ahead of us. Their arms hung down to the ground, ending in giant knuckled fists. Angry red tufts of fur covered their backs.

"You two stay right here with Aleph. No heroics!" Tetora leapt forward on all fours, letting out a loud roar. One ape, larger than the rest, screamed in response and shot forward to meet Tetora's charge. The other two apes hooted excitedly but made no move to join.

Aleph pointed. "He challenged the alpha, so the other redbacks should hang back. When Tetora wins, the others will take off." I nodded as I stared. Were those costumes? No, they were too big. Animatronics? Even Eura shouldn't have that big of a budget! Maybe I was just hallucinating at this point. They looked too lifelike!

The combatants were circling each other now, warily. The alpha ape attempted to lunge forward first, but Tetora dodged to the side. As he landed, he twisted his body and drove his claws into the ape's underbelly. The ape screamed again, though this time it was filled with agony.

Tetora pivoted around the ape in a fluid movement, jumped onto its back, and drove his right fist, claws and all, into its side. The ape collapsed to the ground with a howl, and Tetora jumped back. With a synchronized grunt, the other apes cautiously melted back into the stone forest. As the alpha glared at Tetora, it slowly got to its feet and backed away to join its companions.

Nora suddenly shouted, "Over there!" She pointed, and both Aleph and I turned. To the right, two giant alligator-like lizards left the tree line and ran straight towards us.

"Megalanies!" Aleph shouted as he charged forward, poised to strike. One of the giant lizards veered off to one side while the second darted the other way in a flanking maneuver. Aleph smashed his war hammer into the skull of one while the other came at him from behind.

Nora aimed the orb of her staff at it. "Fulgura!" she shouted. A bolt of lightning shot out from the orb and coursed through the tail of the giant alligator, shocking it throughout its body. The monster stopped moving entirely. Aleph took the opportunity to strike the other alligator again in the eye, throwing it back as it let out a pained hiss. All I could do was gape at Nora in disbelief, though she seemed just as surprised as I was that her spell had worked.

"Behind you!" the voice inside my head screamed as it seized control of my body, whirling me around. Another ape had taken advantage of the chaos and hurled itself at me.

"Better to meet this head-on!" I found myself running towards the new challenger. Unlike the other apes, it made no audible challenging calls.

"We're going to have to kill this one outright. It no longer eats or thinks rationally." I noticed its jaw appeared to be hanging somewhat slack. A fragment of bone was sticking out from the side of its cheek.

Kill it? Are you crazy? I don't have any weapons! Despite my silent protests, I was still running forward.

"You have your fists, feet, and teeth, don't you?"

There's no way I'm going to bite that thing!

"Then stay out of the way and let me handle this. No point in getting injured so early in our journey."

The enraged ape threw up its arms to smash me to the ground, but my body moved on its own as I dove under them and drove an uppercut into its injured jaw with all the force my arm was capable of. Despite how the ape crested my height even when it was on all fours, my blow forced it to stagger backward. I drove a front kick into one of its exposed knees while throwing up my arms to block counterattacks. Tucking my feet under myself, I launched myself backward to put space between us. Blood was pouring from its mouth, and the leg I had struck collapsed slightly inwards. Just how hard had I struck it?

"Not hard enough. Tetora is correct. You need to train."

As if the voice had summoned him, he jumped from behind me, smashing his clawed right fist directly into the ape's eye. It quivered, then fell to the ground dead as Tetora retracted his claws. He was puffing, and I could see him trembling with anger.

"What did I tell you?" His voice was dreadfully quiet, contrasting with what I assumed was his usual yelling.

"It w-wasn't me…" I stammered.

Go on, talk to him, Raelynn!

"I'm not Raelynn."

Then who are you?

"Raeonna, Third Appointed Hero of Legend."

Raeonna? A predecessor of Raelynn?

"Well, I'm waiting for an answer. If it wasn't you, then who was it?" He was snarling softly now, his tail flicking side to side.

"Raeonna." He blinked and considered my answer for several moments. Maybe he never heard of her?

"Tell him he should stop favoring his right side so much. One of these days, he will get knocked on his back permanently."

Now doesn't seem the best time to criticize him!

"Nonsense. Do it, or I will."

I swallowed and repeated Raeonna's message. Tetora's anger slipped away, replaced by sheer astonishment. "But Raeonna's long gone…"

"I know it sounds crazy, but…"

Maybe I am crazy.

"No. You would not say this if it were not true. To think Raeonna's spirit is still with us…" Tetora bowed deeply, looking like he would take her few words of advice to heart. Before I could ask who she was, Aleph and Nora joined us.

"Rae! You punched that redback in the face and broke its jaw!" Nora shadowboxed for a moment.

"It was already broken… Wait, why are you so surprised about what I did? You just cast a… spell! Y-you summoned… lightning!" There were several expletives I omitted at the last moment.

"You've never used animus before?" Aleph asked Nora.

"No, that was my first time!" she said, and I could almost hear her thinking *And it won't be my last!*

"You may need training even more desperately than Raelynn." Aleph frowned thoughtfully. "Let's keep moving. It would be best to reach the village before the sun sets."

CHAPTER 12: RAEONNA

The four of us walked together now, our eyes alert for additional predators.

"Is Raeonna still there?" Tetora asked tentatively.

"I'm not sure."

Are you?

"Do not bother me right now with useless prattle."

I grimaced. "Uh, I think she's busy."

"I see." He sounded disappointed for a moment, but then he snorted happily. "To think I received such praise from Grandmaster Raeonna!"

"It sounded to me like she was criticizing you," Nora remarked.

"Haha, yes, but if that is all she had to say to me, then I know I am doing just fine!"

Then my lips were forced open as Raeonna used me to shout, "Your lack of humility is my biggest concern!"

Tetora turned to face me. "I knew you were still there, Grandmaster." He bowed to me, or rather her, respectfully.

Raeonna had me point to my body. "This one is weak, and many chakras are impacted. The solar plexus chakra is almost completely blocked. Past wounds were treated improperly, allowing animus to solidify in the viscera. There is lingering sickness in the connective tissues and humors as well. You will need to teach this one meditation and training. I will demonstrate the proper exercises to start with shortly."

I would have had a few choice words to say about all of that, but I was stuck impatiently waiting to have control of my body back.

"It will be as you say, Grandmaster." Aleph also bowed to us.

"Hmm. Tiger and Ox together," Raeonna mused, glancing at Aleph. "You have overcome your incompatibility. It is good to know that those believing themselves to be the authority on others' relationships are once again woefully ignorant." Aleph and Tetora exchanged a long, somewhat apprehensive glance.

Then we looked at Nora and waved our hand contemptuously. "Do not seek a mortal master, mage. They will try to limit your understanding under the deceptive guise of tutelage. Life experience is your teacher for now."

Did you just tell Nora she didn't need guided instruction? You're just going to let her do whatever comes to mind with dangerous magical explosives? Do you even know *her!?*

"She will be just fine. It is you *that worries me."*

Great. Just great.

We reached the village just before true darkness overtook the sky. I was hesitant to agree that it was indeed a village. There were only half a dozen wooden hovels with thatched roofs scattered about in the dirt, tied together with lines to hang linens. We entered one of the larger ones, where Aleph and Tetora lit several lamps to light up the interior. The wooden floor creaked as we walked across it.

Raeonna sat us down on the floor in front of a long, squat wooden table. "I have little time. Partake of a small meal with proper devotions, but do not linger in grand conversation. This body must train before my parting." Raeonna then let me go for the moment. I saw Aleph and Tetora heading into another room. Given the sounds from there, I guessed it was the kitchen and they were preparing dinner for all of us. I could hear them whispering excitedly, but I could not make out what they were saying.

"Say something else mysterious and commanding!" Nora exclaimed, looking me in the eyes.

"Uh, I can't! She's taking a break." I could only hope that she'd forget to come back afterward. Or that I would wake up.

"Oh good, you're back." She sat beside me. "What's it like being possessed by a fallen hero from the past?"

"Um. Disconcerting? That's the right word, I think."

"Thought so. Do you let her take over, or did she just sort of…"

"It's weird. It feels like… she's shoved me away from the microphone while I'm on stage."

"She seems rather direct."

"Nora, I don't remember anything about her in the story. Did I forget something important?"

"Mmm…" Nora looked towards the kitchen momentarily, then leaned in to whisper. "*The Last Rae of Hope* only briefly mentioned Rae's past lives. All it said about Raeonna was that she trained a lot with the different beastmen clans before attempting to defeat the demon king."

"Her nickname would have been Rae too, huh?"

Nora nodded. "A recurring theme between all the legendary heroes."

"No need to make them distinct, huh?" I kind of felt bad about that.

"I mean… they're all supposed to be reincarnations of the first hero, so…"

I sighed loudly. "This can't be real, you know. We're drunk. This is a fantastic virtual reality environment, and we can't pull off our headsets. We're alternate reality substitutes. We fell and hit our heads. We're dreaming. We were hit by truck-kun. Tell me which scenario or scenario combination this setup is!"

"I don't know Rae. I remember walking up a mountain and going through a portal."

"Eura pushed you, and I held your hand, right?"

"Yeah," Nora answered.

"I'm definitely not Raelynn."

"Maybe… maybe not."

"You're kidding, right?" I blinked.

"I'm just saying we should keep an open mind about everything."

"Any more open, and your brain's going to fall out! This isn't real!" I shouted, just as Aleph and Tetora carried in a tray of small dishes.

"This must be very confusing for you," Aleph said quietly as he portioned the food for us. It mainly consisted of vegetables, though here and there some dishes were sprinkled with little bits of meat.

"That's an understatement. I'm just a normal person, not a hero. I don't belong here."

Tetora grabbed a pair of chopsticks and went directly for the meat on the dishes before him. Between one mound of food and the next entering his maw, he declared with a dramatic finger point, "You are Raelynn Lightbringer."

"No, I'm Rachel Emily Smith," I responded.

"Gold dragon, born in the year 3500." He shoveled rice into his mouth.

"Uh, Cancer, born July 10th, 2000." I ate some seaweed from a soup bowl.

"You are twenty-two years old."

"I am twenty-two years old," I conceded. "But it's a coincidence."

"Um, Rae…" Nora whispered. "You're also a gold dragon."

"How do you figure?"

"Chinese zodiac. 2000 was the year of the gold dragon. You know… natural, straightforward, uh, prone to continually changing emotions."

You just *had* to add that last part.

I sighed. "How do you know all this?"

She shrugged. "Fanfic research."

"But specifically for my birth year?"

"Dragons are cool?"

I couldn't argue with her logic on that one.

"What are you then? A rabbit, right?" I remembered learning that from a chopstick wrapper.

"Earth rabbit," Nora clarified.

"What does that mean?"

"Intelligent, independent, calm, hard worker. You know, just awesome all around."

"They always list at least one negative trait. Fess up; which one is it?"

"Um. Sometimes, we appear arrogant. Because of all the awesomeness."

"Huh. Imagine that."

"Eat faster, talk less," Raeonna said inside my head.

I let out a resigned sigh and thought, *Yes, Grandmaster.*

As soon as I was done eating, Raeonna took over again without even bothering to mention she would do so. She simply stood me up, waved curtly for everyone else to follow, and walked me through their house to the backyard. It was less an actual yard and more of a flat dirt pit.

"I don't have time to tell you what these are. Just let your muscles learn them. Forget words. Tetora will explain later."

I stepped outside—well, Raeonna walked me outside, anyway—and my body started striking different poses as I worked my way across the field. Here and there, I noted I would punch, block, or kick with various swift movements. She would stop often, shifting my stances and pulling an arm or leg back into more solid stances before starting again.

Tetora and Aleph had brought some lamps outside so we could see the ground in the dark.

"Relax. You are making this more complicated."

This feels awkward!

"You are unbalanced. Lifting weights alone does not satisfy the requirements for good overall health."

Maybe it's just the alcohol?

"There are no traces of alcohol in your body."

Really?

"Focus."

We practiced for what felt like hours. I was getting exhausted, and I knew my muscles were fatiguing. Even if I didn't see the purpose of my fighting movements, I could tell I was slipping. She finally stopped at one point and sat me down in the dirt.

"I will be gone soon."

Wait, you're leaving?

"Yes."

I need a teacher! You saw those things in the woods, right? I don't have the first clue how to defend myself!

"*You need a proper teacher. Not a fake like me.*"

A fake? They don't just hand out the title Grandmaster, you know.

"*I'm an exception. My biggest regret is that I selfishly took knowledge from my masters and did not give back to the next generation. However, if I can set you on the right path… I can finally move on.*"

Raeonna was silent for a moment but came back with a commanding voice.

"*Meditate with Aleph. Train with Tetora. Teach them who you really are. Do not die prematurely. Live the life you want without too many regrets.*"

I swallowed heavily. *Thank you for your instruction, Grandmaster.*

"*Hahaha! You will not be so thankful tomorrow! Good luck, Rachel.*" And then she was gone.

CHAPTER 13: MORNING AFTER

I woke up on a thin cotton futon. Sunlight was streaming in from a small open window onto my face. I went to push myself up, but I couldn't.

"Oww! Ow ow ow!" I greeted the morning angrily. Nora was already up and dressed in a gray cotton robe. I carefully looked at myself without risking elevating my head and saw I was wearing similar attire.

"Don't worry, I was the one that helped you change," Nora assured me. "They didn't see anything."

"Thanks," I said in relief, vaguely recalling Nora dragging me back into the house last night after my mandatory midnight calisthenics with Raeonna. Who knew fighting your own body weight could be so exhausting? Sure, she had varied the intensity throughout, but it had taken a lot out of me for not even lifting a light load. I moaned again as I eventually forced myself to sit up.

"What hurts?"

"My everything," I replied sourly. "I swear even my hair hurts."

"Maybe that's all the lingering sickness coming out."

"Sore muscles from breaking down the connective tissues between them," I corrected with a sigh. "I'm definitely out of shape."

"Too bad you can't just do a simple training montage!" She started making ridiculously dramatic fighting poses while dropping a catchy beat and repeating the word "Montage!"

I laughed, which was a big mistake. "Oh, my abs! I can't see them, but I feel them!" I tried to stretch out my cramping core.

"When you can sit up, I'm supposed to have you drink this." She held up a dark amber glass bottle.

"Okay. I'll get there, eventually."

"Take your time," Nora said as she sat on the floor. "I think they're going to be out for a while."

"Good. Let's review the plan then." I rolled onto my stomach and tried to execute a cobra stretch.

"You have one?" she asked in an astonished voice.

"Hey now, sometimes I have good ideas. Just not… this time." I lowered myself down to the floor again. "All I know is we're not supposed to be here, and someone's making a big mistake."

"Are you open to a suggestion?"

"I'll listen, I suppose." I wasn't committing to anything yet.

"Let's go along with them. At least until we make it to the holy city."

"You think that's what they're going to do? Take us to Chairo?"

"Definitely. I heard them talking last night after you passed out. They're all for getting the band back together and confronting his evil majesty."

"You're not suggesting we follow the plot line we concocted, are you? We won't be able to pull it off ourselves!"

"How about we meet with Relias like they want, tell him what happened, and negotiate with him?"

"What do you mean *negotiate*?"

"We tell him Euphridia is trying to reach him, and if he can figure out how to send us back, we'll pass on any messages he wants."

"But… what if he doesn't know *how* to send us back?"

"Let's not worry about that for now," Nora said nervously.

"What aren't you telling me?"

"Lots of things. Trust me, let's do it this way first. Plan B is a lot more dangerous."

"Plan B?"

"It's not ready for discussion yet." I took her at her word and let the subject drop, being both slightly terrified and curious simultaneously. An annoying charley horse settled into my left leg, and I switched my concentration to eliminating it.

It was late morning before I could stand up without cramping terribly, and I risked it only because I had to answer the call of nature again. Never mind the trouble I had trying to use the chamber pot. At some point, I drank the bottle she gave me, which contained salty, bitter water with some powdered, grassy herbs that foamed at the top. She gestured to the corner of the room, where more bottles awaited me.

Blech!

"Where did they go that's taking so long?" I asked Nora as she set out some leftovers from last night.

"They're washing our clothes. We're supposed to stay inside until they come back."

"I don't think I could make it outside if I wanted to."

I focused on eating breakfast. It wasn't long before I saw Tetora and Aleph heading back to the house from the nearby window. Before stepping inside, they hung our clothes on the line.

"Good day, little one," Aleph greeted me first, though Tetora practically danced to get in front of him.

"Time to train!" Tetora declared. "Let's go now!"

"No way! I can't move!"

"Nonsense!" He grabbed my arm to get me to stand, and I yowled.

"Tetora!" Aleph barked. Tetora's ears flattened, and he let go of me quickly. "Sorry…" He sank to the floor, his tail curling under him. I reached out slowly and patted his ears a few times before I realized that might have been an incredibly rude gesture. Tetora, however, seemed content and chuffed happily.

I grinned. "Nora wants to fluff your ears, too. Is that okay?" Although she had never said it aloud, it was written all over her face.

"Fine, but don't tell anyone," Tetora grunted sullenly.

I never saw Nora move so fast in my life. "Happiness!" she squealed as she joined me.

Aleph turned away with an awkward look on his face.

After a few minutes, I told Nora, "Okay, we should stop now." She frowned but pulled her hand back.

Aleph cleared his throat. "There is much we should discuss."

"Yes," I agreed. "First off, please believe me when I say I am not Raelynn." There was a long pause.

"We… we believe you believe you are not Raelynn," Aleph countered. "But you should believe us when we say you have the same features and voice as Raelynn."

"I… can accept that much," I lied. "However, I have memories that go back to my childhood, and none involve living in this storybook world." Just reading about it.

"Storybook?" Aleph asked, his eyes cloudy with confusion.

Oops.

"Where we came from, all of this is a work of fiction," Nora explained tersely, gesturing with wide arms as I inwardly panicked.

I had thought letting them know they exist as a web novel in my world would be opening a huge can of worms, not to mention explaining what a web novel is in the first place. I tried to subtly glare at Nora to say she was on the verge of saying too much, but I didn't have enough skill points in subterfuge to pull it off.

Aleph and Tetora glanced thoughtfully at each other. While Aleph just shrugged slightly with pursed lips, Tetora responded with a scowl before narrowing his eyes at me. "Raeonna mentioned you had many wounds that were not properly treated. Is this true?"

I crossed my arms defensively. "I have some scars. Who doesn't?"

"Where are they?" Tetora demanded. "I see some peeking out on your right wrist. How about your abdomen? Right shoulder? Above your left ear?"

I went rigid as he pinpointed each one aloud. "Nora! You said they didn't see anything!"

"They didn't," Nora reaffirmed. "They weren't even in the house then!"

Aleph gestured curtly to Tetora to keep quiet. "Are you willing to share with us what caused such scars?"

Usually, I'd never tell them, as it was none of their business, but the situation was anything but normal. "Someone… attacked me with a knife when I was younger." I mentally braced myself for the forthcoming barrage of accusatory questions I had come to expect.

Aleph nodded. "I'm sorry such a thing happened to you." He sat indirectly across from me. "We will not force you to talk about it."

"Oh… I appreciate that." What a good man! I mentally gave him respect +5.

True to his word, he moved on. "Raeonna asked me to teach you how to meditate. Are you willing to learn this skill?"

I took a moment to consider it. "I know… a little about it already. It's not a bad habit to get back to now. "

Aleph nodded. "It will help draw out the solidified animus. It will take practice, however, so consistency will be key. If you agree, we will practice meditation twice daily for about ten minutes. Once when you rise and once before you retire for the night."

"Alright," I agreed.

"Would it be alright if I joined you, too?" Nora asked a bit cautiously, throwing me off for a moment. Oh, probably because of reiterating my childhood trauma. It was a long time ago, and I'm over it, see?

"I don't mind," I said with a shrug.

"I will train you," Tetora declared yet again. "We'll go over the basics once more. When you can move properly again, of course," he added after Aleph gave him another look.

"Those were just the basics?"

"The most basic of basics!" Tetora laughed. "Do not worry, though. You can practice while we travel to Chairo."

"Travel to Chairo?" Nora and I asked, pretending we didn't know what to expect next.

"Will you allow us to introduce you to Holy Sage Relias?" Aleph inquired. "I believe his counsel will help you with your current situation."

I glanced at Nora, and she nodded enthusiastically. "Alright, but only because you asked so nicely."

CHAPTER 14: PACK YOUR BAGS

Tetora began packing essential items for our trip. Aleph was sacrificing some of his older clothes to patch up the rucksacks we would need when I noticed that all of their clothes appeared somewhat worn and patched.

"What have you two been doing since Raelynn left?" I asked carefully, still trying to emphasize that we were separate people.

"Maintaining your shrine," Tetora responded. "Guiding pilgrims."

"Pilgrims?" I blinked.

"They come to the altar to pray for Raelynn's return," Aleph noted.

"Sometimes, they ask you to do ridiculous things for them, like making someone fall in love with them." Tetora snorted derisively.

Nora laughed. "If she could do that, wouldn't she use that power for herself first?"

"Hey!" I shot back. "Watch it, or I'll steal that future husband of yours and go to space myself!"

"You have someone you are in love with?" Tetora misinterpreted our conversation and dropped a plate. "I disapprove! You are too young to, well, not anymore, but… No! We disapprove, right, Aleph?"

"When she is ready to introduce us to him, we will gladly welcome him with open arms," Aleph said gently. He looked at me with a suddenly sly grin, holding up a gigantic sewing needle. "That way, it will be easy to dispose of him if he does not meet our standards."

"Okay, first, no!" I held up my hands for emphasis. "There is no one I'm in love with. Nora's future husband is still theoretical at this point, and I'm too busy just trying to live a normal life." I glanced down at the ground, suppressing a sigh. "Which is not working out for me very well at the moment, all things considered."

"Is falling in love not a normal thing to do?" Aleph asked in a more serious tone.

"Oh. Well. Yes, I suppose it is, but…" I had tried going on a few dates, but it was just an awkward experience all around. Reading about romance was much less complicated than actually trying to engage in it.

"She has very high standards," Nora noted.

"Good," Tetora approved. "No one is good enough for my gold dragon."

"Maintaining the shrine… what else?" I tried to steer us back to the original topic.

"Protecting this village."

"What will happen when we leave?"

"Our senior trainees will take over. Do not worry. They are masters in their own right. We just dislike telling them so." Aleph smiled.

I looked out the window. Some other villagers were walking around, glancing nervously at our house. None appeared to be fully human.

"Are the others… scared of us?"

"They fear most full-bloods. Please do not take it to heart, little one. Life is hard for them," Aleph apologized.

"Full-bloods?" I turned to Nora.

"Humans. Non-beastmen," she replied.

I saw Tetora scowling darkly. "Wait. Is beastmen the right term?" I asked.

"Please use the term *hybrids*," Aleph murmured in a restrained voice.

"Sorry. The story used that other term. I swear I'll say hybrids from now on." Nora crisscrossed a finger over her heart.

There she goes, bringing up the story again…

"Yes…" Aleph murmured, invoking my anxiety. "This story you mentioned. Please tell us more about it."

Nora nodded. *"The Last Rae of Hope.* It's a fantasy novel from our world that talks about Raelynn's travels through Speranza. Until she left, that is."

"The title is rather ominous… or perhaps it is auspicious." Aleph tilted his head back and forth briefly before speaking again. "Who authored such a story?"

Nora and I exchanged a look. I was about to speak, but Nora cut me off.

"Her pen name is Euphridia, but her real name is Eura Abrams."

"Why did you tell them her pen name!?" This was just going to make it more complicated now. Even I was having trouble with the growing pile of coincidences.

Nora shrugged. "It's the truth, though, right? She might actually be—"

"She didn't look like a goddess!" I interrupted angrily. Why was she taking the wrong side of the argument? "She looked like… well, no, I wouldn't say she was a normal person but… I mean… would a goddess wear such an outdated skirt suit? The shoulder pads could have been stolen from a football player and…" I wasn't even able to convince myself at this point.

"Raelynn." Tetora touched my shoulder, and it was the final straw.

"No! That is the one point I will not concede! I am Rachel. Rachel Emily Smith!" I shook off Tetora's hand. "My mother is Maura Smith. I had a normal childhood until, well, you know… but I got better. I transferred to a new high school, met Nora, studied hard, and graduated college with a bachelor's in business administration."

Feeling the need to stretch, I stood up and began to pace, my movements awkward and tinged with anger. "All I wanted was a normal job. Pay off my debts. Do a little good for the world while I'm at it, or at least not make anything worse by being there. But I don't know the first thing about fighting supernatural beings hellbent on world destruction. The best I have are some corporate buzzwords like synergy, and all they're good for is empty talk in executive meetings!"

I took a big breath before continuing my rant. "What am I supposed to do? Tell the demon king if he wants a value-added experience that promotes his long-term viability, he needs to demonstrate his ongoing commitment to global quality improvement?"

He'd at least want to see the numbers for that strategy, and I didn't have them.

Absolute silence. I knew "execu-speak" probably meant even less here.

"I can corroborate her story, at least from the point where we met," Nora said lamely.

"You've met my mother, too. Don't forget that!" I snapped.

"I have met *Maura Smith*."

"You… don't think she's my real mother, do you?" Nora was always commenting on how different we were. Why would you question *this again* now?

"I don't know what I think," Nora admitted.

"How would you feel if I said that about *your* mother!?" I yelled at her before thinking it through.

Nora froze momentarily, then played with a strand of her hair as she tried to shrug it off. "Heh… I mean, biologically, you'd be right, of course, but…" Nora had tears in her eyes, and suddenly, I regretted everything.

"I'm sorry, I'm sorry. I wasn't thinking right! I would never, ever really mean that!" I threw myself down on the ground in front of her.

Nora forced a smile. "It's alright. This situation is hard on both of us, you know?"

"Yes," I gasped from the floor.

"We're in another world we thought was just a fantasy, right?"

"Right," I agreed again.

"We might never see our families again. Especially if we ignore the big issues right before us." Nora put her hand on my head. "So rather than argue and withhold information from the people who can help us make sense of the situation, why don't we try to work together in a shared reality where we can make meaningful decisions?"

"Okay."

"After all, aren't we dynamic problem-solvers with a proven track record who thrive in a fast-paced environment?" Realizing she was using her resume's ridiculous tagline, I glanced at her face. She was smiling now, having previously wiped the tears away. "Sorry, I still don't know how to work the word 'synergy' into the mix."

"No one really does." I also wiped my tears.

"So… let's just fake it until we make it, okay?" I froze stiffly at her words. Hadn't I told *him* I was going to do just that?

"Rae?" Nora blinked.

"Right. Just… as you said." I needed to change the subject because I couldn't devote another second to those other thoughts. I turned to the other two, who had watched our exchange in concerned silence. "Look, you don't have to call me Rachel." I sighed. "But please call me Rae. That's what the people closest to me do."

***

That night, Aleph led us through our first meditation session. As he guided me through a progression of relaxation techniques, I struggled to silence my thoughts, but I knew that was a common problem and that practice was the only way to get better. After our session, I even reserved some hope that I wouldn't have *that dream* again, but one meditation session isn't a panacea.

Please… I can't die here. Just let me hold on a little longer. Not here. Not here.

I saw a bright light before me, and I lost hope. However, I soon realized that this light was different. It was harsher, overly white, and slightly off-center. A soft, glass-like mask over most of my face also obstructed it. I felt air blowing into my nose and onto my cheeks. My eyes could finally open, but everything was fuzzy. I didn't have enough energy to keep them open for more than a few seconds at a time. Someone in a long robe of white was holding a small silver box and talking to it.

"Rachel Emily Smith…" His voice faded in and out as I fought to stay conscious. "… sustained multiple lacerations and puncture wounds from an apparent knife attack… unknown downtime… CPR performed on scene… endotracheal intubation… treated for hypovolemic shock… subsequent acute

infectious process… successfully extubated but remains very drowsy… continue to monitor…"

I struggled to pull the mask off my face with my left hand. My right was bound to a splint. The man paused and walked over to me.

"Hello, Rachel. My name is Dr. Williamson. Do you know where you are?"

I shook my head weakly.

"Rachel, you're in the hospital. Your mother is here too. I'll have the nurse let her know you're awake."

"… Mom?"

How I desperately wished that could be true.

Dr. Williamson put his hand on my left forearm. "It's okay now, Rachel. You're safe."

"Yes. I made it here.*"*

***

Post-Chapter Omake

Olethros: *Regarding your previous comment about an ongoing commitment to global quality improvement. I ran the numbers. There's little return on investment.*

Rae: *What numbers did you use?*

Olethros: *Current quarter projections.*

Rae: *Well, sure, you start with a deficit, but if you think about the long-term forecast…*

Olethros: *Circle back once you come up with an actionable plan. Execu-speak is useless on its own.*

Rae: *…Which one of you taught him the phrase "execu-speak!?"*

Nora: *He used "circle back" too. He's coming along nicely!*

CHAPTER 15: SINCE YOU'VE BEEN GONE

We left the village around noon with our packed provisions. I was still sore and somewhat sleep-deprived but better than the day before. I got dressed in my travel clothes which Aleph and Tetora had dyed a muted wool gray earlier since they would never be bright white again.

"Here." Tetora handed me a long oak stick.

"A bo staff?" I asked, looking up and down the length of it.

"Yes. It will have many uses on our travels."

"How long do you think it will take me to master it?" I hefted it up and down.

Tetora laughed heartily. "You?"

"Like, a few months?" I tried unsuccessfully swinging it around like I had seen in the movies.

He laughed harder. "Gold dragon or not, I shall master it before you!"

"You haven't mastered it either?" I thought he spent his whole life practicing this stuff.

"Anyone who says that they have is a liar. However, for now, it will help you train. You won't need to worry if you break or lose it, either. It is effortless to make another."

I missed my aluminum bat. "Wouldn't a metal weapon be better?"

"You will not find enough free metal throughout the village to even forge a dagger pommel, little one," Aleph said apologetically.

"Oh, sorry. That must have sounded selfish." I looked back at the wooden hovels. "Is there any industry here? I mean—"

"The ground is mostly barren here." Tetora shook his head.

"Then why even try to live here?" I asked curiously.

"This area… was assigned to us," Aleph said.

"Assigned?"

"We are lucky we had a place to go and that it was close to the shrine. The village receives a small stipend to tend to the altar," Aleph explained.

"It was my idea!" Tetora shouted, startling me enough that I dropped the staff. "I only made him go along with it, so if you are mad, punish me!"

"Eh?" I picked up my staff by kicking my foot under it before lifting it to my hand.

"The stipend is for decorating your shrine with flowers, but…"

"Flowers?" Also, it's not my shrine, but I was sick of trying to win that argument.

"We used it to buy supplies for the village instead." Tetora hung his head.

Nora shook her head. "Rae hates flowers anyway."

"Cut flowers," I clarified. "Who decided plant corpses make excellent gifts?"

"The guy who ran out of animals to sacrifice?" Nora sassed back.

"Then you are not angry with me?" Tetora asked hopefully.

"Why would I be? The money should be for the village. That stone doesn't care if it's covered in flowers or not. But who was giving you the stipend?"

"The Church sends it every season," Aleph replied. "It always comes with a note signed by Holy Sage Relias himself."

Relias! Oh, how thoughtful. "What did he do after Raelynn… left?" I asked.

"Relias ran out of the throne room and sealed it shut with holy amity. The only thing he had in his hands was your, I mean, Raelynn's shield," Tetora explained, glancing at Aleph.

"He told us how *Oliver* had sent Raelynn away to another world. With all the injuries she sustained, it was hard to hope that she would survive," Aleph added. "Laverna was angry that Relias had sealed the room without letting us pay our respects, but he said even in death, King Epiales's corpse was exuding demonic animus."

"Wait. Sealed up? It looked more like that entire area had been leveled."

"That happened later… The General Assembly of Clergy came and purged the entire area before the three remaining holy orders dismantled the castle."

"That must have been quite the undertaking…" Nora frowned thoughtfully.

"Did you leave with him after he originally sealed the castle?" I asked Tetora.

"Yes, but by the time we reached Chairo, the Church had already called for an inquisition."

"Inquisition?" I asked.

"To determine how Oliver had infiltrated our party," Tetora explained.

It was Aleph's turn now. "They blamed many for Raelynn's… unanticipated departure."

"Laverna's past was publicly uncovered, and she was tried for several crimes. Many people tried to say she was Oliver's accomplice." Tetora sighed loudly.

"Laverna!? She wouldn't do that!" I exclaimed hotly.

"She maintained her innocence, but it took a toll on her," Aleph clarified. "We haven't heard from her in about three years now." He then took a deep breath and continued quickly, as if the conversation had turned painful. "The Dark Mage Tower, who had recommended Oliver to Raelynn, was destroyed. Dark mages are still persecuted, even inside the Wastelands. Which reminds me, Nora, you should… do the thing."

Do the thing? That's not how Aleph spoke.

"Doing the thing!" She pulled off her robes with a flourish. Underneath, she had a standard light tan tunic and dark pants. I was disappointed. It wasn't as outrageous as I had expected—not even a single sequin or feather. Was Nora losing her touch?

"Behold!" She flipped her robes inside out. Suddenly, they were just like an ordinary traveler's cloak in a forest green that complimented her eyes.

"They're reversible!" I gasped.

"Of course! Two outfits in one! I like to keep my options open in terms of attire."

"You sly, sly dog, er, rabbit!" I admired.

"I can remove the top part of the staff too, see? It becomes an instant, run-of-the-mill walking stick. I was going to show you at the faire, but after you started swinging it, I got a little concerned you really would use it as a bat…" Nora tucked the caged orb inside her cloak.

"I wasn't going to hit anything with it," I murmured, writing off her multifunctional equipment as the result of mere thrifty happenstance.

Or maybe this was Eura's idea from the start.

Then I turned to Aleph and Tetora. "What did you mean about being assigned to the land?"

"Hybrids… are the outcome of ancient experiments conducted by dark mages."

"Yes, I remember that from the story." Sad origins, but certainly not the fault of the hybrids for existing, right?

"The Church has decided that we should not gather in groups larger than twenty."

"That's awfully arbitrary, isn't it? What are they afraid of?"

"They say hybrids generate too much animus and therefore must disperse to the edges of society to maintain balance in the more populated areas."

"That sounds like a giant load of bull—" I suddenly looked at Aleph. Oh, he might not appreciate that.

"Bull what?" he asked so innocently that I couldn't tell if he was playing me or if that saying simply didn't exist here.

"Uh." I looked at Nora.

"Ackamarackus!" she suggested happily.

"What?" we all asked simultaneously.

"Look it up!"

"I can't. She took our phones!" I retorted. Not that they would have worked, anyway.

"Oh yeah. Sorry, habit. Ackamarackus. Nonsense."

"Then just say that," I fumed.

"Ackamarackus is fun to say!"

"Ackamarackus. Yeah, okay, I see your point," I conceded. "But anyway, haven't hybrids been living together for hundreds of years in large communities all over the world?"

"Yes." Aleph nodded. "However, the environment has changed a lot recently, so the Church passes anything remotely associated with decreasing ambient animus into law."

"Ambient animus…" Nora repeated to herself.

I focused more on the legal implications of his statement. "Law? You said the Church decided?"

"Yes."

"They aren't separate?" I asked.

Tetora snorted. "Separate? How could they be? Priests crown kings!"

"Oh. Yes. I guess that shows who's really in charge, huh?"

Just how much of this world drew inspiration from Earth, anyway?

"As for Holy Sage Relias…" Aleph looked at me with large, sad eyes. "He tried to take the blame for all of our shortcomings. He begged the General Assembly of Clergy to assign him penance commensurate with our collective sins so they would spare us."

Wait, spare you? Spare you from what?

"Collective sins?" Nora inquired before I could register my dissent.

"Had we not sinned, Raelynn would still—"

"What are you saying!?" I fumed. "A demon lord deceived everyone. How is that *your* fault?"

"If we had been more dutiful in our—" Aleph started again.

"Bullshit!" I shouted. "No offense, but ackamarackus doesn't cut it this time!"

"See? Even Rae thinks it's bullshit!" Tetora agreed with me. At least he picked up on that phrase rather quickly.

Aleph's long face appeared to grow longer. "Even I find discomfort in the Church's approach to the situation." He sighed again. "Eventually, the Assembly agreed to his request, and we were free to go, provided we returned to this village. As far as we know, Relias still resides in the north tower of the main temple, where he continues the Sacrament of Penance."

I glanced at Nora questioningly. Organized religion wasn't something I knew much about firsthand. Mother had a particular disdain for such practices, and my only real interaction with religious professionals involved the hospital chaplain after my emergency admission.

"Acts of repentance, assigned by the Church and carried out in quiet devotion," she murmured.

"So he's been in punitive isolation… for all these years?" I felt my stomach lurch.

"Yes," Tetora and Aleph agreed.

"To think we haven't even asked about the demons themselves yet…" Nora sighed.

"Yeah, and just exactly what has Demon King Oleth—" Suddenly, Tetora wrapped his giant hand around my mouth, cutting me off. It tasted *absolutely awful.*

"Never, ever say his name!" Aleph shouted with uncharacteristic heat. "He can *hear you* if you call him!"

Nora jumped with a start. "Okay, that definitely wasn't made explicit in the story!"

Tetora released me, and I wiped my mouth. "Let's… take a break, shall we?" I suggested. "You know, before we get ourselves into bigger trouble."

CHAPTER 16: SAME SKY?

"So, every demon lord has a calling name?" I asked as we settled down by the side of the road so we could concentrate.

"Yes," Aleph confirmed.

"If you say it out loud…" Nora started.

"They can listen in on your conversation and even pinpoint your location," Tetora finished.

I looked at Nora. "Raelynn said the original demon king's name in the story, right?"

Nora shook her head. "She called him The Accursed One."

"Oh, I guess the narrator was the one who used it…" I turned to Aleph. "What else should we know about demons?"

"Only enchanted weapons can banish them," Tetora stated. "So don't try to fight one now!"

I wasn't planning to…

"What does banishment mean?" I asked.

"It sends them back to their respective lord's dark sanctum," Aleph explained.

"So banishment… is only temporary?"

"Yes, though it also appears to be quite painful to them."

That's something, at least.

I considered this information for a moment before asking, "What about exorcism spells?"

Aleph frowned slightly before answering, "Successful exorcism sends them to the Void. Only top-level priests and Holy Sage Relias can do that, and even then, it depends on the demon's overall strength."

Nora half-raised her hand. "But the Will of Euphridia can send them to the Void, regardless of their power? Right?"

Aleph nodded his confirmation. "Yes, if the Chosen One wields the sword, and the weapon strikes true. There are other high-level weapons blessed by Relias that would work on certain demons, though none would be as powerful as the Will of Euphridia."

I was curious. "What other high-level weapons are there?"

"My war hammer and Tetora's claws once held such power, but—"

"It's gone now?" I felt my heart sink at the news.

Aleph lifted one hand from his folded arms and scratched his beard. "I believe the blessings bestowed have faded. Luckily, I have not needed to fight a demon in many years."

I shot forward slightly, hands on my knees. "But aren't they roaming all over creation, causing trouble?"

He smirked. "They are mostly busy fighting amongst themselves far to the south from here."

"Why does King O—I mean, why does the demon king allow that? He's still in charge, isn't he?" I didn't get the sense that he would tolerate unorganized chaos from his subordinates.

"He is the most powerful, but the other lords are strong enough together to oppose him."

I guess they weren't happy with the new management.

I let out a hopeful sigh. "Maybe they'll just keep that up for a few millennia and leave everyone else alone."

"Unfortunately, there are many innocents caught in the middle." Aleph pulled out a map. He pointed out three dark spots that formed a large triangle in the southern portion of the Wastelands. "This dark sanctum is where the general and his army reside. Here is the mistress's cauldron… and the last one…" he pointed to a tower on the map just east of a giant sea serpent.

"The king himself," Nora murmured.

He had built his own towering fortress. At least it wouldn't be hard to find him if necessary… not that I wanted to, right?

Aleph continued plotting our course, his finger moving along the map as he explained. "We will go east across the Wastelands, then down through Turri to avoid detection. We should be safe with the three demon factions embroiled in the southern Wastelands."

"Ah!" Tetora suddenly shouted. "We've been sitting around all this time running our mouths and not training!"

So, he had finally caught on to my procrastination. "Uh…"

"Put your bo staff on your shoulders!" he commanded, and I did so. "Hold it steady!"

"Hey!" I protested. "What are you doing?"

"You carry these travel sacks for a while." He tied them to either end of my staff.

"It's too heavy."

"You're still standing, aren't you? Keep walking."

I grumbled and did what I was told, for a minute or two, anyway. "Shouldn't Nora train too?" I complained.

"Hey! I'm a squishy." Nora objected.

Tetora frowned. "Squishy is no good. You will train too. Copy Rae." Nora gave me a bitter glance, and I grinned viciously as she and her staff were also weighted down. Misery loves company, after all.

***

We continued down the dirt road for the rest of the afternoon. Although we were given brief rests with opportunities to stretch, it was still unpleasant for us as adventuring novices.

"We'll stop for the night here," Aleph said, halting our advance as the sun clung to the horizon. "Let's set up camp."

"Camp? Here? Outside?" Each question I asked was in a higher octave than the last.

"There is cover here," Aleph explained, pointing to a few scrappy trees.

"No! We need to find a place indoors. With a locking door!" I exclaimed. I had hoped we would stop at a cozy inn with fresh linens and a roaring fireplace, not sleep in the dirt where dangers lurked around every corner.

"Even if we walk all night long, little one, we won't be able to find such a place," Aleph patted my head. "The nearest town is several days away by foot."

"I can't do it! No. No camping. It's too dangerous!" Even if I could run—*assuming* I could run—I still wouldn't make it back to the village by midnight.

"I'll take the first watch." Tetora shrugged. "Aleph can take the second. We'll be fine—nothing gets by us!"

"What animals are indigenous to the area?" Nora asked while I continued to panic.

"Small game, mostly," Aleph answered. "The biggest animal we might see would be a wolf, but most packs have migrated away over the last few years."

"What about those redbacks? And those giant lizards?" I hedged.

Aleph looked confused for a moment. "Oh, those are demonic beasts, not animals."

Oh, silly me.

"What's the difference between animals and demonic beasts?" I asked Nora.

"The story didn't make it clear," Nora admitted. "I just figured if a creature had a funny old-world name, it was a demonic beast."

Aleph sat down and began to unpack his rucksack. "Demonic beasts are byproducts of animus experiments conducted by the demons. They are not natural creatures and are much more predatory, especially towards humans and hybrids in particular."

"Okay, so, are there any other *demonic beasts* around here then?" I wanted to have all my fears lined up together so I could freak out about everything all at once.

"The farther we move from the old castle ruins, the less likely we will encounter them. There may be a few apodemus nests… but it's summer now, so they don't need to venture this close to the road for food."

"Apodemus?"

"They're like enormous rats. Not as tasty, though." Tetora sniffed.

"Not as…" I trailed off.

"The meat is too acidic." He shook his head.

"I'll take your word for it," I murmured.

I perched on a large rock and tried to process what we were doing. Aleph and Tetora laid out their bedrolls after searching the ground for a few minutes, looking for a flat spot. My attention drifted away soon after; the rest of the evening sort of became a blur. I recalled eating something for dinner and meditating, but I spent most of the night ignoring anyone who tried to talk to me. The overwhelming urge to scratch my right forearm threatened to overwhelm me, a clear reminder from my body that I wasn't prepared for what lay ahead.

As the last rays of light disappeared from the horizon, I hopped into my bedroll with my bo staff clutched tightly, keeping an ear out for any potential danger. I frequently glanced in Tetora's direction to determine if he was keeping watch. His golden eyes occasionally shined in the night, so I eventually relaxed a little. However, no matter how hard I tried, I couldn't sleep. The ground felt hard and uneven through my bedroll. I tried every position I could think of, but nothing worked.

"Nora, are you awake?" I whispered.

"No," she replied. "Why?"

"I can't sleep."

"That's because you're too busy talking," she observed.

"You're awake too, though."

"My answer to you is still the same."

"You're still mad about the walking exercises?"

"I'll forgive you as soon as my calves do."

I didn't know what else to say, so I rolled over, finding another bump I hadn't noticed when I set up for the night.

"Rae, you know I'm not mad, right?"

"Yeah, I know." I loosened my shoulders a little.

Nora laughed suddenly. "Well, that's interesting!"

"What is?"

"The constellations. I see the Big Dipper and Ursa Major."

I looked up and searched the sky, and sure enough, I saw the Big Dipper, too.

"Actually… I found… Orion, too?" Nora sat up quickly. "Hmm…"

"I believe you," I admitted. "But the Big Dipper is all I know how to find…"

Nora stared silently at the sky for a few moments. "Oh, uh, do you know what this means? I think we're not that far away from Earth."

"How do you figure?"

"Think about it," Nora chirped quickly. "Space is three dimensions, but we perceive the night sky as a two-dimensional projection. If we were really, really far from Earth, then we wouldn't recognize the constellations at all. It looks like our worlds really are next to each other."

"I guess you're right." I didn't want to find flaws in her hasty conclusion.

"Ah, what a relief!" She flopped back down on her roll loudly and sighed. "Night-night Rae…" It was only a minute later I heard her snoring lightly.

Okay, Big Dipper. I'm counting on you to be the real one we all know and love. Just keep holding up the sky while I pin down the ground! I closed my eyes, wondering if we would be able to go back, until finally, I fell asleep.

CHAPTER 17: FAKE IT UNTIL YOU MAKE IT

We had been on the road for the better part of a week before we started encountering small crossroads carrying other solo traveling hybrids. Most seemed to be self-motivated merchants, though their wares appeared dusty and worn. To be fair, we were also dusty and worn. The dirt road had been baked to a powdery crisp, and the slightest breeze caused swirls of fine particles to descend on everything. Aleph had us keep our hoods up at all times. We also wore thin black cloth masks across our noses and mouths to hide our faces and protect us from the errant dust.

"Ho, kinsman," a young, ox-tailed peddler hailed Aleph. "What lies yonder?" He gestured to the path behind us.

"The village of Tun and just beyond, the Altar of Raclynn," Aleph answered.

I hadn't even asked the village's name…

"How long until I arrive in Tun?"

"Two days if you keep the peddler's pace," Aleph replied with a smile.

Just two days? Were we really that slow?

"Not much farther then!" The young peddler laughed. "I'm looking forward to dropping off all these prayer requests. For slips of paper, their weight can add up." He gestured to the basket on his back.

"The villagers will happily accept them, no matter their weight or quantity."

I wondered what they did with them. Did they hang them up on trees? Use them as insulation? Burn them as nuisance garbage?

The peddler seemed to ponder something, vaguely embarrassed. "I also have, um… a personal request for Raelynn. Is there something better I could offer than just a scrap of scribble?"

"That depends on the request," Aleph answered. "What are you hoping she will achieve on your behalf?"

"There's this girl…" He blushed deeply. "You should see her—" He looked at Nora and I. "Um. Her…"

"Personality?" Nora suggested.

"Oh, yeah. Big personality!" He laughed nervously.

"Have you told her how you felt about her… personality?" Nora asked, her voice overflowing with insincerity.

"No… see, I must first earn enough money to gain her favor. That's why I'm picking up these odd jobs."

"Earn her favor?" I questioned.

"Yeah. With enough money, maybe I can confess my feelings…"

"What's money got to do with it?" I asked in a surly tone, even though I knew the answer.

"Everything! I can't ask her to marry me without at least showing I'm financially secure! Being a peddler isn't exactly a grand Purpose," he responded sheepishly, which was a real feat for someone built like an ox.

I sighed. "I think you should tell her how you feel, regardless."

"I'll just ask Raelynn to guide me. Thanks," he politely declined, causing Tetora to snort.

"Ask for Widower Pyo," Aleph said around a mild cough. "He makes ornate charms for such circumstances. He'll be glad to help you out for a nominal fee."

"Thank you for your guidance." The peddler bowed. "Ah, before I forget. It would be best to take the low path around Dark Star Hill. There's a surveyor hanging around on the upper side."

"Your advice is much appreciated." Aleph bowed in return, then we continued on our way.

After a few minutes, once we were out of earshot, Nora said, "So… do you think he was referring to her rack?" She pointed to her temples. "Or her rack?" She made an exaggerated gesture to showcase her chest.

"Obviously, he was talking about her rack." I didn't point to anything in particular.

Tetora laughed heartily, but Aleph gave us all a stern look. "Absolutely incorrigible."

"Which one was he talking about?" Tetora questioned with a wicked gleam in his eyes. "Which rack do ox-men fancy more?"

"You're the worst of the lot!" He whacked him somewhat gently in the head with the passive end of his war hammer.

"Gwah!" Tetora shouted, rubbing his head. "That hurt!"

"It's a good thing we entertained his words, though," Aleph mused as he ignored Tetora's protests. "I was planning to stop by Dunon for supplies, but it's not worth it now."

"Because of the surveyor?" Nora asked.

Aleph nodded. "They're quite difficult to deal with. They'll delay our travel for weeks if we let them."

I scratched my head. "Why would a surveyor get involved with our travels? Don't they focus on land boundaries?"

"Their whole point is to limit hybrids from moving around and congregating together. A group of four adults on the road like us will raise much suspicion. More if they find out that our party is mixed."

"Mixed? So humans and hybrids can't even associate with each other? They should mind their own business!" I snapped.

"That's just what it is, though," said Aleph with a hint of resignation in his voice. "If you anger them, a hybrid could find themself assigned to the Northern Land of Dragons."

"Dragons!" Nora breathed excitedly.

"There's no such thing," Tetora scoffed. "I have never seen one."

"Just because you have not seen one does not mean they do not exist," Aleph warned.

"Ridiculous…" I muttered under my breath. "Someone ought to do something about this. I mean, about the surveyors."

Let sleeping dragons lie.

Tetora's tail quivered slightly. "Well, since we're headed toward Chairo anyway…"

"Tetora… she has enough to deal with as it is." Aleph let out an exasperated sigh.

"What's this now?" I asked.

Tetora pounced, figuratively speaking. "When you get into the inner city, tell the General Assembly to—"

"Tetora!" Aleph admonished.

"What? Her words will carry weight. It's not like *we* can make them stop all this!"

"Why not?" Nora asked with an almost exaggerated tone of curiosity.

"Hybrids aren't allowed past the outer gate of the city anymore."

"Wait, you can't come in with us?" I panicked. "What about Nora and me? We don't even have any identification on us. What do we do, say 'we're travelers from another world, so please let us in?'"

"Your face will open any door in the city!" Tetora answered excitedly. "Just say, 'I'm back.'"

I folded my arms and leaned forward with a cocked eyebrow. "You want me to *lie my way into the holy city*?"

"It's not a lie! It's, uh…" Tetora paused, obviously at a linguistic loss. Even though Aleph and Tetora called me Rae, their opinions hadn't changed. Nora kept saying anything was possible. I had settled on a case of mistaken identity because I could easily deny any plausibility.

Nora looked off into the distance. "Let's say we get into the inner city. Where can we find the Assembly?"

"They'll be on the first floor of the main temple. You can't miss them!"

Nora looked at me. "You'll say something to them, of course?"

"Um," I hesitated. What's this now?

Nora grinned. "We're going there, anyway. Don't you think you should use your looks for the good of hybrid kind?"

Please don't put it that way… now this is my problem, too.

"Looks won't be enough." I sighed, slumping my shoulders. "Acting for me is impossible. Don't you remember when I made our high school drama coach cry?" It was in relief, of course, about five seconds after I confessed I wanted to switch to art class.

"She didn't know how to motivate you, that's all." I looked at Nora's face closely. Even her *eyebrows* looked mischievous. She was plotting something. "Actually…" Nora paused dramatically. "You should probably start practicing now, oh Chosen One!" she draped an arm over her stomach and performed an exaggerated bow.

"Oh no, no, no, no!" I shouted defiantly.

"Oh yes, yes, yes, yes," she countered calmly. "If you continue arguing with me, you'll leave me no choice but to *retaliate*."

I ignored her warning and continued my tirade. "I refuse! There is no way you are going to parade me around like some heaven-sent messiah
to—"

"Boop." She reached up and tapped my nose rather sharply with her right index finger.

I stared at her in silent bewilderment, then yelled again, "If you think for one second that I'm just going to do whatever you say, then you—"

Would you believe she did it again?

"Why are you doing that!?"

"Distracting you. If you had thought about it for a moment, you'd realize that practicing now will make it a lot easier when the final exam comes. Didn't you just point out that we have no good way into Chairo otherwise?"

"But…"

"You have two party members who've spent years with Raelynn. Use their knowledge to your advantage. I'll coach you through it."

I rubbed my nose. "I really hate it when you do that."

"I warned you, didn't I?"

"I know, I know. Just why me?"

"Because there's no one else who can," Nora shrugged. "Unless you'd rather just lead an assault on the city. That might be fun!" Her violet eyes lit up dangerously, and I swore I could see electricity crackling around her in an unholy halo.

"I thought we were supposed to be good guys. At least, sort of good…" I mean, at a level greater than blasting everything first and asking questions later.

Nora waggled her eyebrows playfully. "You forgot to tell me about the ends versus the means, remember?"

"Ugh…" I glanced at Tetora and Aleph, who had watched our lively exchange in suspenseful silence. "Just so we're clear, I'm not admitting I'm Raelynn. So don't be surprised if this doesn't work as you expect."

Nora stepped forward. "It also means you two will explain to the real Raelynn, if she shows up later, that is, that you came up with this plan," she added, surprising me. I guess she was entertaining a multitude of possibilities.

"And… uh…" I stalled. I wanted some more concessions for having to go through all this.

"This counts as training, too?" Nora suggested.

"Yes! No extra training hours!" I agreed excitedly. Great idea!

"Agreed," Aleph said with a self-satisfied smile.

Hey, wait. It was Tetora who initially brought it up. Did Nora know this was coming, too? Did they rehearse this whole thing? I eyed all three of them, but they didn't even bother to look the least bit guilty. I had the feeling they had completely hoodwinked me.

"Damnit," I muttered.

***

Post-Chapter Omake

Date: May 9, 20XX

To: All Employees

From: President Abrams, Cooperative Universal Publishing

Subject: Satire Genre Tag Added to The Last Rae of Hope

After carefully analyzing recent feedback from our readers and reviewers, the Satire tag has been added to The Last Rae of Hope.

Many employees have expressed that the very nature and style of The Last Rae of Hope, with its premise about a fantasy web novel that uses a web novel medium to deliver serialized chapters, explicitly illustrates that it is a tongue-in-cheek satire that needs no tag. However, feedback received has demonstrated the need for utilizing the Satire tag. Other employees fear using the Satire tag, in combination with the Comedy tag, may suggest to readers that CUP finds great fault in the story, such that the web novel medium itself is something to ridicule to the point of abandonment.

Although satire is, in many cases, meant to be humorous, its greater purpose is to promote critical thinking toward the wider issues it targets, allowing for deeper analysis and, ultimately, the generation of actionable takeaways for the purpose of continuous quality improvement. Please note that CUP embraces both comedy and satire as quality improvement tools for important topics that deserve greater social discourse. To be able to find fault while still embracing opportunities to improve something we all hold dear is the ultimate privilege.

Due to the limitations of only having four genre tags active on one story, the Board has decided to drop the Adventure tag. This in no way should be construed to mean that adventure will not be part of the story moving forward; aggregate feedback analysis has demonstrated that adventure is not only expected but inherent with the use of the Fantasy tag, which remains unchanged.

All employees, readers, and reviewers are encouraged to continue submitting feedback on The Last Rae of Hope.

Your feedback will help us to continue delivering quality content.

124

CHAPTER 18: OVERLEVELED

"Again," Tetora instructed. "Who are you?"

I put my hands on my hips proudly. "Raelynn Lightbringer, Knight Captain of the Holy Order of Gold, Chosen One of the Goddess, Seventh Appointed Hero of Legend, and… uh, Wielder of the Faith and Will of Euphridia!" The titles really were tedious—and that last one! Obvious lie.

"Hmmm… You need more confidence," Tetora remarked. "The pose is good, but you don't sound like you believe yourself."

Of course I don't believe myself.

"We're done for today, right?" I pressed. "Let's keep going." Although moving forward would take me closer to the holy city, it at least afforded me a distraction where I could hide behind my cloak and mask. Tetora threw his hands up in frustration but took the lead once again.

"Maybe it would help if we talked about the titles," Aleph suggested after we were well on our way. "It might help you connect to her character."

"Actually… can we start with her name? Raelynn Lightbringer is her name, right? Or is Lightbringer a title?" I asked, thinking her last name could go either way.

"Raelynn Lightbringer is her covenant name." Covenant name? I must have been making a face of ignorance because Aleph continued, "When she was received in joyful fellowship by the Church. It was on her sixth birthday exactly."

"What's her *real* name, then?" Nora inquired, her face lighting up. I admit I was also quite curious. "The story didn't—"

"She never told us," Tetora interjected. "Not that she should have, mind you. That sort of thing is very personal."

"Didn't you guys travel together, though?" I asked. "Wasn't it weird not knowing her real name?"

"Not at all." He folded his arms. "That's normal."

"Is Tetora… not your real name?" I asked in confusion.

He turned his head as his cheeks reddened. "Tetora is not the name I received at birth. Don't ask what it is, either. It's weird to be having this conversation."

Are birth names some sort of secret?

"Uh, okay. So, Raelynn Lightbringer," I said, my tone light but thoughtful, trying to pry for more of an explanation gently. "Quite a name for a young girl."

"She grew into it rather quickly," said Aleph. "Holy Sage Relias gave it to her himself."

"She… met him… when she was only six?"

Oh no. Okay, don't think on that one too deeply—things are going to get *really* wrong *really* fast!

"Yes," Aleph asserted. "Euphridia herself told him of her coming. The entire world was waiting for her return."

Minus the bad guys, of course.

I was about to inquire further, but the sound of raucous laughter interrupted our discussion. Three rough-looking figures were making their way along the road ahead of us. Their armor was rusty, scratched, and piecemealed together with tattered leather straps.

"Put up your hoods," Aleph instructed Nora and me in a hushed, urgent tone, his grip tightening on his weapon.

"Huh? Why?"

"So they don't easily see you're human," Tetora answered for him. "Less likely there will be trouble."

Nora and I complied immediately, pulling our hoods over our heads and adopting wary stances as the group neared. I double-checked the mask over the lower half of my face to ensure my features were also properly hidden there.

The three hybrids, all appearing to be scraggly, unkempt dogs, paused briefly upon seeing us, their faces breaking into grins that suggested trouble was on the menu one way or the other.

"Look at what we got here, boys!" the tall one in the middle sneered. "It looks like we found us a couple of beastgirls. And just when I was starting to feel a little lonely. Come on, ladies, we'll show you a good time!"

Beastgirls? ...Lonely? *Good time!? Oh, heck no!*

"But Boss, there's only two!" The smallest one on the right whined in a high-pitched, nasally tone.

"So what? I want the tall one." The leader pointed at me with his giant oar of a sword. "You guys fight over the other. The smaller ones are usually rats or rabbits, and I ain't into buck teeth!" I could sense Nora's glare from under her hood.

"You always get to pick first," the diminutive swordsman muttered.

"Hey, that's the perk of being in charge," the leader said, giving him a hard pat on the back.

"I don't know about this, guys. What about the big cat over there?" the middle-sized one on the left asked as he gestured at Tetora. "He could be trouble." That was an understatement, of course. But did they not even see Aleph with the giant war hammer? I was starting to think the hybrids' clannish nature had led to some interesting racial prejudices.

"Pfft. Don't think for a moment that you stand a chance!" the leader guffawed at us. "No one around here gives the tiniest shit about what could happen to you. So just do what we say, and maybe you'll live to see tomorrow. But you even think about attacking us, and we'll skin the lot of you!"

I glanced furtively at Aleph and Tetora, but they seemed to relax their stances.

"You two have this one," Aleph said loudly when I caught his eye. Then, as if to punctuate his point, he planted the small end of his war hammer into the ground and leisurely rested his hands on the business end.

"W-wait… but…" I started to complain.

"No reason for us to get involved," Tetora confirmed with a prominent stretch. He had sparred with me almost religiously three times a day since we left, but I didn't think I was ready for a real rumble.

Nora, on the other hand, seemed more than ready. In fact, she was already chanting a spell. I recognized the words to Ventos, the spell to summon a giant wind. Oliver had been a genuine fan of that one, rocketing off antagonists he didn't feel like dealing with anymore with a flippant gesture. However, I doubted Nora could produce the same outcome. We'd only been training for a week, and there were no lessons on magic. Was this supposed to be some kind of test?

I glanced at Tetora and Aleph, who didn't look the slightest bit concerned.

Okay, so they want to see what we can do. And they are still there for backup… so… they wouldn't let anything happen to us. Right?

I ignored the tight feeling in my chest and tightened my grip on my bo staff as Nora continued to chant her spell.

"Dark mage!" the shortest adversary cried, taking a few steps back as if he was about to break into a run. I would have gladly let him go, but he suddenly dipped his hand to his left boot, and as his hand shot back up, I saw a glimmer of steel fly from his fingertips—directly at Nora.

My reluctance to engage was immediately forgotten. In a heartbeat, I leaped into the projectile's path and deflected it with a flick of my staff.

I'll admit, attempting to take out the caster first with ranged combat was only logical. I wasn't in the mood to admire his tactics, though. Nora was my best friend, so how *dare* he try to hurt her! I heard a guttural scream and was surprised to find that it was coming from my own throat.

Blinded by rage, I crouched low and launched myself forward. I spun my staff as I pivoted left and right, the motions feeling as natural as though I had practiced them a thousand times. I think he had trouble tracking my movements because I saw his eyes flick nervously back and forth until I was right in front of him, launching my assault.

"Do! Not! Throw! Knives! At! My! Friends!" I punctuated each word with a whack of the staff, one to each leg, one to each arm, then one thrust to the gut to double him over. I finished with an upward swing that stood him back up, and a final crack over the head collapsed him into a boneless heap, unconscious.

I blinked. Is one down already? Seriously, what just happened?

"Wow… must have been his first day," I murmured to hide my confusion as I glanced in Nora's direction, only to find her juggling the middle-sized goon with her wind spell.

"Up and up you go! Oh, oops," Nora flinched as he fell to the ground. She raised her hand, and up he went again at the last moment. "Up and *down* you go, I mean."

The leader froze with shock and confusion. He looked frantically between his friends, one motionless at my feet and the other screaming obscenities as he helplessly floated up and down at Nora's whims.

Eventually, the leader pulled himself together and set his sights on me. He raised his impractically gigantic sword over his head and gracelessly charged forward. His sword came down in a clumsy strike, which I sidestepped. I couldn't understand why countering came to me so easily. I just felt his movements were very predictable and slow. Nothing like Tetora or Aleph, both of whom had moved with graceful economy and terrifying speed during our lessons.

"Are you even trying?" I asked him, and even to my own surprise, the words came out kind of… bored?

This… *dingus* was nothing, I realized. For the first time since arriving in this fantasy world brought to life, I felt like I knew exactly what to do! Was I… enjoying this? Why?

He growled and brought his sword up and around in a horizontal slash, which I agilely hopped over. He followed up with a kick, which I turned aside with my staff, then indulged myself with a little mockery before finishing him.

"I'm going to give you a two out of ten. Is this your first time using a sword? Or is it a boat oar? I mean, I'm no expert myself, but I'm pretty sure you're supposed to hit with the pointy end."

His face turned scarlet with rage. "Hold still, and I'll show you what this 'boat oar' can do, you mouthy—" He actually said a bit more, but I don't feel like censoring all the expletives. I'm not a fan of profuse swearing, to be honest, because it detracts from those rare occasions where you really do need to get your point across.

He continued saying those not-so-nice things as I danced around a flurry of clumsy attacks until I finally decided I'd heard enough from him. I twisted around a thrust, coming face-to-face with him, and let me tell you, the look on his face was priceless.

He was too close to bring my staff around for a strike, so I let go with one hand, seized the hilt of the sword just above his grip, and yanked it out of his grasp. He staggered backward in surprise.

I hefted the oversized blade one-handed over my head and pretended to inspect it. "Ugh, the balance on this thing is awful. No wonder you're having trouble hitting me. Here, you can have it back." I tossed the sword up in the air, and then, while his gaze followed it, I snapped my bo staff across his face. He howled in pain as he fell to the ground writhing. His frantic movements ceased abruptly when the sword came down—staking into the ground right between his legs. He was frozen either in disbelief or terror. I'm not sure which. I pointed down at him disapprovingly. "That's what you get for name-calling."

With the threat, such as it was, neutralized, I began to feel a wave of guilt wash over me. His nose was definitely broken, his tiny companion was splayed out on the ground, and the other was still bobbing up and down in the air, reduced to being Nora's plaything— which she was still having a *lot* of fun with, by the way.

"And up and down you go, and up and down you go," she kept repeating in a sing-song voice. Part of me felt like I should tell her enough was enough, but she looked so happy I couldn't bring myself to.

I turned my attention back to the leader. "Look, I'll make you a deal," I said sternly, wagging a finger at him. "You leave *right now*, take your two moron friends with you, swear never to come back or hassle any hybrids *ever again*, and maybe *you'll* live to see tomorrow. We'll keep your weapons so you aren't tempted to misuse them again. Clear?"

Unable to speak, the leader nodded furiously. Nora finally let down the amateur skydiver, who ran right towards a pile of scraggly weeds and began vomiting. The four of us—me, Nora, Aleph, and Tetora—all stood around cringing until he managed to pull himself together, then he and his leader quickly grabbed their unconscious friend and carried him off.

Once they were gone, Nora and I looked toward our two companions. Tetora was grinning so widely it threatened to split his face in half.

"That seemed… easy," I remarked, noticing an unexpected tremor in my hands. It felt *too* easy, almost unnaturally so.

"It is because of all the training with your peerless mentors!" bellowed Tetora.

Aleph nodded. "Tetora likes to reserve most of the praise for himself, but in truth, you both did well."

"What gave you the idea to juggle him?" I asked Nora, hiding my tremulous right hand behind me. I knew it would stop eventually.

"I didn't think you'd appreciate me just flinging them away, so… I thought I'd control it a bit. I was trying to get the two smaller ones, but I missed. Next time, I'll get the whole bunch all at once."

Next time? I had two minds about the possibility of the next time. However, skirmishes like these had been peppered into the story in the first place, so the likelihood of more good-for-nothings showing up was probably pretty high.

"It seems you both have natural talent," Aleph continued. "Not that I had any doubts. Keep up the good work."

"Mmm…" I didn't trust myself to speak at that point. Intentionally hurting someone… didn't seem right. However, another part of me noted the jerks threatened our safety first, and I had to admit winning without taking damage felt *good*. It was as if my mind was at war with itself, each side presenting its own arguments. I wondered which I should listen to.

"Just *take the compliment*, Rae," Nora scolded.

"Oh, right. Thank you." I went over to pick up the enormous sword, thinking it might be worth something to one of those wandering peddlers. As I attempted to lift it, I found myself straining to even get it off the ground. Even the most oversized sword should not be this heavy. What kind of dense fantasy metal was it made out of? How in the world had I thrown it up into the air earlier? I glanced suspiciously at Nora.

She deflected the glance back at me. "What's this now?"

"What did you do to me?" I asked in an accusatory tone.

"Nothing lately," she replied. "What do you think I did?"

"Some sort of superhuman strength spell when I wasn't looking."

"There is no such thing on the dark mage side, at least that I know of. Why?" She went over to the sword and tried to pick it up. "What the!?"

"Yeah, that's where I'm at." I turned my suspicion on Aleph and Tetora.

"She's giving the angry look again," Tetora whispered loudly to Aleph. "Should I just ignore her? She'll just start yelling if I try to explain it."

Aleph stared at his companion for a moment before sighing loudly as if he had just lost a bet. "Anecdotally, you seem to use amity to strengthen yourself in times of combat, just like… someone else we know."

Amity. The positive emotional force implicated in using holy magic—emotions like empathy, friendship, peace, and goodwill. Raelynn Lightbringer famously used those qualities to empower herself.

I couldn't prove Tetora right. He already had a swelled head, so there was no need to make him more arrogant. "…Oh." I left it at that. The three of them looked at each other uncomfortably but said nothing.

"I'm hungry," I declared loudly. "Time to eat." I dragged the sword off the road before they even made a move. I had no headspace available to deal with things I didn't want to understand.

CHAPTER 19: GET ME TO THE CHURCH ON TIME

I dreamt about the knife attack in the alley again. It was less like watching a movie and more like scrolling through a series of poorly taken photos. The silhouette of a giant man holding a ridiculously long knife. A monstrous mask covered with slick, matted fur. Blood everywhere. A flash of light, then complete darkness. The pictures stopped, and it was more about other senses than sight. Laying on asphalt. Booming laughter followed by someone swearing. Distorted sirens getting louder. The smell of fresh rain. Cold that settles deep into the bones.

I awoke with a start, only to find Aleph's war hammer poking me in the shoulder. "Wuh?" I asked as intelligently as I could.

"Breakfast is ready," he said almost apologetically.

"I'm not." I rolled over in my bedroll and brought it partially over my head, which earned me another poke.

"Everyone's waiting for you."

"That's so nice of them. Tell them I said thanks." I curled up in a ball so he couldn't poke me in the vitals. I should have just gotten up. Aleph was gentle about it, but…

"Up now!" Tetora tore the bedroll out from under me, flipping me end over end.

"Hey! I was sleeping in that."

"Not anymore. We're going to be late." Tetora avoided making eye contact with me.

"Late for what?" We were still in the middle of nowhere, surrounded by scraggly, half-dead trees.

"Church." As he uttered the word darkly, I heard a bell tolling in the distance.

"Wait, an actual building? Is there more than one?" I mean, churches rarely sprout up by themselves, right?

"Churches are more than just buildings, Little Dragon," Aleph admonished. "They are good places to self-reflect and also—"

"Yeah, but I mean, a solid structure. A place. Other people!" I was excited now, racing to gather up my travel essentials. Maybe some of those buildings had access to semi-modern conveniences! Oh, what I wouldn't give for a nice warm bath indoors. I think Aleph would have evangelized at me some more, but Tetora pulled him aside and spoke in low but heated tones. I strained my ears to listen but couldn't understand what they were saying.

After a few moments of conversation, Tetora abruptly turned his back to Aleph. Aleph moved to put his hand on his shoulder, but he must have thought better of it. Instead, he headed towards Nora and me.

"I'll see you two at the church after breakfast," Aleph said in his usual, gentle baritone. "I'd like to prepare Father Baram for your arrival. He'll probably be able to tell that you're full-blooded humans, and he might misunderstand. Don't forget to put on your masks and pull up your hoods."

"Okay." I also tried pretending everything was fine as I pulled my hair back.

Aleph nodded to Nora with a small smile before slowly going up the road.

"You should warn him I'm coming too!" Tetora shouted after him angrily, snarling.

Oh, this wasn't good.

"Where's breakfast?" I asked, shifting from side to side.

"Here." Nora absently handed me a red apple as she browsed through her small, leather-bound journal once again. She had ritualistically read through her notes from the ren faire every morning since we arrived as if to remind herself of where we came from and where we were supposed to go.

"Apples again?" I felt my nose twitch threateningly into a wrinkle.

"Yup."

I sighed and bit into it. It was leathery and dry, but it was food.

"Some jerky, too." She handed me a canvas bag of the salty meat.

"I distinctly remember the author describing large banquet halls with roasts drowning in their own gravy everywhere," I muttered while trying to tear off a piece of salty jerky with my teeth.

"We'll infiltrate the first large banquet hall we see to validate that fact." Nora nodded firmly. "But really, is that the sort of thing you remember? Verbatim food descriptions?"

"I… like food?" I didn't know how else to defend myself. Besides, authors can fit in a lot of world-building by describing food. Food-building, if you will.

"What else do you remember?" Nora was always asking me that. Pardon me for not being able to recite all the words to every chapter.

"The general plot and the characters…" I answered the same as always. One character vexed me to no end, but I couldn't even say his real name, so why bother bringing him up?

"You'll tell me if you remember more, right?" Nora pushed.

"Yeah, yeah. If it's important." That's right, *he* wasn't important enough to deal with, at least at the moment. Or maybe I just didn't know how we would deal with him… No, stop thinking about it, Rachel. Talk to Relias, and everything will be fine.

The bell pealed again, longer this time. It was a pleasant interruption, and I once again returned to the thought that civilization was nearby. I quickly packed my stuff, put on my black mask, and pulled up my hood before setting out. Tetora reminded me to drag my giant sword trophy with an emphatically curt gesture. I grumbled but dutifully tugged it through the dirt as we walked. The first chance I had, I was going to sell that heavy hunk of rusty junk.

We soon crested a small hill, and the road opened into a small courtyard where a small, wooden church sat squatly. Outside the main door, Aleph was talking with an older male hybrid with massive, curling sheep horns, wearing holy robes. Other hybrids were slowly making their way to the church from the other direction.

"You'll have to wait until the congregation disperses for the day," the priest was saying as he pulled nervously at his robes. "I don't want to alarm anyone unnecessarily."

"Of course, Father Baram," Aleph murmured before turning towards us. "This is Rachel and Nora, and though human, I affirm they are neither surveyors nor inquisitors."

I remembered Aleph's discussion about surveyors, but we hadn't talked about inquisitors yet. Hadn't they already blamed everyone there was to blame? I was about to ask, but Father Baram's face drained of color as his gaze shifted to Tetora.

"Iron Tiger T-Tetora," Father Baram faltered. "I bid you good t-tidings." I guess Aleph hadn't alerted him after all.

Tetora's eyes bore into the priest's face. "Blessings, Father," was all he replied in a suspiciously neutral tone. I noticed his tail was low and motionless, save for just the tip, which swished back and forth slowly. Chester would do the same thing back home for about five seconds before pouncing on his target with his claws extended.

"Ah, um, Father Baram, was it?" I asked awkwardly to break the tension. "It's very nice to meet you!" I held out my hand expectantly.

Not only did he grab my hand, he pulled me into his side, and it took me a few moments to realize he was using me as a literal human shield. "Joyous blessings to you on this fine day!" He nearly shook my arm off, all the while making sure I stayed between him and Tetora.

Aleph glanced at Tetora with contempt. "Drop it now or leave this holy place."

"You expect me to just—" Tetora retorted, but Aleph simply pointed back towards the woods we came from with the business end of his war hammer. Tetora looked between Aleph and Father Baram a few times before snarling and sprinting off, stirring up a giant cloud of dust.

"Let's move our conversation inside, shall we? Father Baram must prepare for his upcoming service." Aleph led us through the main doors, with the priest close behind him. I put on a show of struggling with the giant sword so I could lag behind and confer with Nora.

"What do you think that was all about?" I whispered, hoping only she heard me as I shoved the sword into a forgotten corner. I didn't think anyone would appreciate me taking it into the sanctuary. Given yesterday's events, however, I was determined to keep the bo staff on me.

"No idea," Nora admitted. "I'm guessing it was personal, though."

"This will blow over once we leave here, right?" I worried aloud.

"He's probably just sulking because Aleph told him to knock it off." Nora shrugged.

"I hope you're right…"

We entered the sanctuary where Aleph was waiting for us near the pulpit. "We'll sit here." He gestured to the first row of pews.

"Um, wouldn't it be better to sit in the back?" I asked hopefully. "You and I are pretty tall… I'd hate to block someone's view."

"Nice try, little one, but no. Remember to keep your head forward, and very few will even glimpse your face." I would have been offended had anyone else said that to me.

Aleph left to assist Father Baram with the service, so I slid into the pew beside Nora. She was looking forward with an excited gleam in her eyes. I followed her gaze to the enormous banner hung from the ceiling. Emblazoned on the banner was a downward-facing sword with a small buckler hanging from its hilt. A star at the banner's apex illuminated the scene.

"Look! It's the Faith and Will of Euphridia!" She bounced in her seat.

"I thought the shield was bigger," I commented. "It looks so tiny." I bet the artist had never even seen the actual Faith of Euphridia. Nora turned her head slowly to me, giving me a disparaging look. "Raelynn can change its size any time she wants, remember?"

"Oh yeah, that's pretty convenient," I admitted.

"Okay, I just have to say it." She bounced harder in her seat, no longer able to contain herself. "Lemme do the thing, Rae!"

"I dunno what thing you're talking about, so I'm not really stopping you."

Nora puffed herself up and pointed at me. With a dramatic voice, she recited, "Above all, taking the shield of faith, wherewith ye shall be able to quench all the fiery darts of the wicked!"

"What chapter is that from?" I blinked.

"Ephesians, chapter 6, verse 16."

"Wait, from the Bible? So Eura totally just ripped that off, too?" That sort of irritated me since I had always thought the weapon set had catchy titles.

Nora bobbed her head.

"What a lazy author," I muttered.

"Now, now, they all do it. You can't have a story that doesn't connect to the real world. Otherwise, the audience wouldn't understand it, and isn't a mutual understanding the point of telling a story in the first place?"

"Yeah, I suppose, but that's borderline copyright infringement! Wait… is the Bible copyrighted?"

"Most modern translations are, but that's why I quoted the King James version. Fair use."

"How do you even know something like that?" Just what else was stashed away in that head of hers?

She took a deep breath, but loud murmuring and footsteps from the back of the church interrupted her most likely long-winded answer. About two dozen hybrids, primarily sheep, ox, and rabbit variations, filled in various sections of the pews. We had already forgotten Aleph's warning not to stay turned around for long. We couldn't help it, though. The children were the cutest things I had ever seen. Wide-eyed, happy rabbits with their ears just twitching with excitement. Little baby lambs blatting anxiously for their parent's attention. Some hybrids wore cloth masks like we did since, even inside, there were fine traces of dirt hovering in the air. I'm sure it was weird that our hoods were up, but I think everyone was just being polite enough not to ask us to remove them. Though they didn't speak to us, they did nod their heads slightly in acknowledgment. I heard the word "pilgrims" being bandied about in hushed tones to explain our presence.

"We're over capacity," Nora whispered to me. "Even if we exclude ourselves."

"What capacity?"

"Hybrid count." Oh yeah, we were definitely over the limit of twenty.

"I swear if anyone threatens this flock, I'll bust them wide open," I whispered back heatedly.

Nora just gave me a wide, supportive grin in response. Outside, the church bell tolled again, signaling the start of the service.

CHAPTER 20: BOOK OF ORIGINS

Father Baram walked out from a side door to the front of the sanctuary, and most of the congregation fell silent. Of course, I forgave the littlest ones for their continued babbles. The priest smiled and held up his hands. Given the church's small size, I shouldn't have been surprised, but he greeted everyone by their first name. He called me Rachel just before nodding to and greeting Nora.

"We will start with a reading from the Book of Origins." Father Baram gestured towards Aleph, who had just stepped out of an opposing door holding a brown, leather-bound book. He strolled into the pulpit and placed his book on the lectern. Nora's entire being zeroed in on Aleph, and I couldn't help but do the same. Aleph squared his shoulders and spoke sonorously.

> *Before there was, there was Naught.*
> *Naught is nothing, but has the potential to be anything.*
> *In time, Euphridia traveled alone to Naught only after searching all that there already was.*
> *Weary from her journey, she shaped Speranza from Naught in order to have a place to rest.*
> *She gave our world a Name, for without it, it would be unknowable. She gave our world a Purpose, for without it, it would have no use.*
> *In time, Euphridia filled the world with plants and animals, giving each Name and Purpose even as she created them from Naught. For things without a proper Name nor Purpose are doomed to return to Naught.*

In time, Euphridia created for herself a steadfast companion that would support her in all endeavors.

From Naught, Raela, the first human of Speranza, came into existence. With Name and Purpose defined, Raela flourished at Euphridia's side.

In time, Raela realized she could not create from Naught like Euphridia may, for that was not her Purpose. This was the first lesson humanity learned. That humans may not be as to a God, for that is not our Purpose.

In time, Raela asked Euphridia if she would create other humans from Naught. Euphridia refused, for in studying Raela, Euphridia learned humans struggle with their Name and Purpose. Failing such struggles would doom a human to return to Naught. Raela accepted her answer and continued to abide by Euphridia's decision and teachings.

In time, Euphridia realized that even Raela, who strived to be true to her Name and Purpose, would be lost to Naught, for it is natural upon Death that humans forget their Name and their Purpose. Euphridia, ever compassionate, entered into The Everlasting Covenant with Raela, allowing her to continue on after Death if, in Life, Raela stayed true to her Name and Purpose. In turn, Euphridia would remember Raela's Name and Purpose for her and judge her actions in accordance to them after Death came for her physical form.

In time, Euphridia agreed to create other humans who could join The Everlasting Covenant, and I was the First of Men spun from Naught. I was given the Name Relias, and my first Purpose is to guide all of humanity so none shall be doomed to Naught.

And so I say to you, above all else, understand and cherish your Name and your Purpose and be true to them, for in doing so, you shall have Life beyond Death within The Everlasting Covenant of Euphridia.

No one had made a sound throughout the entire dramatic recitation. It really hadn't been a reading, for Aleph never even glanced at the book he had placed on the lectern. In fact, the congregation's awed silence hung in the air for a full minute before Father Baram realized the show must go on.

"Ah, thank you, Aleph," he said awkwardly, perhaps feeling slightly shown up by Aleph's passionate oration. "I now welcome the Borden family to come forward."

The Borden family stood up in unison, composed of a mother, father, and young boy, all with blush pink pig ears adorning their heads. Somewhat inappropriately, I wondered if they had curly tails too, but their clothes were not in such a fashion to reveal the answer. The youngest clenched his fists and squinted his eyes shut as they made their way to the pulpit. I was reasonably sure he was praying under his breath, too.

Father Baram pulled a golden orb from his robe and offered it to the young hybrid. He glanced apprehensively at his mother and father before touching it. The orb filled with a bright light at his touch.

"In joyful faith," Father Baram announced, "we welcome Everett Borden into our community. May you stay true to your Purpose as a farmer!" The congregation cheered loudly, save for Nora and I. Farmer? How is that a Purpose? Isn't that just an occupation?

Everett's face appeared stricken with grief, and I felt he probably thought the same thing we were. He shook as large tears formed at the corners of his eyes. I squirmed in my seat just as his mother went to enfold him in a hug.

He dodged and let out a shriek. "No! I want to be an artist! I don't want to be a smelly old farmer!" He dashed down the aisle and out the back of the church. No one made a move to stop him. The congregation sighed collectively as the rest of the family returned to their seats. Wasn't anyone going to go after the poor kid?

I couldn't concentrate on the service anymore. Instead, I kept craning my head behind me to look out at the main entrance, but I saw no sign of Everett. At one point, Aleph had sat down next to me, but I didn't notice until he gave me a nudge.

"Little Dragon, you need to look forward," he whispered.

"What about Everett?" I asked.

"He will be fine. He just needs time to adjust."

"He's all alone out there!" I exclaimed angrily under my breath.

Aleph simply ignored my complaint and kept his head forward. Nora also looked uncomfortable, but there wasn't much we could do during the service. The moment we were dismissed, though, Nora and I flew out of our seats to look for the little boy. Again, no one made a move to leave the church.

"Which way do we go first?" Nora asked once we were outside.

I looked around the courtyard. The road we had yet to travel wound its way into a small, empty village. The path we had arrived by led to nothing but desolate wilderness.

"Back the way we came," I finally decided. "If he went to his house to sulk, that's one thing, but if he went out that way…"

"Good thinking," Nora approved.

We walked toward where we had camped the previous night, calling for Everett. Each time I said his name, I doubted more and more that he would respond. Nora slowed down as we realized this might not be a job for us. We were just weird, dirty pilgrims who witnessed something downright embarrassing. What sort of child would just jump out and say "Over here!"

"Um, Nora…" I started.

"Yeah, maybe this wasn't good thinking after all." Nora nodded.

Then, Tetora's voice boomed from behind a large rock. "Even if you found him, what would you say?"

"Tetora!" I exclaimed, relieved.

"Well? Answer your teacher!" Tetora demanded, still hiding.

"That he doesn't have to be a farmer if he doesn't want to!" I shouted before realizing he seemed awfully aware of the situation he had not been present for.

"So he should just ignore his Purpose and do what he wants, and when he dies, he can go to the Void?" Tetora countered.

"Uh… but…" I floundered before tagging Nora to take over.

"Why can't he just do both?" Nora asked. "I don't see why he can't be an artist too."

Tetora was silent momentarily, but he stepped out from behind the boulder. Clinging to his tail was little Everett, covered in streaks from dirty tears. His cute pig ears were plastered down to the top of his head, making his appearance even more tragic.

"See?" Tetora patted Everett's shoulder. "I told you these pilgrims are harmless. The tall one is strong and sincere but simple. Listen to the tiny one. She understands the unwritten rules better."

"S-simple!?" I twitched angrily.

"Yes. Like a young child, maybe even a baby," Tetora confirmed. I'd have understood if Aleph had told me that, but hearing it from Tetora was a low blow from a previously perceived comrade.

"What the f—" Stop, child alert! "I mean, how… how dare you! I'm a sophisticated adult!"

"Sophisticated adults do not stomp their feet and announce they are sophisticated adults. They let their actions speak for themselves."

I took a deep breath in preparation for some witty retort, but Everett suddenly let out a giggle wrapped up in an interrupted sob. I stared at him. One ear had popped up into a half-fold.

"Hmph!" I snorted loudly, crossing my arms and turning my back theatrically on Tetora, casting one glance over my shoulder at Everett. He giggled again, this time without any sobs. Both ears floated up a little now.

Nora knelt and whispered something in Everett's ear. Curious, I turned back around. Everett nodded excitedly and pulled out a large scrap of paper and a charcoal stick from his dusty robe.

"Hey… what are you two doing?" I asked suspiciously.

"Creating a masterpiece, of course," Nora said.

Everett fervently drew with the stick while Nora blocked my view of the creative process. Tetora also crouched and watched, his tail twitching curiously in the dirt.

"Lemme see!" I demanded.

"No!" Everett said with a laugh. "You have to learn to wait!" Now, I was sure he was drawing me. At one point, he even asked how to spell my name, and Nora replied with the letters to "Rachel" in sequence.

"Don't forget to sign it," Tetora reminded Everett as he stood up.

"Oh, right!" Everett plopped back down in the dirt. "Wait, how do you spell Everett?" he asked. Nora and Tetora conferred momentarily, then coached him through the spelling even as he finished the drawing. He then handed it to Nora.

"Why are you giving it to her?" I complained. "I wanna see it!"

Nora cleared her throat and held the drawing up. It was a stick figure, tall, with angry eyebrows and a cloth mask and hood. A single line represented the bo staff I had. "Big Baby Rachel" was written in crude letters at the top. At the bottom was "Everett Borden."

"What are all the waves?" I said with a pout.

"Stink lines!" Everett cackled. I blinked and sniffed my cloak through my mask. Oh, no! He was absolutely right!

"It's not my fault! I haven't had a proper shower in days!"

"Big stinky baby!" He laughed harder as he doubled over.

"See? Now you are a comedian, too," Tetora said, slapping Everett on the back. I didn't exactly agree, but it satisfied me that Everett was safe and having a laugh.

"How much for the drawing?" Nora asked.

"A million gold coins," Everett answered promptly.

"We don't have that kind of money!" I countered.

"Then, uh…" Everett paused. "That big sword you left at the church! I'll take it."

Of course, a young kid would notice a giant weapon even if I did my best to hide it. But it wasn't like he could wield it, so I seriously considered it.

"Let's go talk to your parents."

We returned to the church and found the Borden family out in the courtyard, exchanging pleasantries with others. Everett ran ahead and gave his mom a hug and a sincere apology for running away. The others smiled at him wistfully. I finally realized that his reaction must have been so customary to the occasion that they had learned it was best to let the children have some time alone to accept the outcome. I still didn't understand the point of traumatizing someone so young in the first place, though. Maybe I could talk with Aleph about it once I found him again.

It turned out the Borden family was actually interested in purchasing the giant rusty sword, and I ended up striking a deal, with Tetora's help, for the drawing and a small sack of onions and potatoes. I even managed to get a few coins that were minted from a dark, almost black metal I didn't recognize.

"What do you plan on doing with it?" I asked Mr. Borden curiously as we finished haggling.

"Oh, ah, it'll make a nice plow. Ours is a bit busted up."

"Swords to plowshares!" Nora chortled.

I wrinkled my nose. "What's funny about that? I think it makes good sense, actually…" I looked out over the dry countryside. "It's not like he needs an anchor or anything."

Nora grimaced. "Really. You never heard that saying before?"

"It's a saying?"

Nora shook her head. "When we get back, I'm taking away all of your nerd privileges. We'll just have to start you back at level one."

"I'm keeping the ID card you made me," I muttered.

We waved as the Borden family left the courtyard. Gradually, the other townsfolk dispersed in small clusters as we stayed behind to wait for Aleph. Tetora, who had been holding onto the drawing, gave it to Nora.

"Wait. What do you think you're doing with that?" I asked, gesturing at the drawing. "I paid for it, so I get to keep it."

"No way. I gave him the idea to draw it, so it's mine." Nora snapped her bag shut after carefully placing the drawing inside. "You'd probably just crumple it up."

"I would not. Someday, 'Big Baby Rachel' will be worth a lot of money."

"So let me hold on to it. You'll just lose it." I hated to admit it, but she was probably right.

Tetora paced angrily as the minutes went by.

Nora gave him a side glance. "So, sophisticated adults… do they fight with their companions, threaten priests, run off in a fit, and never talk about their feelings?"

Oh, thank goodness she stopped picking on me.

"I never said I was sophisticated!" Tetora exclaimed.

"Are you an adult?" Nora was relentless.

"Of course. Look at how big I am!"

"I wonder if I can commission Everett to do a 'Big Baby Tetora,'" Nora mused.

"Little rabbit!" Tetora growled. "You would not understand my anger!"

"Not if you don't tell me where it's coming from, no," Nora agreed.

No, don't fight! I walked between them. "Ah… Nora, maybe it's not our business what—"

"It is if it affects the party," Nora said sternly before locking eyes with Tetora. "You need to work this out with Aleph. Don't pretend nothing happened, either. You've been yelling at him since dawn." Had I missed something before I woke up?

"You…" Tetora started, then sighed. "Yes, you are right."

"What about Father Baram?" I asked Nora.

"He's not part of the party, so who cares?" Nora shrugged. I really couldn't ever anticipate where Nora would draw the line.

The church door creaked open, and Aleph appeared, gesturing for us to come inside. Nora led the way, and I let Tetora go next so I could bring up the rear. Instead of going to the sanctuary, we headed to a small office with several chairs. Father Baram was sitting at a small desk with Aleph's war hammer lying across its length.

"I will bless your weapons to the best of my abilities," he said by way of explanation. "Your staff, please, Rachel."

I placed my staff on the table in front of him. Then I looked at Nora's staff expectantly, but Aleph gently shook his head. Father Baram caught our exchange, and his eyes widened slightly at Nora.

"You're a—"

"Father." Aleph cleared his throat warningly.

"Ah…" Father Baram looked away, only to catch Tetora's eye. "Er, I would also bless your iron claws if you approve…"

"Yes." Tetora refused to look at him, but he placed his iron claws gently on the desk. Father Baram stood and held his hands above the weapons gathered.

"In Euphridia's name, I pray. May your weapons strike wicked ones true even as they would spare the innocent." I jumped as a gold light formed around each weapon. Father Baram raised his hands, and their glow intensified before disappearing completely. By the end, he looked quite exhausted, his robe almost translucent with sweat.

"It's been a very long time since I've practiced such rituals," he admitted in a wheezing voice. "I cannot vouch for their duration, but I will pray they last through your journey."

"We thank you for your blessings, Father," Aleph replied quietly.

Father Baram sat back in his seat with a huff and chanced a remorseful look at Tetora. "I wish I could have accommodated your previous request, great tiger. I am sorry for causing you anguish."

"It was *our* request, not just mine, Father." Tetora sneered for just a moment. He then glanced guiltily down at his feet before letting out a frustrated grunt. "I am sorry I blamed you. I know… things are complicated."

"I will pray for change," the sheepish priest promised vaguely, spiking my curiosity even more.

Aleph cleared his throat. "Father Baram has prepared rooms for us here. We should rest for today. Tomorrow, we can head into town and restock."

CHAPTER 21: SUNDAY SCHOOL LESSONS

The room had two beds, a fireplace, and a sizable washtub. It did not, however, have any plumbing. As a result, Nora and I found ourselves hauling and heating water over the fireplace's fire so we could bathe. She cheated here and there, though, practicing with a controlled flame from her fingertips when she thought I wasn't looking. A kind soul had previously donated a few bars of lye soap made with animal fat. The soap was odorless, which struck me as odd, but we were assured it would be effective for our needs.

"Shall we play rock, paper, scissors to see who gets the luxury of washing up first?" I asked.

"You first. You're smellier than I am." Nora waved her hand. My nose didn't agree, but I made no argument. I really, really wanted to get clean.

"Before I forget… Why didn't Aleph have your staff blessed?"

"I'm a dark mage. It'd be counterproductive."

"Oh, is that right?"

"A blessing of amity would weaken a focus of animus."

I tilted my head. "A focus of animus?"

"My staff, for example. It helps me cast spells by focusing my… will? Emotions? Determination? Creativity?" She frowned, and I could practically see the wheels turning in her head as she thought about the process. Given that no one had told her how it worked, I was still impressed she could sling spells so well already.

"So, what are you going to do now?" I asked as I carefully added the last kettle of boiling water.

"Snoop around," Nora answered shamelessly. "I'll come back in about half an hour."

"You might as well take the bucket with you and fill it up from the well on your way back."

Nora nodded, grabbed the bucket, and left. I checked the water temperature, sat in the washbasin, and *scrubbed*. The rough cotton washcloth exfoliated everything it came into contact with, regardless if it was dirt or skin. I also washed my hair with the scentless soap, noting that it had grown even longer. At this rate, it would be down the length of my entire back before the month was out.

I sighed, finding myself alone with my thoughts. I had been waiting for some sign that I was dreaming, but hadn't this gone on too long for that? It wouldn't hurt to try contacting Euphridia straight from the church, right? I mean… I knew she said she was having trouble reaching Relias, but… isn't this precisely what those structures were for? But what would I tell her? How could I strike the right amount of dissatisfaction with my current experience without getting served a pile of divine retribution? I considered the compliment sandwich, where you hide your grievances between hand-crafted, artisanal slices of adoration to get someone to bite. Would she see right through that, though?

Nora's "shave and a haircut knock" startled me before I recognized it, and I almost slipped as I stepped out of the tub. I wrapped a towel around myself and opened the door.

"Much better!" she said in approval as she stepped inside with a bucket of water.

"Well?" I asked curiously. "What did you snoop on?"

"Aleph and Tetora are talking it out, so that's good. I couldn't find a copy of the local bible lying around to pilfer, though, so keep your eyes open on your rounds."

"You want to steal a holy book? From a church?" Weren't we in enough trouble already?

"I said pilfer, not steal."

I frowned. "What's the difference?"

"It sounds better."

I went to put on my clothes but flinched at their smell. I should have washed them too.

"Aleph says we can wear the robes in the big closet." Nora pointed.

I pulled out one for each of us. Mine would be weirdly short, and Nora's would hang on the ground. One size fits no one.

After several iterations of lugging well water and boiling kettles of water, it was Nora's turn to soak. I left her to do the thing, as she put it, and headed for the sanctuary. The sun was setting, but dozens of candles had been lit to keep the room from plunging into darkness. I went under the banner and knelt.

"Um…" I paused. What do I call her? Eura? Ms. Abrams…? Euphridia? Holy Euphridia? What was she to me?

"Eura… Um, Speranza is…" Come on, compliment first as the base. "Speranza… has a lot of nice people in it who are taking good care of me. I've made some good friends and… um… you did an excellent job with your world!" Okay, there's the bread. I hope I did okay. Time to drop a couple of bombs… but *politely*. "However, I can't help but think that I *really* don't belong here, and maybe you've mistaken me for someone else." I paused again, lifted my head, and looked behind me. Good. No one was there.

"I want to go home, please. I miss Mother and Chester, and I'm really… scared. I'm not cut out to fight demon kings and save the world. The longer I stay, the more worried I am that the real Raelynn is still in trouble. So if you hear this, please let us come home. I appreciate any and all assistance you would kindly offer. Thank you." There was no response, but I wasn't expecting one, at least not immediately. Prayers take time to make their way to the recipient, right? I awkwardly bowed at the banner, stood up, and made my way out of the sanctuary.

"It's… you!" Father Baram jumped back suddenly from around the corner, spilling a stack of papers from his hands.

"Oh, sorry, I didn't mean to startle you." I crouched down and started picking up the papers. I tried to hand them back to him, but he had thrown himself on the ground along with them.

"Holy Captain!" he shouted. "You've returned to us!" Oh crap, I had forgotten my mask! How could I have left the room without it?

"You're… you're mistaken! I'm—"

"An accidental impersonator," Aleph's firm voice said from behind. "A full-blood who seeks refuge in the Wastelands, away from unintentional scandal."

Father Baram looked at me from the ground, then stood up slowly. "Yes… now I see the hair is all wrong. Raelynn would never wear it like that." While I was thankful he stopped the immediate hero worship, I was disappointed that it didn't even cross his mind that Rae might want to try an original style. She had been pictured with long, flowing hair past her hips. I didn't even want to imagine the daily routine of taming all that.

"I get that a lot…" I murmured, shoving the papers into his hands.

"Maybe you should cut it short," Father Baram suggested. "There's even less chance you might be mistaken for her."

It was *my* hair, but it seemed everyone had a firm opinion on it, which I found irritating. "I'll consider your *wise* words, Father." I tried to keep my tone neutral, but Aleph must have sensed the barb in it.

"Ah, Rachel… perhaps you could help me prepare dinner if you have a few minutes?" He had already taken my arm and led me into the small kitchen. Inside were my prized onions and potatoes, waiting to be chopped.

"What are we making?"

"Spiced stew." Oh! Aleph's famous spiced stew! The book frequently mentioned it, and the party's opinion was unanimously positive. My irritation faded at the prospect of finally getting a proper meal.

"You… have all the ingredients?" I asked excitedly. Spice equals flavor!

"Yes. I would ask that you…"

"Cut the potatoes into small cubes and dice the onions. I'll start the onions first so you can sauté them with the aromatics!" I grabbed the wooden cutting board and got to work.

"I didn't know you could cook…" He seemed surprised.

"Huh? Doesn't everyone know how to cook?" It also helped that I had contemplated recreating this particular dish, but a certain promise to a certain demon king prevented me from referencing the book for the recipe.

What a fiend.

"But you…" Aleph stopped. "Apologies. I assumed something, but I see I am wrong."

"So what about the protein? What are we going to use?"

"Soybean."

"S-surely, you mean some meat, right? Sliced pork belly… beef… even chicken would be alright…" Not beans. No more beans! I get that they travel well, but the side effects…

"Dried soybeans are nutritious and plentiful."

"Tetora wants meat," I coaxed. I wanted meat, too.

"Yes, and if we had that available, I would add it. The beans will suffice." The note of finality in his voice kept me from complaining more.

With my prep work complete, I sighed and sat on a wooden stool near the stone stove. At least the kitchen was stocked with potable water, so I didn't have to go out to the well again. Once everything was on to boil, Aleph took a seat beside me.

"Now we wait," he said with a small smile.

We sat in silence for a little while until I interrupted it by asking, "Why did Father Baram tell Everett he had to be a farmer? He's just a little kid."

Aleph nodded to himself as if he had anticipated my question. "Today was the day he received his covenant name."

"Wait. What was his name before today?" No wonder he couldn't spell it.

"It is rude to ask that question, Little Dragon."

"Why?" I pressed.

"Birth names… are discarded. They are only temporary, and once you are given a covenant name, it is considered quite the insult to call someone by their birth name."

"But what if someone makes a mistake?"

"Then they should sincerely apologize and strive not to repeat it."

"But what if someone doesn't like their covenant name or their Purpose? It's not fair that they don't get a say in it."

"Six-year-olds do not make the best choices, Little Dragon."

"So why do this at six, then? Why not when they're an adult? Who gets to choose names and Purposes, anyway?"

"So full of questions…" Aleph sighed with a chuckle. "Holy Sage Relias can answer these better than I, but I will try my best. Let's focus on who chooses, shall we? What do you think the answer is?"

"Father Baram," I replied promptly.

"I'll concede he revealed it to the congregation, but he is a vessel of greater authority. I pose the same question to you again."

"Um. The head of the Church."

"And who is that?" he asked me again.

"Uh. The Assembly?"

"And who guides their choices?"

"Logic and empathy?" I answered with more of a what than a who, but I hoped I wasn't entirely wrong. Hybrid shaming aside, maybe the Assembly had some redeeming qualities?

"And who gave them the ability to reason and empathize?" I saw where this was going.

"Euphridia." I sighed. "But she isn't…" Oh, how should I say it? "I mean, she…"

"Just because she is not physically present does not mean she does not guide us in our daily lives," Aleph lectured.

"So you're saying Euphridia decided Everett should be Everett, and he should be a farmer."

"You are simplifying the process, but yes. Do you remember today's reading?"

"Yes." I thought it was a lot of naught, but I didn't dare say that to him.

Aleph pinned me with a soulful gaze. "What did Holy Sage Relias say his first Purpose was?"

Good to know I wasn't the only one who asked a lot of questions.

"Guide humanity." Whatever that means. You might as well herd cats for a living.

"And Relias established the Assembly that oversees The Church of The Everlasting Covenant over three thousand years ago. So my last question is, who created Relias?"

"Euphridia. Okay, you have a point, but…" How could I get him to see it was all so *silly*?

"Let's try something else," Aleph murmured as he stood up to stir the pot. "Let's say we tell Everett to be an artist."

"Alright. What's the worst that could happen if he becomes an artist?"

"He starves."

"What?"

"Who is going to buy his art?"

I furrowed my brow. "Well, if he gets really good, he could…"

"He could be the best artist in the world, but who will see it?"

"Surely the other people in town would support—"

"They can't afford to buy art. They are farmers in a small community in the Wastelands."

I got annoyed, but I couldn't find the words. It just wasn't fair.

"You are struggling just as Everett will." He patted my shoulder gently. "It is easier to begin the struggle when young. He will grow up considering what it means to be a farmer. He will grow a sense of self and of being part of something greater. Don't worry. He has many around him who will help him on his journey, just as you do."

"That's a comforting thought," I started slowly. "But I don't know that—"

Tetora crashed through the kitchen door, ending our lesson abruptly. "When's the food going to be ready!?" he demanded, splaying his arms wide in comedic desperation. "Some of us are wasting away out here!"

***

Post-Chapter Omake

Rae: *Do you remember any silly Sunday school lessons from when you were a kid?*

Nora: *I do. There was this one where we pretended the apocalypse happened, right? We could only save a few people in a limited time, so we had to decide who to rescue. Should we save the teacher? The doctor? What about the one with a broken arm? We had twenty minutes as a group to decide who lived and who died.*

Rae: *What the heck… was the moral of that lesson???*

Nora: *I don't remember. I was just so upset trying to figure out why we weren't using that first twenty minutes to save people who could help us save the rest that I rage-quit!*

Rae: *…How did you rage-quit Sunday school?*

Nora: *It's easy if you can outrun the teacher.*

CHAPTER 22: RESPITE

I had to admit Aleph's spiced stew was delicious, even if it was a lot of beans. It wasn't overly piquant, but its rich undertones added a complexity that forced you to savor it. Spending a week eating tasteless bean mush, salty jerky, and dried-out apples also helped enhance its flavor.

"More," Tetora grunted, still chewing on his last bite as he held his bowl aloft.

"Is something wrong with your legs?" Aleph, seated across from him, asked curiously.

"Ah, no…" Tetora stood up to head back into the kitchen.

"Since you are up, please serve all of us." Aleph handed him his empty bowl, ignoring the frown forming on Tetora's face.

Nora and I snickered in unison as we also held up the bowls. Father Baram decided he was good with the bowl he had.

"Opportunists!" Tetora accused. "Wait your turn." He grabbed Aleph's bowl first but eventually filled ours as well.

When I received my bowl back, it was only half full. "Hey…"

"There's no more left," Tetora growled.

I gave him a wary look. "Did you even divvy it up right?"

"Everyone got the same amount who wanted seconds!" Tetora's tail lashed angrily.

"Just let me inspect your bowl to make sure." I stood up and leaned over the table to gauge. "As I suspected…" His bowl was filled to the brim.

"A surcharge for table-side service. You get what you get!"

"And you don't get upset," Nora finished with a smirk.

"The heck I don't." I struck with my fork, stabbing a sizeable chunk of potato right out of his bowl.

"Did you see what she just did!?" Tetora exclaimed to Aleph.

"Yes. Her reflexes are much quicker now."

Tetora tried to retaliate by helping himself to my bowl, but I put up an arm to block him. "No way. Justice is on my side tonight!"

"To think…" Father Baram suddenly interrupted our antics. "That I thought you were Raelynn." He shook his head slowly. "She never would have acted like this."

I paused and sat down, feeling like I was both relieved and insulted. "How do you know?"

"I had met her once," Father Baram replied simply.

"What was she like?" Nora asked, leaning over the table.

"The Holy Captain was quiet, serious, and determined. She would have taken nothing from anyone else. Not even a boiled potato."

"It was all just in fun…" I had already eaten it, so it wasn't like I could give it back.

Father Baram's serious face disappeared, and he laughed. "I know. Fun suits you, Rachel. If she had ever met you… she might have been envious of your playfulness."

"Really? Hmm…" I reflected on his statement while scraping every bit of stew out of my bowl.

"I hope you meet her one day. She would like you." Father Baram stood up from the table, bowed his head to us, and headed off to his office. As soon as his back turned, Tetora motioned for me to follow him outside. He wouldn't make me train on an overfull stomach, would he? That would be a recipe for disaster.

Once we entered the dimly lit courtyard, Tetora advised, "Do not be swayed by his opinion. Raelynn knew how and when to have fun."

"Oh?"

"Yes!" Tetora grinned in the darkness. "One time, she coaxed a squirrel into Aleph's bedroll, and for the next week, he refused to sleep in it!"

"She pulled pranks?" Oh my gosh, wait until I tell Nora! I may not remember the whole story, but I definitely would have remembered something like that!

"Yes, but only rarely. She was smart enough to make it look like it was someone else, too. Usually me." He snorted, looking out over the little town nestled below. "I think… everyone saw Raelynn differently. If you ask Aleph, he would agree with Father Baram. But if Laverna were here… she would say something different."

"Like what?"

"Hmm. She would say… that Raelynn is uptight, anxious, and always worried about everything."

"I see…" Could you blame her? *So much pressure* there.

He laughed. "That was *exactly* what she would say when Raelynn would refuse to drink with her!"

"Drink? Wasn't she underage?" She was only fifteen when she challenged the demon king!

"Who is going to deny the Chosen One a drink? Only Raelynn herself." Tetora shrugged. "But that did not stop Laverna. She believes the only way to know someone is to drink with them."

"You miss Laverna too, don't you?"

"Of course I do. She…" He turned back to the church for a moment, then whispered loudly, his whiskers tickling my ears. "Her original assigned Purpose… was to be a thief."

"W-what!? That doesn't make any sense." Telling a six-year-old that you're going to be a thief. A criminal. Utter ackamarackus!

"Yes," Tetora agreed. "I wanted to tell you this because I do not think… anyone else would." I had thought the title of "Laverna the Thief" was self-imposed and self-promoted.

"So Euphridia said she had to be a thief?"

"No. A priest did. But he was wrong to do such a thing."

"But I thought the priests were only reporting Euphridia's will."

Tetora snorted. "Just because someone acts as a priest does not mean they act in good faith."

"So Everett got off lucky with just getting told he is a farmer."

"Yes. Some priests are bad. Some priests are good. Like everyone else."

I couldn't help but ask, "Do you… hate Father Baram?"

"No. He is doing the best he can with what he has."

I scrutinized Tetora's face. He was trying to tell me something crucial without actually saying it. "There are bad priests in the General Assembly of Clergy, aren't there?"

"I'm just saying you should be very careful when you meet them. Do not let them use you."

I took a moment to let that sink in. "I'll be careful," I promised.

He patted my shoulder roughly. "I do not think you are so simple. But it was easy to call you simple at that moment. Thank you for acting out earlier."

"Um, you're welcome," I replied, knowing that only the second half had been an act.

"As a rare reward… no training tonight. Go get some sleep."

"Yes!" I shouted to the stars before running back inside to my room. Nora was there, hanging up our clothes to dry near the fireplace.

"Thank you for washing them," I praised her.

"Washing them wasn't so hard. Wringing them out is a pain. Did you find a bible?"

I scuffed at the ground with my foot. "I could tell you I looked everywhere, but that would be a lie. There's no way I'm getting involved with your pilfering scheme."

"Let me guess, you're worried about karma?"

"You're not?" I countered.

She was about to deny such things, as usual, but stopped short. "Hmm. Maybe." Then she shrugged. "I just thought it might help us see what else Relias had to say about how this world works."

"We could always ask Aleph to recite a chapter or two," I suggested.

Nora made a face. "And get lectured again? No thanks."

"So he got you too, huh? About Names and Purposes?"

"No, we talked about Naught."

"What did he have to say about it?"

"It's where the souls of bad people and demons go after they die."

"There's no Hell?"

"I think Naught *is* Hell," Nora clarified.

"Isn't everything made from Naught? Wouldn't that mean Speranza came from Hell?"

"No, everything was created from the potential of nothing that also exists in Hell, the Void, Naught, or whatever you want to call it."

"The potential of nothing…" It's just nothing, right?

"I think the theory is… all souls here are made from Naught, and those unworthy of existing will return to Naught for recycling. However, the process is filled with suffering."

It didn't make sense to me. "Come again?"

"Imagine you're a disembodied soul after death. You know what you are, but there's no way for you to interact with your environment. You exist, trapped, waiting to be disassembled into the smallest elements of Naught with no idea how long you have to wait. It gets worse from there."

"You don't just… fade to nothing? You're still… sentient?" It was terrifying to think about.

Nora nodded, though her face suggested she wasn't entirely convinced by the explanation. "But if you're good and do what you're told, or at least try in good faith… you get to reincarnate. It seems a little random what you come back as, but there's one famous exception, though."

"What's that exception?" I already knew the answer.

"Raela. She always comes back as a human female with the same Purpose. Even her covenant name is almost the same."

"What did Aleph say her Purpose is?"

"The same as the story. Continue to be Euphridia's Chosen One. Kill the demon king and save the world."

"Can you imagine being told all that when you turn six? It sounds completely—" My stomach suddenly flip-flopped. "Oh… I must have eaten too much." It was a complaint I rarely uttered.

"Why don't you lay down? You look a little pale."

"Y-yeah. Sounds good." Maybe Aleph's stew was spicier than I thought. "I'll tell you about my conversations first, though." I climbed into the bed nearest the window. Honestly, I don't remember if I made it through all of my mental notes because I was getting dizzy with drowsiness, but I definitely talked about the squirrel prank first. Nothing else really mattered, anyway.

After I had finished recounting the highlights of my day, Nora pondered, "I wonder where he ended up sleeping for that week. "

"Hmmm?" I drawled, forcing my eyes open.

"Nevermind. Night-night Rae." I'm not even sure I told her goodnight back.

***

Post-Chapter Omake

Nora: *I wonder if we're getting paid.*

Rae: *What do you mean?*

Nora: *I don't remember setting up a direct deposit, and we've been here long enough to earn at least one paycheck.*

Rae: *Of all the things going on, that's what worries you the most? I'm not even sure CUP knows we're here.*

Nora: *Look, if I don't start saving now, my mid-life journey to find myself will just be a mid-life crisis. I want to get paid!*

Rae: *I just want to make it to mid-life…*

Nora: *With money!*

CHAPTER 23: MEMO FROM HUMAN RESOURCES

"Psst," Nora hissed in my ear the next day, jolting me out of blissful, dreamless slumber.

"Too early!" Even though I had no idea what time of day it was, I pulled the blankets over my head to solidify my stance on the issue. It had been a long time since I had slept in a bed, and I was determined to enjoy every possible minute.

"It's important!" she whispered urgently. Why was she whispering? Wasn't it just the two of us in here?

I groaned and sat up, flipping the covers down in our shared room within the church. "What is it now?" Someday, I'll wake up in my real bed, and it will be another lazy Saturday afternoon where no one expects anything of me.

"Read this." Nora shoved a folded, somewhat tattered scrap of striated papyrus before my face. I yawned, snatched the paper ungraciously, and unfolded it. At first, it appeared blank, but then it flashed with a gold sheen before distinct, typed words began to ripple on the surface.

CONFIDENTIALITY NOTICE – This document is intended only for the person(s) named in the message header and is protected from unauthorized discovery through the use of Smart-Gene™ biodegrading ink. Unless otherwise indicated, it contains information that is confidential, privileged and/or exempt from disclosure under applicable law. This document and parts herein must not be shared, reproduced, or copied without CUP's written permission, and the contents herein must not be imparted to a third party nor be used for any unauthorized purpose.

To: Eleanora Beatrice Perez and Rachel Emily Smith

From: Clare Mercure (Manager, Human Resources, Cooperative Universal Publishing)

RE: Status Update Received (Confidential)

Thank you for sharing your recent status update from Location=Speranza_Wastelands_North_Vicus_Church_0 09 via Rachel's 'church prayer.' I am glad to hear that despite recent events, you both have arrived on-site safely.

For future reference, please note that bringing anachronistic and/or prohibited items (e.g., journals that are bound with synthetic leather, with stitched binding using synthetic thread, containing recycled cotton paper and pens of ball-point configuration with plastic shafts and oil-based ink) on-site is against company policy. Given the extenuating circumstances leading up to this policy violation, human resources will take no action and considers the matter closed. However, please be sure to secure these items safely on your person at all times and do not impart them to a third party or use them for any unauthorized purpose while on-site. Authorized purpose includes and is limited to 'taking notes and drawing sketches for work-related tasks as authorized under CUP's acceptable use policy' and 'serving as a secured, interdimensional mailbox for receiving confidential communications from CUP.'

The Human Resources Department at CUP is committed to creating and maintaining a safe work environment for all of its employees, including eliminating potential hazards whenever possible. This letter informs you that Speranza_Current_Ambient_Animus_Quality_Index=150

(Elevated: Unhealthy for Sensitive Groups). I strongly recommend you try to reduce ambient animus at your on-site location. There may be multiple processes available to you in order to do this; however, I request that you take the following actions as soon as you are able:

1) Locate your local NAUGHT terminal (ID: Speranza01, Location: Unknown, Primary Network Interface Status: Link Disconnected, Last Up: 2786 days ago)

- You may require assistance from local sentient beings in order to locate your local NAUGHT terminal.

- Do not discuss confidential information about NAUGHT with any unauthorized party as per the terms of your signed non-disclosure agreement.

- Use corporate-approved phrases to express what you are looking for, such as 'the birthplace of all creation.'

2) Perform a manual reboot of the local NAUGHT terminal in order to update the local instance of NAUGHT.

- Critical updates will run automatically upon successful reboot.

- Do not interrupt these critical updates under any circumstances.

- Do not otherwise interact with the NAUGHT terminal. Only NAUGHT-certified content creators are to access NAUGHT systems.

Failure to follow all NAUGHT instructions may result in any number of unintended consequences.

Once the local instance of NAUGHT is updated, a designated member of management will contact you directly with further instructions via primary communication methods.

In the meantime, you may continue to send work-related informational inquiries to me via 'church prayer' and I will assist you as best as I am able. I also wish to inform you that I have forwarded Rachel's most recent 'church prayer' request of "let us come home please" to Administration for further consideration and will advise you of any subsequent decisions via 'interdimensional letter.' Please note that 'church prayer' and 'interdimensional letter' are considered secondary communication channels and may be unreliable at times.

Please confirm receipt of this message via 'church prayer' ASAP. I look forward to hearing from you.

Cc:

Corporate Compliance – Case No. BDT053-RES007-EBPXXX

Employee file(s)

I struggled to read the corporate jargon several times. "What the…"

Nora leaned over my shoulder. "It's from Clare, right? You can see the words too?"

I nodded rather dumbly. "Where… did you find this?"

"In my interdimensional mailbox." She held up her journal.

I didn't know what to make of the situation or the letter's contents. "Is she helping us… or are we in trouble?"

"Both." Nora plopped down on the foot of the bed.

"We didn't do anything wrong!" Prohibited items? It's not like we knew this was going to happen! *And what about what happened to us?* I may not have read my employment contract in its entirety, but surely I didn't agree to all of this!

"It's HR. That's how it works. But forget about that for now. What do you think NAUGHT stands for?"

"Naught?" It was both a clarifying question and a questionable answer.

"It's an acronym. NAUGHT. What do you think it means?" Nora asked me again.

"It means nothing!"

Nora shook her head in disagreement. "No, it's definitely something important."

"No, I mean literally…"

"I know, but it also stands for something. That's why they capitalized it! Hmmm… this is going to bother me until I figure it out. This is why you define acronyms in writing the first time you use them."

"It's a computer, isn't it? We get blasted for pen and paper, and Eura sets up a computer here!?" How the hell was that fair!?

"How else are you going to publish a web novel? You have to use the right tools for the job." Nora shrugged. "But I'm not sure if it's just a computer."

"…The birthplace of all creation." I huffed, pointing to what the locals call it. "It's where she spun everything from the potential of nothing!"

"It might be even more than that." Nora frowned.

"What? I was just spouting nonsense."

"It sounded good, though, right?"

I blinked. "I suppose… But why aren't you mad about all this?"

"I'm living the dream. My favorite world with magic but also mysterious other-worldly technology overlaying it!" Despite Nora's proclamations that she didn't like sci-fi, she certainly embraced it when it reared its ugly head.

"It's all messed up!" It wasn't supposed to be this way at all.

"I don't think so. The people we've met so far seem nice."

I paused and reflected for a few moments. "Well… yeah, for the most part." I discounted the three goons who attacked us, of course. "The people who live here definitely live, laugh, and love."

"I can't believe you just referenced that slogan," Nora laughed snortily. "You know that's an ironic insult these days, right?"

"Oh…" But Mama Perez had that very saying on a sign hanging in her kitchen!

"So we reboot the NAUGHT terminal like she said then, right?"

I nodded sluggishly. "We have to find it first. But yeah, the ambient animus thing sounds important." Were we part of a sensitive group? What does that even mean? "Relias probably knows where it is."

"We could try Aleph too. He seems pretty keen on origin stories."

I strongly felt that talking to him about it would be a waste of time, but I didn't have any evidence to back that up. "Couldn't hurt to try, I guess."

Nora's eyes suddenly flashed. "Maybe we won't even need to find Relias, then! We'll go straight to the end of the journey. Reboot and scoot!"

I jumped up, startled. "We have to! He needs our help! And the General Assembly…" I said I'd do that, too.

She narrowed her eyes with a slight sneer. *"I thought you wanted us to go home?"* Oh no, I couldn't deny it now. The HR lady ratted out my secret prayer!

"I…"

Nora wagged a finger at me. "You better commit to it or commit to quit. You can't keep vacillating."

"I'll do what I said I'd do…" Just no confronting the demon king! *We can't get anywhere near him. We're not supposed to be here! We promised…*

"No more secret wishes behind my back then?"

"Yes," I replied sullenly.

"Make sure you revise your prayer then, okay? I don't want to be yeeted back to Earth while in the middle of something important." I doubted that was a possibility, honestly. The idea that my prayer was forwarded to administration for additional consideration was probably the corporate-approved phrase for "request denied."

I turned my back on her. "Fine…"

Nora graciously accepted her win and offered me a proverbial olive branch: "Oh, by the way, that was pretty smart of you. I'm impressed."

"What do you mean?"

"Praying to Clare. I don't think I would have thought of that."

I flinched, feeling like I owed her the truth every now and then. "I didn't. I addressed my prayer concerns to Eura."

"Now *that's* interesting…" Nora stood up with a bit of an evil smirk on her face. "Shall we confirm receipt via church prayer location equals sanctuary?"

"I guess…" I moved to the door grudgingly, feeling out of sorts.

Nora grinned sheepishly. "Hey, just don't mention my most recent policy violation, okay?"

I turned to look back at her. "Uh, what'd you do now?"

"I drew a butt in the journal after reading that request. I couldn't help it. Some rules are meant to be broken."

I couldn't help but laugh. I was so glad she was here with me for all this absurdity.

CHAPTER 24: PARADISE LOST

Nora and I went back to the church's sanctuary, taking turns to pray while the other kept watch out of earshot. We wanted to ensure we didn't accidentally disclose something to unauthorized third parties, local sentient beings, or whatever.

I kept it brief, addressing my prayer to Clare and verbally carbon-copying all instances of Eura in case she still had some agency here. I even revised my previous request, asking to come home after finishing all the agreed-upon tasks. Towards the end, I added customary pleas for general safety and peace, leaving it up to them to decide how to make it happen. This was getting to be above my pay grade, after all.

Nora, who had only decided to address her prayer to Clare, took much longer than expected. I began to worry about what she was unloading at CUP. Despite the shady contract situation, they technically *were* still on our side… Maybe. So don't make them *too* angry! Eventually, Nora exited the sanctuary.

"*Now*, will you tell me what you asked for?" I asked.

"Mmm. God-like powers to do anything I want. But also the meaning of NAUGHT, as in the acronym."

"W-what?"

"It's still bothering me."

"My exclamation was about the first part!"

"What? The more unreasonable your initial request is, the more likely you are to get a more innocuous one approved. Ask for the moon, get a moon rock? You have a lot to learn, bestie."

I fixed her with a dry expression. "…Innocuous?"

"Inoffensive, harmless, mild."

Innocuous didn't sound innocuous to me. "Oh."

She opened her journal and leafed through the pages. "Hm, nothing yet. Just the old letter." She folded it back up and stuck it inside the journal sleeve.

"You're going to be checking that all day, huh?"

"Yep."

"Just make sure nobody sees you."

We made our way into the communal kitchen, where Aleph had made a beany porridge with chunks of apple. It needed cinnamon and sugar, but none was to be found. I portioned out my serving and brought it to the dining room.

"Thank you for breakfast," I said to Aleph, trying to be polite while knowing that there are only so many ways to mix and match the same ingredients.

"It's lunch," Tetora rumbled from the seat across from me. "Breakfast came and went while you slept in."

"…I'm okay with that." I shrugged.

Nora sat next to me. "I have some more questions about what we talked about yesterday."

"I will do my best to answer them," Aleph responded.

"Euphridia traveled alone to Naught once," Nora recalled from the Book of Origins. Oh, she was jumping right in before I even finished eating.

"Yes."

"And she made everything from it."

"This world and then all that fills it," Aleph agreed.

"Did she do it from the heavens?"

"Heavens?" Aleph tilted his head. "I do not know the meaning of the word." Have they *never heard of heaven?*

Nora took a long pause, scrunching her face in thought. "Another word for a place where Euphridia might reside."

"Ah, you are referring to Paradise," he said sadly. "Yes, there was a time when all lived there."

Nora exhaled slightly before continuing. "Where is it now? Paradise, I mean… the… birthplace of all creation?" I could feel Clare giving Nora a corporate thumbs-up.

"It is forever lost to humanity," he said, shaking his head. "None may go there now save Euphridia herself."

Suspicious.

Nora tried again. "But… physically, where is it?"

"I know not." I almost thought he said "naught."

Turning, I gave Nora my most arrogant and smug look. *See, I told you he didn't know anything about it.*

"Relias would know, though, right?" I asked Aleph after Nora rolled her eyes at me. "He was there too, once."

Aleph and Tetora exchanged a long glance.

Aleph shifted in his seat. "Most likely, however…"

Tetora turned away. "He does not like to talk about it."

"It pains him greatly to speak of Paradise. It is where he lost her." Aleph's eyes fixated on the table. "Do you know who I am talking about?"

"Yes, I know."

He was speaking about Raela, of course. Even I remembered the prologue. She was the first human of Speranza, compassionate to all, yet she paid the price of being too naïve. Her tale took a dark turn the day she discovered the Origin of Sin in the wilderness and, unaware of his true nature, led him to the Goddess. He repaid Raela's kindness by ripping her heart out in front of everyone before tossing it at the Goddess's feet. Relias had been spared from directly witnessing the evil one's gruesome introduction, but he had been forced to deal with the aftermath ever since.

We all sat in silence, probably reliving the confusing parable that advised against being too kind to strangers, at least ones who were demon kings in disguise. It was the hook that drew me in as a young fan, stirring inside me an indignant, deep-seated rage I couldn't ever adequately explain out loud. That gut-wrenching feeling would dissipate little by little with every dribble of further exposition.

I spent my adolescence obsessively checking the landing page for new chapters, even though I had notifications enabled. When a chapter haphazardly materialized, I would pray that her seventh reincarnation would get one step closer to securing world peace, getting her well-deserved revenge, and finally ending up with her true love. I'd reread the older chapters to see if I missed some hint or foreshadowing of a happy ending. I commented religiously, offering kudos and asking questions that were never really answered. In the end, it felt like I had wasted my time on a story that spiraled endlessly without a payoff.

Except I was in it now as an adult… sort of. I mean, I looked like one, anyway. And I would have to deal with all that past nonsense that didn't concern me, along with the present nonsense I found myself wading through.

"Just forget about paradise," Tetora advised, sighing. "If it had existed, it is gone now. If it did not…"

You would spend a lifetime searching for naught. Oh, I just did it to myself. Enough with this!

"We were just curious, that's all." I focused on my food, hoping to drop the subject for now. Relias, the sage subject matter expert, wasn't here to continue the discussion, anyway.

Aleph, however, did not comply with my silent wish and sternly addressed Tetora. "What do you mean, *if it existed?*"

"Ah." Tetora's ears flattened back. "*Of course* it once existed. I meant to say, here. Physically here *now.*"

"You deny everything you cannot see!" Aleph pounded the table, uncharacteristically agitated. *"When you close your eyes, do you stop existing, too?"*

Tetora snarled at Nora and me. *"Now look at what you two started!"*

Nora put down her spoon. "…I have to pack!" Having discarded the rest of her mush, Nora turned traitor and tail, leaving me behind.

Think, Rachel! Before you get in the middle of this. "Uh… I should clean the kitchen, shouldn't I?"

"That would be for the best, little one," Aleph murmured as he continued to pin Tetora with the glare only a grandmaster could give. Tetora gave me a side glance, mentally suggesting he would double training until further notice. Crud.

I picked up Nora's discarded bowl along with my own and ran for the kitchen.

Father Baram appeared in the doorway, heading towards the dining room with a bowl of the communal mush. "Good tidings on this joyful day, Rachel."

"Oh, you don't want to go in there right now, Father," I warned him.

"Is… there a problem? If there is, I should probably…" He trailed off as he heard the two of them arguing in earnest.

"Er, I thought you might want to eat outside today. *Where it's peaceful?*"

He stared at the door that separated him from the philosophical and/or theological chaos inside. "Yes. That sounds like a wonderful idea."

See? There. I saved one sheep from the slaughter. It was time to leave the church now.

CHAPTER 25: A TALE OF TWO TINY TOWNS

Later that same day, we regrouped, thanked Father Baram for his hospitality, and headed into the nearby town. As we approached, I noticed a thick, black cord driven into the ground in the exact center of the dirt road, dividing it into two lanes. Just outside the town's front gate sat two small, identical desks with small stools tucked under them. A small banner strung between them read "Customs/Hybrid Control – Please Wait Here."

"What's all this?" Nora asked as she kicked the cord that ran under the banner.

"Mmm… a creative solution." Aleph gave a slight chuckle, though little humor was in it. "You'll see."

We made our way to the desks and waited. A female rabbit hybrid skittered out of a nearby farmhouse with a charcoal stick and a few sheets of parchment. "Welcome, welcome! Which town are you planning on visiting today?"

I looked around, but I only saw one town. "Um… this one?"

"Northwick?" she pointed to the side of the rope she was on. "Or Southwick?"

"Aren't they the same thing?"

"Oh my, no! Completely separate. See?" She pointed to the rope that continued through the tiny town.

"But…"

"Full-bloods may visit either town whenever they wish. However…" She glanced at Aleph and Tetora apologetically. "Please tell me your intended destination along with an estimated departure time, rounded to the nearest hour."

"I wish to visit Northwick. Estimated departure being one hour from application approval," Aleph murmured.

"Southwick, one hour." Tetora rolled his eyes.

The rabbit jotted down some details with her charcoal stick. "Do you verbally agree not to cross the line at any time during your visit?" Was that figuratively, literally, or both?

"Yes," Aleph and Tetora said simultaneously, with a dual note of irritation.

"Please remember." The rabbit looked at them with dull eyes. "If an inspector stops you, the rule is—"

"Only twenty hybrids or fewer to congregate in any one location," Tetora snapped angrily.

"Church is the only exclusion," she added as if she read my thoughts about yesterday's service. "And remember, the rope divides these two *completely separate* towns."

"What an asinine rule…" Nora shook her head.

The rabbit hybrid had Aleph and Tetora sign their names onto two parchments. "Your respective applications will be processed shortly. In the meantime…" She smiled at us sweetly as she set one sheet on each desk. "May I interest you in any *duty-free* specialty purchases?"

"Duty-free… specialty purchases?" I asked curiously.

"Well, confidentially… Northwick here has the best produce, so *I suggest* that you stock up with   "

"Don't listen to that miscreant!" Another female rabbit came bounding out of another farmhouse on the south side of the rope. She looked for all the world to be the first rabbit's identical twin, save for slightly lighter hair and ears. "Southwick's vegetables can't be beaten!" She quickly picked up the sheet the other rabbit hybrid had placed on the desk nearest her.

"I see you finally decided to start the day, Lulu," the first rabbit remarked.

"I was just delaying having to talk with you until the last possible second, Lala," the other responded cooly.

"Weren't you two sitting together in church yesterday?" Nora asked suspiciously.

"That's different," Lulu of Southwick retorted. "Business is business!" They then eyed each other menacingly.

"Northwick is famous for its juicy carrots!" Lala yelled.

"Southwick's known for its flavorful potatoes!" Lulu countered.

Lala puffed out her chest and pointed at us dramatically. "Don't come crying to me if you forget to purchase Northwick's white onions!"

Lulu waved her arms to catch our attention. "*Lettuce* know what you want in your salad!"

Lala stopped and gave Lulu a withering look. "You're resorting to vegetable *puns* now?"

"You started it with the line about crying over onions," Lulu snapped.

"Oh, that was unintentional," Lala admitted. "Unlike you, I have *standards.*"

Aleph cleared his throat loudly. "We'll be ordering from *both towns* today."

"Oh, well, why didn't you say so?" Lulu sighed, her bunny ears collapsing to the sides of her head. She then handed the charcoal stick and a paper order form to Aleph.

"It was fun while it lasted." Lala exhaled as she also went lop-eared, giving Tetora the similar items she held.

"Tough times?" Nora asked, her eyes gleaming from witnessing the exchange.

"You're the first customers we've had in weeks," Lala affirmed. "As merchants, it's a little hard for us to stay on our game if we don't have *some sort of frivolous rivalry.*"

Merchants? One of them was a customs agent just a moment ago. But I guess it paid off, literally. What a way to engage captive customers.

Lulu nodded. "We like to spice things up."

"Speaking of spices…" Lala grinned. "I just imported some fresh thyme and sage from the middle of nowhere that might interest you!"

"Hey! I gave that to you because you said you'd cook for Mum tonight," Lulu huffed. "You can't sell that."

"Well… what about the lavender?"

I turned to Aleph. "That could be useful…" I tried to sound only somewhat committed to the idea because I didn't want to drive the price up. I liked the idea of smelling something pleasant for once while on the road.

"Fifty percent to me," Lulu demanded, eyeing me up.

"Thirty-five," Lala countered. "I made the sale."

"*Fifty percent*, and I don't tell Mum about your 'walking companion.'"

"Y-you know about Rex and me?" Lala stammered, rubbing at her right rabbit ear.

"*Everyone* knows about you two. Except Mum… *for now*." She folded her arms with a devious glint in her eyes.

"Fine, deal. Just don't say anything yet! I don't want her scaring him off."

Nora let out a suppressed giggle, and the two rabbits turned towards her, their faces flush with embarrassment. "Sorry." Nora smirked. "But it's just nice to see that some things stay the same everywhere you go. Like how everyone's always trying to keep secrets from their moms." She then kicked her foot into the dirt a little. "I bet this Rex is probably good-looking, right? I'm going to ask around about him. Of course… I hope I don't run into your mother and inadvertently say something… sensitive."

Oh, Nora! That's a bit too underhanded…

Lulu and Lala looked at each other for a moment, and Lala sighed with a slightly sour look spreading across her face. "How would you like our 'friends don't snitch' discount today?"

"How very generous. Forget about Rex." Nora beamed as I held in a snicker.

"Ms. Lala and Ms. Lulu," Aleph addressed them in a tone far more serious than their covenant names required. "There are some additional items we are looking for that do not seem to be on the list, but I think you may have them in stock."

"Oh?" Lala asked.

"Do you have a blacksmith in the town?" Aleph asked.

"We do," Lulu confirmed. "But we're not able to take custom orders right now."

"This is more of something they might remove rather than create." He was dancing around his request; that much was for certain.

"Oh…" Lulu recognized what he was looking for. "We don't have the keys to any, though."

"That's alright."

"Two sets?" Lulu wrinkled her nose.

"Yes."

"You didn't get them from us, understand?"

"Of course not," Aleph agreed.

Lala pointed at us humans dramatically. "You *all* need to agree with that statement."

We all promised not to tell anyone we were getting black-market goods from them. I was concerned about what they were asking for, but it was evident by the way they refused to make eye contact that no one wanted to talk about it any further. Lala and Lulu looked over the rest of their respective parts of the orders.

"Looks like you ordered down the middle," Lala noted. "That makes it easier. It'll take about half an hour to round everything up. Why don't you look around the towns while you wait? Your applications have been approved."

I wondered if we would have been denied if we hadn't bought anything. Of course, we could have just walked around the desolate town, so everything was that much more ridiculous.

As we headed in, I kicked a clod of dirt in the road. "If stupidity like this keeps up, they'll need an Eastwick and a Westwick!"

Walking on the other side of the rope from me, Aleph cleared his throat and pointed at a nearby sign that read "Under Construction – Eastwick Farms."

***

Post-Chapter Omake

Rae: *What a stupid rule. Stupid rules lead to workarounds and even malicious compliance.*

Nora: *Some workarounds aren't all bad, though. Look how they ripped us off with it. It was a secondary gain, sure, but it was clever. Don't always discount a workaround when you see one, but certainly consider what it's actually doing as a result of being put into the process.*

Rae: *I still think that the overall rule is dumb. Where's the rationale for it?*

Nora: *You'll have to ask the Assembly. Remember to voice your concerns when we get to Chairo, right?*

Rae: *I won't forget, but do you really think they'll answer me?*

Nora: *Not with that unheroic attitude! You need to visualize to actualize!*

Rae: *...Sometimes I wonder if you're just mocking me.*

Nora: *It's my sincerest form of flattery.*

Rae: *I thought that was imitation.*

Nora: My *sincerest form.* Me.

CHAPTER 26: TIME WITH TETORA

Aleph and Tetora were careful to stay on either side of the line as we walked through the villages of Northwick and Southwick. The divided main street was relatively short, but a handful of storefronts suggested Lala and Lulu weren't the only merchants around. While Nora and I were permitted free rein, we stuck to the side we arbitrarily chose. At one point, I grabbed Tetora and yanked him with me as I looked over a small shop that had not just one but two tiny bottles of perfume.

"I am not interested in pungent liquids like this," he protested loudly.

"But I am! Which one masks odor best?" I held a bottle in each hand so he could perform a sniff test.

"Why are you so worried about your scent?"

"I-I didn't say it was for me!"

"Then, who are you buying perfume for?" Tetora raised an eyebrow.

"… I don't like being stinky."

"Warriors work hard and sweat!" He pumped his fist. "It is the smell of victory!"

I set the bottles down to show him my coins. "Just tell me how much I can buy with this."

"Two sprays. Maybe."

"What!?"

Tetora shrugged. "Perfume is expensive. Just get used to the smell."

"Are you telling me Raelynn walked around smelling like… well… *me*!?"

"Yes. Exactly the same smell, but worse because all teenagers stink. But it is a sign of health and growth."

Bacterial and fungal growth, you mean!

"The author never wrote about things like that in the story!" I was still having trouble thinking of her as a content creator, let alone an actual deity.

"Because it is a trivial thing. The Goddess does not care if you stink."

"*I* don't like being stinky," I reiterated. "I enjoy taking a shower daily and putting on fresh clothes."

"How did you have time for all that when you sleep past noon every chance you get?"

Calling me out again. "By not mindlessly training all day in the hot, dry sun!"

"No wonder you are so delicate now. Just like a courtier." Tetora jostled my head playfully, pulling off my hood and messing up my hair in the process.

"Don't do that." I scrambled to hide in my cloak again as he snickered at me.

"You fuss over the silliest things, but it is good to see you expressing your likes and dislikes. You…" He stopped and frowned. "I mean, she did not fuss."

"Never?"

"No."

"Not even before getting ready to fight Ep… er…" I knew the old king was dead, but with all the weirdness about names, I didn't want to jinx myself.

He raised his finger to reiterate his point. "She did not complain. Not even once."

I frowned. "I can't imagine that. No one is that stoic."

Tetora shrugged. "She is a hero, so… that is how a hero must be."

I bristled. "That can't be—"

"It is a mask you will need in the holy city," Tetora warned. He looked out over the landscape for a moment before continuing. "I am sorry to tell you this."

"Ah," I breathed, realizing he wasn't buying into the words he had just spoken. "Well, I'll work on it." Pretend that nothing fazes me, though? Impossible. I shattered my mask for that long ago.

Nora suddenly came running over, crossing the line. "Give me money."

"For what?" I shoved the coins in my hand into my pocket, half afraid she'd just help herself.

"Fruit tart." At the mention of dessert, I immediately surrendered it all.

"Thanks!" She ran off.

"You forgot to ask her to share," Tetora noted.

"Crap!" I gasped and ran after her, with Tetora's boisterous laughter trailing behind me.

***

I returned to Southwick shortly after with my fair share of two fruit tarts. "Here." I offered one to Tetora somewhat reluctantly. I might not have had any if he hadn't spoken up, so I figured he deserved one.

Tetora gave me a long look before sneering. "Are you trying to bribe your teacher!?"

I pulled the tart back. "Huh?"

"Do you think giving me such a thing will make me go soft on training?"

"No, I was just trying to be—"

"If you are going to bribe me, do it with something I like! I do not care for the taste of confectionaries." He turned his back to me, and I saw his tail swishing playfully.

I suppressed a chuckle. "Yes, great teacher Tetora."

After I consumed both fruit tarts, one of the rabbits came to tell us our grocery order was ready. Lulu or Lala—I couldn't say for sure if they were not right next to each other.

Aleph and Tetora put most of the goods in their rucksacks, including two bulky items wrapped in coarse burlap. They made several dull, clunking noises as they settled into their respective bags. The rest of the order was salted meats, dried beans, and somewhat shriveled root vegetables. Aleph had also kindly ordered some small honey candies we promised to ration along the trip. Of course, we had to try one now while they were still fresh, so to speak.

"Are all the villages in the Wastelands… like that one? Er, I mean, like those two?" I asked once we were well on our way again. Tun had been too small to warrant hybrid counts, so I had noticed nothing odd besides the residents avoiding us.

"More or less, yes," Aleph answered. "Many villages were established before the rule came out, so they've all tried to find ways to comply. The word *location* is quite vague."

"Does all this help to decrease animus?" Nora asked archly.

Tetora raised his arms. "How would *we* know? We cannot see it or touch it," he said, pausing with a slight twitch. "But animus is real. I know that much." That last part was very transparently an attempt to avoid another argument with Aleph.

"I am not sure the rule does anything except complicate matters for hybrids," Aleph said. "That is why we do not take it seriously."

"Do hybrids generate more animus than full bloods?" I inquired carefully.

"We are told we do." Tetora sniffed. "But I do not think it to be so." But what if it was true? What if it was having a global effect? Then I caught myself, ashamed. There had to be better ways to deal with it at a higher level instead of vilifying the little guy!

Nora's frown deepened. "Very suspicious. What other benefit is there that they'd make such an effort to enforce this stupid rule?" No one had a good answer.

The next few days were uneventful, filled with waking, eating, walking, and training before settling down in the evenings. Nora checked her journal routinely, but she did not receive any responses.

While I had gotten better at focusing during my meditation sessions, I'd still get distracted towards the end about how the hybrids were being treated. The thoughts would keep me from falling asleep at a reasonable hour. *Aleph and Tetora gave up their families, homes, and even their clans to save the world from The Accursed One. This was not how they should have been rewarded.*

***

"Iron Tiger Tetora." Raelynn Lightbringer bowed deeply to the venerated grandmaster. "I beg your forgiveness for interrupting the tournament's grand finale, but I urgently require the skills your clan has cultivated over the centuries."

"Little girl." Iron Tiger Tetora snorted derisively from his throne. "Are you lost? This is a place for warriors!"

"The fact that she has traveled this far into your forest should indicate that she is not a mere little girl," Aleph the Ox-like rebuked.

"My students are forbidden from fighting young children," the tiger beastman snarled as he rose. "As well as weak herbivores!"

"Holy Captain, perhaps a member of the monkey clan would better serve our purpose," Aleph murmured in a low voice. "It does not seem this one holds much in the way of intelligence."

The Chosen One simply shook her head. "He will join us. His pride will be the pride of all clans when the world is made right once again. However…" She gave him a knowing look. "Please instruct him as you see fit."

Aleph nodded, his long limbs stretching as he slowly straightened to his full seven-foot height. "Great Tiger," he rumbled, cracking his neck. "I have been permitted to correct your misgivings about my clan. I believe shared understanding will bring us closer together, so I hope you'll actively participate in the lesson I'm about to teach you."

Without hesitation, Iron Tiger Tetora leapt down from the podium and landed gracefully in the dirt ring before Aleph. "Ha! Show me what you think you can do, beast of burden!" the king of the bamboo forest taunted, beckoning Aleph to make the first move with a daring wave of his hand.

Instead of launching into a wild attack like Tetora and the other tigers had expected, Aleph remained calm and composed. With a sharp inhale and highly controlled precision, he shifted his stance slightly and swiftly struck out with a single fist, landing a powerful blow to Tetora's unguarded stomach. The force knocked the wind out of the belligerent tiger and sent him flying to the ground.

As Tetora lay there gasping for breath, Aleph loomed over him with only the slightest trace of a smile. "Well, Great Tiger?" he asked. "Have you learned your lesson? Or do you need me to repeat my instruction?"

For the first time in his life, Tetora was unable to instantly retort. He gasped for air as he tried to regain his composure. "No one has ever defeated me before!" he finally managed to wheeze as he reluctantly held up a hand in surrender.

"At least you are honest about your defeat," Aleph noted with a hint of solemn respect. "Join us on our journey to defeat the demon king, my dear companion. Together, we can bring glory to all clans and stand unashamed before the Goddess."

CHAPTER 27: RAELINA

Nora kept checking her journal at least twice daily, but we received no reply from Clare.

"N could be for novel…" Nora murmured to herself one evening. She scribbled possible words for the NAUGHT acronym in the margins of her journal. At first, I tried to help, but I eventually gave up. Even if we did figure it out, we wouldn't know if we were right. It was an exercise in futility.

"You shouldn't have asked to become a god," I huffed in response. "Now she's ignoring us."

"You're just upset you didn't think of it yourself." That wasn't true. I was already *well aware* I could never be a god, and that level of responsibility was something I couldn't possibly handle.

I took comfort in the traveling routine we settled into, often opting for the first watch at night so I could sleep uninterrupted as long as possible. The road was getting wider and more traveled as the days passed, with green plants beginning to erupt from softer soil. Grass, sickly at first, began to speckle the landscape, hiding small, skittish rodents within its reeds. We spent a few hours at the first intersecting stream of clear water, taking advantage of all it offered, including another bath and a feast of freshwater fish.

"Even lower than last time." Tetora shook his head disdainfully at the stream, even though it had just filled his belly. "It should flood at this time of year!"

"When's the last time it rained?" I asked.

"I cannot exactly remember when a good rain fell," Aleph admitted. "However, I do not think the Wastelands ever saw much rain."

"But this isn't exactly the Wastelands anymore, is it?" Nora asked. "We're close to the border of Turri, right?"

"You are well informed," Aleph praised her.

"Hehe. I memorized the map a long time ago."

"Turri…" I mumbled sleepily. "Hurry to Turri for catfish curry…"

Nora poked her head in front of my face. "What did you just say?"

"Catfish curry," I yawned.

"What does it taste like?"

I sat up. "Huh? How should I know?"

She narrowed her eyes. "There's nothing in the story about catfish curry."

"Are you sure? Maybe you forgot about it."

Nora looked deeply offended, but I ignored it and continued, "No one has a photographic memory. I'm sure it was practically just a footnote or something. Don't take it so hard."

She wouldn't let it go. Instead, she turned to Aleph and said, "Is that a saying? Hurry to Turri for catfish curry?"

"It is a children's song," Aleph murmured as he scratched at his beard. "An old one."

How did the rest go? "Have no worry, it's ready in a flurry, catfish curry!" I sang the refrain with a satisfied smile, ending it with the customary two claps. See? I remembered *something Nora didn't.*

Now, they were all staring at me. In my defense, I was *exhausted*, so it took me a minute to figure out what had happened. "Written stories… don't sing out loud, do they?" I swallowed hard.

They all shook their heads.

My thoughts preoccupied me for the next few days, focused on the melody I had shared. What a useless thing to have stuck in my head, and it didn't even belong to me.

The border of Turri loomed in the distance, demarcated by a giant wood and stone fortress shoved haphazardly between two cliffs. The ground on either side of the road was lumpy and choked with thick, thorny weeds that curled in on themselves. I had to stop and unsnag myself several times as we navigated through the threatening foliage.

"It's like living barbed wire…!" Nora delighted in the vicious plant's appearance.

"Don't praise it," I complained, freeing myself and inspecting my clothes. There were a few tiny holes, but nothing too noticeable. "It should be ashamed of itself for attacking me."

"You walked right into it. What were you thinking?" Nora said with a smirk. I knew better than to answer with the truth, so I said nothing and continued down the road. I wondered how she avoided it with her long, dark mage robes. Guess shorter legs mean a shorter stride, so maybe that was her secret.

A little while later, I stepped directly into the armed bushes again. Now, why did I do that? I really must not have been paying attention—longer stride or not.

"Rae!" Tetora barked. "Don't go that way!"

I tried to back up, but my legs seemed intent on moving forward. What the!?

"Ignore him. We have to go this way!"

Huh… who are you now?

"I promised my parents I would return once I defeated the demon king. They're waiting for me!"

Your parents? You must be Raelynn! Oh, but are they really this way?

"Yes! We need to hurry! They've been waiting for so long!"

I motioned to the others. "Raelynn! She says her parents are ahead!"

"Rae…" Aleph said carefully. "I do not believe there are any inhabited areas that way."

They must have thought I went mad, as I was leaning towards that conclusion myself.

"He's wrong. The village is just a little farther!"

I sighed. "She's saying there's a village ahead."

Why don't you just talk to them directly?

She ignored my question and started moving my feet for me. She must not have been able to feel my pain because it was as if she was purposefully trampling a path through the thickest part of the razor-sharp vegetation.

"Which way is the church?"

How should I know?

"You can't feel the pull of its holy amity?"

No?

"Do you even know what I'm talking about?"

No, obviously.

"Close your eyes and think of something that makes you warm and content. That's how you consciously activate amity."

I thought about Chester. He was probably snuggled up on my fuzzy pink blanket back home, purring the day away. My hands radiated a soft, white light briefly before fading.

What the…

"Perfect. Now, do you feel anything pulling at you?"

Um… Not really.

"Maybe it's farther than I thought."

Do you think we could try stepping over *the plants?*

"Fine. We'll work together. Just keep thinking happy thoughts. Please, just not that song you've been thinking about all day. It gets old after a while."

Hey, I'm not happy about it either. Wait… you can hear that? How long have you been listening?

"Since some time yesterday."

Great…

This had to count as an invasion of privacy. I wonder if a complaint to Eura would help?

Eh, probably not.

A few minutes later, I found some flagstones underneath the receding thorny bushes.

"Oh… here it is… no wonder we couldn't feel it."

I looked up. It was getting dark now, but I could make out the ruins of several old stone buildings.

"This way. Turn here."

We turned in unison, and I soon found myself in the middle of a forgotten graveyard that clung to the side of a small hill. Rough stone markers of varying heights were spaced evenly apart under a thick cover of ivy. A path out of the other side of the graveyard wound down into a thickly wooded valley. Curiously enough, the path had a few fresh, awkwardly placed footprints. I didn't have time to investigate because she pulled me deeper into the graveyard instead.

"Mother! Father!" she called loudly in my voice. "It's me, Raelina!"

You lied to me!

"No, I didn't."

You're not Raelynn!

"I never said I was."

But you let me assume you were!

"It was necessary. The best lies you can tell come out of the minds and mouths of others."

That doesn't sound like something a hero would say.

"Not out loud anyway, no."

She started pulling vines off the various gravestones. "Mother! It's me! Where are you?"

The others had finally caught up to me. Nora was levitating a ball of light a few feet above her hand, once again impressing me with her sudden skills. They huddled briefly and started pulling the weeds off other gravestones.

"These markers are ancient…" Aleph murmured. "Who should we be looking for?"

"Amatus. Dominic and Isa Amatus," Raelina answered as she took us down another row. I couldn't do much now except worry that this fallen hero was slightly *off*. If we're looking for her parents in an abandoned graveyard, they couldn't be *alive*, right?

"They promised to wait for me. But I must tell them to go on without me because our work isn't done."

Our work?

"Yes. Our work is to make things right."

"Over here!" Nora shouted. "I think I found it."

I ran over to the small gravestone Nora had cleaned. Sure enough, at the top of the marker was carved "Amatus."

"Mother and Father! Please come out!" Raelina urged, guiding my hands to rest upon the gravestone. For just a few moments, a hazy image shimmered before my eyes. I saw a woman with brown hair coiled into a messy bun, kneeling with open arms, ready to embrace us. Beside her, a man with cropped black hair stood with arms folded in satisfaction. Between them, a stone hearth crackled with inviting flames, above which hung a pot of catfish curry, its aromatic scent tantalizing my senses…

"My family… finally welcoming me back home…"

Suddenly, light erupted from my hands, causing the gravestone to emanate a similar glow. From the earth behind the marker, two ethereal, formless figures spiraled upwards, emerging as if summoned by my touch.

"Who dares to once again disturb our restless slumber!?" the first one roared angrily, causing me to stumble backward.

"Dear, if you say restless first, then it's not slumber at all, right?" the other rebuked in a feminine voice. "So this isn't really a disturbance."

"Not now, Isa. I've had enough of these *loitering drunkards*, coming and going whenever they please!"

"Aren't we technically the ones loitering?" the shade of Isa pondered. "Our time was up long ago, after all."

"Father!" Raelina shouted, waving my arms. "It's me!"

"Victoria?" Dominic, I presumed, loomed closer towards us with a featureless face.

"It's Raelina now, Father!" She crossed my arms with a huff.

"Nonsense. Victoria suits you best. My little Victoria, all grown up and… uh…" the shade paused awkwardly.

"You seem to have changed your face, dear," Isa supplied. "How did you manage that?"

"It's a long story, Mother…" Raelina said with a soft sigh.

"I liked the old one better," Dominic grumbled. "Your eyebrows are way too thin."

There was no way that was true. I had nothing to pluck them with here!

"Father… You're being ridiculous. This is the style now, that's all."

Dominic puffed out what would have been his chest proudly. "The locals said you killed the Origin of Evil years ago."

"Yes, that's right," we answered with false enthusiasm.

"So where have you been, titan of titans?" Dominic asked. "You didn't forget about us, did you?"

"Dear…" Isa said in a deceptively quiet tone. "I'm sure the Chosen One has been *very busy* putting the world back in order."

"She should still get married and start a family. I want grandchildren!"

"That's not your choice to make, is it, *dear?*" Isa turned dark.

"Ah… Of course, you're right, Isa, my love." Dominic shriveled up to about half his previous size.

"Mother… Father… I'm sorry you had to wait so long…" I felt a sudden shock of endless sorrow course through me, pushing tears out of my eyes. Raelina wanted to hug them again to feel their warmth and loving touch, but she knew it would be forever impossible.

"Now, now, none of that." Isa shook her head back and forth. "We're just glad you're okay."

"Yes. I'm fine now," she lied with my entire being. "It's because of all the great people I have by my side supporting me. So you can go now with no worries!"

"Are you sure, love?" Isa asked.

"Yes!" I smiled even as more tears poured out of my eyes. "And take Father with you. He's just worthless without you."

The two shades joined what I could only imagine were hands, and Dominic shouted, "We love you, Victoria!"

"Raelina!" we shouted back defiantly.

The two began to fade, but then Isa re-solidified with a shudder. "Wait. One of your friends was here recently." She turned to Dominic, who had also stopped dissipating. "What was her name again?"

"Honey, you know I don't remember much."

"This is important."

Dominic's form quivered. "Did she even say her name? She was so drunk I couldn't make out most of the words she was saying. She just kept saying Rae-Rae."

"Perhaps you were too busy *appreciating the view*." Isa's outline filled with tiny barbs.

"I'm telling you, I just never saw anyone be able to drink so much and still breathe!"

"Vernie? Laverna?" Tetora demanded of the shades as he stepped forward. "Red hair? Big…" Tetora looked at Nora. "Big personality?" He ended his line of questioning somewhat lamely.

Nora shoved him a little. "Just say chest! *He* doesn't know the meaning behind that phrase."

"She has both," Tetora said defensively.

"That definitely was her then." Dominic nodded, prudently moving out of Isa's immediate range.

"You should probably check on her. She's been hanging out with a dangerous crowd," Isa said, pointing down into the dark woods. A tiny light deep within winked in and out of existence as if to validate her words.

"Anyway… Time for us to move on," Dominic said in a slightly embarrassed tone.

"Be happy, sweetheart." Isa waved. "Congratulations on saving the world!"

"We love you, dear." Dominic also waved.

"I love you too…" Raelina's last words faded from my mouth as we watched them dissolve into nothing. Then, I fell to my knees and started to cry in earnest.

***

Post-Chapter Omake

Nora: *So… Speranzans pronounce curry like /ˈkəreɪ/?*

Euphridia: *Uh. Yeah, I guess. Why?*

Nora: *Shouldn't it be more like /karee/? Why an American English pronunciation?*

Euphridia: *...Then you lose the rhyme.*

Nora: *But Turri like /ˈtʊrɪ/ doesn't rhyme with hurry, curry, flurry, or worry...*

Euphridia: *They're almost rhymes.*

Nora: *Which means they don't.*

Euphridia: *It's close enough! Singers and songwriters butcher the pronunciation of words all the time!*

Nora: *So just because others do it... Makes it okay for you to do it, too?*

Euphridia: *Insufferable!*

Nora: >D

CHAPTER 28: MEMORIES OF MOTHER

"She'll be gone by morning." Tetora folded his arms crossly. "You know she never stays in one place for long!"

"It's too dangerous in the dark," Aleph objected.

"I can see just fine. Let me go!"

Aleph gripped his war hammer tightly but agreed to his demand. "Just be careful. We don't know who she is with or what she is doing."

Tetora shrugged, pulling out his iron claws. "I am always careful."

I heard their conversation with only half a mind as I tried to get my tears under control.

"If you don't find her within an hour, you must return," Aleph said. Then he added, "Promise me."

"I promise," Tetora repeated, holding up a hand.

"Say *all of it* when you promise," Aleph said in a stern tone.

He sighed. "I promise I will come back within one hour."

"Go then," Aleph said, then watched Tetora bound off into the dark woods.

Nora patted my back as I continued to sob. "I'm sorry… I'm trying to get it under control," I mumbled, still pushing away all the sorrow after Raelina had left. By our crude calculations, her parents had been waiting in that graveyard for over a millennium for her triumphant return. No wonder she didn't want to tell them the whole truth after all that time. Guiltily, I realized I couldn't remember the last time I had hugged Mother or even just thanked her for taking care of me. Would I ever get to do so again?

"There is nothing to apologize for, little one." Aleph gently put his hand on my shoulder.

"I don't… I don't cry like this, you know. They're her tears, I'm sure."

He squeezed my shoulder comfortingly. "Shedding tears is nothing to be ashamed of."

"Did Raelynn ever cry?" I asked, sniffling. "I don't remember ever reading any part where she did."

Neither Nora nor Aleph answered me outright, but they pulled me into a supportive embrace instead. After a few minutes, my tears dried up. "Thank you." I breathed slowly. "Again, I'm so—"

"Honey candy!" Nora shoved it at me.

I took the carefully wrapped confectionery. "I thought we were out?"

"I saved mine. Here. It's no fruit tart, but…"

I stuck it in my mouth, thankful I had an excuse to avoid apologizing or talking about my feelings.

We moved back out of the graveyard and into the village's stone ruins. One exceptionally sturdy shelter retained most of its walls, and we huddled for the night inside it, using a small campfire to keep us warm.

"So, living with Tetora…" Nora's gaze drifted to Aleph. "What's his worst bad habit?"

"Nora!" I gasped, almost swallowing the candy outright.

"What? We have to pass the time somehow."

"You can't just gossip and dig up dirt on him the moment his back is turned."

"It's *exactly* the best time."

"That is a troublesome question to answer…" Aleph frowned. "There are so many bad habits to choose from, yet I don't know where to start."

My incredulous eyes shifted to Aleph, and I saw him suppressing a grin. He winked at me and continued, "Perhaps it is that he is forever making a mess, yet he turns a blind eye to it when I tell him it is time to clean. Or that he acts before he thinks. He yells when he speaks for no reason. He argues with his students long after they have proved him wrong just for the thrill of it."

Nora cackled in sheer delight, and I soon found myself smiling as Aleph continued down the list of Tetora's shortcomings. It was the typical banter I so desperately needed.

"You two really get along, don't you?" I snuggled up in my bedroll, suppressing a sniffle. "I'm glad you have each other. This world seems tough to deal with if you're all alone."

"…I believe no truer words have ever been spoken," Aleph agreed softly.

I glanced at Nora. "Should I tell you about *her* worst bad habits?"

Nora cleared her throat. "I don't have any bad habits. Also, you can't tell him now because I'm *right here*."

"I don't mind saying them in front of you."

"But I do!" she said somewhat indignantly. "If I hear about them, you might expect me to improve myself. It's hard enough living up to your idealistic expectations already."

"*You* don't have to change," I advised, suddenly worried I had taken it too far. "I like you *just* the way you are." My old neighbor always said that to me, and I found great comfort in hearing it.

"Oh geez, do you *see* how utterly impossible she is?" Nora asked Aleph. "She's just too saccharine sometimes."

Whew. We were still good.

Aleph chuckled and shook his head. Tetora came back shortly after.

"Did you find her?" Aleph asked immediately upon his return.

Tetora eyed him contemptuously for a moment and then flopped down in the middle of the stone shelter to warm his hands over our tiny campfire. "Aleph *always* asks ridiculous questions when the answer is obvious. He also nags me to no end about silly and unimportant things. Last, he always forgets that I can hear everything he says, even from a distance, because of my *great tiger ears*!"

"I did not forget." Aleph shrugged. "I simply felt it was time to remind you again."

"If I could go *just a day* without hearing about it…"

"Well?" Aleph asked again. "Did you find anything at all?"

"Maybe. Maybe not."

"Tetora!" we all shouted at him in exasperation.

Tetora grinned viciously. "What is it worth to you?"

Aleph, Nora, and I exchanged glances before shrugging slightly out of sync.

"Forget it." Nora sighed.

"We can check again tomorrow," I followed up.

"I'm sure we'll have better luck in the daytime," Aleph concluded.

"H-hey! No, I did find something!" Tetora protested.

We all sat up quickly.

"What?" Aleph demanded.

"This." Tetora held out a flat throwing knife about five inches long. Its center was hollow, but the edges appeared razor sharp. An angry red monkey was painted at the bottom of the handle. "It was embedded in an old stump."

"That's her mark, but…" Aleph paused. "Why would she just leave it where anyone could find it?"

"I am not anyone. I am Iron Tiger Tetora!"

Aleph folded his arms. "Was it hidden or not?"

Tetora sighed. "…It was very obvious. I think it is a message for someone."

Aleph scratched his beard. "Or a trap. I guess we'll find out tomorrow. Let's get some sleep."

***

"What were you doing out so late at night in your pajamas?" Detective Harris asked me again. "Were you meeting with your boyfriend?"

"As I disclosed previously, I do not have any such suitor. I do not recall why I was in that dark alleyway…" I gripped the bed linens tightly, trying to keep myself covered as much as possible, as the hospital tunic was scandalously short. The machine tethered to my arm let out yet another piercing wail. I took a few slow breaths, hoping it would be subdued into silence again. How could I get him to leave? It was almost time to watch the upcoming television program on the station that was my trusted window to the world. It needed contributions from viewers like me, but I could only watch in appreciation for now.

"Do you have a habit of going out late on school nights? What did you bring with you? Who were you planning on meeting?"

"I don't—"

A loud crash outside my room caught our attention. Mother simply stepped around the overturned cart of meal trays, performed the customary hand cleansing at the door, and entered my room.

"You were right, Clancy. He's here," Mother said aloud as she adjusted the audio transmitter in her ear. "That's up to you, of course, but I won't see him again."

"Ms. Smith." Detective Harris turned away from me to confront Mother. "Rachel already gave me her permission to—"

"Harass her as the victim? I doubt that's what she agreed to." Mother folded her arms.

"Ma'am, I'm just trying to piece together what happened that night—" He paused as the mobile communication device strapped around his chest crackled in warning.

"My office, NOW!" the device erupted.

"You might want to call and tell him you're on your way. I suggest you do this from your squad car." Mother pointed imperiously out into the hallway.

"Mother?" I asked.

"In a moment, dear," she said, holding out her hand while gesturing for the detective to leave with the other.

Detective Harris gave Mother a stern look but left quickly.

Mother turned her gaze to me. "You should have called me. That's what your phone is for."

I considered the smartphone on the bedside table for a moment. "Yes, I understand." I hadn't followed standard protocol again.

"You... know how to use it, correct?"

"Yes, Mother."

"For my peace of mind, please show me."

I sighed and called her smartphone, struggling to manipulate the touch-responsive screen with my stiff fingers. "I just... didn't think of it at the time."

After verifying that I could indeed use the device, she said, "Very good. I'm just making sure."

"If he comes again, I'll call immediately," I promised, returning the phone to the bedside table.

"He won't, so don't worry about it. But if you need anything, all you need to do is ask, alright?"

I frowned. "A hug, maybe. If it's not too much."

"Of course." She gently hugged me, though it felt strange, probably because of all the "ivy" tubing in the way.

"Thank you. I'm fine now." Everything was returning to normal, and I hadn't missed the program's opening. It would be another beautiful day in the neighborhood, I was sure.

***

I sat up, bringing most of my bedroll with me. It had been years since I had *that* dream. Avoiding any more thoughts of Mother, I tried to imagine whatever had happened to Detective Harris. I comforted myself with the idea that he most certainly hadn't been called to the office for a promotion.

CHAPTER 29: FIRST ENCOUNTER OF THE DEMONKIND

I sensed a sort of uneasiness from Tetora and Aleph as they led us through the forest. It was in the way Tetora would sniff the air, followed by an exchange of furrowed glances between the two hybrids.

"So, what's the plan?" Nora ventured, perhaps seeing what I was seeing.

Aleph sighed, stroking his beard but not offering an answer.

I decided to give it a try next. "Think we'll be able to find Laverna?"

"Perhaps…" Aleph said shortly, once again glancing warily at Tetora but not exactly answering my question.

At this point, I knew for sure something was going on. If there was going to be some kind of trouble up ahead, shouldn't they explain their thoughts to us?

Tetora abruptly stopped with a resigned sigh. "There are many human and hybrid scents here."

Aleph nodded. "Yes, and we are too close to the border to tell friend from foe easily."

"So that means…" Tetora raised his gaze from his slumped shoulders. He looked like he was told to stay indoors and clean his room when he only wanted to go outside and play.

"I'm afraid so," Aleph answered almost apologetically.

Nora and I shared our own exchange of glances. Aleph and Tetora being at odds for whatever vague reason wasn't uncommon, but I had never seen Tetora so… resigned.

Aleph cleared his throat and hoisted his rucksack off his shoulder, placing it on the ground. "It will be easier to explain them as an embarrassing ruse than to accessorize in an emergency."

I leaned to see around the big ox-man for some hint of what they were getting at. What he eventually pulled out absolutely shocked me.

Two giant wrought iron collars, hinged in two places and held together by chain links. A threaded lock was built on the side of each one.

Nora's eyes widened. "Slave collars!?" I had erroneously thought their black market purchases would be handcuffs for future encountered outlaws, but the truth was even more disturbing.

"These are for us. Do not worry." Aleph put the collar around his neck, bending the lock shut. He then pulled on it a few times. Satisfied it was secure, he turned to Tetora. "Your turn."

"…Help me with the lock," Tetora ordered with an authoritative tone, perhaps to salvage some of his dignity. Aleph complied wordlessly, grasping the iron and fusing the lock shut on Tetora's collar with a twist of his fingers.

"If we encounter anyone, you two are in charge," Tetora advised, pointing at us like it was not up for discussion. I could only stare, mouth agape, my emotions boiling into righteous indignation on my friends' behalf.

"If you leave your mouth open like that," Tetora cautioned, "eventually something will fly into it."

I stammered, "B-but I can't just—"

Aleph silenced me by raising his palm. "Just command us to speak to them on your behalf if you don't know what to say."

"Don't use our names," Tetora added. "It's Tiger for me and Ox for him. We'll forgive you for your rudeness." He tried to smile, though his eyes burned with anger.

"I…" I wasn't prepared for this. How could they talk so nonchalantly about this? *This was wrong!*

"They are just iron rings," Aleph stated calmly. "You cannot activate them without their tethered focus, so they are not harmful."

Nora frowned. "Tethered focus?"

"It is a magical key with which to suppress our strength. The collar is merely deceptive jewelry—nothing more." Aleph shrugged. "So do not let it upset you."

"Easier said than done!" I nearly shouted.

"Our well-being depends on it," Tetora warned.

I swallowed hard and glanced at Nora again.

Nora stamped her feet indignantly. "Before you ask, no, *none of this* was in the story!"

"It is a newer practice in Turri. It will not last." Aleph turned to Tetora and intentionally changed the subject. "Show us where you found the knife."

We continued through the forest in silence until Tetora led us to a fallen tree. "The knife was at ankle height here, on this stump. She usually scratches three diagonal lines with a cross-out to mark her trail. Keep your eye out for anything unusual, though."

We had several false starts as we searched for trail markings, but nothing of any real substance. After an hour of inspecting the forest, I announced, "We should probably take shelter soon. She won't be out in the storm, anyway."

"Storm?" Nora looked up. "What are you talking about?"

"It's going to hit us any minute. Can't you feel it?" I shivered as an icy wind blew through us. From the east, two slender wisps of inky black fog slithered from around the trees, coalescing slowly into spinning orbs of deep, star-speckled midnight. Splashes of color then erupted from the core-like center of their respective dark spirits, shaping limbs and filling in a humanoid appearance.

"Ohhh…" exhaled the first figure, its mouth taking shape to form the words. "A Tiger…! How fortunate for us!"

The other had a velvety, dangerous voice. "The Ox is also well-built! I told you it would be worth it to come all the way out here!"

With their physical forms solidified, they now bore dark red military fatigues with gold epaulets pinning a half-cape to their backs. Antlers had sprouted from their skulls. It was their eyes, or rather the lack of realistic eyes, that truly unsettled me. The first demon conjured yellow ones with slitted, goat-like pupils. At the same time, his female-appearing counterpart simply sculpted hollow eye sockets before filling them with eyes containing ever-burning orange flames.

I heard Nora inhale sharply from behind me even as Tetora and Aleph scrambled to get in front of us, weapons drawn.

The first demon shook its head. "We're not here to kill *you*, Tiger and Ox. We're here to liberate you!"

"Oh?" Aleph questioned. "Liberate us?"

"Don't you want to escape your *human oppressors?*" the demoness asked with a sultry shrug.

"Swear allegiance to the Great General, and we will remove your collars!" the other demon proclaimed with a haughty salute to the air before him. Was he referring to General Ragnerus? I had thought he only ever accepted fellow demons into his ranks.

"And if we decline?" Aleph asked, his jaw tensing.

"Oh, even I think you know the answer to that one, Ox," the demon answered with a giant, fanged grin as he held out his hand, summoning a floating spear of inky darkness. "After all, we are only obliged to ask *once*."

"Nora," Tetora warned. "Do *not* engage these demons. Stick back with Rachel." It was the first time he *ever* called me that.

"Ah! You're going to attempt to *fight us*? How wonderful!" The demoness buzzed loudly, and her form phased in and out of existence as she charged toward Tetora, slashing with fans of razor-sharp blades. Tetora skittered backward, leaping this way and that as he watched for an opening to strike.

The male demon appeared abruptly beside Aleph, thrusting his spear in rapid succession. Aleph, with controlled precision, trapped the spear's tip in his war hammer's claw and yanked it off course, sending a spray of gold and black sparks into the air. The demon momentarily convulsed, with cloudy vapor dispersing, before he pulled himself back into a solid mass with a flickering shudder.

"Their weapons are blessed!" the male demon shouted in alarm.

The demoness cackled her response as she swiped at Tetora. "So much the better. An actual challenge for once!"

The two demons, probably deciding Nora and I were mere fodder, initially ignored us. No other Raes seemed to want to take center stage, either. At least, I didn't think so.

Anyone there?

Nope, no takers. I guess Tetora and Aleph really did have this covered.

The male demon, after a forceful exchange with Aleph, taking a few solid, sparking blows from the ox-man's war hammer, seemed to decide on a new course of action.

He shot towards me, spear poised to strike. "Show me your despair, human girl! I hunger for your screams!"

Time to think happy thoughts like Raelina said! Uh, catchy Japanese pop songs with a driving beat! Finding a long-forgotten pint of premium ice cream in the freezer late at night! I felt a surge of strength as I knocked his spear aside with my bo staff, summoning more sparks and temporarily stunning him.

The demon swore loudly as his spear fizzled away. "Even the oafish human girl has one!"

Oafish...? Ah, don't let him get to you, Rachel. File that questionable feedback for review later.

He extended his right hand, unleashing a blast of sheer force in my direction, which I wasn't exactly prepared for. I lost my grip on the staff as I collided back into a tree trunk, sliding down to the ground with a stifled grunt.

"I said *scream!*" He translocated himself in front of me and hauled me off my feet by the front of my hooded cape, slamming me into the tree trunk again. Reeling with the scattered thought that I should *really* invest in a helmet, I did the only thing I could think of. I dropped my head and bit his hand as savagely as possible. Surprisingly enough, it seemed to affect him, and *he* ended up being the one to scream as he tossed me away. I stood and spat, frantically wiping at my now-burning tongue. Raeonna had said to use my teeth if necessary, but I can't exactly recommend it as a best practice.

"H-how...*you... hurt... me!?*" He gasped as he pulled back to look at his hand, which dripped watery black blood. A dark miasma wafted off him upwards into nothing, and he shuddered back and forth between a solid and spirit form. "What… What did you *do to me?*"

I didn't bother trying to come up with an answer. However, he was still between me and my blessed staff, and rectifying that little situation was the priority. I tried to dart around him, but even with his disorientation, he cut me off.

He inhaled, swelling in size as his mottled, ever-phasing form took on a beast-like shape. His muzzle sprouted a mouthful of needle-like teeth jutting out every which way. I was sure I had seen worse in my dreams, though, so his efforts to frighten me into submission fell flat.

With a sneer exposing way too many canines, he growled. "I'll teach an ugly, pathetic human like you to fight b—"

"Private Belgaldi!" the demoness shouted over her shoulder in disdain as she slipped around Tetora. "Pull yourself together! *I can see right through you!*" He *was* looking rather flimsy, all things considered.

"Y-yes, Sergeant Bodil!"

Would you believe he turned away in deference to his superior? He even took a moment to salute her—completely exposing his right flank! And he thought *I* was the oaf!?

"Don't you *dare* lay a hand on me again, you *glitchy ghoul!*" I yelled, seizing the opportunity to deliver a powerful, glowing vertical punch to his exposed side. My light aura and his black shadowy essence exploded upon contact with each other—the resounding impact knocking both of us back. I was able to get up quickly, but he seemed to have taken additional damage. His form began to melt away in earnest, exposing his spiritual core that sparkled for all the world like a tiny, starry nebula.

"You're *not supposed to be able to do that!*" he shrieked as he tried to reform himself. "You can't—"

Rising behind him like a roiling sea of angry determination, Aleph took advantage of the demon's disruption and slammed his gigantic war hammer into his core sideways. I watched in awe as the screaming demon erupted in golden flames before he dissipated utterly.

Tetora deftly dodged and weaved; he was a blur of motion in his battle of speedy strikes against the demoness. However, when her compatriot's final wail ended, she suddenly disappeared from view.

I sighed with relief, bending down to pick up my bo staff as I prepared to congratulate everyone on a job well done. However, as my hand reunited with my weapon, a rustling of leaves grabbed my attention, and I looked up.

"You're thinking one down and one to go…" Her voice drifted eerily from the treetops.

"But I'm not low-level like him!"

I shot around, thinking her voice had come from behind me, but nothing was there. Aleph took a step closer to me, so we were back to back.

"I am everywhere yet nowhere!" She laughed from the ground in a mocking echo. Nora, who had been observing from the sidelines until now, tensed her hands on her staff.

"But you haven't taken a turn yet, dear!" In a sudden, startling manifestation, the demoness reappeared right before Nora. Her face now grotesquely stretched in a mockery of human features. "Is it because you're frightened? Or maybe you're just *useless*?"

Nora clenched her fists around her staff to hold herself back just as I rushed to strike, but the demoness disappeared again, leaving a shadowy haze as an afterimage.

Suddenly, she pressed herself against Nora's opposite shoulder. "You have quite a few secrets, don't you?"

Nora jumped back, but the demoness continued, leaning on nothing. "I can sense your anger, fear, and oh! *So much guilt!* But… why aren't you exuding any animus?" Aleph swung but missed as well. Clearly, she was toying with us, dissipating with only dark miasma to mark where she had been.

"Hmm… maybe I'll sell you to the Dark Mistress instead. She just *loves* dissecting secrets." The demoness was upside-down above her now, with her bladed fans almost pressing on Nora's temples. Tetora leapt over Nora as she ducked, but the demoness evaded his strike.

She was no longer visible, but we could still hear her. "But I wonder, are my words even understandable to a *shameful little ankle-biter like you?*"

Oh no… shameful little ankle biter? That's what those nasty girls in high school used to call her… how in the world… Was it a coincidence? Or…

Nora's eyes flashed, and she began to emit a dark aura herself. *Oh no!*

"Well, what do you know? You *can* understand me!" The demoness snickered.

"Nora! What are you doing!?" I gasped as the shadowy haze around her thickened. It wasn't a good look for her.

Nora ignored me, flaring her nostrils upon standing straight once again. After we heard the telltale buzz of the demoness's translocation, Nora swung her staff the moment the demoness reappeared. "Ignis!" she screamed in a ferocious tone I'd never heard from her before. Upon contact, both her staff and the demoness burst into an angry conflagration.

"Ha… ahahahahahahaha!" The demoness crowed as she began to absorb the magical fire. "I was getting tired from all the back and forth! You have my sincere appreciation, my diminutive, dim-witted dark mage! But it's time we end this."

"N-no!" Nora stumbled backward with a sudden shake to clear her head, realizing her mistake. She had actually fed the demon her own ill-will, boosting her skill. The demoness leapt at her with bladed fans poised to strike. It was Tetora who intercepted the demoness with a deep roar and bore the brunt of her slashing attack.

Her blades sliced cleanly across his chest, spraying blood as he pulled her into an angry hug. "Begone!" he bellowed, shoving his claws into her back and grappling her to the ground. Black blood spurted from her body as he pulled them back forcefully. Her flesh began to melt around the wounds, and I saw her exposed core sparkle gold.

"*All in all, this has been quite entertaining!* Let's agree to suffer together, Tiger. Together!" She laughed hysterically even as golden flames engulfed her, burning her essence away.

"Tetora?" Nora stepped forward, reaching out her hand fearfully.

"I told you… not to… engage." Iron Tiger Tetora stood slowly and turned, blood dripping from the ugly purple lacerations strewn across his chest and abdomen. "You owe me… a new shirt." He managed just one step forward before his shoulders rolled.

The earth shook as his heavy, limp body crashed to the ground.

CHAPTER 30: SICKBED CONFESSION

Aleph inspected Tetora's unconscious form in a brisk, business-like manner. "Demonic poison," he confirmed. "We will need to act quickly in order to stabilize him. Please assist me."

"O-okay." I knelt across from Aleph and laid my hands on Tetora's stomach.

"What are you doing?"

"Isn't this… how you heal someone? I just think good thoughts and…"

"Rae. You are not a priest."

"But they use amity, too. So maybe…" I tried to picture *Chester. Cotton Cheesecake. Hanging out at Nora's house.* Nora…

Nora was curled up in a ball a few feet away from me, her tiny form wracked with silent sobs. My good thoughts faded. Sometimes, you just can't fake it.

"I appreciate the effort, but we must use another tactic. Start a fire, and boil a tin of water, please." I got up and quickly gathered what I needed to comply with Aleph's request. He then opened his sack and pulled out a small leather bag.

"Put these in the tin." He handed me various sachets of herbs he had pulled from the bag. I dropped them in and watched them boil. After a few minutes, I retrieved them as instructed, and he placed most of the concoction directly on the wounds before bandaging them. Aleph put one unboiled sachet directly under his tongue, however. Afterward, he opened up a small wooden box full of needles. Tetora soon became a pincushion, with Aleph swiftly inserting them all over the front of his body with practiced skill.

Aleph pointed. "We must keep him warm, so keep the fire going."

"Are we… safe here?" I asked as I added firewood.

"For the moment, relatively speaking. It will be a few days before those demons reform completely, and the sanctum we banished them to is far away from here. Ragnerus's recruiters come in pairs but eliminate any competition, so it's doubtful others are nearby. The animus they discharged will be enough to keep animals and even some demonic beasts away as well. However, we did not find the other hybrids and humans in the area we were searching. We will still need to be alert."

"I see…" I said, considering the smoke from our fire, which definitely took some stealth points away from our makeshift outdoor sick room.

"How is your head?" he asked, as if he just remembered my short-range flight into the tree trunk.

"Ah, it's as hard as ever! Just… a little tender on the outside." I then glanced meaningfully at Nora's backside before turning back to Aleph. He nodded, silently dismissing me to attend to other things. "Hey." I sat next to Nora. "Do you want to talk about it?"

"No," Nora sniffled, wiping away tears with her sleeve.

"Is it okay if I give you a hug?"

"I don't deserve it."

"Sure you do. You're my friend. You can have all the hugs you want, no charge."

"It's all my fault Tetora got hurt."

"Is that so?" I tilted my head to the side. "I thought the demoness was the one that hit him, not you."

"But if I had just listened to Tetora and—"

"She still would have attacked someone, most likely Tetora again. He's the fastest and arguably the most dangerous, though I think Aleph is just as much of a threat."

"But I didn't listen! *I completely lost my temper*, and I ended up making her stronger! *What the hell was I thinking!?*" She punched the ground in frustration. Honestly, it *was* strange. As long as I had known her, she had never been so angry that she lost her reasoning. It was a completely different story for me, though.

"Well…" I scratched my cheek. "Did you do it intentionally?"

"No! Of course not."

"There you go then." Leaning back against a tree trunk, I recited the words I had read many times before: "Sometimes bad things happen, and there's no way to prevent them. Sometimes, there are things we can do to keep them from happening again. Either way, that doesn't mean you should keep punishing yourself."

"I thought you said you didn't remember much from the story, but now you're quoting it."

"It's… coming back to me?"

"…All of it?"

"I just remember certain parts. You know, the ones that helped me through some tough times."

Nora sat up slowly and held out her arms. "I want that hug now."

"Yeah, yeah." I hugged her tight. "Just *don't wipe your snot on me*, okay? I really hate it when you do that."

She settled into my embrace and softly asked, "He's going to be okay, right?"

I didn't know for sure, honestly. "Aleph's doing everything he can to help him."

"Just tell me everything's going to be fine."

Oh, what would Raelynn say in *this* situation? "Everything will be as it should, so long as we do our best."

"That's *not* what I asked you to say."

"I know."

"Stop saying her lines and say your own!"

I cringed. "Sorry."

"I'm waiting."

"Everything's going to be just fine." I hoped with all my might that it wasn't a lie as I squeezed her tight.

A few hours later, Tetora regained consciousness, though it was clear he had developed a fever and didn't know where or who he was with. We applied additional boiled poultices, and Aleph stayed glued to his side. Nora tried to act normal, but I knew a few minutes of telling her it wasn't her fault wouldn't fix everything.

"You two should get some sleep," Aleph said. "I can handle things for now."

His words were more of an ironic curse than an actionable plan. No matter how much I tried, I couldn't fall asleep. My mind lingered on the demons we encountered. They were raw, half-formed entities that delighted in tormenting their enemies and feeding off their fears. Worst of all, they seemed to be just playing with us. Had they wanted to kill us outright, I felt there wasn't anything we could have done to stop them. Deep down, I wondered… Was *he* anything like them?

Aleph tapped my shoulder. "Rae, it's your turn to take watch."

"Right," I said as I stood up.

"Keep the fire going and wake me up if he becomes too much to handle."

What does that mean exactly?

"Okay." I walked over to Tetora and sat down.

His breath shifted slightly. "Where'd he go?" His tone sounded weak and delirious.

"He just needed to rest for a little while. I'll sit with you."

"Noooo. I want the handsome doctor back." Tetora rolled over sluggishly so his back was facing me.

"Handsome? …You think so?"

"…Isn't it obvious?" He turned his head back slightly to gauge my reaction, and I could see his eyes were focusing correctly again.

"I guess. He's not my type, though. I kinda think of him as a father figure." A father I never, ever wanted to disappoint with my actions or contrary beliefs.

"Oh, but he's mine!" Tetora sniffed. "Just… so you know."

"Does *he* know?"

"What do you mean, does he know? Of course he knows." Tetora's voice was considerably stronger now.

"Does he feel the same way about you?"

"Another question with an obvious answer!"

"Hey… You say it's obvious, but *you two are the ones who define your relationship*, not me." I just hated it when people just assumed that sort of thing. Nora and I had been accused of being more than friends many times in the past, and honestly, I felt it insulting and debasing that two girls couldn't get along without fighting over romance or being in one with the other.

"We are together," Tetora confirmed. "I thought this was a good time to tell you."

Was his injury even more severe than I thought? I felt a nauseating fear rise from my stomach. "Why are you—"

Tetora waved his hand. "I could have blamed it on the demonic poison if our relationship upset you."

I sighed with relief. "*You cheeky cat!* But why would you think it would upset me? I'm happy for you two."

"It upsets many people, so…"

"Ffffttttsss!" That's the closest I could come to spelling out the indignant sound I made.

Tetora groaned as he rolled back over. "I always wanted to tell Raelynn. I would not have met Aleph had it not been for her."

I looked up at the sky. "She probably knew and kept quiet about it, especially if you're right about it upsetting people. I'm sure *she* wasn't upset about it, though."

"Maybe. We were more careful back then, even with each other. We were going to say something after… the defeat of the demon king. If anyone could convince the Church to allow two grandmasters to marry, it would have been her."

"Wait, *that's* the problem people have with your relationship? Because you're both grandmasters?" I was *way off* the mark.

"Romantic relationships would interfere with our Purpose."

Oh, for the love of… Aleph and Tetora!

"Walk me through *that* one." I resisted the urge to palm my face.

"We are to train our juniors and lead our respective clans. Cross-clan marriage at that high a level would distract us and those we serve."

"And just how much training and leadership have you been able to provide to your clans, *living in the middle of nowhere?*"

Tetora grunted. "… Aleph says we are setting a good example as educators and leaders by following the Assembly's will."

"You don't seriously agree with that, though, do you?"

"I think we need to do more, yes."

Damn the General Assembly! They isolated Relias, banished Aleph and Tetora, and tried Laverna for crimes she didn't commit! Not to mention subjugating hybrids and persecuting dark mages.

"Ugh. I'm trying to be a believable Raelynn." I sighed. "But I kinda just want to beat the *absolute tar* out of the General Assembly. That's not all that heroic, is it?" I mean, she never did *that* in the story. Of course, now that I thought about it, I wasn't sure she ever even met them.

Tetora grinned. "Did I not tell you once that if a hero does something, it must be heroic? So do not let semantics stop you from doing what you think is right."

Violence alone probably wouldn't solve everything, though, even if *the Goddess herself* believed so.

Aleph came to check on me a little while later. "So… too much to handle?" he asked nervously.

"Not at all. Is it okay… to tell Nora?" I yawned. "When it's time to wake up, that is."

"She already knows. Oh, that he's awake and talking, too."

Nora's really good at picking up on things that I'm not…

Just to reassure him, I flashed him a sleepy smile. "I'm glad you two have each other. I think you balance each other out."

"Yes… well…" Aleph cleared his throat several times. "I suppose that's one way to look at it." He then gave me a meaningful look. "Now, isn't it time you retired for the night?"

I stifled another yawn. "Yes sir. Heading off to bed now."

"Sleep well, Rae," he called as I set up my bedroll for the night.

***

Post-Chapter Omake

Rae: *All this time, you knew?*

Nora: *It was pretty obvious, after all.*

Rae: *Really?*

Nora: *If you were paying attention, anyway. Of course, Aleph knows acupuncture! Remember how he held up one of those needles when we were packing?*

Rae: *That wasn't an acupuncture needle. It was a giant sewing needle. It's totally different! Acupuncture needles aren't nearly as wide, and when inserted correctly, they are practically painless. But... is that what we're supposed to be talking about here?*

Nora: *Well, what else should we be discussing?*

Rae: *...Absolutely nothing.*

CHAPTER 31: DREAMING OF YOU

Once again, I found myself inside Olethros's rotunda of lavender twilight. The main entrance was sealed off with a dark miasma that sluggishly undulated up and down in striated patterns. His giant scythe was ensnared in a humming barrier of shadow, hovering above the golden magic circle ingrained in the center of the dark marble floor. Multiple wooden bookshelves had been ripped from the walls and thrown violently to the ground, where they lay with cracked sides.

I was about to step around one such splintered ruin to get a better glimpse of him at his desk, but I heard him talking to someone else. Maybe I should have made an appointment? I really wasn't trying to come here again, though. Honestly, I was avoiding him because I didn't want to conflate him with the real antagonist.

Olethros's voice, laced with disdain, echoed through the space. "You're telling me you have *absolutely nothing new* to report?"

A distorted, anxious voice responded, "Your Majesty, if you could just provide more specific guidance on your concerns, I could—"

"Concerns? You think I am merely… *concerned?* No wonder you're not taking your orders seriously!" Olethros flared his voice in anger.

"I mean no disrespect, Your Majesty… but I am unsure of what more I should be doing…"

I felt a little sorry for the minion at that point. He sounded so pathetic and out of his element… Wait. That would mean *he's another figment of my imagination, too*, wouldn't it? What part of my personality would he represent? Imposter syndrome!? *I'm doing my best, you know!*

"I'll give you just one minute to rethink your last statement to me." Olethros tapped the seconds out on his desk in appreciable irritation.

I reminded myself once again that this was *just another weird dream* and that anything that happens here is my brain trying to cope with recent events. To solidify that fact, I glanced down and ensured I was transparent. All I had to do was wait this out and apologize for our last rough encounter, right? I'd concede he was right, and I should have listened to what he was saying, maybe flatter his intelligence a little, then hit him with recent circumstances and ask for his sage advice. Ah, but don't say "sage" to him. He might take that as an insult.

"Perhaps I should…" the voice hesitated after his time was up.

"Just tell me what that *damnable priest* has been up to!"

Definitely skip the word sage.

"Which—"

"Relias!" I heard his fist slam into the desk. *"Who else would I be asking about!?"*

"H-he spends most of his days locked in the tower, Dread Lord!" The voice sounded somewhat tinny, as if he was broadcasting across a distance.

I carefully peeked around the bookshelf and saw his dark majesty slowly scraping his claw-like fingernails along deeply carved ruts on his desk while sneering into a magic orb. His silvery lavender locks were in complete disarray, which I once again found particularly bothersome. I know you're a busy demon king, but take some time out for self-care once in a while.

"Most? Not all? When does he leave? What does he *do? Who is he meeting with?* I have all these questions, yet your report *does nothing to address them*!"

"I'm… not sure of the answers… The holy barriers obscure—" The voice he was talking to seemed to be coming in fits from that magic orb. Although Olethros must have been able to see something I couldn't because it was just filled with green fog.

"Must I instruct you on every task, *Amos*? Obtain their calibration schedule from Councilman Vetus and slip inside the inner city during staggered maintenance. I'm sure *the others* are already well ahead of you."

Amos? Vetus? I couldn't remember either name from the book. *But Vetus still sounded familiar…*

"Your Majesty, Vetus died two months ago…"

Wow! Fastest NPC death ever?

"And you've neglected to report it?"

"He was just a regular human… he wasn't even highly skilled in using amity."

"Tell me his cause of death. Was it suspicious? Did they… find him out?" He peered nervously into the orb with glittery green eyes, but its center remained foggy.

"Sir, he was *ninety-four years old*. No one investigated his death. It was a foregone conclusion."

Olethros exhaled exaggeratedly. "Inutilis wouldn't have access to that information. Procul is currently away inspecting Fort Turri… What about Councilman Pravum? Have you tried bribing *him* yet?"

How am I supposed to interpret this dream if you're using names I don't know, brain?

"The amount of gold he's asking for is—"

"Irrelevant. Just give it to him. Promise him anything he wants and get that schedule. I want to know what's happening in the Inner Sanctum. Nothing makes sense!"

"Yes, Your Majesty," the voice responded sullenly.

"I expect tomorrow's report will contain *useful* information."

"T…tomorrow? Your Majesty, the risk I'm taking each time I contact you—"

"Is nothing compared to what will happen if you fail."

"Please, Your Majesty! I'm doing my best to change things!"

"And yet you've done *nothing* to improve your incompetence. It's as

if—" Olethros shuddered, and both of his eyes suddenly flicked open. The whites had given way to darkness, with tiny wisps of black smoke leaking from the outer corners. "You're working with *her,* aren't you?"

"No, I swear, I've not been in contact with Mistress Aziza—"

"Not her. *Her!*" he shouted angrily, slamming the desk again as he stood up.

The distorted voice stayed silent for a moment before proceeding with clear apprehension. "Your Majesty, there's no tangible evidence that she has returned. Every reported sighting turned out to be unfounded. You need to forget about—"

"Enough." He grabbed his head with both hands, his features blurring behind a dark veil of shadow. "Our conversation is over. Do not contact me again until you have something *productive to report*!" He ended the call by forcefully swiping the magic orb off its pedestal. The resounding shattering of glass crystal echoed throughout the room, momentarily stunning me.

"I know you're here, Rachel," he murmured in a low, malevolent tone that caused me to tremble in fear. He definitely wasn't in a place to talk meaningfully with me, and I wasn't ready to deal with whatever this dream was actually about. "You can't hide from me for long." Oh, thank the heavens… he didn't know I was *"here"* here!

"This wasn't supposed to happen," he continued, his voice rising with every syllable. "None of this was supposed to happen. *You weren't supposed to come back*!" He suddenly disappeared with an angry buzz, only to reappear directly in front of the magic circle. Now, the darkness surrounding him seemed to emanate from his entire body.

"Plus animus! *Ego vi!"* The magic circle hummed louder, and his scythe pulsated in response to his unhinged shouts. "I refuse to be the next victim in all of this!"

He shrieked mindlessly as the room filled with the dark vapor spewing from his physical form, clouding my vision.

✳✳✳

I awoke covered in a cold sweat, strangely thankful for physics and any other related sciences that made it impossible for me to jump out of my own skin.

"What the… why was he acting like a two-bit antagonist this time?" I mumbled to myself to play off the stupid dream as I rolled over, only to find Nora inches from my face.

"Who are you talking about?" she asked quietly.

"I-I have no idea!"

It wasn't him. It couldn't have been.

"You're having weird dreams again, aren't you?" It was so comforting to hear that she had once thought they had *gone away*.

"You know me." I laughed nervously.

"You're still not going to tell me about them, are you?"

"Nora… They're just dumb dreams. They rarely make sense, and…" *I don't want you to think less of me.*

"The last time you had them bad, your mother sent you away for the summer," Nora reminded me. "So even if you can't talk to *me* about them, you should consider—"

"I've been lying to you," I interrupted quickly, not wanting to hear her latest advice for my chronic sleep problems. "It wasn't Mother's decision to go away for therapy. It was mine. I just… didn't want you to blame me for ruining our summer vacation plans." Sorry, Mother. It was so easy to blame you for my issues. Then, I didn't have to deal with them myself.

"You… lied to me? And I *believed* you?"

"I'm so sorry!" I was probably making her lousy day even worse now.

"I can't believe it… You lied to my face with *your face*! I didn't know you had it in you."

"You're not… mad?"

"Everyone lies. I just thought you were really, really bad at it."

I stared at her for a few moments. "Uh, thanks, I guess?"

Nora took a deep breath. "If you need help to deal with them…"

"I'll ask for help when I need it. I promise," I lied again.

***

Post-Chapter Omake

Olethros: *You're out there somewhere, Rachel, and I'll find you.*

Rae: *No, you won't!*

Olethros: *Yes, I will!*

Rae: *Nope!*

Olethros: *Oh, I suppose I'll just forget the whole thing, then.*

Rae: *Really?*

Olethros: *No!*

Rae: *…You definitely need a hobby. Something that takes you outdoors.*

CHAPTER 32: A WALK IN THE WOODS

Tetora's wakeful state, while appreciated, did not immediately progress to one where he was fully ambulatory.

"Meat," he whined incessantly the next afternoon. "I would heal quicker if I had meat."

"The more you yowl, the less I believe you are actually suffering." Aleph exhaled.

"This is a forest. I am sure there are tasty animals *somewhere* nearby. Bring me some. Otherwise… I might faint again." He was on his back and still covered in sweat. However, his tail twitched playfully in the dry leaves. Hopefully, his overacting wouldn't exhaust him more.

Aleph rolled his eyes while turning to me. "Let's go see if we can set a few traps. At least it will give our ears a rest."

Nora, who had been squeamish about talking with Tetora, looked at me with haunted eyes. I betrayed her silent request to switch by giving her a covert but enthusiastic thumbs-up.

I started following Aleph deeper into the woods. "You'll have to show me how to set one."

"It isn't hard," Aleph replied, though he made no move to do so.

I waited until we were out of earshot. "Did you two come up with this, also?"

"What do you mean?"

"You said before that no animals would be around because of the demons," I reminded him.

"You are far too generous to Tetora. He *does* want us to find meat."

"So you're saying it was just you, then?"

"They need to talk alone. I am just taking advantage of Tetora's ridiculous request."

We walked silently while looking for trail markings, but not bothering with any traps. As we progressed, the woods thickened around us, but at least the sunny sky was still visible through cracks in the canopy.

Now was a good time. "Aleph…" I took a big breath. "There's something I've wanted to ask for a while, but… you might not want to answer." Could I have been any more vague?

"You won't know for sure until you try."

"What… What was *he* like?"

He's not like how I had imagined him, right? What I had dreamt couldn't actually be…

Aleph stopped walking and turned, blocking my view of his face. "I do not know to whom you refer."

"I don't know if I am allowed to say his other name. You know, the one he used when pretending to be a dark mage."

"It is not his true name. It has no power."

I hesitated. "What was *Oliver* like?"

"It does not matter what he was like. Oliver did not exist."

"But he was—"

"Whatever I thought Oliver was *is not the truth*." His tone was harsh, I could tell he didn't want to talk about him, but I couldn't help myself. I had to know.

"The story made him seem intelligent, even witty. Is that how he seemed to you, too?" He's not some mindless, mustache-twirling villain, right?

"Oliver was a persona adopted by a powerful demon lord. He was *not real*."

"Well, his persona then. What was it like?" Crafting a persona requires intelligence and wisdom, right? Wouldn't that mean… he could be reasoned with?

"It doesn't matter what it was like! *He never existed!* To spend even *one moment* considering his past influence only adds to his demonic power!" Aleph slammed his war hammer into a nearby tree, splitting the trunk with a resounding crack.

I swallowed hard, frightened by his uncharacteristic rage. "I…" I took a few steps back, and Aleph's eyes widened in sudden remorse.

"Little one, I didn't mean to hurt you."

"No, no, I was just startled, that's all. I'm sorry." I scratched my right wrist absently at first. Once I realized I was doing it, I tried to stop but had little luck. "I shouldn't have—"

"I am the one who wronged you. Do not apologize to me."

A slurred and shaky voice called from the treetop, "You should apologize to *me*!"

I tensed, regretting not grabbing my bo staff. Were the demons back?

"Knock softer next time!" the voice yelled again.

My tension dissipated at Aleph's incredulous chuckle. "Vernie? Is that you?"

"Pretending to know me won't work. Full price is off the table at this point."

"Please, just come down here so we can talk."

A weighted rope dropped from the tree's canopy, and a middle-aged woman slid in fits and starts before plunging the last several feet to the ground noisily. Her dark leather outfit was skin-tight, leaving absolutely nothing to the imagination. She swept her wild red mane out of her face and stood up with a cat-like stretch, followed by a fluid motion to regain her balance after a near stumble.

"Ho…? Not what I was expecting at all…" She looked me up and down with bleary, chartreuse eyes. "But looks can be deceiving." She then turned to Aleph, staggering slightly and counting off wavy fingers as she spoke. "The standard slaver bounty, minus a three-day late fee for making me wait, comes to—"

"Slaver… bounty?" I looked between the two of them.

"Did you think you'd make some money off the suffering of others, kid?" She pointed dramatically at me, wobbly knife in hand. "Not that I blame you for wanting to get rich, but you chose the wrong side. Let's see how *you* like wearing a collar!"

"Laverna!" Aleph's voice thundered. "Sober up and try again."

"Eh...? Aleph?" She blinked several times before grinning widely. "So, you've finally woken up! It's about damn time, you pathetic pacifist!" She punched him in the shoulder roughly with her free hand.

Aleph tried again. "Laverna, we really—"

"Wait, where's the furball?" She started looking around wildly, jumping here and there in a comedic fashion. "You wouldn't have left him behind! What happened?"

Aleph groaned. "*Just how much have you had to drink today?*"

"Today? Ah, I don't know. Business has been good, so..." She shrugged, her black leather halter top bouncing along with her shoulders. "Probably more than enough. Why, you want some?"

"No. Just..." Aleph rubbed his temples. "She's *not* a slaver."

"Issat so?" She turned to me again, then frowned, drawing in her plump, overly red lower lip. "Wait. Take off your mask."

I glanced at Aleph dubiously for a moment before answering. "Put the knife away first."

"What knife?" she asked in confusion.

"The one in your hand!"

"Oh! No, I wasn't going to..." She tucked it into a sheath on her hip. "See?" She held up her hands, twirling her fingers. "All good now."

I pulled off my mask and tensely waited for her reaction.

"Never mind." She turned away abruptly and said, "Put it back on. I'm mistaken."

"Uh, sure." I pulled it back up, thoroughly confused. Were Aleph and Tetora... only seeing what they wanted to see in me? I should have felt relief, but... all I felt was awkwardness.

"Where's Tetora?" she demanded again of Aleph.

"Not far. We encountered demons yesterday, and he took a hit of poison."

"Demons? In *my* forest?" She straightened considerably. "And they managed to *hit him*!?"

"Army recruiters," Aleph confirmed. "We banished both. One was a sergeant."

"Fuck!" she swore loudly as she pulled out a whistle. Three long, loud tweets later, we heard frantic movement around us. Humans and hybrids, mostly dressed in brown and black leather, started popping out from denser areas of foliage, only to run deeper into the heart of the woods.

One young man ran up to her and saluted sharply. "Orders, Boss?"

"Full evac! Red mountain. Vulture's in charge. You have five days to move the entire operation, tops." She looked at Aleph. "Supplies for how many?"

Aleph made a strange gesture before answering. "If you're joining us, we'll be five."

Laverna also gestured back, even as she agreed. "You heard him!"

"Do you have any curcumin?" Aleph asked the henchman. "I'd like to incorporate it into Tetora's treatment."

I thought that was just a spice?

"Yarrow would also be helpful."

"Anything else?" Laverna asked. Somehow, she exuded a sense of authority even though she couldn't stand straight without waving about.

"Any priests in your employ?" Aleph inquired.

Laverna snorted. "As if!"

"Yes… I understand," Aleph replied somberly.

"Um… Tetora wants some meat, too, if possible," I added.

"Yeah, of course," she answered, though she refused to look at me. Did I offend her? I'm the one who should be mad—being mistaken for a slaver!

The young man saluted again. "On my way, Boss! I'll be back soon!"

We all watched him run off and quickly disappear behind a large bush.

"You're not going to ask her name?" Aleph asked.

"I'd just forget it," Laverna slurred.

"She looks like someone you know, doesn't she?"

"No! I don't hallucinate anymore!" Laverna declared.

"That is very good to hear, but she certainly looks like Raelynn to me."

At that, Laverna turned to look at me, tears shining in her eyes. "Rae-Rae?"

"Um…" I didn't want to mess with her, but I was beginning to openly question everything. "Maybe?"

CHAPTER 33: LAVERNA

Laverna seemed more in control as we walked back to camp, making me wonder if she had really been drunk. Aleph carried the bulk of supplies, though I too found myself belted down with several canvas packages from her subordinates. They both continued to share strange gestures, making it apparent that they were silently talking about me.

"Just say it out loud, Aleph…" I sighed.

"I do not wish to upset you. I'm merely briefing her about our current situation."

"I can handle it…"

"Of course," Aleph agreed, though the gestures then ceased.

"Rae-Rae," Laverna addressed me. "What about the time we fought those brigands out in Lios? Remember? You stole the belt off that hairy one in the middle of the melee! It was the nastiest thing I ever saw. Bet he never forgets his underwear now!"

"Laverna…" Aleph shook his head. "*You* did that. Not Rae."

"I did? Ha! But you were there too. Remember, Rae-Rae?"

"That's hilarious, but no. Sorry." It would have made a fun chapter in the web novel.

"You know, it was right before we went to the Dark Mage Tower to recruit O… Oh! Oh well, anyway. It was good fun!" She slapped me on the back, almost causing me to drop some supplies.

"Sounds like it." I nodded awkwardly.

We made it back to camp, and to my relief, Nora and Tetora were sitting together. Tetora had propped himself up under a tree, and Nora was taking notes in her journal.

"The shirt needs to be made of the finest silk. Embroidery on the cuffs. Gold buttons down the front! On the back, I want—" Tetora's demands suddenly cut off as he looked up.

"Vernie!" He tried to stand quickly but shuddered in pain before he could straighten.

"Bowing in my presence, hmmm? As you should, as you should!" Laverna gestured grandly to Aleph and me. "I come bearing gifts."

"Just get over here!" Tetora shouted. "What were you thinking, disappearing suddenly like that?"

Laverna, ignoring his apparent injuries, head-locked him in a rough greeting. "You *know* how it is! It was time for me to leave. But now…" She turned to look at me with sparkling jewels for eyes. "Things will be different!"

Oh boy. Not another one. I felt the pressure mounting across my temples. "Before you get your hopes up, I—"

"You're very tiny." Lavena had already moved on to Nora, who had also stood up. "Let me have a good look at you!"

"I'm tiny but mighty!" Nora declared hotly. "Don't underestimate me."

"Yes. You are perfect," Laverna agreed with a laugh. "You can probably get in almost anywhere unnoticed, with the right training, that is. What do you think about becoming a thief?"

"Oh…!" And now Nora's eyes were the ones shining. "Yes! Teach me."

"Hmm…" Laverna tilted her head. "Aleph said you have one of my knives?"

"Er, yes." Nora started to pull it from her boot, startling me.

"Keep it, for now. I'll show you how to use it in a pinch."

"Nora!" I exclaimed. "You're considering multi-classing already?"

Multi-classing wasn't really a thing in Speranza, given the singularity of people's assigned Purpose, but it was certainly a rule that needed to be broken. Basically, if you had inherent skills in amity, you were a priest or a knight. Animus? You were relegated to dark mage.

Except, nothing's ever that simple, right?

"I won't be useless ever again," she snarled, obviously still reliving our recent encounter.

"Nora…" You weren't useless. It was just a bad matchup. I still wanted to know how in the world the demoness knew to call her a shameless ankle-biter, though. That was a personal trigger for Nora.

"Alright now, time to celebrate our reunion." Laverna blithely ignored the tension and pulled a large bottle of wine from her canvas sack.

"No wine!" I gasped in response.

"But… you promised to have a drink with me."

"When was that?"

"Almost eight years ago, and I've been saving this for a special occasion."

"But—"

Vernie waved her hand. "It's just a toast to celebrate. Join me!"

I wavered, overwhelmed by the sudden feeling that I couldn't disappoint her. "One glass, but just because I'm drinking this does not mean I'm admitting I'm Rae-Rae, Raelynn, or whatever."

Laverna opted to pour me a glass instead of arguing. "Cheers on defeating the demon king, Rae-Rae!"

I sighed and clinked glasses with her before taking my sweet time to consume it. At my request, Nora stayed sober to monitor its effects.

"Well, remember anything yet?" Laverna asked.

"No… That's not how brains work."

"Obviously, you need more." She filled my glass again. "You're not even slurring your words yet."

"Laverna…" There was no way I was going to lose my wits completely—not after the last time! "I said, *one glass!*"

"It's Vernie. You need to call me Vernie. Also, it's still the same glass I'm using, so refills don't count."

"Fine, Vernie. As in, Vernie, I'm not drinking any more wine. The last time I got drunk, it only took one glass, er, fill."

Vernie scoffed. "You can't get drunk on one glass of wine."

"Some people do."

"No. You have a bigger frame. I'm thinking… three to four should do it."

"No! If you're not going to respect my wishes—"

"You're Rae-Rae. Just even more stubborn now." Vernie picked up the glass she had poured and downed it in one swift swallow. "Thanks for keeping your promise, even if you don't remember the details. I can die happy now."

"Why are you talking about dying?" I sat up suddenly, my nerves unraveling.

"It's just a saying."

"No! I don't like it! No!" Sweat trickled down from my hair.

"Don't worry. I don't plan to die soon—not before we get our revenge against Oliver. So tell me, what's the plan?"

"Uh. Go to Chairo and talk with Holy Sage Relias?"

"Then what?"

"Then…" Threaten the General Assembly? Search for Paradise? Await further instructions from my other-worldly bosses? None of it was going to make sense. "I don't know."

"I thought you might have gotten better at this sort of thing when you came of age, but you aren't a grand strategist," Vernie commented. "Lucky I found you when I did!"

Wasn't it the other way around? "Yes, very lucky."

"I'm not…" She leaned back, grimacing as she searched for the right words. "…*Looking forward* to seeing Relias, though. You're going to have to help me make nice with him. Just like old times."

"Make nice? What happened between you two?"

Vernie folded her arms as she laid back, looking up at the evening sky. "Don't you think, of all of us, that the *wise and ageless holy sage* should have realized Oliver was a demon?"

That was one of our initial criticisms as well. We had even taken care to outline a clear growth arc for Relias, suspecting his hesitant nature stemmed directly from the deep-seated trauma and despair of losing a loved one to the original demon king. In fact, I believe it was number three on NoRaeNoWay's *33 Opportunities for Improvement*. Nora, however, also verged on calling him just generally incompetent, but I chalked it up to Oliver being, well, Oliver.

"*He* seemed pretty good at hiding his true intentions," I remarked. "I'm sure he knew how to keep Relias from getting suspicious." Nora had immediately identified that he was a demon, but she had the audience's perspective. Living in the moment and seeing things unfold firsthand would offer a different view, right?

"Of course you don't blame Relias either…" Vernie sighed. "But *I did*, and I said some pretty terrible things to him before he was locked away."

"And you're sorry you said them?"

"… Maybe," Vernie mumbled. "A little." She sat up and gave me a big grin. "So, you'll apologize on my behalf, right?"

"No way. You have to say it yourself. But…" I squirmed some, not wanting to get more embroiled in party politics. "I'll help… and be right next to you when you do it." Crap, what is *wrong* with me, picking up side quests every time one pops up? I'd never get home at this rate.

Vernie grinned at me. "Thanks, Rae-Rae."

Nora, who had been silently observing, finally asked, "So, why do you call her Rae-Rae?"

"Because Rae-Rae-Rae-Rae-Rae-Rae is ridiculous!" I noticed she missed a Rae, but I didn't want to interject. "She's the seventh Rae, but I simplified it! Rae Rac." It was embarrassing to realize that even the story's characters thought the naming convention was absurd.

Aleph, who had just finished another round of Tetora's bandaging and acupuncture session, drifted over to join us. Tetora came closer, too, opting to curl up near the campfire.

Vernie turned to me and said, "It's my turn now. Tell me… what was Euphridia like?"

"Demanding!" I answered immediately. "And pushy. But I'm not sure that—"

Aleph gave me a startled look even as Vernie laughed loudly. "Just as I imagined… always asking more and more of her followers."

Aleph huffed. "Holy Euphridia's ways are just not like those of humanity, and we cannot begin to understand—"

Vernie rolled her eyes as she interrupted him. "If she wanted to save the world, she'd just step in and get rid of the demons herself."

"I don't think she can do that," Nora said. "She seemed like the type who would if she could."

"Then what good is she?" Vernie jeered. "Gods and priests and the Church, too! What good are any of them?"

Oh, I could only *begin* to imagine what she had said to poor Relias.

Aleph's face was full of unspoken anger, but he took a deep breath before responding in a soft, somewhat forced tone. *"She brought her back to us, didn't she?"*

Vernie looked at me for a long moment, then sighed. "But she doesn't remember us. Why didn't she fix her head?"

I have to admit that it stung a little. "Hey now… I'm not—"

"If I could just give my Rae-Rae a hug once more…" Vernie looked off in the distance, sighing.

Maybe that would help her realize I wasn't exactly who she thought I was. Or maybe… Well, in any case, I stood up and motioned for Vernie to do the same. My attempt to hug her was initially pathetic, mostly because I didn't know how to do it without coming into awkward contact with her ample bosom. Vernie, however, had no such qualms about personal space and forced me into an embrace that I could only classify as a friendly submission hold. Several moments later, she loosened her grip to put a surprisingly gentle hand on my left cheek, peering deeply into my eyes with a mournful expression. "My poor dear Rae-Rae… Look at what he did to you…"

Well, that backfired splendidly. "Vernie… I'm trying to show you that—"

She broke off her stare abruptly and pulled away. "Do you realize how many times I could have taken your life in the last few hours? You're just too trusting, letting someone *you don't even remember* have full access to all your vital points. Or I could have poisoned the wine you just drank! Memory loss I can accept, but what happened to your *common sense*? You're backsliding into your first life as Raela!"

"You… you would never do something like that!" I protested, confused by her sudden change of heart.

"How do you know that for sure?" she asked me pointedly. "Aleph even told you that half of Speranza is convinced I cooperated with Oliver to betray you, yet you never entertained that thought for more than half a moment!"

"Because you're Vernie! I—"

"First lesson! Trust no one here, Rae-Rae, especially those who want to get close to you! I don't want to go through *losing you again*!" She then pulled out her whistle and blew it twice, startling all of us. A few minutes later, her young minion appeared at the edge of camp. She spent a few minutes talking with him in quiet but heated tones.

"She has a point," Nora murmured.

"But… she's *Vernie*!" Deep down, I knew that Vernie was wholly innocent and that she would never intentionally hurt me. "She's like a big sister you can rely on for anything! Not a double-crosser!" Sure, she drinks too much for her own good, but none of us are perfect.

"Vernie aside, I think we need to stop thinking that the narrator was reliable about things in general," Nora warned. "Too many issues were glossed over or omitted completely. *So listen to what she's saying, and don't hug strangers anymore.*"

"Alright…" Vernie wasn't a stranger, though. I knew the difference.

Vernie returned to our campfire. "More supplies will arrive tomorrow. I'll feel better once you both have some proper protection."

I sulked for the rest of the night before going to bed alone, not even wishing anyone a pleasant goodnight.

***

Raelynn Lightbringer, Champion of Humanity, knelt to question the condemned thief. "Tell me in truth, what was your crime?"

237

The red-headed savage, her face full of scorn and contempt, spat directly into the Holy Captain's face before responding. "I followed my Purpose and became a thief! Just as I was told!"

"What did you steal?" Raelynn inquired calmly as she used her cape to wipe her face.

"What didn't I steal? Gold, silver, jewels, supplies, food! Everything I could get my hands on!"

"What did you do with everything after you stole it?"

The thief laughed humorlessly. "That's what matters to you, eh? Too bad you're never getting it back!"

"You didn't keep it for yourself. That much is obvious." Raelynn stood up and gestured to the executioner. "Release her into my custody."

"Holy Captain… this criminal is—"

"That's an order."

Laverna attempted to flee the moment her chains were unlocked, but even she could not escape the Hero of Legend.

"Laverna the Thief!" Raelynn's voice thundered throughout the square. "Holy Sage Relias accompanies me to officially change your Purpose! You are to join us on our quest to defeat The Accursed One!"

Laverna suddenly tripped and fell to her knees even as Raelynn came up from behind, placing her gauntleted hand on the thief's shoulder. "Rise, dear companion, and join us in grand celebration!"

"I humbly apologize." Holy Sage Relias bowed deeply. "For all you must have suffered. Though it may not begin to make up for your tribulations, the priest who originally assigned you such a false Purpose has been defrocked so that no others may suffer so needlessly."

And there, in the square for all to see, did Laverna the Thief weep even as her fate was once again entwined with the Chosen One of the Goddess.

CHAPTER 34: DEMON DEBRIEF

The next morning, we lingered about, waiting for the extra supplies Vernie had called for. I tried to ignore yesterday's little friction with her, knowing that team building can be rough at first.

"We're not going to try to go *through* Fort Turri, are we?" Vernie asked in an exhausted voice. "There are better ways into the kingdom."

"We are open to alternatives." Aleph nodded. "As long as we find a priest to nullify the poison."

"There's a path between the mountains to the village of Kopria." Vernie yawned. "It's not exactly… *pleasant*, but we could avoid going through Turri's official border crossing altogether."

"Wouldn't we be able to find a priest faster in Fort Turri?" I asked, recalling it was relatively close to us.

Vernie frowned. "Mmm. Yes, but…"

I envisioned a barrage of wanted posters plastered across its inner stone walls. "Let me guess. You're pretty famous there?"

"Infamous is probably the better word…" Vernie scratched her cheek nervously. "Kopria's *smaller* and a little more in our ultimate direction. There's less chance of raising a ruckus."

"How much climbing?" I asked, looking at Tetora. Could we keep pushing him?

"No climbing. There are some inclines, but nothing so steep as requiring hand grips. Trust me, it's much safer in the long run. It's the priest part at the end that's going to be a little difficult, though."

"There aren't any priests in Kopria?" I asked, almost rejecting her suggestion outright. Health comes first!

"Oh, there's sure to be one," Vernie said as she twirled her knife. "They'll just take some convincing, that's all."

Tetora grunted. "We can just go straight to Chairo. I don't need a backwater bishop."

Aleph held his tongue even as he rolled his eyes. Perhaps he was suffering just as much as Tetora but for different reasons.

"I think it sounds like a good idea. Going to Kopria, I mean. Right?" I asked everyone else, who more or less grunted before turning back to breakfast. I looked at Aleph in particular, thinking he would make the final decision.

Instead, Aleph clasped his hands together. "We'll do just as you decided, then."

Wait, no. I'm not the executive decision-maker here. Betrayed by my fake father! I knew nothing about the upcoming terrain, distance, climate, possible encounters, just to name a few. Right, Nora?

Oh. I suddenly realized Nora was still moping. She'd been reticent ever since the incident with Tetora and currently had herself absorbed in the journal. I glanced over and saw a page filled with sketches of the two demons we had recently encountered in various terrifying shapes, with several messy notes scribbled in between. In big letters underneath, Nora had written "Ask Clare for more information on demons." What could Clare possibly know, though, all the way back home? It's better to ask the frontline subject matter experts first. But first and most important…

"I bet that one would look better with a mustache, don't you think?" I pointed to the demon holding the spear. "It would hide his thin lips."

Nora mumbled something unintelligible in response. I picked up her pen and started drawing it in. "See? Not nearly as disturbing. Let's give him a bad toupee, too!"

"How can you joke about him?"

"Oh. Well. It's because I wanted to take away his power. That's all."

"Take away his power?" Nora blinked. "How does a *fake comb-over* do that?"

"Those two were scary, right? And even though they're not here now, they're *still hurting you*. So… you, you know, make them silly and dumb in your head, so they can't live there rent-free anymore. Talking about ridiculous things is easier when you can separate *them* from your real self." That's how I did it, anyway. It's not a cure-all, but it can help stop the terrible memories from returning and overwhelming you.

Nora took back her pen. "She… needs a clown nose."

"Don't forget the wig," I agreed.

Nora drew for a few moments more before speaking again. "We need to discuss them as a group, don't we? You were just waiting until I was ready."

That was giving me too much credit. I just wanted her to feel better. "Well… I mean, I have a lot of questions, but I can hold off."

"No… You're right," she confirmed. "Even though it's a little late now, we should debrief."

"Debrief?" Vernie sat up quickly. "In front of everyone?"

"It's… not that kind of debrief…" I winced, still feeling awkward about yesterday's impromptu lesson, calling out how stupid I was being.

Nora set her shoulders, becoming all business. "We encountered two demons the other day. I want to talk about how this encounter went. The goal will be to talk through what happened and how it happened so we can avoid a similar outcome."

"Oh. That doesn't sound nearly as interesting." Vernie sighed as she settled back against a tree trunk and closed her eyes.

Aleph cast his gaze down to the ground. "It was my fault for—"

I cleared my throat. "We're looking for improvements, not shame and blame. Where I come from… usually we start by talking about what went well."

Aleph and Tetora exchanged a long look.

"We all survived," Tetora noted.

"Our blessed weapons all worked," Aleph added.

"I don't think any of them recognized us, either," I stated as Nora took notes. "They called us Ox, Tiger, and human girls." Aleph and Tetora would be famous in demonic circles, right?

Nora frowned. "Why didn't they just kill us?"

I immediately froze at the heavy-hitting question, knowing they could have done so quickly.

Aleph exhaled. "They value our suffering over our death."

"What… do they get out of it?" Nora asked.

"Power," Aleph confirmed. "Their strength grows from the animus they extract: anger, ill will, sadness, despair. But our death is the end of all that."

"It's just a game of power to them…" I sighed, feeling my shoulders sag.

Tetora sniffed. "And a matter of pride… taken to extremes. They often boast about how long they can extract animus from their victims."

Nora drew a big breath. "Let's talk about the private for now. Why was he flickering so much after Rae bit him?"

Aleph put on his lecturing face, so to speak. "Demons… gather and store animus in their spiritual core to strengthen themselves and create a physical form. However, direct application of enough holy amity can disrupt a demon's hold on their animus. Usually, we use blessed weapons, *and not our teeth*, to do that."

I felt my nose wrinkle. "Well, what else was I supposed to—"

"I know you had no choice, Little Dragon," Aleph said mournfully. "I purposefully delayed proper instruction on fighting demons, thinking it would only cause you more anxiety. I also… underestimated the risk of a demon appearing before us so early in our journey. Perhaps it is time I woke up, as Vernie has suggested." He sighed, lowering his big brown eyes.

"A-ah no, I didn't mean anything by it. We're taking the time to learn now, so it's all good." I got up and hugged his broad shoulders tightly. Don't be sad, other-worldly dad.

"When we find a priest," Tetora mumbled, "we should get them to bless Nora and Vernie's knives. They'll need to defend themselves, too."

"Yes," Aleph agreed, patting my head reassuringly. "I believe the proper knowledge and tools would help to improve our outcome should such a situation occur again."

"So. The demoness." Nora gritted her teeth. "What did she do to me?"

I glanced expectantly at Aleph and Tetora, but they hesitated.

"She *did* something, right?" Nora continued. "I wasn't myself."

"I saw a black haze around you, too…" I finally admitted both aloud and to myself.

"So you're able to see high levels of concentrated animus again!" Tetora's head shot up.

"Wait, what?" I blinked. "Then… you guys… didn't see it?"

"I told you before, we can't see animus," Tetora admonished. "But now *you can again*. This is a *good* thing!"

I refrained from refuting his statement or thinking about it harder. "Back to Nora's question. What did the demoness do to her?"

"Dark mages are sensitive to animus by nature," Aleph replied. "Demons take advantage of this by using their own animus to enhance their victim's negative emotions, forcing them into animus overload."

"Animus overload?" Nora asked. I felt a chill run up my spine as her face filled with consternation.

"A state in which rational thought is no longer possible. Sentient beings in animus overload often lash out violently without distinction. In extreme cases, the afflicted become paralyzed with rage. It can happen to almost anyone, but certain groups are more sensitive to it… hybrids and dark mages included."

"Animus overload…" Nora mumbled again.

"You didn't know about animus overload?" Tetora snorted. "It's the first thing they teach dark mages."

"How would I know something like that? I've only been a dark mage for a few weeks."

"You know powerful incantations, but not the basic tenets? Did the story not instruct you?"

"It wasn't an instruction manual!" Nora huffed. "It was a *lousy*…"

Lousy what? Lousy teacher? "Nora?"

Nora shook her head with an exhale, refusing to continue with her comment. "So, you're saying I'm susceptible to animus, and all it takes is a few negative words to set me off?"

"From a demon, anyway," Aleph confirmed. "You will need to counteract their attempts to provoke you mentally."

"The words she used to upset Nora were *very specific*," I grumbled defensively. "How did she know about them? Is she a mind reader?"

"In a way," Aleph said thoughtfully. "Strong demons can pick up words and short phrases tied to extremely negative emotions. If we reencounter her, she will surely use the same phrase against you, Nora. It is best to disengage those trigger words from your feelings. I will help you do so."

Nora nodded with a sigh. "I'll have to work on that. I don't want to feed her a spicy snack again next time."

Vernie, who had been seemingly half-asleep, opened her eyes. "Spicy snack?"

"I stupidly… tried setting her on fire with dark magic."

Vernie looked at her for a long moment, obviously late to the party. "Huh. So, even *aliens* are susceptible to animus overload. You learn something new every day!"

Nora twitched. *"What did you just call me?"*

"An alien. That's what you are, right?"

"I'm not an *alien!*"

"You fell from the sky from another world. Alien," Vernie concluded with a shrug. "I'm *just saying.*"

Nora, at a loss for words, shot a brief glare my way before turning her exasperated gaze to Vernie.

I couldn't hold it in any longer. "My best friend's a magical alien!" Nora would get the inside joke, as we had read another web novel with that *very same* title.

"Rachel Emily Smith!" Nora exclaimed as I continued to cackle. She jumped up and tackled me to the ground with mock ferocity. "Not you, too!"

Of course, that was precisely when two of Vernie's henchmen appeared in our camp, carrying a large wooden box between them.

"Uh. Boss?" I recognized the younger one from yesterday. "Are we… interrupting something?"

"What, haven't you ever seen a debrief before?" Vernie replied coolly.

***

Post-Chapter Omake

Rae: *Our debrief here was more than a little loose. No one should use what we did as a model for a structured debrief.*

Nora: *Right. But it's important to ask what went well, just like you did at the beginning. Debriefing should be a timely opportunity to acknowledge successes and challenges for learning opportunities after a critical incident occurs.*

Rae: *Above all else, please don't use them to shame people or to place blame.*

Nora: *Yeah, there are so many other processes available for doing just that!*

Rae: *Uh…*

Nora: *You know I'm right.*

CHAPTER 35: INVENTORY AND EXPECTATION MANAGEMENT

With our debrief derailed, we gathered around the box her associates delivered.

"What's inside?" I asked curiously.

"Protection!" Vernie declared. "What was Euphridia thinking, sending you two here with no real offenses or defenses?"

"To be fair, she was aiming for the holy city," Nora remarked. "I'm sure we were supposed to suit up there."

"Rae-Rae's old armor isn't there, though." Vernie shrugged. "Some scoundrel stole it a few years back after they pulled it from the castle ruins."

"Scoundrel?" Nora bobbed on her tiptoes. "Maybe one with flaming red hair?"

"So you've heard of her, eh? Of course you have. She's the legend that fought alongside the hero. The thief who can steal anything. The unrivaled leader of the Red Monkeys!" Vernie shot her a grin before continuing in a more serious tone. "They had it on display for the public, still covered in dried blood like some gruesome sideshow attraction. Couldn't let that stand so…" Vernie trailed off with a shrug.

I stepped back from the box. "I don't want to see something like that…"

"I didn't *leave it* that way. It's all fixed up now, good as new." Vernie clapped sharply, and her two goons lifted the top off the box. The inside was thickly padded and lined with purple velvet. Vernie drew off the top layer of fabric with a dramatic flourish, revealing a silver half-plate ensemble that had been polished to a mirror sheen.

The cuirass, gauntlets, pauldrons, and tassets were embossed with an ornate gold inlay along their edges.

"Oh, my!" Nora gasped. "It's beautiful! Rae, you *gotta* try it on!"

I picked up the shimmering cuirass with trembling hands. Raelynn wasn't the type to be overprotective of her possessions. In fact, she hated to see things go to waste, especially if someone had a need for it. "As long as I take good care of it and give it back as soon as I'm done with it… then it's all good, right?"

"Give it back?" Vernie crossed her arms. "What are you talking about? It's yours to begin with."

"Haa…" I sighed. "Well, let's just see if it fits, okay?"

It was like it was made for me. Even the straps only needed minimal adjustment. Everything fit together so perfectly, and it wasn't nearly as heavy as I thought it might be. I needed some help to get into it, though.

"Um, how do I look?" I asked as I put my hands to rest lightly on the tassets covering my hips.

"Squeal!" Nora cheered in a high-pitched voice. "If you had her monastic scapular, you'd be all set!"

"Monastic… what?"

"Sometimes mistakenly called a tabard?"

"Umm…" It sounded familiar, but…

"Like a surcoat?" Nora continued.

"You mean the apron thing with all the fancy embroidery?" There's no need for a giant bullseye, thanks.

"Apron thingy? You can't call it that."

Are you mocking my word choice? You just shouted "squeal" out loud!

"But you knew what I meant, so…"

"Never again!" Nora insisted.

"Alright, alright. But anyway…" Reality settled back into my thoughts. "Isn't this armor, even by itself, pretty distinctive? Even if I keep my mask on, it will attract attention." Unwanted attention.

"Only criminals wear masks in Turri. Dumb ones, anyway," Vernie clarified as a side note. "You'll have to get rid of it."

"How about I trade it for a helmet?" I asked hopefully, recalling that the slight bump on the back of my head was still there.

"Rae-Rae, you don't wear a helmet. Then nobody could tell you're *you*." She was missing the point. Both of them, actually…

"I think I should protect my head… or at least what's left of it…" I grumbled. "And I think it would be best to keep hiding my face for now."

"… The best I can do is this," Vernie murmured, handing me a polished steel circlet. "Just don't let anyone hit you in the head anymore, and you should be fine." It's not like I purposely got hurt.

I grunted and pulled off my mask, balling it up and stuffing it in my rucksack before donning the circlet. "I can still wear my cloak over the armor, right? I'll just keep my hood up, and my hair pulled back."

Aleph nodded. "That will help you hide, for now."

I didn't like how he tacked on that "for now" at the end.

"What about Nora?" I asked. "How can she protect her assets?"

Nora tittered. "Now that one, I like. Asset protection."

"There's still more in the box," Vernie asserted as she turned to Nora. "Help yourself."

Nora rummaged around momentarily before pulling out an intricately banded set of brown leather armor. Its wide, overlapping straps were encased by chainmail, while a more traditional soft leather backing allowed for a nicer feel against the body.

"The banding allows for a greater range of motion," Vernie explained. "In case you find yourself in tight spaces, as we discussed."

"Fantasy armor that adds plus five to defense *and* charisma? I'll take it!" Nora smirked. Why did she call it fantasy armor? Oh, no chest plate.

"Shouldn't there be a little more coverage here?" I asked. "I mean…"

"You always were a prude," Vernie remarked sharply.

"Not a prude! Pru*dent*!" I folded my arms. What's the point of wearing armor if *those* are exposed?

Vernie pulled out a small metal chest plate and snapped it in place. "Better now?"

"There goes my charisma bonus." Nora sighed whimsically. "I've never seen armor you could do that with, though."

Huh? Really? It seemed standard fare to me.

"It's adjustable for different occasions." Vernie waved her hand in the air. "However, neither armor set would survive a direct attack from a powerful demon, so don't be fooled by a false sense of security."

Nora and I nodded a bit numbly in response. It was going to take us a while to get used to Vernie.

"I want to see if I can put this on myself," Nora said as she stepped away for some privacy.

"Get used to carrying around a sword again." Vernie handed me a longsword sheathed in an engraved scabbard she had dug from the bottom of the box. "It's no Will of Euphridia, but it'll do for now."

I drew the sword from its sheath. It wasn't physically heavy, but it felt cold and somehow draining. My bat back home was a blunt weapon that had other purposes. I had even hit a few home runs with it back in the day. Swords have only *one* purpose, though, right? "Ah…"

"Don't worry, we'll retrieve your real one soon enough," Vernie claimed, misinterpreting my apprehension. "Now, where was that targe…" She practically dove into the box, rifling through the loose padding.

I was going to be over-equipped. How could I possibly manage it all *and* my rucksack? "It'd be weird… to walk around with a sword, a shield, and a staff, right?" I suggested. "Better to keep the blessed weapon on my person, I think. I mean, demons and all…" Then I could ditch the sword and shield and forget about the advanced level of hero dress-up we were playing.

Vernie gave me a look that mixed concern and pity in equal doses. "Rae-Rae. You need quick access to everything. *Different tools for different situations.* Turri is not very forgiving right now."

I glanced at Aleph, and he nodded slowly. "… Alright," I murmured as I absently buckled the sword around my waist. I planned on ignoring it for now, seeing as I wasn't sure I could use it with any skill or grace. As for the targe, I opted not to buckle it to my forearm but to slide it through the carrying loop of my rucksack, turning it into little more than dead weight.

Tetora rumbled behind me. "We will review basic sword and shield movements… soon."

Not too soon, I hoped.

Aleph cleared his throat. "Yes, *Rae and I* will do exactly that."

A snap of electricity appeared between the glare they shared, but Tetora was the first to break it. "Fine, start with the beginner's course. When you're ready, I'll show you some proper moves."

Aleph looked at me with chestnut eyes, his face lost in thought. "The first lesson is in just a few minutes. The sooner we start, the better," he murmured before moving to set up an area to practice.

Before I could really protest, Nora snapped her fingers from behind us, and I whirled around to see her strutting for all the world like a runway model. She even had the haughty expression of someone who refused to look you in the eye because you just weren't worth her time. I clapped dutifully just as she stopped before us, put her hand to her hip, and struck a pose. Her green cloak fluttered around the armor, and I was just a little suspicious she had used Ventos again under her breath.

"Very classy," I noted.

"Multi-classy," she agreed. "Soon, I'll be the queen of all trades. Then I—oh! Sword! Show it to me."

I drew the sword and handed it to her, handle first.

"Hmmm…" After brandishing it, Nora considered the blade. "Not for me." She gave it back, and I returned it to its sheath. "Ranged attacks are more my style, I think. Let me change what I said. I'll be the queen of all *suitable* trades."

"Ahh… I guess I better learn something about this then." I sighed wistfully as Aleph waved me over.

Aleph's first lesson was intentionally short, probably because I started off by saying, "I don't want to kill anyone. I know swords aren't toys, but slashing down people isn't really—"

"The first lesson will be how to avoid using it that way. We'll go over how you can use the blade's flat side to strike someone without causing too much damage."

"Wait. Isn't it live by the sword, die by the sword?"

He looked at me curiously. "Why limit yourself to those two choices?"

"No, no, the code of the blade and do or die or…" I paused, thinking about every self-insert swordmaster epic I had ever read. Your sword is your destiny? Kill or be killed? Isn't that the inevitable end of all those who wield one? However…

I paused, then said, "Raelynn… used her sword as more of a symbol, didn't she?"

"Wherever she could get away with it." Aleph smiled. "This conversation is very nostalgic, in fact."

"Huh?"

"By the time I met her, she already knew how to kill. She worried about that more than *anything*. She wanted to learn *careful* weapon handling. *Sometimes, the most important lesson is knowing that we can use a tool in more than one way.* Hmm…" he paused, folding his arms. "We'll skip the shield for now. Instead, why don't you show me how you would hold your sword?"

I huffed but drew the blade again, gripping it as tightly as possible with both hands.

"No," Aleph said firmly, taking the sword from me. "Let's try a handshake grip. Offer me your hand in friendship." That sounded easy enough. I held out my right hand expectantly, and he placed the sword hilt in the curve of my palm. "Now, grip the sword with your other hand as well. No. Too tight. Relax your right-hand grip and move your hand down away from the hilt just a little. That's right, you can even put your right thumb on the back of the hilt for extra control."

I looked up and down the sword shaft, trying to note my hand placement. "Now what?"

He picked up a stout stick and broke off several leafy side branches. "Parry me. When you can tap my shoulder with the flat of your blade, the lesson's over for the day."

"What if I hurt you?"

Aleph laughed for a moment, then frowned. "Oh, you're being serious. I apologize."

He wouldn't dare laugh harder… but still…!

"You won't," he said. "I know you, and I know that you're scared right now. Remember to relax your grip and have fun while you learn to work the sword like a lever."

Have fun? This is your idea of fun?

I *did* try to tap his shoulder, I swear. But eventually, my arms were just too exhausted to keep going. I slapped his stick with the flat of my blade several times, but his shoulder… Well, that was a very lofty goal, figuratively and literally.

"Let's call it here." Aleph smiled again. "And look. We're both still very much alive. Next time, we'll talk about a pommel strike."

"Pommel strike?"

"Yes. In fact. I suggest using it when you're in… the ox stance!" I stared suspiciously at his face for a moment, trying to discern if he was teasing me. Again, he had such a serene poker face!

"Is that even a real thing?"

"I wouldn't mention it if it weren't." He shrugged. "But enough lessons for now. Let's get moving."

✳✳✳

Post-Chapter Omake

Nora: *And then she called it an apron thingy.*

Olethros: *Did you not explain to her it is a monastic scapular?*

Nora: *Repeatedly and at length. It's like she was trying to come up with the most ridiculous names for it.*

Rae: *Armor poncho?*

Nora and Olethros: *You're not supposed to be here!*

Rae: ...*I've been getting that* a lot *lately.*

***

Post-Chapter Omake 2

Rae: *I hate it when someone tells me to just don't let it happen next time or be more careful, like Vernie did after I hit my head on that tree.*

Nora: *Advice like that assumes that lack of knowledge was the only contributor to the event.*

Rae: *Yeah! I already knew that bashing my head hurts. Probably better than almost anyone else!*

Nora: **facepalm**

Rae: *And now you do, too!*

CHAPTER 36: OH CAPTAIN, MY CAPTAIN

That afternoon, we prepared to leave the forest in earnest. We were well provisioned now, but that meant more to carry, especially since Tetora could not bear any extra weight.

"I'll be fine. At least let me carry my rucksack," Tetora demanded.

"No," Aleph replied bluntly.

"It is a *command*, not a suggestion."

Aleph raised an eyebrow. "Show me you can lift your arms above your head and hold them there for thirty seconds."

Tetora hesitated, then turned and snorted angrily.

"Just as I thought," Aleph murmured. "We'll take breaks every fifteen minutes."

Our pace was slow, but it was necessary. Although Tetora refused to complain about his injuries, he was clearly feeling their effects. His legs would twitch now and then, and sweat began to form on his brow.

Nora let him know she was concerned in her own unique way. "Are you sure you're a tiger?"

"What nonsense are you spouting now, magic rabbit?"

"Cats don't sweat like that. But look at you! Your fur looks like you just went swimming!"

"What do you mean? Sweating is normal, woman! I'm just fine." He patted her head roughly, purposely fuzzing her curly brown hair before he laughed. He *wasn't* fine, but there wasn't much more we could do about it right now.

Vernie led the way confidently, with Nora close to her side. Although I wasn't privy to their entire conversation, I caught Vernie demonstrating how to hold and throw a knife properly. Nora was so absorbed in her words I couldn't help but feel a bit jealous.

"Do not worry. She won't steal your friend away from you," Aleph teased me with a smile.

"I know…" I sighed. "I just… I don't know how to take her sometimes." Bonding with me one minute, pointing out my most significant flaws the next… and before I knew it, she was outfitting me in a full armor set. What would she insist on next?

"When you figure it out, please tell me the secret too."

"Aleph!" I said a little too loudly.

"I worry for her," Aleph admitted. "She has had a rough life. But she does not desire such pitying feelings from me. So I struggle instead to meet her where she needs me to be." He took a deep breath. *"It is a location that moves often."*

"I see…"

We reached the rocky foothills of the Turri Mountains just as sunset arrived. Tetora was excused from all the camp chores as we prepared for the night. While setting up my bedroll, I spotted Vernie with a flask inches from her lips.

"It's just a nightcap," she protested, even though I hadn't said anything.

"Okay."

"It's not like I *need* it."

"I believe you," I said as carefully as I could.

She exhaled angrily, took a sip, and capped the flask. "See? I'll be just fine without it."

Where does she need *me* to be right now? I pondered over my next words then said, "I'm proud of you."

"What?"

"Things have been tough, right?"

Vernie shrugged, her smirk showing a hint of defiance. "I'm still here, aren't I? That means I'm even tougher. Oh, and before I forget…" She put up a finger as if an afterthought just struck her. "She passes. Temporarily."

"Huh?" Who passes what?

"Your friend Nora."

"Wait. What about Nora?"

"She can stay in the party, for now. But if—"

I shot up. "How was that *ever even in question?*" I felt my heart leap with instant irritation.

Vernie let out a patronizing chuckle. "Well, I'm not going to trust *your* judgment right now. I'll be the one who decides who stays and who goes."

Okay, wow, no!

"You're not in charge!" I shouted.

"Then who is, Rae-Rae?" She turned her head innocently. "Who's the leader?"

I paused, trying to center myself. Her little nickname for me suddenly felt like a huge insult. "We don't need—"

"We do," she interrupted, her voice firm. "If you're not going to take the lead, *I* will. This is your last chance."

Forget being nice or meeting her in the middle.

Tetora was out; he was too sick. Aleph was wise, but there were certain other-worldly complications Nora and I couldn't tell him about, which would limit his decision-making capacity. Nora was just getting over her guilt, so she didn't need the burden of leadership. Above all else, there was no way I would let *Vernie* take the lead.

"Fine. I'm in charge!" I declared. "That means you have to follow my orders, right?"

"Aye aye, Holy Captain!" Vernie laughed in delight as she gave a mock salute. "So, what are they?"

"Don't ever do that again!"

The humor faded from her face as she took me in. Good, at least she was listening.

I took a breath and then expelled some harsh words. "I never want to find out that you or anyone else felt the need to judge or test another party member behind my back. We work together. That means no hazing, stupid rites of passage, survivor-style pranks, infighting—nothing like that! This is already hard enough. You said I'm too trusting? You don't trust my judgment about others? *Well, congratulations. Now you can spend your time working on earning* my *trust!"* I mean, she was the one who said don't trust her before, right? So, for once, I would listen to someone else's advice.

Vernie inhaled sharply. "Anything else, *Captain?*"

At least it was only the holy part that got dropped.

"No. Dismissed!"

***

"For homework, I want you to draw yourself," the occupational therapist instructed. "Let's test your pencil grip. I don't think you need to practice outlining with the bigger highlighters anymore."

"Home… work?"

"Oh, poor word choice. I know you'd rather do it at home," she said with an apologetic smile. "But this is an exercise that will help you to get to that destination." She placed a piece of white paper in front of me, which contained the outline of a woman, before putting a sheet of tracing paper on top. "You can use this as a base, but make the drawing yours. Take your time, and don't worry about any mistakes."

Right. The artist on the TV called them happy accidents, *which I found endearing.*

It was hard, but I was glad she left the room to let me work on it by myself. I knew my inability to manipulate the pencil wasn't the reason I was still here in the hospital, but it was nice to feel I was accomplishing something while I waited for my bloodwork to stabilize. I focused on creating a new me on the page, so absorbed that I did not hear the behavioral health nurse step back in.

"Tell me about your drawing," she said, catching me off guard.

"It's me," I said rather bluntly, never knowing what she was digging for.

"I like the shoulder pads." She smiled. "Very detailed."

"They're called pauldrons."

"Tell me about the other pieces of armor." So I did, pointing out how they fit together and worked as one for self-protection.

Oh, no one here has need of things like this anymore, do they?

"It looks so heavy to wear," she noted.

"It's not really. Not if it's made well and adjusted correctly to your shape. It can be a little warm, though, especially in the sun."

257

"It would be nice if we could walk around in armor all the time, wouldn't it? Then we would be protected from things that could physically hurt us."

Oh, it's one of those discussions.

"It can't protect you from everything." I sighed, trying to rush her through whatever she needed to say so she could document accordingly. "And sometimes you need to take it off."

"When do you take your armor off?"

"When I feel safe."

"What do you need to feel safe, Rachel?"

I almost said "my armor," but that would probably get me kicked out of group therapy again, and I enjoyed listening to the others. I wasn't ready to talk to them about myself yet, but knowing others were trying to figure out how to be normal in this world gave me a great sense of relief.

"Control," I said hesitantly. "When I'm the Captain, I can protect them all."

"Who?"

"Those that I care about. But I can't be the Captain they need anymore, so I had to let them all go."

***

I sat up in bed. Looking over at Nora, I contemplated waking her, but she had starfished and needed her sleep. Tetora was curled up in a ball next to Vernie, who was snoring fitfully. Aleph was on watch, leaning back against the flat of a large boulder, looking up at the night sky.

Since I didn't think I'd be falling back to sleep, I got up and walked over to him. "I had a strange dream about something that happened to me a long time ago," I admitted to him quietly as I took a seat, absently scratching the scars on my right wrist.

"Do you want to talk about it?"

"No." Just acknowledging it would be enough for now. I could fly apart about it later *when things were back to normal again.*

"Do you want to talk about something else?"

"Yes, please."

He gave me a soft smile. "Then shall we discuss cheesecake as the perfect dessert again? I look forward to trying it with you one day."

CHAPTER 37: FETID FOOTHILLS

Vernie avoided me as much as possible the following day. I also refused to look at her, at least when I thought she'd notice. It was the customary silent treatment plus complete denial of existence between two sullen females, each side having perfected an imaginary barrier that simply negated the other's presence. If I talked to Aleph, she would purposely disappear from the edge of my view. When she went to Tetora, I avoided them both like the plague. And never were our paths to cross that morning.

It did feel weird to be decorated in all the safe luxury a good set of armor could afford, though, especially when it was given to you by the person you were having a cold war with. She was still trustworthy, of course; I just didn't appreciate being treated like someone who needed to be carefully handled and manipulated. Therefore, I could not apologize first, even if I felt somewhat guilty.

Nora sat beside me, disrupting my imaginary isolation barrier as I ate my breakfast in heavy silence. "Got a reply," she said cryptically as she handed me her open journal.

I glanced down, and sure enough, another sheet of papyrus was shoved between two pages. The top contained the default confidentiality header, so I quickly skipped down to the meat of the memo.

To: Eleanora Beatrice Perez and Rachel Emily Smith

From: Clare Mercure (Human Resources)

RE: Nora's Request/NAUGHT Advertisement

Thank you for confirming receipt of my first letter via 'prayer request.'

The following attachment is in response to Nora's *'informational inquiry'* regarding NAUGHT.

Please note that Human Resources is in no position to grant "limitless, god-like powers to be used without consequence" to *anyone* and does not condone the use of such reckless powers by its employees, clients, volunteers, or customers.

ATTACHMENT: NAUGHT Advertisement

NAUGHT: Not A Universal God Hand Tool
NAUGHT is nothing on its own, but in the hands of content creators with working knowledge of *The Rules**, it has the potential to do anything.

NAUGHT-certified content creators use NAUGHT to bring their stories to life. See our customer success stories available on the DivinitEpub platform.

Interested in becoming a NAUGHT-certified content creator? Please contact Client Services at Cooperative Universal Publishing.

Together, we can adopt and adapt best practices throughout our shared realities.

Cooperative Universal Publishing
Connecting your world to ours.
**The Rules are subject to change without notice. CUP strives to index and document these ever-changing rules in real-time to ensure the optimal NAUGHT experience.*

The address for the North American headquarters was intentionally blurred out at the bottom of the document. I reread the document several times, scowling harder and harder on each pass. "What does this mean?"

"Yes, er…" Nora scratched her head. "They named NAUGHT… something it's not."

I bristled at that one. "You did that on purpose!"

"No, I think *they* did."

"They? You mean CUP?"

"Yes. Or the creator of the tool. I think it is a cautionary tale."

"Eh?" I asked as intelligently as I could.

"NAUGHT is nothing on its own." Nora pointed to the advertisement. "This next line makes me think it's a powerful tool in the hands of someone who knows what they're doing, but it isn't everything."

That was the God-hand part.

I scowled. "And how does this help us?"

"I'm not sure yet," Nora admitted. "But we asked and got an answer, at least. We still need to find NAUGHT, even if it can't do everything, because we need it to do *something*."

More nonsense. Great!

With careful slowness, I reread the advertisement. "The Rules… Didn't President Abrams say something about 'The Rules?'"

"He said he didn't know all of them when he was younger. But this says they're ever-changing," Nora replied.

"It'd be nice to know what they have to say right now," I mumbled speculatively.

"We should ask for a copy," Nora agreed. "I thought he was talking about publishing rules, but now… I'm not so sure."

"It would count as an informational inquiry, right?" I sighed. "Oh… but maybe it's only for content creators."

"We won't know until we ask. The worst she can do is say no."

And admonish us in HR-speak for even asking. But that still didn't have any real bite here. What was she going to do? Summon us to her office?

After breakfast, Aleph insisted on another sword lesson. I sighed again, realizing he wasn't going to let me just coast. The second lesson was more of the first, though he told me often to stop moving my hand past the hilt as I transitioned grips. He even showed me the *ox stance* (or, as Nora clarified, the Ochs stance), where you hold the sword in both hands, keeping it level with your head while sort of standing next to it. The technique made it easy to transition into a pommel strike, though again, there was no way I would connect with him. Aleph paid more attention to adjusting my footwork and repeatedly reminded me to control my swings. If I heard "it's not an ax" one more time...

I caught Vernie glancing at me now and then during the sword lesson, but Aleph was ensuring I paid a price every time I got distracted. A quick thwack would come with a stern reminder to "Keep your eyes on your opponent."

Nora watched the whole thing, though she was gracious enough not to comment on my flailing. Instead, she opted for encouragement. "Hey! Looks like you're getting the hang of it!" Ironically, I took the supportive gesture as a sign that I was doing worse than I thought.

"I'll believe that when *he* says that," I grumbled.

We broke camp a little while later. Vernie assumed the lead before I could even issue orders, signaling that not only would this be a long day, but likely the entire journey ahead would be equally taxing.

Nora hung back with the rest of the group, idly playing with the knife she received earlier. Tetora's determined but sickly gaze fixed on the landscape in front of us, and after a few dismissed attempts, I gave up trying to talk to him about how he was feeling. Aleph once again carried the bulk of our supplies without a single note of dissent.

The rocky foothills were just as sunny and dry as the wastes, though curly brown moss covered most dirt surfaces, which may have helped keep down the overall level of particulate dust.

As we continued deeper, I noticed a foul odor reminiscent of leaking sewage.

"What is making that *awful* smell?" I asked the party as we took another brief rest in the late morning.

Vernie shot me a withering look. "We're in malodorous mustelid territory. Don't even remember that much, huh?" It wasn't worth responding to her, even if the words out of her mouth made no sense.

Nora jumped up from the boulder she was sitting on. "Will we get to see one!?"

"Probably not," Vernie answered. "They rarely come out in the daytime."

"Rats," she sighed, sitting back down.

"No, more like giant, stinky mongooses that walk on two feet," Vernie corrected, wiping some sweat off her brow with a trembling hand. Had I upset her that badly? No… It's just warm out—and I'm not feeling guilty.

"Let's get moving," Tetora snapped, chafing at our slow pace. "We're wasting time."

The smell worsened the farther we progressed, and I knew there was no way I would eat anytime soon. Vernie still led the way, but she now stuck closer to the rest of us, her eyes darting back and forth as a slight frown settled on her features.

As we approached a hill, Vernie ascended ahead of us, and a particularly pungent wave of stench wafted past my nose, causing me to dry heave. "Uuuh, how long until we get through here?"

Instead of answering my question, Vernie suddenly took a few quick steps backward down the hill, positioning herself in front of me and causing all of us to halt. Before I could question her on what she was doing, she shouted "Incoming!"

As I craned my neck to look over her shoulder, my heart jumped at the sight: at least three dozen small, filthy creatures, about four feet tall, crested the hill, all poised for attack. They were a ferocious sight—sharp claws, pointed snouts, and jagged teeth. Some even clutched rocks in their clawed paws. Their meerkat-like features were marred by angry, ringed eyes that seemed to weep sorrowful tears.

"What are those?" I asked.

"Malodorous mustelids," Vernie answered curtly.

Oh, so that wasn't just random gibberish earlier.

Suddenly, one emitted a belligerent squawk, which the others reacted to as if it were a call to battle. In a frenzied blur, they surged towards us, pouring down the hill like a tidal wave of fury and claws.

I grabbed the hilt of my sword and began to pull it free, but something stopped me. Vernie's hand gripped my forearm, preventing me from drawing.

"Vernie!" I yelled, struggling as her firm grip on my arm held me back. Why was she stopping me? What kind of petty game was she playing? Now wasn't the time for this! Or...

A terrible thought gnawed at the back of my mind as the creatures rapidly closed in... She did say not to trust her.

"Vernie!" I shrieked. *"Let me go!"*

CHAPTER 38: MALODOROUS MUSTELID MELTDOWN

The malodorous mustelids poured down the hill at us in a ferocious wave of stench and hostility. My gaze shot between them and Vernie, who watched the approaching horde stoically, my arm still seized in her grasp.

Nora stepped forward. "I've got this. *These guys* are *definitely* flammable!" She began to chant the words to Ignis, obviously wanting to prove herself after our last skirmish.

"Enough!" I yelled at Vernie, feeling we couldn't waste another second with… whatever this was. I made a heartful attempt to pull free and draw my sword.

Vernie, however, yanked down, pulling me off balance. Her lips were near my ear as she implored, "Rae-Rae, this isn't right! These creatures *don't* act like this. I *know* them. Something is very, very wrong!"

The urgency in her tone gave me pause. Did she know demonic beasts? What exactly *had* she been up to these past seven years?

I resisted the urge to dismiss her statement outright, searched her face, and saw a mix of sincerity and desperation. "Okay," I agreed uncomfortably. "But we've got to stop them somehow." Their screeches signified they were out for our blood.

"I know, I know, but we can't just *murder* them. Stop Nora before she burns them to a crisp!"

Murder? Exterminating those angry, smelly beasts equates to murder in her mind? No one ever said being the Holy Captain would be easy.

"Nora!" I shouted. "Uh, crowd control—non-lethal?" It was a suggestion more than anything, but I knew better than to order *her* around.

Nora's brow furrowed with concentration as she continued casting her spell, but she managed a nod. As the wave of mustelids drew closer, Nora's chanting crescendoed, reaching a climax when the creatures were about fifty feet away.

"Ignis! Impedimentum Ignis!" Nora roared, slashing her hand from left to right across the path of the malodorous mustelids, then up, back, and down, forming a perfectly square box of ten-foot-high flames around them all.

Impedimentum? I guess adding the fancy-sounding words and articulate gestures made all the difference.

I heard a few angry screeches as some braver mustelids tested the walls, quickly learning through searing pain that this barrier was no mere illusion spell. The scent of singed fur mingled with the breeze, further exacerbating the already foul odor of the area.

Nora sagged from the effort she had just made. "That should hold them for a minute or two, anyway." She took a moment to catch her breath. "I don't think I'll be able to pull that off again for a while, so everyone else needs to take their turn *this round!*"

Did she think we were just playing some tabletop game?

Raeonna… She helped me with the demonic beasts back when we first arrived, but I hadn't heard a peep from her since then. Maybe I could call on her wisdom once more?

Raeonna?

…But there was no reply. I remember Raelina seemed more focused on doing anything she could to find her parents, but she was a local… albeit an ancient one. Maybe she had dealt with them in the past?

However, she too was nowhere to be found. Was my head really that empty?

"Vernie…" I finally focused on the person who claimed to be an expert. *Do you have any ideas about what their problem is?* I asked. "I mean, other than us, apparently."

"The matriarch must be upset. If we can calm her down, the rest will follow." Vernie squinted at the roaring flames. "She's not with the others in there… but she should be somewhere close by with direct sight over the battlegrounds."

It was Tetora's sharp eyes that spotted her first. "There." He pointed resolutely. "At the top of the hill, in the eastern mountain's shadow. I'll go knock some sense into her myself."

Aleph loomed in front of him, blocking his path. "You will do *no such thing*. You are still in no condition to engage in combat."

"I am a warrior, not an invalid. Get out of my way!"

No, none of that now. Damn it. Everyone is supposed to get along. But even I was failing at that. "Iron Tiger Tetora," I bellowed. "Stand down!"

"You *dare* to question my—"

"I don't question your ability, skill, strength, commitment, whatever. But I *am* questioning your judgment. Of course, you would *win*, but at what cost? Have faith in your companions, and let *us* handle this. Stop trying to shoulder everything yourself!" Hypocrisy isn't an uncommon trait for a fledgling leader, right?

"… Fine! Just take care of it quickly," he conceded with a snort. What a stubborn, obstinate fool. That's probably why I got along with him so well.

The matriarch was dancing with anger at her thwarted attack. She was beyond listening to reason like most enraged beings, but I felt I could almost understand her indignant hisses and screeches. Perhaps it was because she was standing on two feet, or maybe it was just her body language. In fact, her flying fastball fists of furry fury might have even been comical if… wait. *Comical…*

Irrational inspiration struck me.

"Nora," I asked tentatively. "Do you have enough juice for a wind spell?"

"Juice?" she gave me a flat look, signifying once again I had uttered something outside of her range of preferred word choices. "Yes, but how would that help, exactly?"

"Um… fastball special?" I suggested, already trying to picture myself as a strong, aerodynamic superhero who laughs in the face of danger. Oh, right, the sword. One or two practice sessions were not enough to make me proficient. I quickly unbelted it, choosing the staff I could control better instead. Too bad I didn't have a virtual inventory to hide the sword in, but I'd probably just fill it up with shiny rocks and other useless sundries. Although… some rocks I found here and there but had to leave behind were nice… Wait. Focus, Rachel. Superhero, remember? *Superheroes can do anything they put their minds to.* "Ready for takeoff!"

Her face lit up momentarily before a slightly worried frown appeared. "You better stick the landing," she warned.

I *can do* this, I told myself again. I just have to. Thinking back on my fight with the boat-oar-sized sword-wielding brigand, I focused on how I had felt at the moment: strong, confident, and empowered by the trust my friends and teachers had in me. Those very feelings came rushing back, and a warm, glowing aura appeared around me. "I'll stick like glue." Maybe not exactly *Raelynn's* words, but I was sure I captured her general sentiment. That was the trick, right? Visualize to actualize!

"Wha—" Nora stopped short, leaving her question for later. "Start sprinting. On three, jump!"

I ran, focusing all the power in my lower half. When Nora hit three, I leapt as high as I could. My amity-assisted jump would have earned me gold, even before Nora's spell caught my backside.

"Ventos!" Nora yelled.

As I rocketed toward the mustelid matriarch, I heard Nora's voice receding behind me as she added, "Good luck! Don't splat!"

Splat? *I could splat?* Why did she have to *say* that!? *That would hurt!* I stumbled at the thought of injury, my aura momentarily flickering.

Fortunately, I was able to catch myself before tumbling out of control, but I then realized I had overshot the matriarch by a few yards. I sprung to my feet and turned just as the giant mustelid was on me with a blur of teeth and claws. She was too close to bring my staff in for a full strike, but between it and my armor, I turned away her speedy blows with a few lucky but mostly intended moves of my staff.

Her assault continued in a relentless stream of swings and cuts with her razor-sharp claws, her natural weapons flashing high and low. What I initially assumed to be erratic attacks revealed a coordinated effort, the matriarch searching for an opening in my defenses. Her jaws snapped bites at my face to drive me back, and it was clear that her fangs were sharp enough to put a quick end to my part in this story.

At first, I mistook shadows from a nearby mountain for obscuring her form but then realized unnatural darkness covered her. A gloomy, almost sticky miasma had surrounded her, oozing from the outer edges of her eyes. I wracked my brain even as I gave up ground, trying to troubleshoot her malady. Was it… concentrated animus? Could it be disrupted, just like how I managed with that enlisted demon? But the staff hadn't sparked even once since it had come into contact with her, so I remained doubtful.

While still doing my best to avoid every blow and snap of her jaws, I tried to formulate a new plan. I dared to glance back down the mountainside and saw the wall of flames had diminished to half of its original height. A few mustelids were successful in high-jumping over them. Attrition was out; I needed to end this quickly.

I needed to just get in for a punch or a slap somehow… Well, it'd be worth a try, anyway. Otherwise, I'd have to end up doing something even worse. A hazardous idea came to my mind, and I executed it before I could second-guess myself—allowing her to chomp down with those teeth she was so eager to use. With a wet slam, her jaws closed on my staff. *Perfect!*

Releasing my grip, I caught the next slash of her claws with a chest block, sweeping my other hand up and grabbing her arm. The surprised creature lost precious moments fighting with my staff, allowing me to pull her close to me while retracting my blocking hand for a punch before she could disengage. As expected, she didn't bother trying to escape but went for a bite to my throat instead. *Fancy armor, don't fail me now,* I silently prayed as I jerked my upper body to the side, taking her teeth on my shoulder pauldron.

She hissed in frustration, but it cut off abruptly as I drove my fist into her gut. I put only a little strength into the blow, instead focusing on pushing my inner amity out through my fist. For a tense moment, I wasn't sure it had worked, but then she convulsed in my arms, fell limp, and slumped towards the ground. Oh no, had I done… the unspeakable!?

I eased her down as best I could, anxious to find any signs of life. Thankfully, she took a breath, and then I could see the other changes in her. The thick miasma seeped away until fully dissipated, and her face no longer contorted in rage.

Her eyes opened, and at first, panic gripped her even as I backed away. She hissed several times as she started retreating before suddenly freezing in place.

"H-hey now…!" I said cautiously, my hands up nonthreateningly.

She sniffed tentatively at the air, and her mangy ears popped up, one after the other. When she finally realized I was no longer interested in exchanging blows, she let out a languid sigh. She even managed to look embarrassed about the whole thing by flattening her ears to the side and giving a sidelong glance.

"It's okay. I know you weren't exactly yourself just now," I murmured. Then I turned toward the bottom of the hill, where the walls of the flame cage were dying out. I pointed both awkwardly and urgently. "Um… Can you please stop them before someone gets hurt?"

Even though she didn't speak, she immediately seemed to understand what I wanted. She bounded up to a cliff edge and let forth an ear-piercing screech, causing the rest of the mustelid pack to freeze in place. Half a dozen had already managed to encircle Aleph and Vernie, but they suddenly fell back at the matriarch's resounding cry. Aleph, however, quickly snatched one of the slower ones by the scruff of its neck, perhaps as insurance for the others to keep themselves in check.

"Um. So… how about we negotiate a peace treaty?" I asked hopefully.

The matriarch gave me another suspicious look, then bounded toward her pack. After she turned back and screeched at me insistently, I carefully followed her down the hillside.

***

Post-Chapter Omake

Nora: *Fastball special?*

Rae: *Fastball special!*

Tetora: *A secret fighting technique from the next world. I wish to master it!*

Rae: *Uh… It'll be a little hard to get you the serialized comics, er… sacred scrolls…*

CHAPTER 39: SECRET TUNNEL

After careful negotiations with body language, the mustelids pulled back farther from the party. We also regrouped ourselves, though Aleph kept one mustelid firmly clasped in his arm.

"Let him go," I advised. "Let's not make the situation worse."

"Rae." Aleph frowned. "These are demonic beasts. It's impossible to reason with them."

"Aleph, she *just* did!" Nora snapped, pointing at me. "Besides, if they can't be reasoned with, then holding one hostage is *pointless.*"

Aleph opened his mouth to speak but then looked back at the group, his eyes troubled. "This is a trap, to be sure..."

"I told you, I *know* these guys," Vernie argued with wildly gesticulating arms. "Do as the Holy Captain says!"

Oh, the full title came back now...

Aleph's ears twitched with irritation, but he warily lowered the mustelid to the ground. As soon as it was free, it quickly darted off to the matriarch. After a quick sniffing session with the previous prisoner of war, she stormed forward.

"Ssakrak!" she admonished Vernie.

I turned to her. "What does that mean?"

"How should I know?"

"You're the one who *just* said you knew them."

"I can't *speak* with them. I just know how they act." Vernie shrugged.

"Just apologize for whatever you did!" I demanded.

"I didn't do anything! I just—"

"Skraak!" the matriarch interrupted angrily.

Vernie blinked and gave it a shot. "Er... I'm... sorry?"

"Charakas?" she questioned before sighing. "Krestakkok…"

Maybe I still had some brownie points to spend. "Uh… ma'am? We need to go to another place called Kopria…" I tried pointing to the path we had been traveling. "Through these hills up—"

The matriarch started chittering angrily at her subordinates, and some returned her… words? One large mustelid, whose fur was noticeably singed, appeared to be arguing with her. She let it continue for a moment before rising off her haunches and slapping it forcefully across the face with an openly clawed paw. It yowled, then lowered itself to the ground submissively. *Ouch.*

She snorted derisively, then pointed to a path off to the side that looked like a small game trail.

"Oh, I don't think that will work for us…" I started, once again unsure if my words were working.

"Critakak." She gestured again imperiously.

I set my jaw. "Up that way!" I pointed again.

"Chatah!" With that command, all of her uninjured minions lined up to block our path, assertively aiming their rears at us.

"Wait, wait." I held up my hands. There was no way I was going to be a target of *that!*

"She's going to lead us through their burrows!" Vernie inhaled suddenly. "Why would she do that?"

"Burrows?" Oh Goddess, how smelly would it be in such cramped quarters?

A gust of wind blew down the mountainside, and Tetora's ears flicked back as he seemed to snarl without sound. "Against my better judgment, we should take her up on the offer. There are several men up in the hills, and they're covered in blood."

"Wait. We need to help them." I balked instinctively before realizing we wouldn't be much help without a healer.

"Not their own blood, but mustelid blood. We'll be next, if not for any good reason except simple association."

"Wait, are these guys at war with someone? Who?" I blinked. A loud brass horn pierced the air as if to answer, reverberating through the entire area. "What was that?" I gasped, half-deafened by the frightening sound. The mustelids quickly headed towards the game trail with flattened ears and tucked tails.

Vernie hauled me towards the side route even as the matriarch took point. "Now's not the time, Captain. Ask inane questions later."

The small trail wound around the shadowed side of a hill and under a few outcroppings of stone before ending at a short, hidden crack on another small cliff face. A group of mustelid sentries guarded it, each one almost as big as the matriarch herself. The unarmed sentries, save for their claws, eyed us nervously, but we were allowed to pass without any sort of scuffle. They darted inside after us, pushing rocks and camouflaging vegetation across the opening.

I believed it would be a tight squeeze once deeper inside, but I was mistaken. As we entered the passage, it was clear their living space was a network of expansive, interconnected caverns. Nora summoned a bouncing ball of light that followed her movements perfectly, keeping our immediate surroundings well-lit. I noticed several glittering stalactites dripping from the ceiling, turning the uneven yet smooth stone floor into a slip-and-fall lawsuit waiting to happen. Now and again, we heard the call of the brass horn, which would cause us all to freeze. I found myself more and more anxious every time I heard it, though.

"Rae?" Nora asked for the fifth time.

"Sorry, sorry. It just sounds…"

"Like they're moving away from us." She nodded confidently.

I was going to say "terrifyingly familiar," but I decided to keep it to myself.

We eventually stopped for a short break in a large, wet, underground gallery, where everyone seemed to relax slightly. "So, now, can I repeat my question? Who were they?"

"That was the call of the Holy Order of Blue," Aleph answered with an absent stroke of his short brown beard. "They must be at odds with these demonic beasts."

Holy Order of Blue… It didn't sound ominous on its own, but for some reason, the phrase made me bristle.

Vernie crossed her arms. *"They're not demonic beasts. They're just* misunderstood."

"They're hostile to—"

"Of course, '*demonic beasts*' will be hostile!" Vernie spat. "It's right there in the name. It's such a *terrible thing* to be named so poorly. But it's just a designation. There's no truth behind it."

"Their names and labels did not come first." Aleph shook his head stubbornly. "Their origins and behaviors did."

"They were hostile towards us an hour ago," Tetora snapped. "Or did you conveniently forget that?"

"They probably just confused us for those holy knights," Vernie argued. "Besides, *they* started it. You act hostile towards an intelligent creature, and you'll get it back in spades."

"Explanation, please," Nora interrupted. "What do you mean, *they* started it?"

"Demonic beasts and, uh, *other creatures*, like malodorous mustelids, used to roam the wastes," Vernie said unsteadily. "But the holy knights routinely cull them for 'training purposes.' There aren't too many left these days. This might be the last bastion for them."

Aleph raised his head. "Demons engineered demonic beasts to attack human and hybrid settlements! They did not stick just to the Wastelands, either. Historical records clearly show they attacked settlements all over Speranza. It's *only natural* that the holy knights would—"

"When's the last time a demonic beast attacked a settlement?" Nora interrupted.

"You saw the redbacks when you arrived. Proof right there!" Tetora grunted.

"Who was there first?" Nora pressed the argument forward, but neither Tetora nor Aleph answered in words, just derisive snorts.

Nora continued, "As I recall, they weren't in the village limits, either. They were in that weird stone forest, next to the old demon king's ruined castle in the middle of nowhere."

The party stopped talking abruptly, and we mulled over the others' arguments. Aleph and Tetora's faces contorted with subtle frowns as they exchanged frequent glances, though they often observed the mustelids as if expecting them to turn on us. I felt

Vernie silently reflect on something else, mostly because she caught my gaze for a moment before looking down at the slick stones before her feet. After a few minutes of awkward tension, the matriarch chittered at us again and began to advance deeper into the underground passageways.

"Well, I'm going to do what *she* says." I stood up with a sigh. "She seems like she knows what she's talking about."

***

Nora's Journal

Unreliable ~~Malodorous~~ Skreethi Mustelid to English Dictionary

Ssakrak: What the hell, I thought we were partners!

Skraaak: You led those @#$%#s here.

Charakas: You have no idea what I'm saying, do you?

Krestakkok: Ignorant hairless monkeys.

Critakak: This way, if you don't want to die.

Chatah: Now listen here, you little...!

CHAPTER 40: REBRANDING

We continued through the caves, which had broken into numerous small side galleries where significant bodies of water gathered, though it was too dark to assess their proper depths.

"The water's probably too cold to bathe in," Vernie warned me as she caught me eyeing a rather serene-looking pool.

"I prefer privacy anyway…" I wasn't sure I could dismiss our forceful tour guides. Either way, trying to get the stench off now would be a grand exercise in pointlessness.

"Thanks…" Vernie said mutedly.

"Huh?"

"For believing me earlier. I know I haven't earned your trust yet, but—"

"That's not true," I interjected guiltily. "I do trust you… I was just, you know." Annoyed that you would *even think* that Nora might not be trustworthy. But I supposed that from her point of view, an *alien dark mage* might be somewhat suspicious…

"I told you not to, though."

"Yeah, well, that doesn't mean I have to listen." I shrugged, taking a seat as we took another break. "And… to tell the truth, I owe you an apology also. I did have a moment where I thought the worst of you… when you first stopped me from drawing my sword." I sighed as I reflected on it, a fresh wave of guilt coming over me.

Vernie smiled. "No, that's good! I'm glad you listened at least a little."

I laughed and shook my head, feeling the tension between us vanish so completely that I wondered why it was ever there in the first place.

"Can I keep calling you Rae-Rae?" Vernie asked with a playful glint in her eyes. "Holy Captain is too formal."

"…I never said you couldn't."

She cleared her throat and continued, more relaxed now. "I know they *stink*, but they're great sentries. I've been giving them food in exchange for alerting the gang about potential slave raids. Of course, they just informed us about anyone coming back down the other way into the forest. But still, they work for cheap!" She pulled out a bag of old apples and tossed it to our escorts.

They tore the bag apart, snapping up the contents in seconds. Two of them savagely fought over the last apple, while a third one, scrawnier than the rest, looked onward with hopeless desire. The matriarch snorted loudly, inspiring the bigger two to split it in half to share.

Nora held out an apple of her own carefully, offering it to the third one. He sniffed it tentatively, then plucked it out of her hand. Nora then turned her piercing gaze towards me. "Malodorous mustelids… they really *do* look like 'the toxic trio of tyranny,' don't they?"

The toxic trio of tyranny. Three particularly obnoxious girls with high-pitched voices we had the displeasure of knowing back in high school. They had a terrible habit of humiliating their peers publicly for likes on social media. They were also the ones who used to call Nora a shameful little ankle-biter. Me? I was an "ugly goliath." It didn't mean anything to me, though, since I had never considered myself ugly. Awkward? Sure. Weird? Yeah. But ugly? I mean, as long as I kept somewhat covered… I didn't think I was *ugly*-ugly. And goliath? Well, if you're tall, you're tall. It's just simple genetics and a bit of RNG. Just give up on finding cheap pants that are long enough.

While absently scratching my head, I focused more on Nora's observation, which gave me a bit of déjà vu. Have we discussed their similarities before?

"Yeah, I totally see it," I finally responded. "It's the screeching chitters and that heavy, clumping mascara they used to wear. But honestly, I think these guys are nicer than them, so I can't think of them as *demonic*. I mean, I'll admit they seemed rather rabid at first, but after I discharged the matriarch's animus with a punch, she—"

"*You did what?*" Tetora interrupted me.

I quickly explained, to the best of my ability, anyway, about the dark miasma that had surrounded her and how I had counteracted it.

"Rae. Demonstrate your attack on me," Tetora ordered.

"You want me to punch you…?"

"Yes. With amity! See if you can punch out the poison." I had never heard anything so ridiculous come out of his mouth before.

"But I don't see any animus around you…"

"Punch me," Tetora insisted.

Since no one moved to stop me, I repeated my earlier performance with a glowing fist, aiming for his upper arm instead of his abdominal wounds, but to no effect.

"That was not a punch," Tetora grunted. "Harder!"

"The punch isn't the point." I had pushed my amity straight into him just like I had done with the matriarch. No reaction, nothing.

"Just try again." I switched sides, but again, nothing happened.

"You're not doing it right. Do it again."

Aleph finally stepped between us and put a hand on Tetora's shoulder. "Could you tell me exactly *why* you are insisting on this idiocy?"

"I want to be sure I do not become enraged as she did." Tetora gestured to the matriarch. "I do not want to lose my ability to rationalize." So you finally admit the mustelids also have such an ability…

"Your temper and intelligence are the same as always," Aleph said, shaking his head, "short and lacking."

"What was that!?" Tetora demanded.

"Your evidence. You did not strike me for uttering a provoking verbal insult, so you are fine."

Tetora blinked several times, then turned away, his tail swishing wildly. "Hmph."

Nora cleared her throat in exasperation. "*You were saying*, Rae?"

"Oh, yeah. If we tell the holy knights about what happened, maybe they'll…"

"They won't stop," Tetora muttered, his back still turned. "It's part of their Purpose to kill demonic beasts."

"To hell with some randomly assigned Purpose!" I screeched. "What about critical thinking skills!? Where is that in all of this!?"

"You're a genius!" Nora suddenly stood up. Oh, I had never been accused of *that* before.

"What?"

"Critical thinking skills. Malodorous mustelids… are considered to be demonic beasts. Name, Purpose. They're historically linked. So, let's just stop calling them by that name. That's all. Then their Purpose becomes, well, whatever. I say we just don't bother giving them one at all."

"What?" I repeated myself.

"Let's just come up with a new name for them and leave it at that," Nora repeated. I glanced at the mustelids.

"But *we're* not allowed to assign those things, are we?" Also, how would that change anything?

"Relias is a priest, right? We'll get him to finalize it."

Great, another side quest.

"But first," Nora continued, "let's come up with a new name. Don't want to have him work too hard and all…"

Was she serious about all this? Does it work that way for cr… animals, too?

I began to ponder. "Too bad we can't ask them what they *want* to be called…" The whole thing with renaming people against their will was still prickly in my mind. If your name isn't something you can identify with, why shouldn't you be allowed to change it? I mean… through the proper process, of course. But what was the appropriate process here?

"Skreethi." The matriarch pointed directly at me.

I blinked. "Did she just—"

"Skreethi," she insisted again, patting her belly.

"She just wants your apple," Vernie explained with a shake of her head. "She knows there's some left."

That was some pretty universal body language right there again… Are they *just* animals? I was beginning to doubt that demons had anything to do with these indeterminately intelligent creatures.

The others also began to mimic her, making noises that came very close to sounding like "skreethi" while patting their bellies.

I pulled out yet another less-than-fresh apple I had saved from lunch and tossed it to her. She caught the apple quickly enough and downed it in just two bites. The others slumped some, but no one was in a position to argue with her about the serving size.

"Skreethi… doesn't have any meaning to us, right?" Nora frowned. "But that actually might be a good name for them. No preconceived notions." She opened her journal and clicked her pen audibly, which caused me some anachronistic anxiety. "We'll get Relias to re-assign their Purpose if they *really* need one, but let's just list their discerning features." She started writing while she spoke. "Matriarchal society. Communicate with vocal sounds and arm gestures. Observed using tools."

"Tools? When?" I asked.

"They threw rocks, remember?"

"Oh, right."

She drew a sketch in her journal and labeled it "Skreethi Matriarch."

"Nora…" I frowned some, looking at her sketch.

"What? I'll finish it up later. Pencils, oh, er, charcoal sticks, would be better for this, anyway." She put the pen away quickly.

"The way you drew her…" She had outlined the matriarch in the "cute woodland animal" style, blunting her snout and enlarging her eyes while minimizing her teeth and numerous claws. She had also given her a full, pristine coat of speckled fur that gave her a plush, inviting look. "You're taking an awful lot of creative license with this."

"They're gonna need the marketing." She shrugged. "Think of it as a re-brand."

"You *really* like them, huh?" Maybe she felt bad about wanting to incinerate them earlier?

"More than the toxic trio, so, yeah. This isn't much, but maybe it's a start. I'd hate to see them disappear."

"I still think you need to warn people about their stench, at least," I advised.

"Musk," Nora corrected haughtily.

"Because… that sounds better?"

"Yep."

Nora jotted a few more notes and then closed the journal. "Lead the way, Skreethi Matriarch."

The matriarch, who had been lounging and completely ignoring the latter half of the discussion, stood up and stretched before slowly waddling onward.

CHAPTER 41: TARGE TUTORIAL

It was hard for me to measure the time we spent with the Skreethi, primarily because we spent long periods traversing underground. Sure, we returned to the surface intermittently through the rocky foothills, but it all got somewhat confusing with how the sun seemed to shift around every time we saw it. We just ended up proceeding slowly and sleeping when it seemed appropriate.

Along the way, I realized there were many more Skreethi than I could have imagined. Whole families appeared and disappeared from view in the caves. Some watched us nervously while others ran up close as if they had been dared to do so. A few snarked at our backs, but it only took a look from the matriarch to make them scatter. Here and there, though, Skreethi would exchange some cuter-sounding wordless banter with us, then shake their heads as we didn't seem to get their meaning.

Aleph took time during our frequent breaks to give sword lessons. It was the lightest of taps, but during one such training bout within a large stone chamber, I finally managed to hit his shoulder with the longsword.

"I'm done now, right? Can we stop with the sword lessons?" I gave him my very best "reward me" smile.

"Of course," he agreed, just a little too quickly.

"O-oh! Then, why don't we—"

"Get your targe." Although his voice was as gentle as always, I found myself unable to argue, even though I really, really wanted to. The "dad effect" was strong with him.

I fiddled with my rucksack strap and freed the leather-bound shield. As I started to slip my left arm through the double straps, Aleph cleared his throat.

"Give it to me," he said as he held out his hand. I complied without protest, secretly hoping this lesson would be all talk and no work!

"Now, try hitting my shoulder again," he instructed as he equipped the targe himself. Oh, for the love of…

I had no words, and neither did he. Instead of explaining anything about the history, composition, or general usefulness of the targe, he simply showed me how effective it was at deflecting everything I had just learned with the longsword. After I stubbornly learned that lesson, he started on the next topic without any introduction. Without warning, he used the targe to deflect my sword thrust and then swiftly countered, knocking me back with a solid bash.

"Hey!" I shouted as I stood up with an angry start. "That's cheating! You didn't tell me you were going to do that!"

"Oh? So I should tell you I'm going to strike back? As your opponent, you should take that as a given."

"Just give it back!" I demanded, wiping my wet, muddy hands. "I'm gonna show you!"

"Of course." He held out the targe, and I snatched it away carefully, half afraid he was setting up a trap. "You're not… going to tell me about this thing?"

Aleph picked up my previously discarded staff and started wrapping some padding around one of the ends. "The targe you're holding is constructed of thin wooden boards held together by wooden pegs. The rim is made of iron, and its front is made from cowhide that has been riveted in place. The back of the targe has been padded with straw and cloth to absorb impact. The straps have been replaced at least once, possibly twice. And while I don't have a specific tool of measure, it appears its diameter is about nineteen and a half inches. The most fascinating thing about this particular targe, however…" he paused as he looked directly at me.

"Yes? What?" I waited expectantly. Was it once owned by some legendary warrior? Did it have some epic backstory? The rivets had an intricate design on the front; maybe it was a famous maker's mark?

"…is it has *finally* captured your attention as a necessary tool for offense and defense!"

I scowled at him intensely as the rest of our group burst out laughing. Even the Skreethi Matriarch, who had been lounging on her side, chittered enthusiastically. She *definitely* understood more than she could say.

"What is this, '*Gang up on Rae Day*?'" I snarked as I equipped the targe.

Aleph blissfully ignored my grumpiness. "Now, I want you just to practice deflecting my attacks with the shield. I will go slowly at first, and we will pretend this is a spear." Aleph brandished my padded staff. "Are you ready?"

"I suppose…" I started to re-sheath the sword.

"No. You'll be using that, too."

"But… I'm clumsy! I should learn the shield by itself, then put them together later."

"No," he insisted. "Focus on the shield for now, but keep the longsword in your right hand and use it when you feel it's appropriate."

He didn't strike with the makeshift spear all that quickly, but I still had trouble deflecting it at first. Trying to meet each thrust dead on with the center of my targe was my first mistake; directly opposing forces don't like to turn suddenly after crashing into each other. I also realized I had to push a little. He wasn't just tapping anymore but putting weight behind the shaft. However, when I caught the hit just right, it didn't take all that much effort to turn aside the strike successfully, and it even seemed to add something to my counters.

Sometimes, he struck at my sword arm, and I deflected blows there as well. If I set it up right, typically more from dumb luck than a concerted effort, I could also get the shield in the offensive mix, but overall, it was still weird trying to manage the sword and shield together. When I finally established the rhythm of blocking with the shield and then attacking with my sword, Aleph destroyed my entire worldview.

"If you keep that up, you'll surely lose."

"What do you mean I'll lose?"

"The shield is not merely a counterbalance to your sword. You are leaving yourself wide open. The shield should protect you even as you attack, not just before and after."

"But…" That's how it works in video games.

"Well… I did warn you this time. Remember that."

I did not exactly listen. Or maybe I just didn't understand. In any case, he spent the next several minutes showing me my mistakes by hitting me with the padded end of the staff almost every time I attacked, even when I parried him with the shield first. Frustration overwhelmed me. I couldn't keep everything in my head at once and lost my stances. There were just too many things to consider. However, there was one way I knew of to show him what I could do. *Just imagine yourself as a superhero again.*

I felt the amity flow through me, providing a sort of sureness in my muscles. My armor and sword felt lighter, also making me feel I could move faster. A soft golden aura surrounded me as I straightened my posture, ready to engage. Enough getting knocked around! Time to show I'm not completely pathetic!

"I forfeit." Aleph held up his hand.

"Already? But I didn't even——"

"Even with the worst technique imaginable, you will surely win without gaining any benefit from the exercise. Therefore, it is not appropriate to continue until you stop using amity." He resolutely turned away from me.

"But… it's too hard otherwise."

"It is very likely that you will encounter opponents for whom amity alone will not be enough, but I am not one of them. There may also be times when using amity to its fullest extent is simply not a wise choice. You cannot just train what you are good at. You must train various skills to respond appropriately to different threats."

I sighed, finding my glow already dissipating. "It's all just too much…" I still couldn't get it right. I took a few hits from the padding, and while they did little more than sting, it was just a constant, crushing reminder that I was just a fake with no natural talent of my own.

"Rae!" Tetora's voice cut through my thoughts.

"What! What now? I get it; I'm stupid. Okay!?" My voice cracked, and tears welled up from frustration. My arms and feet just couldn't coordinate themselves.

He folded his arms. "You're not stupid. Just stop thinking so hard."

"What do you mean, just stop—"

"You're getting in the way of yourself!"

I took a moment to kick at the stony floor in frustration before righting myself and trying again.

Tetora yawned, slapping his tail on the ground. "Just do better. Don't think about anything else."

I hoped his students didn't have to *pay* him for his teachings. *Git gud. Gee, why the hell didn't I think of that!?*

Except it worked.

As long as I focused on other things, my movements became more natural, like a choreographed dance triggered by my opponent's actions. If my mind got in the way, though, it just kept short-circuiting on the idea that *I'm never going to figure this out.* Once my brain and I finally agreed not to think about the whole situation too hard, we were happier with what we needed to do: getting this embarrassing show over with!

I made great strides once I realized that both my arms could indeed move independently of one another. My left arm, equipped with the targe, deflected oncoming attacks before, during, or even after my right attacked, depending on the opportunity presented. Of course, this is not to say I didn't use the sword defensively, either. There was a certain rhythm to sparring, though the tempo varied quite often. I started comboing the blocks, chaining a moderately successful strike here and there in faster succession.

"Much better," Tetora said approvingly after four successful deflections in a row, scratching at his ear.

"This is a good place to stop," Aleph agreed. "Let's not get too tired and pick up bad habits."

A weltering of various emotions filled me, but ultimately, exhaustion won out. "Okay. Thank you, Grandmasters." I bowed to them both, maybe even a little sincerely. The matriarch, interestingly enough, stood up, turned to them, and also bowed. Was she making fun of me?

Time passed as we continued our underground and aboveground journey through Skreethi territory. We ate several small, cold meals interspersed between four long rests before daylight again poured in from around the corner of another cracked cavern wall.

The matriarch thumped her tail, and two scrawny-looking Skreethi darted through the opening on all fours. It was a few minutes before they returned, striding casually on their hind legs.

"Seras," one of them reported to the matriarch.

She turned then and glared at Vernie. "Krreshat!"

"Uh, right then?" she responded with little conviction.

Her response must have been satisfactory because they all suddenly ran off back the way we came. Vernie also peered out the exit carefully after letting her eyes adjust to the daylight.

"Well, I'll be... it's Lake Potiri! Looks like we took a smelly shortcut. But this is the perfect place to clean up."

I didn't notice their smell anymore. Had I gotten used to it, or had I just stopped associating it with something bad? We started to head towards the lake, but I just couldn't get over the abrupt abandonment.

"I feel like we should have at least said thank you..." I murmured, adjusting the rucksack on my back. An apple, which I had saved as it was fresher than the others, fell out from the poorly secured top and bounced several times, taking on a few dents. I could have eaten it before it developed a bruise, but I was just so sick of apples. "Ah... I'll just roll this back in the cavern. I'm sure some lucky Skreethi will find it."

"Don't dawdle," Vernie warned as the others approached the inviting lake.

As I returned, I found the same two Skreethi lookouts swinging sticks at each other. When we locked eyes, they gasped and darted around the corner as if I had caught them red-handed.

"You know… I think you were on to something earlier with those rocks as ranged weapons," I called after them as I rolled the apple farther in. "Your arms are a little too short for close combat, and your enemy rides horses, right? But if I were you, I'd sharpen some sticks and learn to throw them. Then you wouldn't have to get in so close."

The two slowly returned around the corner with flattened ears and low tails, chewing on the apple's last bits.

"You guys… understand every word out of my mouth, don't you?" I finally asked.

They made a show of looking at each other awkwardly for a few moments but avoided making any noises in response. On the off chance that they didn't, I took one stick and gestured at its end. "Sharp. Like teeth." I pointed to one of my canines. "Then throw." I hurled it at the wall, wondering if it would work for me, too. But then that would mean *even more training* for yet a different weapon proficiency.

The one on the left bowed, while the other turned with a startled jump before smacking them several times. The first one reciprocated in kind, and they both devolved into a dust devil of teeth and claws.

"Uh," I started, and they both paused, breaking off from each other.

"No, it must have been my imagination. Too bad… But thanks for everything!" I waved and left them to practice in private. I wouldn't rat them out to anyone. It wasn't any of my business, anyway.

CHAPTER 42: PARTY OF FIVE

We were now well within Turri's borders, way past Fort Turri, and hopefully way, way past the holy knights bent on depopulating the world of the newly rebranded Skreethi. Outside the caverns, we found towering pines buffeted by continual gusts of wind coming down from the edge of the mountains. We took some time to bathe in Lake Potiri, and I spent the better part of two hours trying to scrub out any possible lingering musk that had worked its way into my clothes. A smoky, somewhat petulant fire from sappy, green firewood helped warm and dry us out overnight before continuing towards the east.

Unlike the Wastelands, the winding dirt roads we eventually intersected were full of travelers, mostly humans, many riding horses in pairs. Occasional wagoners passed us, usually shouting barely understandable curses at us for forcing them to slow down a little. Vernie took the lead, sandwiching Nora and me in the middle of the group before Tetora, and then Aleph brought up the rear.

"So rude," Nora muttered as yet another pompous ass drove his galloping horse too close to her. "What the heck is everyone's problem? *Can't they see we're walking here!?*"

"Want to switch sides?" I was a bigger target, bound to cause more damage if they hit, so maybe they'd give us more space?

"No, then I wouldn't get to complain as loudly. But really, it's like they speed up *after* they see us!" She was right about that last part, though, funny enough.

"Eh… they just expect us to step aside for them." Vernie put her hands in the air. "But I pretend I don't know local customs. Ah!" She then bent down, picked up a coin, and stuffed it in her pocket.

I looked off to the side of the road. "We're supposed to step in the muck?"

"We're not going to, though." Vernie shrugged. "So don't worry about it." She picked up another coin.

"You seem to have quite the luck today…" I noted as she picked up yet another coin.

"The seam tore on that traveler's saddlebag. He should fix it." She reached down and snagged a fourth coin.

"That's karma for you." I snickered.

"So you're starting to remember!" Vernie gasped happily, turning around to look at me.

"Eh?"

"Karma!" She pulled out the large dagger from her hip sheath.

"Your dagger's name… is Karma? Wait, you did that?" I didn't know whether to praise in awe or rebuke. But the overdressed jerk had it coming, so I just gave a slightly disapproving grunt.

"You always act so surprised every time I commit a crime." Vernie rolled her eyes.

Nora made a strange sound, and I quickly glanced at her. "Don't *you say anything.*"

"I was just clearing my throat."

"Ungh!" Tetora let out a frustrated growl tinged with pain, and we all stopped.

"I just tripped, that's all," he lied as we re-grouped.

"It is a good time to stop anyway," said Aleph. "We won't be able to make it to Kopria before the sun sets tonight, but we'll have time enough to reach it before nightfall tomorrow."

When I heard those words, a shiver of delight ran through me. "Do you think we'll be able to sleep indoors tomorrow?"

"If Vernie has gathered enough coins," Aleph confirmed.

"I take back that previous grunt!" I declared quickly.

Vernie nodded absently. "We should be good for a night's stay at an inn…"

"What about finding a priest for Tetora?" Nora asked, glancing at him.

Aleph answered, "We'll stop at the church first. It's along the way. It's strange to be headed back there after all these years…"

Tetora, however, did not seem to be reminiscing. He pulled fitfully at the iron slave collar still around his neck. "Don't forget. You must call us Tiger and Ox around others. You're our owners here."

That grunt I dismissed threatened to come back around with a vengeance, but I stifled it. "Right…"

We returned to the road, and I distracted myself with the passing scenery. There were plants of all types, with adequate water and soil to take root. The pine trees had thinned away in spots the farther east we headed, giving way to sprawling farms, their patchwork pastures blanketing the landscape. One large field approached the road, and I could see several ox and rabbit hybrids working the land. They kept their heads low as we passed by. One ox hybrid, his beard tinged with white, collapsed in the middle of the field. A man ran out to him, but instead of offering aid, he cursed incessantly.

"If you're going to die, do it in a ditch! Don't mess up my rows!"

"Forgive me, Master." The ox-man exhaled in exhaustion. "If I could just be excused to get a drink from the trough…"

"Last time I let an ox do that, they tried to run. Do you think I'm stupid!? No water breaks!"

"Little Dragon, hold your strike." Aleph was behind me, surreptitiously holding my arm as I had my sword half-drawn. "If we intervene, it will only get worse." He pointed to a small hill, where at least half a dozen men sat, crossbows drawn. He pointed not only at the older ox hybrid on the ground but also at the other hybrid workers.

"Well, what are we going to do about this?" I asked, quickly shoving the sword back into place angrily.

"We should not—"

"I got this." Nora waved her hand. "Just keep walking."

Against my better judgment, I kept marching along the road, silently seething.

"M-my lord! The roof, the roof!" one armed sentry screamed after we passed, pointing to the main house. "The roof is on fire!"

Black tendrils of smoke were pouring out of the clay tiles near the top of the chimney. Then, the terrible excuse for a landowner started shrieking.

"Everyone! Go get water! Don't let it burn down! *That's my house!*"

"Ah… that's not how the song goes…" Nora shook her head. "But I guess this works too. At least he's going to get a drink now."

"Song?"

She gave me a wide-eyed stare. "Seriously, Rae?"

I turned away from her before answering, only to see everyone on the farm heading towards the well. Another ox helped up the older hybrid even as they made their way to battle the growing conflagration. The hybrids moved quite a bit slower than what appeared to be the hired help.

"Anyway…" I changed course again, feeling I had missed something I shouldn't have. "Did *you* do that? I would swear an oath that I didn't hear you utter a single word!"

"I didn't need to *say* any words of power. I know sign language." She wiggled her fingers. "Pretty cool, right?"

"How did you know that would work?"

"I didn't," she admitted. "But it was worth a try."

It was a short-term solution, that was for sure. But the whole setup didn't bode well. Those ox hybrids were just going to undergo a different torture tomorrow. "That farm…" I began.

"You're going to ask why there are so many hybrids on the premises?" Aleph finished.

"Yes."

"In Turri, there are exceptions to the rule. Owners can provide for many hybrids, as long as they pay an animus offset to the Church."

"*Provide for!?*" Nora screeched. The word he should have used was *enslave*.

Aleph's face contorted. "Their words, not mine. But change is coming. The Holy City has issued several proclamations already condemning the practice of—"

"Proclamations ain't worth the parchment they're printed on!" Vernie declared. "Sending a note does nothing."

I mean, she was right. I briefly imagined Clare writing the note she sent us about the acceptable use of Nora's journal, which only resulted in its intentional defacement.

"Why aren't the holy knights doing anything about this?" I asked. Sure, Rae was the Captain of the Gold Order, but there were still the White, the Blue, and the Silver. They also welcomed all that could pass their trials, hybrid or human. Demons, of course, needed not apply.

"They're busy," Tetora rumbled. "The Three Orders are split between the upper and lower entrances to the Wastelands, defending against the demon king's inevitable invasion."

Nora and I exchanged a long glance. We had a lot to dissect with that declaration.

"Doesn't that mean the hybrids outside those borders… have no protection?" Did they just choose risky freedom over imposed slavery?

"The Three Orders routinely patrol the Wastelands," Aleph murmured. "To say there is no protection would be an… oversimplification." However, we hadn't directly encountered them in our travels, and we even managed to pass by their giant fortress. As I contemplated the significance of our stinky shortcut, I found it more than a bit troubling. I was about to ask how *routine* the word "routine" really meant, but Nora was faster with her next callout.

"I thought there were four orders in total," Nora remarked. "Which one's missing?"

"Ah…" Aleph paused. "Raelynn *was* the Holy Captain of the Gold Order, but…"

"The entire order disbanded?" I asked with a sinking feeling.

"You… could say that…" Vernie looked up at the sky thoughtfully. "But you're getting it back together."

"Huh?" I didn't remember promising to do a side quest of that magnitude.

"The Gold Order is almost complete. Once Relias joins, we'll be at full capacity!" Vernie laughed flatly.

I swallowed hard. "Wait, the whole Gold Order… was just six people?" Or… five plus one other?

"That's all it ever was," Vernie replied.

That's… not an Order. *That's a party making dinner plans! It wasn't even close to the upper limit of the two-pizza rule.*

We had more pressing issues to clarify since it seemed like Aleph was holding on to even more information than we had realized. "Has the new demon king already declared war?" I continued.

"You're expecting him to act like a human!" Tetora shouted, straining himself. "When he's ready, he'll just attack everyone without restraint. It's as simple as that."

No. No, he wouldn't do that. That would be stupid, and he *isn't* stupid. Waging a war on several fronts without any solid allies? Stupid.

"But it's been seven years already…" Nora sighed. "Political shake-ups with the other demon lords aside… what could he possibly be waiting for?"

"Seven years is hardly a blink of an eye to him. He's just consolidating power now. When he gets bored with that, he'll strike."

"Isn't that all the more reason to have a united front and stop blaming each other for all our problems?" I questioned, but my words were met by an uncomfortable silence that lingered as we continued along the road. Before we could find a less emotionally charged topic to debate, the sun began its inevitable descent, forcing us to make camp for the night.

CHAPTER 43: FIRESIDE CHAT

We had moved a bit off the road and into a small cluster of protective pines for the night, not wanting to call too much attention to our party. The smell of bean stew wafted in the air, but trust me, it wasn't so bad. First, I had finally gotten used to eating and digesting beans—a phrase I thought I'd never actually write down. Second, it was correctly spiced since I was in charge of preparing it.

"Dinner's ready!" I announced. "Everyone come—"

I dodged to the side, seeing a sudden flash of silver pass my right.

Thock!

A throwing knife buried itself into the tree a few feet away.

"Bullseye!" Nora cheered, standing next to Vernie.

"Which one of you just did that!?" I demanded of them both.

They immediately pointed at each other as the last rays of sunlight hit both of their guilty faces.

"I see…" I marched over and pulled the knife from the tree. "Well, I guess I'll just hold on to this for now, then. Maybe you'll pick a target a little farther away from my face next time." Honestly, it wasn't all that close, and I could tell by the way it hit dead on that it was Vernie who threw it, showing Nora how to get it to tumble end over end correctly.

"Told you she'd get mad," Nora muttered.

"You saw, though, right?" Vernie whispered back.

"Yeah," Nora agreed quietly.

I frowned. "Saw what?"

"You sensed it even before it hit," Vernie explained nervously. "You turned and dodged, even though it was unnecessary."

I had?

"Are you seriously trying to get on my bad side?" I gave her an exaggerated mad-dog stare, complete with a dramatic eye twitch.

"No! No! I'm just… trying to show you that… you're extraordinary, even when you don't try to be."

I was filled with a somewhat warm and squishy feeling even as I contained my instinctive rage that demanded I throttle them both. "Just… no more throwing weapons at party members or in their general direction, okay? *Someone might get the wrong idea.*"

"Yes, Holy Captain," they agreed petulantly in unison, crossing their fingers over their hearts.

After we ate, Aleph tended to Tetora's wounds again, which had begun weeping a dark serous fluid that stained anything it touched. Aleph also showed signs of moderate stress now, often opting out of casual banter to hover protectively around Tetora. They had both decided to retire early tonight, though I could hear them whispering back and forth quietly.

Nora, Vernie, and I sat around the campfire, overstuffed on dinner but too lazy to get ready for sleep. We watched the ruddy orange flames dance for a little while in silence. As the burning wood crackled and popped, I couldn't help but think of the farmhouse fire from earlier. Had they put it out before it spread too far? Who would be blamed for it? With a silent grimace, I concluded that all we did was force that landlord to overcharge for water. What use is a substitute hero who doesn't confront blatant villainy when she sees it?

I exhaled with annoyance again for about the thirtieth time and changed into a different slumping position.

"I'll take the first watch," Vernie volunteered with a wave of her hand. "You kids should get ready for bedtime."

Nora and I exchanged a purse-lipped glance.

"Who are you calling kids? You're the one who got your toy confiscated before dinner." Nora then stuck out her tongue, purposefully negating her argument.

"Hey now, you helped, remember?" I nudged her with my elbow. "I'm almost positive you talked her into it."

"I know I don't look it," Vernie said dramatically, tossing her hair back with an audible flick as she stood up. "But I'm your elder, and you'll always be kids to me." She paused then, looking nervously toward where Aleph and Tetora had settled in for the night. "One more day 'til we find a priest for him…"

Nora and I mumbled our agreement as Vernie climbed a tree to get a better view of the area.

I took a deep breath and stood, but Nora tugged on my arm.

"Rae… What's Kopria going to be like?"

I almost asked "Why are you asking me?" but from her tone, I surmised she was looking for reassurance. "A normal village, I guess… I bet the inn will be nice. This area has a lot of vegetation, and the climate's not so bad…" I took a natural pause as I sat back down across from her, but Nora didn't seem satisfied with my answer.

"What about the priest there?"

I sighed. "Well, if he's anything like Father Baram—"

"I don't think he will be anything like Father Baram." Nora frowned. "I think we should be wary."

"Wary? Why?"

"Hybrid slavery's legal here. Do you think the priest will just heal Tetora with no questions asked?"

"That's… what they do, though, right? I mean, Tetora's sick. Demonic poison. If that's not the *Purpose* of a priest…"

"Maybe…" Nora said without conviction. "But do you understand what Aleph was saying about animus offsets?"

"Mmm… sounded like some sort of exemption," I answered vaguely to hide my ignorance.

"Landowners pay the priests money so they can have more than twenty hybrids as slaves," Nora clarified. "Vernie said it's a practice spreading all over Turri."

"So they're just bribing them to look the other way?" I straightened in surprise.

"They *say* they use the money to fund activities to reduce animus, but who knows what that means…"

I frowned. "Well, we can skip the inn and pay the priest instead. Or maybe barter. I think maybe some of my armor might fetch a—"

"Don't be stupid!" Nora flicked my forehead. "Personal protective equipment is a necessity. Do you have any idea how much you scared me going one-on-one with the Skreethi matriarch? You could have been ripped to shreds by a giant skunk!"

"That does… sound like an idiotic way to go, huh?" I tried to play it off lightly so she wouldn't get upset.

Nora folded her hands in front of her and cleared her throat softly. "Rae. I think we need to have a serious talk." *Oh, I don't like those.*

"Um…"

"Do you recall a character by the name of Prelate Dolus?" Nora asked.

I blinked several times. "No, never heard of him."

Nora nodded. "Me neither. But Vernie has. And it seems he's in charge around here, causing all sorts of trouble."

"Wait, shouldn't she be talking to *me* about this?" I mean, I'm the captain, right? She practically made me captain!

"She's having enough trouble keeping herself together. Haven't you noticed you two have been butting heads lately?"

"Well, yeah, but…" I thought we were doing better now? Oh… I looked at the knife I had confiscated.

Nora's eyes crinkled slightly. "She's also stopped drinking cold turkey recently. The last thing she needs is to get into a religious argument with you."

I grunted. "Fine, just tell me what you know about this Dolus person."

"Mmm… the nicest phrase Vernie had for him was '*corrupt inquisitor.*' Apparently, he's one of those who promoted the theory that hybrids generate more animus than other animals."

"Wouldn't it look really bad for him if he refused to help someone attacked by a demon?" I hedged. "We should at least try to talk to him first."

"Fine, but then what? What are we going to do if he stonewalls us?"

I didn't know how to reply, so I just stared at the ground for a little while, not using my eyes to see anything in particular.

"I know what I'd do," Nora sniffed. "But I think the decision should come from you. We'll back you up, regardless."

"I'm… not going to give up if that's what you're worried about. Tetora needs healing, and he needs it now."

"Just don't kill the prelate, okay? Or break his jaw. You seem to have this thing for punching things in the jaw, but I think he might need his to cast. Not all of us can talk with our fingers."

"I'm not gonna beat up *a priest!*" I gasped in surprise, utterly horrified at what Relias would think of me. "I'm the—" I stopped myself. I almost said it aloud. *The big lie. The lie I was starting to fall for myself.*

"Rae… you *might not* have to resort to violence," Nora murmured. "But it will require you to do something you've been avoiding. You're going to have to *do the thing.*"

"What thing?" I was already gritting my teeth, well aware of the answer.

"*Be the hero I know you already are!* Eura told you to do whatever you need to do to make things right! So namedrop, start glowing, and order him to comply! Maybe he'll even listen."

Sure, it's one thing to say, but something totally different to do. And there was no coming back from it.

"… I'll consider it." I stood up abruptly.

"Rae, I'm not saying that you're really—"

"I'm going to bed now." I resolutely walked away from the campfire, not wanting to continue the conversation aloud. I couldn't stop it from continuing in my head, though, with vehement arguments from all sides.

After a few moments, she called after me. "Friends forever?"

"…Friends forever." I didn't look back.

CHAPTER 44: KOPRIA

Sleep did not come right away that night, but after I got my thoughts to quiet down, I was blissfully rewarded with dreamless slumber, a rarity I never forgot to be thankful for.

I was even the first to wake the next morning, a fact that seemed to startle everyone.

"Emergency meeting," I announced as we started eating breakfast.

"Who's sus?" Nora asked as she plopped down on the ground next to me.

"Dolus is sus…" I looked at everyone else, noting their general confusion. "I mean, suspicious. But there are other things to talk about, too. First, I think we need to establish some ground rules as a group."

The others looked at each other and nodded tentatively. Aleph's face, however, appeared quite dark.

"I'm… sorry. For not exactly being approachable lately," I began. "I thought I was improving, but I realize I must improve my communication skills… I should start by saying I'm still uncomfortable being in charge, but… anyway. I want to ensure everyone feels like they can speak up directly about potential hazards to me and the rest of the group."

Vernie kept her gaze on the ground. I at least tried to avoid calling her out specifically.

"Sometimes…" I continued awkwardly, "I just get mad or irritated and don't always listen. So… I want to introduce… 'stop the line.'"

"Stop the line?" Tetora asked, his ears pinned down in bewilderment.

"Think of it as a catchphrase that gets my attention, no matter what," I explained, somewhat embarrassed. "If you say those words, I have to stop and respond to your concerns before continuing what I was doing. I've been getting a little too caught up in some big feelings I'm having, and, well… this is a way to get around that."

The group exchanged several glances with each other but nodded slowly.

"I get to use it too, though, so it's a two-way street." I took a deep breath. "So, can we agree that those words should be reserved for discussing something that affects our immediate safety?"

They murmured their general agreement.

"So, I'm going to do it first." I folded my hands to hide my nervousness, even while willing myself not to scratch my wrists openly. "Stop the line. We need to talk about this Prelate Dolus. It's important."

Aleph went rigid with rage. "I have heard of *Father Dolus*. Do not tell me he is in the area!"

Vernie hadn't even told Aleph, either? Uh oh… This just might not be about me, then.

"I haven't been in Turri proper for years," Vernie confessed with a quiver. "But the reports I've been getting say he's been making a name for himself operating out of Kopria itself."

"We should have gone to Fort Turri instead!" Aleph bellowed, causing me to jump. "Why did we listen to you!?"

Vernie inhaled sharply, her face paling. "I'm dead if I go there! And anyone else associated with me. It's not like I lied about it. I just… didn't want to get left behind…"

Aleph's face contorted in anger. "You should have told us this sooner! You're always downplaying the trouble you cause! What was it this time? What did you do?"

Vernie sat up. "First of all, I didn't do anything wrong. Helping ex-slaves across the border is not wrong! I'm not ashamed of what I did, and I won't let you make me feel bad about *my life choices like you always do!*"

"If you had done it legally, there would not have been a problem!"

"How do you legally help a slave not be a slave?" Nora asked pointedly.

I groaned out loud. This wasn't what I wanted to focus on. "Enough! Slavery is bad. Helping people is good. *Also, Fort Turri is not an option now.* We need to focus on getting Tetora healed up, which means figuring out how to engage this Dolus character."

"He's a skinflint," Vernie mumbled. "Charges for everything; pays for nothing."

"He doesn't see hybrids as anything more than tools." Aleph snorted again, refusing to look at Vernie.

"So, how do we get him to help us?" I asked with genuine concern, hoping someone would have a sneaky solution to the sticky problem.

However, nothing new came from the discussion that followed. We could ask nicely, which was my lame contribution; we could bribe him, try intimidation, or engage in a whole confrontation.

"Alright," I finally said, as the situation threatened to degenerate into a shouting match. "This is how it's going to go. I'll talk to him first. No one else. I'll try appealing to his… *standup character as a priest,* then bribery… and then… um…"

They all froze just to stare at me. I swallowed hard. "Just… if I have to… I'll do it, okay? But promise me you guys will stay out of it."

"We should be assisting—" Tetora started.

"No! I can just imagine the headlines now! Dark mage, wanted felon, and two hybrids attack innocent priest!" I shouted in exasperation. They probably would substitute the slur beastmen for hybrids, though.

"Stop the line," Tetora said firmly. "We work as a team, Rae. We do this together for all of our safety. This time, we're not leaving it all on you."

This time? What was he talking about?

"…I won't convince you otherwise, will I?" I sighed.

"No. Captain or not, you are still my student, so you'll just have to accept my instructions." Tetora grinned weakly for a moment before turning to Aleph. "Apologize now," he commanded. "You've put it off for way too long already."

Aleph's ears hung low as he looked at Vernie uncomfortably. "…Sorry. I have made it hard for you to approach me because I have judged your actions while not understanding the whole story many, many times now. Please forgive me, Vernie."

"I should have told you why I wanted to avoid that place…" Verne admitted. "I thought one man would be easier to deal with than the whole Blue Order."

Vernie must have had run-ins with them before, given her current wanted status. I guess we'd better put them into the category of potential antagonists.

"Your rationale does make sense, in hindsight…" Aleph scratched his cheek.

Vernie glanced at him briefly before throwing herself into his side. She sobbed loudly in apology as they hugged, making me feel both relieved and anxious for the day to come.

***

Kopria's building planner must have been… How do I put this? He was either a dark servant dedicated to chaos, habitually high or intoxicated, or, most probably, never existed in the first place.

The church was built into and around the front gate, though the main doors leading into its genuine interior were bolted shut. Beneath the grand archway lay a stone square, its surface intricately etched with silver runes, much like a holy circle of blessed protection. It was pretty, of course, but otherwise useless since neither Nora nor I could sense any magic from it. I wasn't exactly an expert, but I felt like I had started being able to see and feel things that others couldn't. In any case, we concluded that the placebo effect worked wonders here.

A stone plaque in front of the central archway leading into a courtyard read "Let Faith Defend and Guide Us." It was troubling to see such a blatant disregard for fundamental safety and security measures. Even Disney World had a better reproduction gatehouse! Not to mention, it had front gate attendants and security guards readily available. Why bother to have a walled town with no functional gate?

After trying every door we could find, we gave up on getting inside the church.

Churches are supposed to be sanctuaries, with priests as their hallowed keepers. I thought their gates were open to all, not just a privileged few.

Was this the outcome of recent events?

Or was I just naïve? "What now?" I asked. "I don't think it will help our case if we try to break in…"

"It's a little late." Aleph glanced at the sky apprehensively. "We may wish to see if we can find some lodging until tomorrow."

"That would mean fewer coins to bargain with, though…" I mumbled.

"A daytime discussion would still be better," Vernie agreed, pointing at the walls. "Those are spyholes. I know I haven't been here in a long while, but they're new since my last visit."

Do churches *need spyholes*?

We continued through the church's courtyard, which led to the residential district. The homes here were mainly wooden constructions, poorly shaped with uneven plaster and in various levels of disrepair. More complex buildings seemed to be scattered randomly about, with their overhanging second floors invading each other's space to provide shaded, crooked alleys ripe for waylaying. Several of these structures also served as sudden endings to wide streets. We had to go around in jug-handle fashion more than once. But where were the inns?

Even weirder were the residents' reactions. I had been worried about how I would act while in town as a well-to-do hybrid slave owner, but I never even got the chance to audition. As soon as anyone even glanced our way, they ran. Some shuttered windows, while others slammed doors.

"Do we still smell bad?" I wondered aloud as I turned back to Tetora.

"No, Master," he said with uncharacteristic softness, his gaze fixated on the ground. "Not any worse than that garbage pile over there, anyway," he whispered.

It was awkward and unnerving to be called Master while depopulating an entire neighborhood. I kept a steady grip on my staff as we entered the eastern part of town.

As we rounded yet another corner, we startled an older woman who was hawking her second-hand wares in an impressive voice. She took one terrified look at us, lifted the stationary end of her two-wheeled cart, and tore off with incredible speed. As she rounded a corner, something furry fell from her cart.

Nora walked over and picked it up with a startled gasp. It was a puffy hat made from a Skreethi pelt, its long tail hanging off the back as decoration. The fur was still spotted, denoting that it was from an adolescent.

"I'll just… make sure to give it a proper burial…" Nora said in a low voice, respectfully storing it in her rucksack.

Eventually, we found the Blue Lion Inn, a two-story, rough-hewn, rectangular building with a dilapidated barn jutting off one of its sides. A garish mural coated the inn's exterior, depicting a beast that only the most drunken of patrons would even consider being a blue lion feasting on a large hock of ham. Posted out front was a crude sign with an entire row of open locks hanging on bent nails.

The Blue Lion Inn is for human patrons only!
All beastmen must be properly collared and immediately secured
in a locked barn stall, where they must remain until checkout.
Anyone not complying with these rules will be immediately reported
to the town watch.
No meals or blankets will be provided to beastmen.
No exceptions!

"What the hell!?" I finally exploded aloud.

"It's even worse here than I thought it would be…" Aleph murmured, covering his mouth.

"We'll just go *elsewhere*!" I declared before anyone could speak, storming forward. Elsewhere, however, it was the same. All the inns had converted other nearby buildings into shabby seconds where hybrids were to remain caged. Trying to talk to anyone about the rule seemed futile as well because even here, anyone looking at our party immediately ran off, seemingly stricken with terror.

"Let's just get out of this turd of a town and return to the church in the morning…" Nora sneered as her fists shook in irritation. "Before I become an arcane arsonist again…"

We had already missed our mark and would never have the chance to talk to the prelate in private. As we retreated to the church's courtyard, we were finally met by the local welcoming committee.

A mob of furious residents blocked our path, wielding the customary lit torches, pitchforks, and shovels. A few brandished some tatty brooms as well. At the front stood a tall, stern-faced man with eyes full of fervor. His pristine white and gold robes rippled audibly in the evening breeze as he stepped towards us.

"You dared to bring a *traitorous tiger* into our peaceful village!?" the mitered man shouted, raising his bejeweled right hand. "May Euphridia forgive you for your wickedness, for we, the righteous, shall not!"

CHAPTER 45: THE HERO APPEARS?

Prelate Dolus struck the butt of his staff down against the ground, summoning a bright, glowing light from the crystal orb at its apex. The light began to infuse with his weakly flickering aura. Behind me, I heard Aleph and Tetora gasping for air. As I turned, I saw them both fall flat onto the cobblestones, their neck collars emitting a blazing white light.

For a dreadfully long moment, I couldn't tell if they were alive or not. I held my breath until I saw them draw theirs slowly. Despite their attempts to resist, a powerful force kept them pinned to the ground. Before I could fully process this, the clamor of the mob erupted around us. I couldn't make out much of what they were saying because of a nearby bell tolling, but I caught a few one-liners that helped fill in the details.

"The one with the sword is the ringleader!"

"Overgrown filthy heathen is probably from the south!"

"Prelate Dolus! She was the one talking to that loathsome tiger!"

Prelate Dolus let the crowd continue on his behalf for a bit before holding up his right hand, ushering in a wave of silence from the group. The ringing I heard continued, louder now.

"Outsiders!" the prelate boomed. "You stand accused of entering town limits with dangerous livestock, failing to dehorn your ox, and consorting with an enemy of humanity!"

The wind whipped across the courtyard, and I saw dusky clouds of hazy animus billowing around the crowd. My gaze returned to the prelate, but he didn't appear to be the swirling source of darkness. His shimmering silhouette indicated he was talking animatedly, perhaps orating an impromptu sermon, but I couldn't hear it. The ringing had turned into a high-pitched screech that drowned out everything else. My vision began to tunnel and fade somewhat as I felt the increasing tension in my temples.

Nora was still behind me, pulling at my cloak. She appeared to be shouting at me as well, and I considered that perhaps *she was the one to blame for generating animus*, but no, she was just *distracting me from my target*. Surely, the source of this obfuscating chaos and ill will was a demon of significant rank, right?

But it wasn't.

It was me.

I wasn't simply frustrated or irritated. *I was filled with a dark, all-consuming rage.* The blatant exploitation of the vulnerable and marginalized. The dehumanization of hybrids. *The unprovoked and unwarranted attack on my friends!* And in front of me was the one profiting off the whole damn system. But I could end it all in just a few seconds. The world would undoubtedly be better off if I did. Wasn't I told to do whatever it takes to make things right?

"You could chop off his head and put it on a pike to deter others. I'm sure there's a lot more where he came from."

It was the softest of dispassionate whispers, yet it cut through the distracting noise buzzing between my ears.

What did you say?

"Hang his corpse from the wall? Drain all the blood out first to make it last longer."

Th-that's—

"Why is that so upsetting? You've already decided to break your promise to Nora about not killing him. If you're going to go that far, why just stop there?"

I won't… I won't kill him. It was… I mean…

"I know. It's not you. You're the type to save that as a last resort."

But I won't let him get away with all of this!

"I wouldn't expect anything less from you."

Are you—

"No."

Then who…

"Doesn't matter. I was just passing by for the moment. Just think of me as a distraction."

A distraction from what?

"No one can avoid having intrusive thoughts sometimes. Accept them as they are and move on, but don't give in to them. Don't lose yourself. We'll talk again later when it's more convenient."

"Rae!" Nora's insistent shriek hit me from behind as the darkness enveloped me and ebbed away, its last tendrils dissipating off my limbs.

"What just…?" I asked, still disoriented.

"It seems you have nothing to say about your misdeeds!" The prelate slammed his staff again, catching my attention.

"You're… accusing *me* of wrongdoing?" I blinked several times to shake off my sweaty shame and confusion. "After what you've wrought here? You've codified slavery and turned against your fellow man!"

"Just who do you think you are to come here and judge our customs, outsider?" someone shouted from the mob as others jeered at my use of "fellow man."

And there was the opening I couldn't ignore. I glanced at Nora for some last-second reassurance before turning to… Vernie? But she wasn't anywhere to be found.

"She said to tell you to draw this out as long as possible," Nora whispered. "Also, shout it loud enough so she can hear you."

What was she up to now?

I took a deep breath and steeled myself.

"Who am I?" I said, taking a marginal step forward and raising my head high. "I have many names and titles, and some of you might even remember them." I unbuttoned the clasp of my cloak with my trembling left hand. My voice rose, not with rehearsed theatrics, but with genuine fervor. "*I am Raelynn Lightbringer*, Knight Captain of the Holy Order of Gold, Seventh Appointed Hero of Legend, and Chosen One of the Goddess. I am the Champion of Euphridia!" I tore off my cloak and flung it to the side, hoping I pulled off a dramatic flair as I did so. The mob's sharp inhalations were moderately satisfying, but the scoff from the prelate sobered me from any hope of an easy verbal victory.

My tone dropped to absolute zero. *"Release my companions at once!"* I swept my fierce gaze over the crowd, locking eyes with anyone who dared to stare back. Some laughed, others elbowed each other as if they were enjoying a show. Well, then… let's add some special effects.

To focus my amity, I didn't think about selfish things, like ice cream or sleeping late. I thought about how Aleph and Tetora have looked after Nora and me since our arrival, accepted us into their home, shared meals, and even agreed to travel with us as we navigate this world.

Nora let out a high-pitched squawk. "Rae! You're…"

"Finally adulting?" I murmured so only she could hear as I handed her my bo staff for safekeeping.

"I was going to say shining like starlight." It was the first time I saw my own bright aura radiating out several feet in all directions in a slow, pulsating fashion, dulling the prelate's own. A few mob members started to take me seriously at that point. *"It's… the Chosen One!"*

"H…Holy Captain…"

"Feel free to help me bluff this one," I said through clenched teeth to Nora as I assumed a Wonder Woman pose before shouting, "Let them go, or I will hold all of you fully accountable for *your reprehensible actions!*" Okay, I have to admit, that pose really does help. Even imagining it can make a difference.

Prelate Dolus wasn't about to lose his hold over the crowd that easily. "Beware the *Face of Sin*, who masks itself in the illusion of authority!" He leveled his blazing staff at me in case anyone was confused about who he was referring to.

Was he calling me ugly now, too?

Nora cackled loudly in retort. "That's exactly what I wanted to say! How much would you say you've bankrolled from *normalizing such deviant behavior?* I mean, I'm not a priest, so I couldn't pull off such a devious con… but your finery suggests you've been doing rather well until now!"

The mob muttered darkly, and a few people started pulling back from the rest of the crowd. Others dressed noticeably better than the rest shouted their unwavering support for Prelate Dolus. At least it was easy enough to identify his professional guards. It would take more than mentioning morals and money to turn them, though.

"A paid comedian, no doubt, for surely you jest!" the prelate snapped. "But your jackal-like japes do not distract the virtuous from their duty!"

It was much too serious a moment to make a joke about duty.

"I'll say it again!" I retorted. "Release *Aleph the Ox-Like and Iron Tiger Tetora!*" The murmurs only increased as I name-dropped them, too.

"Aleph and Tetora!? Here?"

"I… think we made a big mistake…!"

"F-free those imposters, and they will surely destroy us all," Prelate Dolus retorted in a shrill voice. "Everyone knows the tigers have sided with the demon army after their grandmaster disappeared!"

Okay, now, that was *unexpected* but irrelevant at the moment.

I was getting tired of repeating myself. "Anyone not supporting this terrible excuse for a priest, leave immediately or suffer my righteous wrath!" I thundered while drawing my sword from my scabbard with a steely hiss.

Maybe I should have given the mob the option to flee *first*. A good dozen denizens took off after realizing they wouldn't be treated as innocent bystanders anymore.

Prelate Dolus quivered with fury. "I refuse to acknowledge your authority. You're nothing but a heretic! The real Raelynn Lightbringer *died* because of those do-nothing, deceitful beasts! The Goddess won't return until we eradicate every last one. *Humanity must be purified!*"

Did he… actually believe the words coming out of his mouth? I had assumed he was spouting rhetoric, but the truth was even more horrible.

I had enough of both of us posturing. Although I doubted he knew what I required him for, it was time to drop the *hammer*.

I leveled my sword at him. "By the authority of Euphridia and the power she bestowed upon me, I, Raelynn Lightbringer, declare you,

Prelate Dolus—*Excommunicate Traitoris*! By your thoughts, intents, and actions, I find you guilty of treason to the Will of Euphridia. Submit or die!"

∗∗∗

Post-Chapter Omake

Nora: *Now I can finally cross off "proclaimed a heretic!"*

Rae: *What are you doing?*

Nora: *Playing Female Protagonist Bingo.*

Rae: *Hey…*

Nora: *I could win easily if you'd just heal someone with the power of your love!*

Rae: *…You bought the deluxe magical girl edition, didn't you?*

CHAPTER 46: PRELATE PANDEMONIUM

Prelate Dolus took on a stance of stubborn indignation as he inhaled, preparing himself to unleash what I could only imagine was a scathing counterargument. However, as he opened his mouth, his aura flickered before extinguishing entirely. His eyes widened as his face took on a sickly gray cast, yet his staff continued to radiate with an unwavering, defiant brilliance. He raised it high into the air as if to call upon its power and leveled it at me, but nothing happened. Sweating for a moment, his gaze darted wildly between Aleph and Tetora, still prone behind me. He shook the staff a few times, but again, it seemed as if it wasn't obeying his most recent unspoken commands.

Whatever just happened seemed to be more than mere performance anxiety, but at least he most likely can't cast any more spells right now.

Cornered and without any other recourse, Dolus barked an order to his loyal lackeys in long-skirted gambesons, commanding them to attack me even as he withdrew behind them. Everyone else in the courtyard had enough sense to scatter to the eight winds.

Three men in the courtyard's center formed a protective half-moon a few feet before the prelate. The remaining two fighters, positioned on either side, initiated a daring diagonal approach. The leftmost figure ignored the short sword strapped to his waist, opting to brandish a longer spear instead. Still partially in shadow, the fighter on the right held a thick wooden club with a spike on the end. They kept their relative distance from me at first, taking measured steps while the other skirted sideways, trying to divide my attention.

"Look, whatever he's paying you for this, it's not enough!" I snapped loudly. None of these people were superpowered demons or amity-assisted holy knights. They weren't even experimentally enhanced hybrids. While I didn't exactly understand their motivations, I was troubled by the nagging thought that they were obligated to obey orders and were little more than disposable pawns. Unfortunately, they decided not to heed any of my warnings and continued their advance. I was going to try my best not to inflict any fatal wounds, focusing instead on disarming and incapacitating them.

Sir Spear's first move from the left was a deceptively simple thrust, lulling me into a false sense of security. But this was just a feint I unfortunately fell for. Within the blink of an eye, he disengaged from my shield block, leaving me to rely on my amity-infused chest plate to take the brunt of a potentially lethal strike. The bruising impact reverberated through my body, forcing me to stifle a groan as I reminded myself not to underestimate *anyone*, even pitiful NPCs. No more foolishness! It was time to focus on defense and quick takedowns as priorities.

I jumped back to put more distance between us, but Sir Spear continued his advance relentlessly, showering a flurry of stabs at me. The control of his weapon was noteworthy, but I felt he was moving in slow motion. As annoyed as I was about this stupid fight by proxy, I carefully observed his techniques, identifying several to exploit later. Amity was probably helping me cheat here, but I didn't feel very guilty about it.

He must have fallen for my face at one point since he shifted tactics to try and skewer it mercilessly. This was why I needed a helmet! Not a fancy circlet or shiny tiara!

His repeated attempts to maim momentarily distracted me from his companion, who closed the distance between us swiftly. However, a loud grunt caught my attention at the last second. I opened some distance by stepping back and turning to face my opponents. The one who grunted had a brightly gleaming silver knife poking through the gambeson covering his shoulder, answering why he halted—it was Vernie! She must have returned and kept them in check from the shadows. I momentarily wondered about what she could have possibly been up to, but I only had time to settle on the idea that it was probably both beneficial and sneaky.

Let's hope it's reinforcements.

Sir Spear came forward with a series of rapid thrusts, but he overextended himself, and I seized the opportunity by sidestepping and striking his straightened forearm with my sword. Although his gambeson remained intact, he yelped in pain as his right hand lost its grip on his spear, dangling limply.

From the shadows, the wielder of the club launched another quick assault, his weapon gleaming ominously as it arched forward.

"Watch out!" Nora called from behind. "That goedendag has a vicious point!"

I skittered to the side to distance myself from the club wielder. "What the hell is a guten… tag…?"

"Spiked club!" she clarified quickly.

"Then just *say that first*!" Fancy foreign words are too hard for me right now.

"But that doesn't accurately describe all the deadly nuances of the g—"

"We can talk about this later!" The spiked club wielder paused and jumped back as another knife flew across the field.

Meanwhile, Sir Spear recollected himself and renewed his sinister, single-handed assault, albeit with diminished strength and accuracy. Before he could pull back from his latest spear flurry, I grabbed his weapon with my left hand, just behind the metal tip.

I don't think he expected that, but that was just one significant benefit of the targe. You could keep your fingers free, and your opponents might not know about it until it was too late. Thanks, Aleph!

With a forceful tug, I yanked the spear out of his hand and kicked him solidly in the gut with my right foot. He doubled over and collapsed to the ground, gasping for air.

I took a moment to twirl the spear in my fingers before aiming in the general direction of the spiked club wielder. I wasn't trying to skewer him as much as to frighten him off. With a swift motion, I hurled the spear; it whizzed past his left side, embedding itself in a nearby tree. Instead of thinking twice, the spiked club wielder seemed to take the toss personally, surging forward with a clear intent to cut me off from further advancing on the incapacitated Sir Spear.

"Graaaaaagggh!" His battle cry belied his intelligence as he furiously swung his gigantic club again, forcing me to give up ground. I drew a deep breath to bolster my confidence and went on the offensive. I lashed out with a barrage of my own attacks, which may have put him on his back foot, but he was too good at evading my onslaught, countering and sidestepping my rapid, measured strikes with almost effortless grace.

I had to admit it: trying to subdue the brute with the flat of my sword was proving futile. I needed to change my strategy. With all the strength and amity I could muster, I slammed my longsword purposely into his club, deflecting it just long enough to pivot and bash him in the face with the edge of my shield. He stumbled back, then toppled over, hitting the ground with a sickening thud.

"It… was just the rim?" I muttered, tensing with anxiety as I looked over his unconscious form, complete with blood trickling out of his nose. I had been so worried about seriously stabbing someone that I had again forgotten the perils of blunt-force trauma. Suppressing a small wave of nausea, I returned my attention to Sir Spear with my guard still raised.

He had gotten to his feet and was now pulling out his short sword as his last option. He started retreating some, glancing back at the three who had yet to make their move. Something seemed to pass between them, and he suddenly broke off from the fight, making a mad dash back into town.

Oh good, the coward's probably just… oh no. Going for trained reinforcements! Vernie's blades marked him twice, but he still kept going.

I almost gave Nora the signal that *I screwed up, so give him everything you got.* Except this was my fight, and I was the one who was adamant about her not using magic unless necessary. Instead, I sprinted after Sir Spear and jumped into the air.

It wasn't skilled weapon handling or a martial artist's secret technique; it was an act of desperation. When I landed on him, we bounced, tumbled, and skidded in the dirt together, tangling even as we kicked up a cloud of dust. My fingers instinctively grabbed a fistful of his hair as I prepared to knock some sense into or out of him, but his eyes had already rolled back into his head.

I stood up, ignoring the throbbing ache in my chest as I turned back towards the three defenders and Dolus, leaving Sir Spear to his slumbering devices. The one in the center motioned for the others to stand their ground, but the man on the right began to tremble nervously.

"Are you having second thoughts?" I fixed my gaze on Mr. Trembles, taking a single step menacingly towards him as I made a show of bringing my sword back into a long point position before me. "Now would be the exact last moment to surrender."

"Forgive me, Holy Captain!" he wailed in lament as he sprinted and stumbled forward. I didn't trust him, so I pulled my targe defensively across my front and pulled back into a plow stance.

"I knew this was all wrong!" he confessed loudly as he threw himself on his knees. "I should have never paid Councilman Procul to look the other way!"

Procul…? That sounds…

Before I could demand more information, Dolus swore loudly and reached into his robes with his right hand. In one quick motion, he withdrew a bullwhip and lashed it forward, striking the blubbering footpad square in the face.

What kind of priest carries something like that!?

Nora and I weren't the only ones to gasp in surprise. More people must have been hiding in the nighttime background than I had thought. The whipped man's screams were wet and thick with blood, and it was all I could do to tear my eyes away from his stripped face. For one moment, I cursed my ability to glow with holy light that illuminated too much of the battlefield.

During my sudden shock, another mercenary from the group had shortened the distance between us while wielding another short spear of his own. *Didn't he even care about his comrade who just lost several layers of flesh?*

He assessed my legs with an unmistakable intent to strike. *No way are you messing with my best features!* He lunged forward with his spear, but at the very last moment, he veered down and zeroed in on my right foot. Reacting on reflex, I swiftly raised my leg to evade before decisively driving my foot downwards, shattering the spear shaft and throwing him off balance. He scrambled to regain his footing, but I felt obliged to take him out with a mighty but merciful kick from my other foot straight into his head before he could stand erect.

With just one defender left, Prelate Dolus loomed anxiously behind him, clearly looking for an escape route. However, Vernie's knives appeared around Dolus's feet at routine intervals, so he hadn't found one yet.

"What are you waiting for? Kill that imposter!" the prelate screamed at his final henchman, who had relaxed his defensive stance.

In a sudden twist, the remaining hired hand abruptly turned on the prelate and tackled him to the ground with a shriek before he could snap the whip again. "That was *my brother* you hit, you disgusting pig!" The angry man continued his assault even as I considered how or even *if* I wanted to intervene. He swung his dagger with wild abandon as he desperately tried to re-sheathe it in the prelate's face.

"Wait!" I yelped in concern as I finally dashed forward. "If you kill him, we can't have him heal your brother."

"His powers are gone!" the man bellowed in rage. "He has no value to anyone now!"

"No… he just lost his confidence…" I faltered, realizing that my words might have had a greater, more permanent effect than I realized. *Order of operations matters! I should have done that after I had him heal Tetora, not before! I screwed up again!*

As I started to swear sulphurously under my breath, at least a dozen citizens surged forward from the shadows to pry the two men apart. Miraculously, most of them pinned Dolus himself, though a few switched over to hold the angry brother back with visible reluctance. Within moments, the group manifested several lengths of rope to tie Dolus in place. One particularly stout fellow, who I would have sworn wasn't in the mob previously, wrested the staff from Dolus's hands, cutting him off from his last focus of power.

"Ah… Captain Lightbringer…" the man started nervously, his hands tightening around the still-glowing staff. "Certainly… you'd explain to your friends on the ground that we meant no *real harm*, right? If we had known *they were with you* from the beginning…"

"That's not the point!" I held out my hand expectantly. "No one should be treated like that without reason!"

"Oh, yes, of course, my thoughts exactly!" he agreed with a nervous, high-pitched laugh as he handed me the staff, clearly playing the mediating suck-up.

How was I supposed to turn off this damnable thing? I fumbled with it for a moment.

"Ah, dear Captain, if you just twist—"

"This orb, right?" With my gauntleted right hand, I squeezed at the glassy sphere until it cracked and then some, rendering a good portion of it into a fine crystalline powder. It was nice to have something inanimate to vent my frustrations upon.

I dropped the staff with a purposeful clatter and brushed off my fingers, even as Tetora and Aleph slowly rose from behind me. "Now tell me," I sniped suspiciously at the new man before me. "What is it that *you* want from me?"

CHAPTER 47: MAKING AMENDS

"Please call me Reynard, Chosen One." He bowed awkwardly. "As a long-standing member of this community, I simply wanted to offer my gratitude for your timely intervention."

"Is that right? Well then, your gratitude is duly noted." I grunted in dismissal, not wanting to get involved in whatever his political agenda was. My mind was trying to figure out what I needed to do next while still stuck on what just happened. What if the mob just untied him the moment I turned my back? Who was going to make sure this didn't happen again? How was I going to get help for Tetora now?

"Ah… perhaps we can talk again in a little while. You seem a little busy right now…" he murmured in retreat. At least he knew when to back off.

"Holy Captain," Aleph said resolutely after clearing his throat. "It would seem that Kopria at large has passed your test. We should embrace them with open arms as we rejoice in their attempts to make amends."

I spun around to give him an incredulous stare. Test? *Passed? Amends? They're only helping now because it's the path of least resistance! Less than an hour ago, they would have skinned you alive and laughed about it.*

Aleph put a steady hand on my shoulder and smiled wistfully as he whispered, "Steady now. Let's not snuff out the smallest strides for change."

"Alright…" I sighed, still distrustful that they were suddenly on our side.

Tetora stepped forward and savagely mussed my hair with unsteady hands. "Finally found your dragon breath, I see."

Glancing at Tetora reproachfully, I found myself whispering in shame, "I think I made a big mistake, declaring Dolus a traitor to the Church, and now—"

"Give me back my powers!" Dolus screamed fitfully from his bindings. *"You have no right to take such things from me!"*

Nora, who had been unusually silent, zeroed in on him and scoffed derisively. "If she didn't have the right, it wouldn't have worked, now would it?"

"The people of Kopria need my healing abilities. There's not another priest for leagues in any direction!"

He probably drove them off himself, finding him as obnoxious and offensive as we did.

Nora turned to Reynard, tilting her head slightly. "Is that true?"

"Ah, yes." His head bobbed quickly. "It's been hard to keep the good ones around, at any rate."

"Hmm…" Nora eyed me for a moment, then leaned in and whispered, "Any way you can give him back his heals, even temporarily?"

"I have a thought…" I murmured back hesitantly. "I think I could do what Raelynn did back at that orphanage. But he'd have to be slightly sorry for what he did."

"The… orphanage?"

"You remember that, right?" I asked. "It was the first time she manifested her powers."

Nora's eyes darted back and forth suspiciously. "Let's say, for the sake of argument, I don't."

"The matron," I reminded her quickly. "You know how she made the kids beg on the streets for money? Patching them up just enough to go out and get roughed up some more? Remember, she said that if she healed them, no one would feel sorry for them, and their daily take would disappear."

"Sure…" she said without conviction. "Then what happened?"

"Well, Raelynn was taken there after her parents died from the plague. But she wasn't about to be used as some street urchin, so she confronted the matron and sealed her powers like I did to Dolus. But the matron confessed someone else was extorting money from her. That's when Raelynn granted her *Absolutio Partialis.*"

"…Absolutio Partialis?"

Did we not read the same story? "Raelynn can't forgive on behalf of Euphridia." I shook my head. "But she can set people on a different path if they repent, seeking restoration in The Covenant. I'm not seeing that happening with Dolus, though, so I doubt it'd work."

I mean, there are Rules to these kinds of things. A person can forgive someone without them being sorry. But as for Euphridia? Well… actions speak louder than words, and even then, there are no guarantees.

Nora absently twirled a curl of hair around her index finger. "So all we have to do is get him to say he's sorry…" With her nose twitching, she snapped her fingers twice, then marched purposefully over to Dolus, with Vernie emerging from the shadows at the very last moment to join her. "Apologize, and maybe your healing powers will be reinstated." Nora then glanced at me with a hesitant look. "You'll have to be *sincere,* of course."

The angry brother, tearing himself away from the group holding him back, renewed his assault, slamming the bound Dolus onto the cobblestones again. "Beg for forgiveness, Dolus. Convince us both you have some worth to society, or at least give me the satisfaction of hearing you scream!"

After obliging with some fitful yelps, Dolus was hauled back into a sitting position, glaring at me as if he had swallowed a rotten lemon. "I… I seek absolution for my *sins,*" he hissed between trembling teeth.

"Oh! I think we can do a little better than that, don't you?" Vernie declared as she stole center stage. "Because if you don't change your ways, the only sect that will accept you is the Order of Eunuchs!" she laughed harshly, gesturing grandly with her dagger. *"I'll even help you sing soprano!"*

"It's… Laverna! Laverna the Emasculator," an older man from the sidelines shouted gleefully as the crowd cheered. I heard Nora stifle a snort, but I wasn't so sure it was a joke.

"E… emasculator?" Dolus's voice cracked in more of a falsetto than the soprano Vernie had mentioned. "Wait! Wait! Forgive me. I won't ever target hybrids again!"

That's what it takes to get you to take things seriously? Not the threat of death but the threat of…

"So…" Nora eyed me. "Think he regrets his actions *now?*"

I considered him for a moment, trying to convince myself that he genuinely was sorry on some level. Honestly, it seemed more likely that he regretted the predicament he had landed himself in, but maybe that'd be enough. I'd benefit if he got his powers back, too, truthfully. But, just in case, I was going to make sure he was in the *best position* to learn his lesson with some significant community service.

"I'll grant you *Absolutio Partialis,* provided you offer your woefully mis-bestowed healing powers free of charge to any and all that request them." At least, I hoped I could… Visualize to actualize?

"…All?" he squeaked, flinching as I glared at him. "Of course, all…"

"Swear it!" I folded my arms awkwardly, my chest muscles rejecting the painful movement.

"I swear never again to mistreat beast… I mean, hybrids, and I will heal all before me that are in need." He choked on about half the words, but he did manage to finish his oath.

"Then… I grant you *Absolutio Partialis,* with healing being the only skill you are authorized to use."

"That wasn't part of the deal," he shrieked. "I require *all my amity skills* as a priest!"

"Oh, I didn't say you could return to being a priest." I snorted, helping myself to his abandoned miter on the ground. "And I doubt I ever will. So get to work, You have a lot of customers before you already." I might not have the Church's authority behind me right now, but I'd rat him out to Relias to ensure it was all official and permanently binding.

I'm sure he called me something vulgar under his breath, but I ignored it, glancing at Tetora instead.

"Have him tend to the battle wounded first." Tetora gestured towards the courtyard shakily.

"But…!"

Tetora quirked an eyebrow at me and tilted his head, playing stoic and waiting for me to continue.

With a sigh, I loftily signaled for the mob to bring the others forward. They began by dragging over the battered brother, who had lapsed into semi-consciousness despite their efforts to administer first aid. Dolus's palms began to emit a soft glow to my instant relief. "As Euphridia guides my hands, I heal thee," he intoned flatly.

Sure, the brother's face was physically healed almost immediately, but his eyes still showed the horror of his recent betrayal. It doesn't matter how great of a healer you are; you can't fix it all as if nothing ever happened. Anyone who promises otherwise is nothing but a detestable liar.

After a tearful reunion, the brothers tried to slink off together, but Nora intercepted them. I watched anxiously for a moment before I realized she was gathering intel. Although I couldn't quite make out the specifics, their body language clearly showed that they were divulging all sorts of incriminating information. Some mob members also crowded in, but I suspected they were simply seeking gossip. The other men, whom the citizens had previously secured, were also brought forward and healed in turn.

"Now for my companions," I demanded. "Heal them, too."

Aleph slowly shook his head. "I am not in need of healing. Please proceed with Tetora."

Tetora fought against but ultimately lost to his emotions, making a disgusted face as he lowered himself next to the prelate. Dolus then snorted derisively. "So this is why you came here, of all places…"

Guess he didn't think this was a charming little hamlet, either.

"Oh, look. My dagger's a little dull." Vernie sighed as she tested the blade's edge. "But it'll still do the job…"

Dolus jumped but then hesitated after placing his hands on Tetora. "Demonic poison…!" he gasped. "They've made it this far east?"

At that, every mob member fell silent, gripped by trembling fear.

"Now you have something far more significant to concern yourself with," Tetora snapped. "Hope you're on good terms with the Order of Blue. You'll require the support and protection of all the *humans and hybrids within their ranks.*"

"I'll dispatch a letter of request immediately," Reynard declared from behind me, causing me to whirl around in surprise.

Still hanging around looking for an opportunity, huh?

Dolus, his hands trembling, took a deep breath before focusing his aura once again. It took longer to heal him, but Tetora eventually hopped to his feet lithely, patting himself as if to ensure all parts were restored. "You begin the path to make amends, Father," he said in his most neutral tone. It was neither a thank you nor forgiveness—an observation, at best.

I would have felt much better if he had told him off, though.

"You're injured too, are you not?" Aleph asked me with concern.

"It's nothing I can't handle." I set my jaw pugnaciously, refusing to allow him to put his hands anywhere on me. "Maybe it will serve as a reminder not to be so stupid next time…"

"There is no need to be so hard on yourself." Aleph sighed. "But I share your revulsion at letting one such as him touch you. So it's your choice."

"I'm just a little sore… It'll pass." I flashed him an appreciative smile, relieved he didn't press the issue.

"Now then." Aleph raised his voice, mainly for the mob's benefit. "Let us pray in the sanctuary and ask for Euphridia's forgiveness for resorting to violence."

Oh, Aleph… I was sure she didn't give the *slightest damn* about what we just did.

Tetora snorted. "Perhaps then we can also find someone willing to ensure Dolus continues on the right path."

Reynard stepped forward once again. "Would you care to leave him in my care? I can assure you I'll make sure he appreciates the lesson you taught him." Various townspeople swiftly agreed, with a few more standing behind him. As I looked at the mob, I realized there were more people here now than even at the beginning, with most of them dressed in more muted colors. Something was fishy, and I wasn't dumb enough to take them at their word. "I don't think—"

"I trust him, Holy Captain," Vernie agreed quickly before turning to Reynard. "Would you help us enter the church?"

"Why, of course, dear lady!" The stout fellow chuckled. "I'm sure Holy Euphridia eagerly awaits your prayers!"

"Friend of yours?" I muttered suspiciously as we headed across the courtyard behind him.

"Just met him today." Vernie shrugged almost imperceptibly. "Turns out we're kindred spirits."

"You're… gonna explain this all later, right?" I felt a pit forming in my stomach.

"You'll see." Vernie smirked mischievously.

The church door was still closed but no longer locked from the inside. Nora had joined us at the last moment, her eyes burning with enlightened excitement.

"So what's the latest gossip?" I asked as the others filed inside slowly.

"Later, when we're alone. Then I'll dish, promise!"

As I brought up the rear of the group, Reynard bowed in grand obeisance as he held the door for me. *He couldn't have appeared any more suspicious if he tried!*

My eyes fell on the interior of the church. "What happened here?" I stared at the disarray in front of me in utter disbelief. The floor was littered with stomped papers, furniture lay overturned, and the walls were stripped bare, save for the occasional nail here and there.

"Dolus must have had someone gather up all the church's valuables," the jolly fellow shouted in a sudden, booming voice behind me for the mob's benefit. *J'accuse!*

"But how could he have possibly—" I started to say before Nora stomped on my foot in warning.

"Holy Captain!" Reynard dropped to his knees piously while still somehow propping the door open with his body for all to see. "I would like to request that our community undertake a thorough investigation of this atrocity as well."

Even though I was sure this wasn't under my authority, I internally shrugged. "Granted, I guess… though I'm still not sure—"

"Lock him in the tower until we finish our investigation!" The fellow scrambled to his feet and pointed as the townspeople dragged Dolus away, kicking and screaming. The fellow turned then and flashed an unabashed smile at us. "Our *investigation* will be quite thorough, I assure you."

"Anything else we should know before heading out, Reynard?" Vernie asked in a hushed but severe tone, crossing her arms.

"Not really, no." Reynard's eyes twinkled. "Nora has the gist of everything; she can fill you in. Just don't take too long with your show of piety. I won't be able to hold them off forever." He began to close the door behind him, but Vernie stuck her foot against it.

"You did make those other arrangements, right?" she questioned in a dangerous voice.

"Would I double cross you?" he asked, mostly to himself. His entire demeanor changed as if someone had just yelled "cut," and with a chuckle, he answered his own question. "Probably, but not over something like this. I do hope you'll request my services again, Laverna. Tonight was *very profitable*… for me, anyway." He bowed to us again, and then he smirked at me specifically. "If I were you… and I'm ever so glad I'm not… I'd run away from here as fast as you can. I'll try to keep things quiet, but you know how rumors spread." He laughed as he closed the door, separating us from him and the villagers on the other side.

"What just happened?" I rubbed my face, watching in disbelief as Vernie moseyed through the ransacked church.

"These people just want someone to blame for all their troubles. Since we're removing the idea that hybrids are to blame, we should give them someone else to focus on instead. They don't need specifics like *evidence*; they need a body. I knew you wouldn't kill him because that's not what you do. Taking away his power was pretty neat, but we must also take his profits. Otherwise, he'd cause trouble somewhere else."

"So… you arranged for the church to get raided? While I was… grandstanding?"

She shrugged. "Among other things… like gathering support for you at the end."

Wow, she works fast. That's almost scary.

"Don't worry. They'll put that money back into the town eventually. They're all locals, anyway. Next time, try to distract them on your own so I can help myself to some spoils, too."

Next time?

I turned to look at Aleph and Tetora. "And what do you two think about all of this?"

"I don't condone stealing…" Aleph said in a soft voice. "Good thing I didn't see it happen."

Tetora growled. "It's just a shame he's still breathing!" He looked at me then with a troubled gaze. "Not that I wanted you to dirty your hands on him, Little Dragon. I know you wanted to."

"A little too much so." I shook my head wearily, secretly glad my companions were acting more like themselves again now that we were out of the spotlight.

"I still take it as a sign of respect." Tetora sniffed.

Nora tapped my shoulder. "Hey! Why didn't you ask me about *my thoughts?*"

"I know what you're thinking! You approve of all of this."

"Not officially… until now!" Nora grinned and gave Vernie a big thumbs-up. "Nice."

"Let's hurry…" Vernie advised, unable to hide a grin of her own. "We don't want to hang around here for long."

I knelt in front of the sanctuary's banner. Nora, Aleph, and Tetora joined me in quiet prayer while Vernie busied herself with searching for anything valuable. I kept my prayer as more of a status update. However, I thanked Euphridia and CUP in general for the opportunity to meet Vernie and heal Tetora after our unexpected encounter. I also apologized for frequently losing my temper and letting my animus briefly get the best of me, even though I knew I wouldn't work on changing my behavior too much. I skipped the part about someone ransacking one of her churches, thinking it unimportant in the grand scheme of things.

Nora's prayer took the longest, with her mumbling quickly but mostly unintelligibly. I also noticed she was white-knuckling her journal as she prayed, with the word "demon" popping up more than once. When she finished, she stood up with an audible exhale. "All done," she confirmed.

"So… we're leaving now, right?" I asked.

"Fleeing quickly would be the most prudent course of action." Aleph frowned. "Even if this place is…" he stopped, his face twisting with difficulty.

"Um… *Rustic*?" I offered.

"Kinder than any other words I could find. But yes, we should make haste regardless. Outrunning gossip is probably a fool's errand, yet we cannot help but try."

"I suppose we'll be walking for a good portion of the night, won't we?" I mumbled as I half-successfully stifled a yawn, feeling a wave of exhaustion creeping up on me.

"Guess again!" Vernie threw open the door, and an oversized wooden war wagon was waiting for us in the bright moonlight. Four giant shire horses were hitched to the front, waiting patiently for us as their new owners. An elegantly inked drawing on the sideboard showed an angry red monkey on one side of a scale, perfectly balanced with a black fox on the other.

"You're lucky that scoundrel came through." Nora snickered. "Otherwise, you'd look silly, opening the door to nothing."

My mouth fell open once again in pure disbelief. Damn, she— *they*—work fast.

CHAPTER 48: SUCCESSFUL GETAWAY

"Who gets to drive?" I found myself stumbling over to the horses excitedly.

"Oh no, leave it to me," Vernie declared quickly, jumping up on the driver's bench. "Get in the back, and let's get out of here."

But… horses! Beautiful, majestic horses!

I fought down a wave of irrational disappointment and headed to the back. Aleph went first, unlatching the tailboard and carefully crawling into the back of the wagon in such a way as to prevent his horns from catching on the ceiling. Tetora went next with an agile leap that might have been his way of showing off his newly restored health. Nora scrambled up, and I stumbled in last, pulling the tailboard back into place. The wagon was partially filled with hay and supplies, including a few spare wagon parts. Sighing, I found myself a place to curl up between two barrels and started to close my eyes until…

"Cheese?" I sat up suddenly, half afraid I was hallucinating the smell. The wagon lurched as it started rolling forward, and I lost my balance, crashing into Tetora.

Tetora was holding a giant wheel and was secretly stuffing his face. "Ah… Just checking if it's still good," he said.

"Cheese!" I demanded, grabbing his arm.

"Alright, alright," he surrendered, ripping off a hunk. "It's a little salty."

"Little" was an understatement. But it didn't matter. It was *cheese!* Not beans, vegetables, dried-up bits of meat, or mushy apples.

"Already you forget to serve others before helping yourself," Aleph chided as he held out his hand.

"Hey… I can finally eat normally again, so I must build back my strength," Tetora countered as he passed around more portions of the hard cheese.

Nora opened a small wooden slat on the front of the wagon. "Want some?" she asked as she passed a chunk to Vernie.

"I didn't ask him for cheese…" Vernie replied loud enough to be heard over the horses' hooves even as she helped herself to it. "Ugh. Probably going to say I owe him a favor in the future…"

"You might get lucky and never see him again…" Nora shrugged.

"One can only hope…" Vernie exhaled after taking a bite. "He was too easygoing with everything… *I don't trust him.*"

You put a lot of faith in someone you didn't trust… though I suppose he did come through for us.

Aleph and Tetora glanced knowingly at each other and chuckled dryly.

"Let's just hope no one in Kopria is close with any local knights," Aleph added, his tone slightly more serious. "The Order of Blue will be adamant about questioning all parties involved, and I would not wish to explain our current circumstances to them… or try to come up with a lie convincing enough."

Tetora snorted. "We didn't do anything wrong."

"Not from our perspective, no." Aleph sighed. "But I cannot fathom how they've allowed such matters to deteriorate like this within their own jurisdiction."

It couldn't be possible that they were simply unaware of the hybrid slavery all around them, could it? And Tetora mentioned they had hybrids in their ranks… Were they treated as slaves there, too? Or did they have an entirely different class system? Maybe they simply turned a blind eye because it was sanctioned by the Church.

No matter the answers to my questions, getting involved with them now would only complicate our journey. Even the thought of encountering the Blue made me uncomfortable.

Let's just focus on food for now.

After overindulging on cheese, I settled back in my comfy corner, padded it with hay, and laid down. Once again, I found myself closing my eyes…

"What's this Councilman Procul like, by the way?" Nora asked, jolting me awake. *Procul!*

Tetora stood up and quickly closed the slat. "He's the one who tried to convict Vernie," he snarled.

"That political platform earned him a seat on the Assembly a few years back," Aleph added grimly.

"Did those two men have anything else to say other than him accepting bribes from Dolus? Having some physical evidence of his affairs would be nice, but…"

"He's in Fort Turri for the moment." Nora frowned. "He's there under the pretense of an official inspection, but those two brothers said he's been letting the nobles know he's willing to look the other way on almost anything… for the right price. I just wonder what kind of person he is and why he needs so much money…"

His dark majesty's words echoed in my ears, filling me with icy dread… *Procul is currently away inspecting Fort Turri…* There's no way I could have *known* that… So, how did I *dream* it?

"Nora… you've never heard of him before, have you?" I asked with a shiver, desperately hoping for an answer that proved me wrong.

"I'd most certainly remember him if I had!" Nora puffed up defensively.

"You mean… not even from the story?"

"Like I just said…"

"Right…" I didn't bother to try to convince her otherwise. Even if he were in the story, it wouldn't explain the part about being in Fort Turri now. *Just what other lies have I been telling myself to cope with everything?*

"Hey… You're not allergic to hay, are you?" Nora's brows furrowed. "You kind of look funny."

"Too much cheese…" I lied absently.

Nora pointed at my wrists. "You're scratching again."

"I'll just… put my gauntlets back on." My shaky hands, however, wouldn't cooperate. "Never mind." I turned to Aleph. "Uh. How fast… can this wagon go?" *We're moving too slowly.*

"A little faster in the daytime… but it would be foolhardy to press the horses long term." Aleph gazed at me. "Is there something we should know, Rae?"

Tell him I've been in contact with him? *Tell him he knows I'm here? That he's manipulating the Assembly to put his minions within striking range of Relias? That… that I've* talked *with him on several occasions? That I'm an utterly unreliable idiot?*

"I think…" I swallowed hard as I ran through all the previous conversations I could remember, pulling out the most critical issue. "I mean, I just have this horrible feeling that Holy Sage Relias might be in imminent danger…" And us as well, especially if any of *his* minions caught wind of what we just did. I silently prayed that Amos was as useless as King Olethros had made him out to be.

"Foresight!" Tetora's ears shot up. "Did you have another prophetic vision?"

Another…?

"I'm not sure… I didn't understand it before, but now…"

"Leave it at that and let them draw their own conclusions."

You again? Will you tell me who you are now, "passerby?"

There was no reply, and I realized that this one seemed to have a light touch. I definitely preferred that over being remotely controlled, though.

"Raelynn's were very much the same." Aleph patted my shoulder gingerly, mistaking the confusion on my face. Or at least a part of it. "Do not worry. We will make all haste."

Nora's face, however, clearly showed that my vague attempt at deceit had not convinced her. No matter how hard I tried, I couldn't shake the heavy feeling of her suspicious gaze.

After a few minutes of oppressive silence, Nora finally spoke again. "Tell us about the other council members. Are they not usually confined to Chairo?"

"Mmm… they occasionally travel to their homelands…" Aleph scratched his ear. "Procul is from Turri, so it's not suspicious that he's in the area. Inutilis hails from Porta, but other than that, I know almost nothing about him. From my understanding, he doesn't say or do much of his own accord."

"How many members make up the Assembly, anyway?" Nora glanced at me again, and I quickly busied myself by braiding some strands of hay, finding my fingers soaked in sweat.

"For the Assembly itself, there are only four councilmen leading it, with Holy Sage Relias acting as a voting member only to break ties. Otherwise, he's not privy to their discussions."

"Isn't he the one who established the Assembly?" I asked as my voice cracked. "Why would he exclude himself?"

"He felt the Assembly needed to be made up of the very same as those they would serve."

"Why only four councilmen, though?" Nora inquired. "It's an even number."

"To represent each of the four countries. Technically, I believe Relias speaks on behalf of Paradise, but since it is no longer truly accessible… he merely constitutes the tiebreaker in worldly affairs."

"Who represents Ecclesia and Lios?"

"Pravum was born and raised in Ecclesia," Tetora grumbled. "He's the one you need to watch out for. *Nothing* gets done without his blessing."

"Vetus of Lios would be the best one to talk to first," Aleph advised. "Don't be fooled just because he's old. He's quite receptive to new ideas."

I flinched as I stifled a gasp. Vetus died two months ago, but I couldn't say so as I had no way to explain how I knew that without revealing too much.

"But he was the one who recommended *him* to Raelynn," Tetora grumbled.

"I am sure he was deceived, just as we all were…" Aleph replied mournfully. "Don't forget it was *him* who convinced the Assembly to let us go in the end."

"That went by a little fast," Nora admitted. "Are you saying Councilman Vetus told Raelynn to seek out Oliver in the first place?"

"Yes. I still remember the letter of recommendation she received." Tetora raised his hackles in a show of aggression before imitating the voice of someone much older. *He's a young and promising sorcerer who has already worked his way through the first three Circles. He's a little full of himself, but that's almost considered a requirement in the Dark Mage Tower!* Tetora snorted and took a swipe at an innocent barrel, only to knock it down with a self-satisfying crash, demonstrating once again he was a cat at heart.

Aleph looked at Tetora disparagingly before sighing. "The last dark mage to be part of the Golden Order abandoned the hero's party over fifteen hundred years ago. Poor Raedine... she was never the same because of it and ultimately gave into despair and rage before losing to the original demon king. We were hesitant to include another such dark mage at first, but... Councilman Vetus convinced us it would be helpful if someone knowledgeable on the properties of animus accompanied us."

"This time, though, we have a dark mage vetted by the Goddess herself." Tetora winked at Nora, though she didn't acknowledge it.

"Another reincarnated hero..." Nora was distracted enough by backstory to stop glaring at me. "How often do these heroes show up, anyway?"

Tetora eyed me. "Every five hundred years or so. With one exception."

"Go on," I mumbled, too tired to argue about my identity.

He shook his head. "Raelynn showed up over four hundred and fifty years early. Luckily, we were ready for her."

Nora also gave me a scrutinizing look, but I just shrugged.

So she was a little different. That's... not necessarily a bad thing, is it?

"Well, back to Raedine," Nora said with a sigh. "Which one was she?"

"The fourth Chosen One," Aleph answered. "Legend says she was very self-effacing, even modest."

"Always said her success was because of those around her." Tetora righted the barrel under Aleph's judgmental gaze. "Never used her titles. She always said she was just passing by when someone asked who she was."

Oh… So that's who you were… I'm sorry you had such a bleak ending…

The wagon suddenly bounced several times as Vernie veered off the road into a secluded grove, displacing us all.

"Next time, warn us first!" Tetora snapped loudly as he scrambled back into a sitting position.

"Yeah, yeah." Vernie dismissed his complaints with a small laugh through the now-open slat. "Good to see you're back to yourself again."

"Why did you stop?" Aleph inquired.

"We're all tired, and this is far enough for now. Let's get the horses settled and rest."

"Tetora and I will help you." Aleph practically crawled out of the wagon. "You two may stay—"

"I want to help with the horses!" I shot up frantically, not wanting to be left alone with Nora and her inevitable interrogation. Karma was instantly rewarding this time, causing me to bang my head on the wooden ceiling. "D'aah!"

"Alright…" Aleph chuckled, misconstruing my false enthusiasm. "Just be sure to stay calm, and I'm sure you'll make friends with them in no time."

"I'll stay here." Nora's nose twitched threateningly. "I'm feeling rather tired from all the *recent drama.*"

As I passed her on my way out of the wagon, she muttered scornfully, "We'll just have to have our *private girl talk* a little later, won't we?"

CHAPTER 49: THE STORIES WE TELL [OURSELVES]

Seeking serenity within the company of our new horses was moderately rewarding, though I did little other than pet their necks for mutual reassurance. I was beyond exhausted, of course, but I was terrified of sleep. One of the shire mares with a chestnut coat was kind enough to allow me to lean on her side, where I fought with all my might to keep my eyes open.

"It'll be okay…" I murmured aloud, more to myself than her. "Keep up the good work, and we'll all make it through. We'll get to Chairo, then Paradise, and get someone else to deal with all the other problems… Right?" Amos might be my problem, though. And what if Relias won't accept any substitutions? …What if we get there too late? …What if *he* figures out where I am?

"Reynard said her name is Cinder," Vernie said as she wandered over, holding up the note that had been attached to the wagon.

"Cinder is a cute name." I straightened myself slowly, forcing myself to concentrate on Vernie's words.

"The brown mare over there is Tana. The bay next to her is Sela, and the black mare who has already settled for the night is Maren." Vernie put her arm on my shoulder. "Maybe we should do the same?"

"Oh…" I nervously glanced back at the wagon, wondering if Nora was still awake. "I can… take watch first."

"The only thing you could watch right now is the back of your eyelids! You *need* sleep."

"Did Raelynn… ever have nightmares?" I asked hesitantly.

"Nightmares?" Vernie pursed her lips. "Is that what you're worried about?"

"Yeah."

"Putting off sleep's only going to make it worse." Vernie sighed. "Trust a professional. Let's set up for the night, get you out of your armor, and I'll tell you about my first big heist. It's my favorite! Everything was almost worth it to get to tell it again." She gave me a playful wink.

"…Again?"

She grinned and scratched her neck. "Right, never mind. Just get ready for bed, okay?"

I followed her suggestion, mostly because I didn't have the mental stamina to develop a believable reason why I shouldn't. However, I drew the line at taking the armor off.

"I just feel better with it on for now," I said after she returned from the back of the wagon with my bedroll. "I'm sure I'll get used to it."

"Suit yourself! Though… I guess you already have." She laughed. "A bed of hay in the wagon might be more comfortable without it, though."

"I don't want to disturb the others…"

"No noise you'd make would come close to Aleph's snoring," Vernie retorted. "He's finally able to stop worrying about Furball."

"I'll stay under the stars tonight," I reaffirmed, carefully rolling out my shabby bedroll. I made quite a show of pulling out the corners and getting it just right without ever attempting to rest in it.

"I'm waiting," Vernie said, sitting cross-legged in the grass, her arms folded in front of her. "No stories until you lay down. "

"I *am* an adult, you know," I groused sleepily.

"Yes," Vernie agreed. "A very stubborn one. Come on now. You'll enjoy it."

I sighed heavily and plopped down with a clatter. "There. Regale me with the tale of your greatest heist."

"No, I said the first one, not the greatest."

"Oh? So it's not about the ring?" The web novel always had her talking about the time she swiped the signet ring of the King of Turri and used its most salient feature to fuel a shopping spree that even the wealthiest archduchess could only dream of. Neither the ring nor any reasonable facsimiles she had made from it were recovered, either. Ultimately, the king had to recommission his own family crest. Depending on the goal, certain story parts would be shared or omitted from each subsequent telling. I liked to hear about how all the stuff was given away capriciously to those in need. It helped make it seem it was done with an altruistic outcome in mind instead of just sheer skill and selfish will alone.

"This was way before that little escapade!" Vernie chuckled. *Little escapade?*

"So… what was it, then? What did you steal?" I couldn't help but ask after reviewing my hazy memories of other heist tales.

"Guess you'll just have to listen to find out." Vernie smiled and cleared her throat.

> *I found myself in yet another village with a forgettable, throwaway name. By this point in my life, my reputation for being a skilled pickpocket had already preceded me. But this tiny town held a trove of treasures, and I knew securing its pinnacle would only add to my prestige.*
>
> *It wouldn't be easy. My colleagues had made numerous attempts to abscond with just one item from the hoard, only to be caught and sentenced to the severest of lashings. The meticulously crafted treasures were under the surveillance of a whole cadre of gruff, battle-ready professionals, so I would need to enlist the perfect partner to carry out my objectives.*
>
> *The dapper elder I found in the shadows was simply known as Whiskers, a moniker suited for his frame and form. He was not interested in splitting the prize with me, but he demanded his hefty service fee upfront. Luckily, I had enough coin to meet his demands.*
>
> *Our roles were well defined: I would handle infiltration and extraction while he took center stage as a master of distraction. We'd hit the target location at the change of shift in the late morning when general disarray would cloak our movements.*

"What was the target location?" I asked with a frown, trying to imagine where this was going.

"Later, later." Vernie silenced me with a wave of her hand. "You're interrupting."

Whiskers made his grand entrance through the front door. He was purposefully overdressed in the most ostentatious bowtie specifically selected for the occasion, catching the eyes of everyone in the establishment. Their raucous laughter was the signal for me to get ready. When I heard the heavy footsteps on the other side of the back door fade to the front, I snuck in on silent feet, sticking to the shadowy corners.

Navigating the small labyrinth stealthily, I avoided the lesser treasures scattered about. I had my sights set on the grand prize, and for that, I'd have to reach the pedestal it sat upon. I resorted to stacking several heavy canvas sacks as carefully as possible to climb up to where it lay upon a precious-looking silver-colored trivet encrusted with sea-blue glass baubles.

"What was it?" I asked impatiently. "And why did the no-name village have a silver trivet?"

Vernie held up her hand. "Silver-colored. Not silver."

As my nimble fingers slowly lifted the treasure from its resting place, the proprietor caught sight of my crime in progress. Armed with a butcher's knife, he advanced on me with dreadful intent. Quick as a flash, I leapt from my improvised ladder, darted back through the maze of noisy traps, and slammed the heavy back door shut behind me. I had strategically placed a doorstop within arm's reach to buy myself a few precious seconds to escape and successfully deployed it.

Sprinting and weaving up a narrow back alley lined with boxes, I paused momentarily to watch Whiskers escape out the front door and melt back into the shadows he found safety in. Although our paths never crossed again, we had accomplished the unimaginable as my first grand heist. I held in my trembling hands Baker Baxter's famous oversized blueberry pie!

And I ate the whole damn thing!

"A… blueberry pie?" I blinked as I stared up at her from the ground. "You *paid someone* to help you steal *a pie?*"

"Whiskers was a cat." Vernie shrugged. "I couldn't put on the bowtie and scoot him in the front door without a treat, now could I?"

"You managed to put a bowtie on a cat?" That was probably the most unbelievable part of the whole thing. Chester would have never *ever* let me do something like that.

"Yes. The polka dots didn't exactly go with his tabby coat. That's why everyone was laughing."

I thought hard about the unspoken details. "Where'd you get the bowtie from?"

"Now that's a story for another night." Vernie smirked.

"… How'd it taste?"

"I've never had a better blueberry pie," Vernie admitted before looking at me seriously. "Probably because I got so sick from stuffing my face with it back then. I still can't stand them to this day."

I'll admit I have a weird sense of humor. The idea that karma was so instant to her made me laugh uncontrollably, with tears of exhaustion and giddiness running down my cheeks. Even if she had embellished a bit, even if it wasn't the truth, it was still a great distraction from everything that didn't make sense. Finally able to relax a little, I found myself nodding contentedly into a late-night slumber.

***

Her high heels clicked down the tiled hallway at a slow, staccato pace. She entered my room, pulling the heavy but silent wooden door behind her. She clicked the lock shut as always, though we both knew the nurses could easily override it from the outside.

"Hello, Mother." I turned away from the window I had been gazing out of. "It's nice to see you."

"It's nice to see you up and moving around, too." Mother's eyes shifted behind her glasses to the cityscape scene outside the window.

"Dr. Williamson says he plans to discharge you home tomorrow."

"Yes," I agreed with a smile. "I'm looking forward to going outside."

"The only problem is…" Mother took off her glasses and tucked them in her front breast pocket before folding her arms in front of her. "I'm not sure where your home is, exactly."

"What? No… I live with you, of course. You're my mother."

The one I'm supposed to trust.

Mother's gaze turned sooty. "We both know you've been hiding things, even from yourself. But you're going to need to make a decision. I can look into sending you back now that you're medically stable, or you can continue to live here."

"No… I'm Rachel. Your daughter! I live with you and—" A welter of images filled my mind. Home was a small stone room with a grated window built into a towering fort. A crowded dirt lodge filled with other young orphans. A wooden cabin with a warm stone hearth. A cotton futon lying on a woven grass mat. An ornate, golden temple with cathedral ceilings. A noisy farmhouse with an ever-busy kitchen. A dark and drafty cave lined with animal pelts.

"You don't know the truth, do you?" Mother's voice was tinged with the slightest hint of concern.

"I can't… remember right…" None of the flashes of memories, however, showed Mother. Was she not…? "I don't even know who you are!"

"I'm the one who first found you in that alley." Mother shrugged. "That's all."

"If you don't know me… then… Why have you been helping me?"

"I promised him I would follow The Rules while residing here. In this world, you're still a minor, subject to certain protective rights. I've been tasked with your safety and security until you come of age. If you want to go back, that's ultimately your choice, but with your memory loss, the situation is a bit complicated—"

"I can't go back!" I clutched my heaving chest as the room spun around me. Her story wasn't adding up. I needed answers, the truth. "I—" Then everything faded into a murky gray abyss as I collapsed to the polished, chilly floor.

CHAPTER 50: PALTERING

"How long are we going to let her sleep?" I heard Tetora demanding loudly.

"As long as she wants." Aleph's tone was unyielding. *"She had a busy day yesterday."*

"Just toss her in the back, and let's go. I want to know why everyone thinks I disappeared and my clan has turned traitor!"

"You realize that remark could have been simple slander, right?" Vernie said skeptically. "None of my men reported any such intel to me."

"No one I spoke with in Kopria had seen a tiger in years, though," Nora interjected. "Isn't that a little concerning?"

"Tigers aren't all that common in this region," Aleph pointed out. "Their forest is far from here."

"I did disappear…" Tetora muttered guiltily, then let out an exasperated snarl. "But I charged my sister with keeping things under control. She had better be doing exactly that!"

"You have a sister?" Nora asked excitedly. "What's she like?"

"Strong, fierce, determined!" Tetora laughed proudly. "Taika is even more stubborn than I am."

"Don't believe him," Vernie countered. "At least she can be reasoned with. She also *thinks before she speaks.*"

"I think before I speak. I just do it faster, and no one notices because I am like the wind!" *A blustering wind…*

Once more, I found myself drenched in cold sweat; its unpleasant aroma combined with my armor became somewhat nauseating. If I moved, though, there were bound to be problems. First and foremost, I could feel the tender bruises under my chest plate from yesterday's nonsense. Second, they would know I was awake and assume I would want to engage in the discussion. I half-hoped someone would indeed pick me up and toss me into the wagon, but as their conversation drifted, that outcome seemed less likely.

Instead, I remained as motionless as possible, plotting how to deal with Nora. The phrase "private girl talk" sounded an alarm in my head. It meant I would need more than my regular tactics to suffice. Rather than avoiding or blowing her off, I'd have to go on the offensive. She wanted the truth, and I decided to give her only the bits I was ready to disclose.

Mainly, I didn't want to tell her about *him*. I was sure I had my reasons, though if you asked me to put them into words at this point, I really couldn't. My feelings were too raw and unanalyzed, leaving me unable to discern what was the truth and what was merely my own projection of our fake relationship built on intentional misinformation and misdirection.

Cinder, the chestnut mare I had half-collapsed on the night before, started sniffing at my face.

"Alright… I take it you're in a hurry, too?" I asked as I sat up with a surrendering groan, carefully keeping my hair away from her mouth. It had reached my hips now, and I suspected its growth cycle was somehow tied to my use of amity. I knew people at home would pay for such a wealth of hair, but I found no value in it. Cutting it made no difference now either; it would be back to the same length when I awoke again.

"Did I miss breakfast?" I called to the group as I cautiously caressed Cinder's muzzle. Thankfully, she seemed accepting and allowed me to stand up without interfering too much with the painful process.

"Just be thankful Aleph saved some for you," Tetora barked back at me. "I wanted seconds, but he insisted."

"Thank you, Aleph… and you too, for showing such restraint." I took the hint to express my gratitude to Tetora as well, and he seemed pleased. After rinsing my hands, I helped myself to some cheesy bean gruel. The cheese honestly made all the difference, turning what was normally a bland breakfast into a comforting blend of creamy beans and melted cheese that warmed me from the inside out. Then again, the bar for what I considered a good meal had been significantly lowered since the start of my adventure. I was just grateful for the cheese.

After taking the last bites of breakfast, I finally chanced a glance at Nora, whose face was arranged like a poor man's Picasso. "Can I talk to you privately in the wagon? I need your help deciphering my vision before we share it with everyone. You're usually good at helping me understand my weird thoughts, no offense."

Nora blinked, successfully caught off guard. "Alright…" She was halfway out of her seat before a suspicious glint reappeared in her eyes. Well, the battle wasn't over yet. I climbed in first and offered her my hand to help pull her up, but she ignored it.

"You're mad at me because you know I was hiding things from you," I quietly conceded once we sat opposite each other. "But I didn't know I was hiding them until last night. I'm sorry."

Her eyes darted back and forth as she processed my statement, almost like she was looking for something to disprove. I waited patiently until she gave up trying to deflate my defense.

"Well… what were you hiding, then?" she asked in a more mollified tone.

"Remember when you asked me who I was talking about that night when I had a weird dream?"

"Yeah…"

"In my dream…" I paused, getting to the tricky part. Paltering, more commonly known as lying with the truth, is an art best suited for professionals like politicians and CEOs. I didn't have enough experience with it to be called a master, but I had picked up on the basics. "I overheard a conversation about those four councilmen… er, three now."

"Three?"

"Vetus is dead," I said softly. "He won't be able to help us when we get there."

"Did someone kill him?" Nora's eyes went wide.

"I don't think so. They seemed to think it was due to natural causes. But there's a bigger problem."

"Lay it on me." Nora started to spin one of her brown curls around her finger.

"I'm pretty sure at least one of them was a demon trying to penetrate Chairo's inner barriers and reach Relias." I didn't even want to think about what would happen if he managed to pull it off.

Nora blinked again, several times, and I continued quickly to cut off any more questions. "I didn't see him, though, so I'm unsure. *I only heard his voice.* But he was told to find a way in by bribing Pravum for the barriers' maintenance schedules. Someone called him… um, a name I don't recognize, though I doubt that was his true name, by the way the other said it."

It was still too risky to say the name aloud either way.

"Someone?" Nora asked with a raised eyebrow.

"Neither one said the name of the other." I tried *my damndest* not to look away or sweat. Nora's eyes lingered on my face for a moment before she looked at my hands resting peacefully in the confines of my lap. However, the urge to scratch my wrists was almost overpowering, so I forced my toes to curl painfully inside my boots to override my nervous response.

After a few dreadfully long moments, Nora finally exhaled and pulled her journal from her cloak. "Write down his name."

I scribbled "Amos" into her journal with a shaky hand.

Nora squinted. "It is a rather plain name. It might be a cover. Maybe not even a demon. He could be a dark mage or hybrid with a vendetta."

"Maybe he's even human," I added. "But we should suspect the worst, right?"

"You're right." Nora took a deep breath. "Sorry… for doubting you."

"No, I understand…" I shook my head. "I'm beginning to think that some of my memories and my dreams, maybe even my thoughts… aren't my own. They're all confused and…"

Stop. That's too much truth. She'll ask more questions…

Nora shook her head. "And let me guess… you don't want to talk about it?"

"I just don't know where to start," I admitted. "I think this is something I will have to figure out over time, on my own."

She opened her mouth several times but caught herself before uttering a single syllable. Finally, she murmured, "It doesn't help that you have strange visitors stopping by unannounced."

"Oh. About that. I had one drop by when we encountered Dolus."

Nora nodded, letting out an absent grunt. "I thought that might have been the case, too. You were quite distracted. Who was it, and what'd they say?"

"Raedine," I confirmed. "She told me not to fly into a rage and kill Dolus… and all the others…" I looked down. "I was a little upset. If you know what I mean…" I paused, once again ashamed at my murderous thoughts.

"Hmmm. They do *seem* to be helping, at least," Nora mused. "But I think they have an agenda of their own."

"Doesn't everyone?" I asked rather plaintively.

"Um, yes, I suppose so." She glanced away as she padded her makeshift seat with extra hay.

"When that demoness disrupted you with animus…" I started, recalling the moments before Raedine routed my rage. "Did you hear anything before you got angry? Like a high-pitched shriek?"

"Hmm. I heard a throaty roar, like from a giant beast." Nora shook her head. "Angry… but a bit grief-stricken."

Grief-stricken? "Oh… I was just wondering if it was the same as what I heard. Guess it's different."

We sat silent, listening to the others break down the camp.

"Speaking of demons…" Nora wiggled uncomfortably again before offering me a piece of parchment plucked from her journal.

"No papyrus this time?" I skipped the confidentiality introduction.

To: Eleanora Beatrice Perez and Rachel Emily Smith

From: Clare Mercure (Manager, Information Technology, Cooperative Universal Publishing)

RE: Demon Inquiry (Confidential)

I received your 'prayer request' for 'more information on demons.' Please see the result and error below. An IT support ticket has been opened on your behalf to troubleshoot the error encountered. Please note that a full restore of the Speranza Sentient Being Type (SBT) database is not currently possible. I will attempt to manually reconcile data inconsistencies to repair your local NAUGHT instance upon successful reboot and critical update installation.

Speranza SBT Database: Your query: demon returned 0 results and 1 error:

SBT= "demon" OR SBT= "daemon" OR SBT= "devil" OR SBT= "fiend" OR SBT= "hellion" [...]

Error: Critical Data Fault Exception

A foreign key constraint violation has been detected. This should not be possible and must result from actions by a user with super administrative privileges to edit the database files directly. Data corruption has already occurred. To reconcile data inconsistencies, a full restore of a database backup that predates the corruption will need to be performed, or manual intervention by a database administrator will be required. Please contact your database administrator IMMEDIATELY.

I didn't understand the error, but they better have made it a high priority to fix!

"Are they saying… there's no such thing as demons?" Try telling *them* that.

"Mmmm… no. They're saying they don't have any information on them in their database. The fact that they got that error when running the search suggests foul play, though."

"Foul play?"

"Yeah. I think this error means *someone* illegally deleted entries about them from the database."

"What database?" I fretted. "And why is Clare the manager of IT now? I thought she was Human Resources."

"She probably wears many hats," Nora said as she lounged back into the hay. "The fewer eyes on this stuff, the easier it is to keep it confidential."

The parchment paper turned brittle and flashed brightly before disintegrating into a cloud of fine, golden dust between my fingers. "Gaah!"

Nora let out a nervous chuckle. "Guess that's what she meant by self-destruct in the header!" *Like in the cartoons?*

I swallowed hard and reminded myself never again to skip over a single line of text from CUP, no matter how short, stupid, or insignificant it appeared.

Nora patted my shoulder reassuringly, instinctively picking out my greatest fear. "I'm sure that Relias knows how to take care of himself. He's been around for a while, right? Don't worry. We'll find him, and he'll help us make sense of the situation."

I inhaled, wondering how he'd react upon seeing me. Half the time, I settled on him immediately discarding the idea that I was Raelynn. The other part of me fretted, thinking he was going to be tricked, just as the others seemed to be. Honestly, I couldn't decide which scenario was worse.

"Sounds good," I eventually replied, still reluctant to open up about my deeper thoughts.

CHAPTER 51: CALL OF THE ORDER

"Well?" I heard Vernie ask the others as Nora and I hopped out of the back of the wagon a little while later.

"It certainly is… different," Aleph answered dubiously, tugging at his right ear.

I stopped in my tracks, and Nora bumped into me from behind. Vernie was sporting the world's worst dye job, and her now raven-black hair was made slick by crude, dark oil that had rubbed off in smudgy streaks around the nape of her neck.

"It's not that bad, right?" she asked both of us. Oh no, it was much worse than simply *bad*. She was a red base, and she'd used a blue-hued black. Any warm color from her pale skin was simply gone now, and the light freckles she had looked like the faded remnants of a sickly pox.

"What was your intent?" Nora asked, one eyebrow cocked up in disbelief.

"A disguise," Vernie admitted as she pulled up the hood of her cloak. "Red hair's a bit of a striking feature. If I'm going to drive the wagon, I should try to blend in some. Don't want to catch the Blue Order's attention. Pretty sure someone's going to boast about seeing me around here."

Nora's nose wrinkled as she fought with the truth. "You certainly don't look like yourself, so… you've achieved your objective. Right, Rae?"

"Uh, yes," I agreed, relieved I didn't have to add my opinion. "But shouldn't we take turns driving the wagon? Bouncing on that box seat for hours doesn't sound like fun…"

"Mmmm…" Vernie exhaled nervously. "Nora can probably learn… but other than that…"

We finally realized why the other travelers had been rude on the road. Even if Aleph or Tetora could sit comfortably on the driver's bench, it would add unnecessary complications. Kopria probably had the market share of racial prejudice, but that didn't mean their practice was confined to any particular boundary.

I looked at the team of horses with anticipation. We could move faster and rendezvous with Relias in no time. "What about me? I could try—"

"You are absolutely forbidden to touch the reins!" Tetora declared, folding his arms crossly. *"Your driving is terrible."*

"You don't know that!" It's not like driving a team of horses is anything like driving a car. They had brains; they'd eventually figure out what I wanted them to do.

Nora started cackling, and while I should have been relieved to see her treating me like normal again, I *knew* what she was thinking about.

I folded my arms as I defended myself. "I'm telling you, that driving instructor purposely hid that four-way stop sign behind a tree branch. That's why I failed!" It was true!

"You want to go fast?" Tetora looked at me disdainfully. "Ride the horse *yourself*. Leave me and the wagon out of it."

Ride the horse myself… Would Cinder let me do that? I twitched a little. *Maybe soon… Oh, but the wagon might be too heavy for the other three without her…*

"I also abstain from such rides unless it's a true emergency," Aleph agreed. "Let's not test the idea of breakneck speed… ever again."

"Horses like to run…" I muttered under my breath. I didn't, at least on my own two feet, but horse riding is… what, exactly? How would I know… about the exhilarating thrill of being of one mind with a powerful creature, passing by all the numerous but ultimately tiny problems that just blurred in the distance so you could finally see the great expanse of the world before you?

To just keep going, never looking back…

We helped with the last part of the clean-up before we prepared for our day's travels. As we packed the wagon, I briefly summarized the redacted version of my "prophetic vision," which was again couched as a vaguely overheard conversation. After showing everyone Amos's name in Nora's journal, we concluded no one recalled such a being. I also shared the updates I had heard about the council members.

"To think Vetus has passed…" Aleph shook his head. "This changes things."

"A new councilman to throw in the mix?" Nora asked. "Any ideas who?"

"No, actually. Electing a new councilman takes about a year and a half…" Aleph's ears twitched in irritation. "And that's only if no one contests the results."

Nora shoved the last of the supplies into the wagon. "A year and a half? There's no interim succession plan in place?"

"They're all supposed to be able to cover for each other until another is elected." Aleph shrugged as I settled in the back. "They'd know best what needs to be done."

In a perfect world, maybe, but this place was far from it.

"So with Procul back here and Inutilis being rather inert, it's Pravum as default, isn't it?" Nora mumbled.

"Yes… Pravum and Relias don't have a friendly relationship," Aleph admitted. "To be honest, none of them do."

"Of course not…" I sighed, feeling bad for Relias in particular. "I'm guessing being the tiebreaker doesn't win you anything except the losers' disdain."

Our travel pace was annoyingly sluggish, and my worries only grew as I bounced along in the wagon while Nora and Vernie rode up front. We were traveling faster than before, but not nearly enough, in my opinion.

"Why don't you rest, little one?" Aleph eventually asked. "Soon, you'll be out of hay to braid."

I flinched a little, tossing aside my impromptu handicraft. The only way I had learned to enter a dreamless slumber and avoid… you know, was to stay up past the point of exhaustion first. "No… I think I got enough last night, thanks."

I made them tell me more stories about Raelynn. Many of them were already familiar to me from the novel, but their added commentary gave me more dimension to who she was or… perhaps who *I* was. Still… it sounded like she never wavered even once, and that was probably the biggest difference between us. Wasn't she ever scared? Or anxious? She just… did what she had to do. None of their stories included Oliver, of course, though I had been secretly hoping they'd let something slip about him.

How would I deal with him if I didn't know his true characteristics and weaknesses?

"What the… No!" I suddenly shouted out loud at myself for such a troublesome thought. *I don't* want *to deal with him!*

Tetora scowled. "Are you really so hungry you can't wait another hour? If we stop now, we'll lose the daylight."

They must have been discussing tonight's schedule. "What? Oh… no… I don't know what I was thinking. I can manage." I sighed and shook my head.

The evening was filled with disappointment. Although Cinder let me climb up her back, she didn't seem keen on going anywhere, really. I couldn't blame her since she had put in a full day's work, but I had been hoping she had wanted to go for a short trot after dinner. I gave up pressuring her and instead participated in the evening grooming ritual with everyone else.

With Tetora back in action, nighttime training resumed under Nora's bright ball of bouncing light. While Aleph had allowed me to explore different sword stances with a range of acceptable variations, Tetora was convinced that if a move was not executed perfectly, it was an utter failure. I silently amassed several derogatory names to call him should I ever find a good opportunity to do so.

The days passed as our new routine settled around us. With the wagon, no one tried to run us off the road like before. A few people exchanged brief pleasantries with Vernie and Nora. There was also the occasional threatening or vulgar proposition that necessitated Vernie to brandish her knife, but no one ever took her up on her counteroffer. Although it was never openly discussed, Aleph, Tetora, and I, being the most recognizable members of the party now, stayed in the wagon during daylight hours to minimize the chance of being spotted. At Nora's insistence, we broke the tradition of hiding one quiet afternoon to bury the Skreethi pelt we had found with full honors.

She'll probably protest when she reads this, but she can be just as sweet and sentimental as me… maybe even more.

After a week or so, I found myself particularly antsy from the moment I awoke. We proceeded as normal, but another hour or so passed until I finally put my finger on what was bothering me the most. "No one has passed us by…" I quickly peered out one of the triangular openings along the wagon's side. "Where are the other travelers? No one's coming from either direction."

"Stop the wagon!" Tetora ordered, though he didn't bother to wait until it came to a halt. He bounded out the back and dashed a few hundred feet down the road before pausing. His ears first flattened, then turned in several directions. His lips curled up into a sneer, and he took a few breaths as if he were tasting the very air itself.

"There's no one around," he reported back tersely.

"No one?" Aleph repeated in dubious disbelief.

I glanced at the landscape. There were no farms here, just vast, open fields, unmarred by any tools and overgrown with various plants fighting to reach the sun.

"We passed a few offshoots on our way here… but this is the main road to the east…" Aleph stared into the distance.

"No. They're… hiding themselves," I stubbornly disagreed, instinctively focusing my aura. "They're nearby, hiding in the brush to the north. No, wait. To the… west?" There were hostile intents all around us, for sure.

Aleph turned. "Rae, I know you're worried, but—"

"Look!" I pointed into the distance, where several birds had darted off from one of the fields in unison.

"Get in the wagon!" Aleph boomed. "Nora, in the back. Vernie! Get us to the foot of that hill!"

As we took flight ourselves, I heard a familiar blood-chilling call of a brass horn from our distant left. It was immediately answered by another from behind, leaving no doubt in my mind.

The Order of Blue was *closing in on us*.

CHAPTER 52: CHIVALRY IS DEAD

The wagon's increasingly ominous creaks and high-pitched squeals rose above the thrumming of the horse's hooves, distorting my sense of time and distance. The wagon shuddered as we overwhelmed its steel and leather belt suspension, and I found myself holding my breath to the point of seeing dark spots before my eyes. Rivulets of sweat had gathered on my forehead, and with every resounding call of a brass horn, they would cascade down into my eyes with a painful, salty sting.

Tetora grabbed my shoulder roughly, pulling me away from one of the triangular side holes I had fixated on. "How many are there?"

Reminded by his presence to breathe again, I inhaled with a choking half-snort. "I have no idea?" I responded once I could muster enough concentration to reply. "They're still too far away for me to see."

"Close your eyes and count them!" he ordered urgently. "How many blue lights do you see?"

Blue lights when I close my eyes? Shutting my eyes tightly, I initially saw nothing out of the ordinary. The customary flickers of color were there, like always, but ophthalmologists told me countless times that seeing phosphenes was expected. They shifted and swirled as I concentrated, desperate to identify anything blue or some meaningful pattern among them.

"I can't…" I trailed off, suddenly distracted by a sea of azure holy stars rising from the darkness. They hovered in place, radiating a pale blue light as they slowly spun on their axes. One star, larger and brighter than the rest, set the scene ablaze with a sudden lash of electric blue flames, knocking out my vision completely. As everything faded into a swirl of neon blue light, a severe and commanding shout of "Captain Raelynn Lightbringer! Surrender immediately or else!" pierced through my mind, filling my heart with dread as I realized they were after me in particular.

I had heard that stern, terrible, and eternally unappeased voice before in my nightmares, constantly reminding me of my numerous shortcomings.

"Half a hundred at least. I couldn't count them all," I admitted after a few moments with an uncontrollable shiver. "There was a big one that just took out the rest." Feeling like I had just stared into the blazing sun itself, I rubbed my eyes without relief. *Surrender immediately or else…*

Aleph began smashing the more useless barrels in the back of the wagon with his war hammer, tossing their sharp remnants onto the road behind us.

"We need to lessen the load on the horses. Discard anything that isn't essential."

Nora peered out the back of the wagon briefly before gesturing slowly in a wide arc. *"Ventos pulverulentus…!"*

At first, I thought it was simply the horses kicking up extra dust from the road with their faster gait, but the dust billowed out in a rippling, u-shaped pattern behind us. Again and again, Nora repeated her words, filling the air with a dirty, smog-like haze. "How much… longer… till we get to the hill?" she asked between ragged breaths.

"Keep it up for a few more minutes. I'm going to cut across the fields," Vernie screamed, and Nora readjusted the pulsating waves of dust in response. The wagon then seemed to jump and hover momentarily as we broke off from the road onto a grassy plain.

I didn't have the heart to tell them we probably weren't fooling anyone. Makeshift caltrops from broken barrels? Clouds of obscuring dust? Clever in thought, but probably just mere annoyances to a mounted cavalry communicating our movements almost instantly between squads.

The others needed to get away. Somehow, I just knew they'd be used against me.

"Which one of us do you think they're really after?" I asked Aleph quietly to gauge his perspective, realizing I could hear a thundering counterpoint in the distance to our horses' gallops.

Aleph took too long to answer, pretending he was looking for more debris to throw. "It's hard to say."

"Guess it doesn't matter…" I replied solemnly, knowing we both knew the truth. We weren't going to say it out loud, though.

The wagon lurched to an abrupt halt with a loud screech, dumping us all towards the back tailgate. Tetora and Aleph jumped out and raced each other up the hill to get a better look while the rest of us followed in their wake.

The view was undeniably beautiful, except it was marred by the encroaching tide of swarming blue pennons from all directions. Moderate breaks were visible in their formations to the north, but they were disappearing at an alarming rate as they closed ranks around us. Weren't there any other options?

I slammed my eyes shut and willed myself to concentrate on the swirling, pulsating colors that checker-boarded before my eyelids. The blue stars converged, but I saw tiny pin-pricks of silver way off to the west.

"Silver… silver stars now as well," I said, pointing in defeat at a distant mountain pass. "There's a bunch of them just beyond there…" Now, a second army was in our path. We were completely screwed.

"Ecclesia's Order… this far west?" Aleph said as he doubled back to the cart and turned to Vernie, his brow suspended somewhere between concern and wonder. "Do you have any intel about this?"

"No!" Vernie replied emphatically. "But don't look a gift horse in the mouth! And speaking of horses… Let's not burden them so much," she advised, already disengaging them from the wagon. "I swear, I would have told you if I had known anything like that!"

"Rae," Aleph called out urgently as he quickly tacked the horses, readying them for riding. "We might have a chance if we just get to them. The Silver Order is much more reasonable."

Wait, we could trust them? Oh, but we wouldn't make it unless…

I promptly mounted Cinder the moment she was free. "Let's make a break for it!" I replied in a falsely optimistic tone as I watched the others follow my lead. *I really am a hypocrite, saying we should stick together and speak up when there's a concern. But I was the leader and had to act like everything would be okay. They needed "that Rae" of hope to make the impossible happen.*

"Hey, gimme a hand up!" Nora called from Cinder's flank.

Simple math alone should have prepared me for this issue. "I think you should ride with Vernie." I frowned. "She's probably more skilled at riding double." *No, I was* not *making any sort of innuendo there.*

"I want to ride with you!" Nora insisted. "I'll be useful, too! They're too far away now, but I'll hit 'em with Fulgura once they get close!"

"Lightning sounds like an easy win," I replied. "But are you okay with roasting a platoon of holy knights alive in their armor? And that's only if you catch them off guard, which I wouldn't count on…"

Nora opened her mouth in retort, then pulled it shut with a sigh. "It's like we're doing this on hard mode. Ugh." She scratched her cheek.

"Somnia… Somnus…"

"Ultum Somnum," Tetora muttered. "*He* would use that to put our enemies to sleep—" He stopped short with a half-roar, turning away. "Just use those words when the time is right."

"I'll target their horses," Nora declared as her eyes glittered. "You're okay with that, at least?"

"Yes," I agreed. "Just be sure to hold on tight to Vernie."

Nora shouted, "I *just said* I'm going to ride with y—"

"No," I said firmly. "Captain's orders."

Sorry, Nora, but this is where we part.

Nora mouthed something most likely condescending under her breath, but she ultimately mounted Vernie's horse with her assistance.

Focusing on my posture, I adjusted the grip on Cinder's reins and urged her forward with a throaty cluck. "Spread out a little and look for weak openings! Do whatever you can to break through!" I commanded as if I knew exactly what I was talking about.

They obliged with the bare minimum of spread, still crowding me more than I was comfortable with. I was about to complain, but once again, that blusterous, blood-chilling horn resounded throughout the now-stale air. Trembling, I urged Cinder to go faster.

No matter how swift Cinder was, she couldn't outrun a well-trained warhorse. She tried her best, though, as the rest did, cascading across the expansive grassy plains before us.

Nora, holding on for dear life, her arms wrapped around Vernie's waist, turned and gave me an apprehensive look. "Fog?" she mouthed in exaggeration.

Perfect. I nodded emphatically.

Her fingers wiggled almost imperceptibly, and a sudden fog whipped up in swirls around us.

"Stick together!" Aleph shouted in alarm as they continued to gallop off.

I figured the fog would only last a few minutes, as she would soon need to put the enemy horses to bed, so I pulled back on Cinder's reins. No holy knight, no matter what Order or rank, would shoot someone in complete surrender. I couldn't take half a hundred of them, anyway.

Cinder and I slipped away from our companions as we retreated out of the fog, searching for a wide-open space.

Cinder trotted to a stop as I watched the cavalry move in like a wave, their silhouettes ghosting through the last remnants of fog, getting clearer as they approached. I threw down my weapons and supplies as loudly as possible. My heart raced, not just from the chase but from the uncertainty of what came next.

There, in the open, I stood alone, my hands raised in a universal gesture of surrender.

"I, Raelynn Lightbringer, request quarter!" I shouted at the top of my lungs as I pulled down my hood. The cavalry's advance halted as the wind died around us, causing their flags to droop. A squad of the most decorated knights closed rank in front of me, their agile horses appearing to walk sideways, snorting and stamping restlessly.

A giant black warhorse shoved its way forward, breaking the line. Its rider pulled off his decorated helmet, revealing a short crop of platinum hair and the hardest eyes I had ever seen, devoid of anything remotely resembling warmth. His chiseled features were harshly sculpted into a face of eternal discontent. He waited a moment, his chilling gaze paralyzing me. I tried to summon my aura, but something oppressive hanging about the area halted me. *It was as if there was no goodwill to be found.* He turned to his right and snapped his fingers once.

The mounted knight beside him abruptly aimed a crossbow. Before I could react, a bolt flew from the bow, striking Cinder. With a soul-piercing scream, she bucked me from the saddle. As I slammed into the ground, she continued thrashing wildly as she roared and whirled.

"You forgot to kneel," the captain explained emotionlessly. "Be thankful I have rectified this lapse in your conduct so I can properly grant you the quarter you requested." *The captain who threatened me to surrender!*

Dizziness and nausea engulfed me as I tried to rise from the ground, where I saw the swirling smoke of disappearing dark runes around my feet. *Had someone cast a spell on me?* Pain radiated down my right shoulder into my hand, with my wrist hanging gruesomely out of place. I stared incredulously at the both of them while they ordered the others to secure my horse.

Once Cinder was trapped, the horse shooter shouted, "Get one of the priests to silence it, then send it back for proper training."

"At once, Lieutenant Balor!" one of the other knights responded. *Balor… Balor the what? What was he, again?*

"How could you… do such a… terrible thing!?" I spluttered in fear and anger at them both, my rapid breathing threatening to overwhelm my speaking ability. *The heavy tension in the air continued to press down on my thoughts, forcing me to keep my mouth shut about my darkest suspicions.*

The captain drew himself up in his saddle, folding his arms crossly. "First, you refused to include my Order in the final assault on the castle of the demon king. And now you have the audacity to return and think you can *circumvent my authority in Turri?* Why must you persist in being such a disappointment? I've raised a truly disobedient daughter."

364

CHAPTER 53: ABOUT FACE

If Nora and I knew *anything about anyone* in this fantasy story, it was that Raelynn's parents were *dead*. She was an orphan, one of many young survivors of a terrible plague that had run rampant across Speranza. She made her family *where she found it*; she never would have broken bread with such an arrogant extremist! *He's just manipulating me.*

"You're *not* my father!" I shrieked in pained disbelief.

"And yet I personally invested six years into your military training, though I remain unrewarded for my exhaustive efforts." The captain shrugged indifferently. "But not for much longer. I am the one who found you first this time."

Is there… some reward for my safe return?

"Captain Garvith!" a young knight with short blonde hair called as he led his lathered horse to intercept the line. "A report from the scouts!"

The captain sighed impatiently as he waited for the knight to dismount, walk over, and bow to him. He then took the parchment the knight offered and promptly shoved it under his saddle without a cursory glance. "Just tell them to return to base. We got what we came here for," he responded curtly before a contemplative look spread across his face. "Belay that." He paused before turning to his lieutenant. "Switch them out one more time. Her companions might decide to double back sooner than expected."

"As you command, Captain Garvith!" Balor responded, leading his horse off with an unnecessarily strong snap of its reins.

Garvith eyed the blonde-haired knight. "Secure the prisoner… And splint her wrists. But be sure to tie the bonds as tight as you can. She has a way of slipping out of tight spots."

The weary young knight looked at me with unwanted pity in his eyes. "Shouldn't we call for a healer?"

"No. It's a reminder to keep her from doing something stupid," Garvith retorted.

The young knight balked a bit. "But… Captain… she surrendered…"

"So what? She's not to be trusted. Understood?" Garvith declared to the entire line, who saluted sharply in response.

"What about Cinder!?" I yelled at him.

"You can have that *"horse"* back once we reach our destination," the captain replied with a hint of callous amusement. "Behave, and I might even spare your inevitably interfering companions. But understand, it depends on you doing precisely as you're told… for once in your life."

Just who the hell was this guy, and why was he such an asshole? And why were the others all listening to him? Most of the other knights remained helmeted, so I couldn't search their faces, but I did catch the eye of the now-terrified young knight once again.

"Just do what you have to do," I hissed. He would probably scream just as much as Cinder did if *he* were hit with a crossbow bolt.

He nervously dashed to his saddlebags, procuring a few wooden sticks and linen wraps. I gritted my teeth as he splinted my wrist as ordered. "Arms behind you…" he motioned sadly when he was finished, and I reluctantly complied, willing my tears not to fall.

"I'm sorry, I'm sorry," he whispered repeatedly as he bound my hands sloppily behind my back. They weren't genuinely constricting, but it was enough to be uncomfortable. My wrist continued to throb threateningly, and I knew eventually I wouldn't be able to take the pain.

A few other knights, some hybrid, some human, dismounted and gathered my weapons, snorting with contempt at their simple design. Captain Garvith, however, shot them a disparaging look, and they ceased with their side commentary.

"Since you two are now well acquainted, you'll be riding together," Captain Garvith asserted as he turned away. "I advise you again, Raelynn, to keep your aura in check. Otherwise…" he stopped, and I felt his frontline draw in their holy focus in unison. "Do you understand, *Daughter?*"

Raelynn spent six years with him? I couldn't stand six minutes.

"*Understood, Garvith,*" I said with a sneer. The most insulting thing I could afford was not acknowledging his rank or claim of having some relationship with me. Rather than react, he wordlessly led the column toward the south.

There is almost nothing more humiliating than to be hauled up and unceremoniously deposited onto the back of a warhorse. I was somewhat proud of myself for not screaming during the harrowing process, biting my lip angrily as they secured me in the saddle with additional rope. Each forced movement sent a wave of pain erupting from my broken wrist, even with the splint. With a growl forming but never escaping my throat, I started to regret the chain of decisions I had made that had led up to this point. Why had I held on to the naïve belief that the code of chivalry was strictly followed? Once again, I had foolishly assumed that people would uphold the same principles as I did.

I wasn't worried about losing my life; I was sure his anticipated reward was commensurate to my overall well-being. It was that I let my friends operate on a false set of assumptions just because I knew they'd disagree with my plan. My thoughts started to go dark with smoldering rage directed at myself and, to some extent, my captors as well.

"*Again already?*"

Raedine! You're back!

"*I said I was just passing by before… but I don't like going in circles. Do you?*"

I screwed up again.

"*Everyone does. But dwelling on your anger alone won't solve your problem.*"

How do I solve it then? If I try to power up now…

"*If you can't determine an appropriate action, you probably lack information or a timely opportunity. Put your energy to good use and watch for your moment.*"

A sigh escaped my lips, but I took her breezy advice to heart. Information and opportunity…

"Well…" I tried my best to keep my voice level. "What's your name, Sir Knight?" I asked my "voluntold" riding companion, whose horse kept pace with the one I was tied to.

"Volker," the young blonde replied quietly. "But I am no knight, Captain Lightbringer."

He was certainly dressed like one. "Uh," I began in confusion.

"I am merely part of Captain Garvith's retinue," he murmured. "Only those with the inherent blessing of amity can hope to become true knights of the Order."

"Oh… I see." *Makes sense, I guess.*

"You can tell the difference by looking at the pendants we wear over the surcoat," he explained. "Although we wear similar livery, the holy knights are the only ones who may bear Euphridia's Star."

"Do they… pay you well?" I asked, trying to distract myself from my discomfort.

"Room and board, at least," Volker confirmed. "I take on odd jobs that are… ah…"

"Beneath the others?' I supplied.

"That's one way to put it," Volker murmured. "Let's not say it too loud, though."

We rode in awkward silence for a bit after that. He seemed nervous about his assignment as my babysitter, and I didn't know precisely what would constitute a policy violation at this point. I wanted to get someone on my side, however. That would be the best inroad for an informative exchange with these professionally sanctioned mercenaries. But what could I offer up at the moment? I wasn't about to tell them about my friends or anything else that could be used against me.

"Did you forget your celebrity status? You're playing Raelynn, the returning hero, back from the unknown. Impress him with an epic tale that can only be told by you."

What would a holy knight consider an epic tale that only the hero could—oh…

"Feel free to embellish it a little. I know you can't remember all the details."

"Everything's so different now," I stated loudly, gazing into the distance with what I hoped was an air of aloofness and mystery. "I had hoped Speranza would have changed for the better after I defeated King Epiales." I let out a sigh of disappointment and regret. "But I suppose my victory remains unsung, given the world's sorrow at my, uh…" I fumbled my words.

"Unanticipated exodus."

"Unanticipated exodus," I repeated aloud. Raedine's corporate-speak was even better than I had realized.

"N-not true, Holy Captain!" Volker straightened in the saddle considerably. "We all speak of it, and we know of your sacrifice. It's just… well… the captain… and some other holy knights… They were looking forward to participating in the ultimate quest for glory."

Can't get a nice reward if you don't participate, right?

"I didn't want my sacrifice to cost the world anything greater than necessary, but I could see how some must have been disappointed, unable to join the final battle," I falsely conceded while suppressing an eye roll. The *last* thing she needed was a bunch of violent hotheads calling attention to her actions.

"What was it like?" he asked in wonder, completely hooked now. *"The final battle?"*

I chose my next words carefully, shamelessly plagiarizing from the serialized novel. "He was a grotesque fusion of nightmare and malice." I exhaled, trying to straighten in the saddle but failing as the rope held me in place. "His face and body were covered in a hideous, matted fur, and with two baleful eyes, he regarded me as less than nothing before his abject might."

"What did he say to you? What was his reasoning for seeking to destroy the world?"

I shook my head. "The only words he could scream were, *'You are not Raela. You are even less than her. Tell your Goddess to send Raela next time!'*"

The knight tensed his grip on the reins. "To think he only wanted to destroy again that which was most precious to Holy Euphridia…"

I couldn't disagree with him there. It was as if a singular, destructive obsession had utterly consumed the old demon king.

I put on my proverbial story-teller hat and recounted the scene while adding a little drama to my word choice. "There was no use in talking with him. I advanced, my shield high to ward off his vicious first strikes. He swung his claws as his weapons of choice, unleashing wave upon wave of dark energy that crashed against my shield. Though each blow staggered me, I held my ground." I paused, noting that a few more knights had slowed their horses to fall in step with ours.

"But you fought back, wielding the Faith and Will of Euphridia," another knight took up the story from me. "Relias himself testified that as your blade met his twisted flesh, he felt pain for the first time in his miserable life!"

That… was plagiarized straight from the novel, too!

"I think you have that idea in reverse, Rachel."

I swallowed hard. "Yes… Although my memory cannot serve me correctly, I vaguely recall his unearthly screeches piercing the air as I drew more and more ichor from his body with every successful swing. His claws raked across my armor, denting and shearing the metal even as he called upon the darkness itself to ensnare and poison me."

"Relias also gave his all. He maintained the barrier of holy light that protected you from the evil toxin that fiend exuded." It was an older knight now, holding his helm under his arm as tears unabashedly shined in his eyes.

Word for word…

"The Holy Order of Blue has quite an oral tradition. I'm not surprised they've memorized the official lore."

"Tell us of your fatal strike!" yet another demanded. "That's the missing part. How did you manage to pierce through his armor?"

"His armor?" I questioned in confusion.

"Forged from the darkest of fallen stars and absorbing all holy light that touches it," the venerated knight in charge of me recited, his voice taking on a solemn tone. "It is the armor of ultimate despair."

Oh, right, *that armor*. Huh. Technically, the charged final blow went straight through his armor into his chest, where one would typically find a heart. The wound was described as gaping, with nothing behind it except sludge-like oil. But how had she managed to disable its ability to negate amity attacks? What trick did she pull?

"This is the part you have to embellish. I'd go with something powerful but vague."

I locked my jaw and set my gaze toward the horizon. *"When one faces the true abyss… the righteous do not falter, but call upon the great powers of all those who support them in their courageous endeavors."* Is that vague enough? I wished there was a system where I could have bonuses to deception.

Glancing to my side, I saw that two of them were crying openly now, tears silently streaming down their faces. Even though they were my captors, powerful knights that were dutifully carrying out the orders of a jackass, I felt a twinge of guilt. My bound and throbbing wrist, however, opposed any permanent forgiveness.

"How long until we reach Chairo?" I asked after a long silence. "It's imperative that I reunite with Relias as soon as possible." I gave you the information you wanted; now reciprocate! Are you going to rendezvous or clash with the Order of Silver? What's the next step in your action plan?

The half-dozen knights who had listened to my tale exchanged furtive glances before nodding to Volker.

"Holy Captain… we're not headed for Chairo," Volker said with a wince, having pulled the theoretical short stick.

The oldest knight bashed his fist into his chest plate, and I couldn't help but notice it was already quite dented. "We are returning to Fort Turri, where we will begin negotiations with the Holy Capital. They need to remember that *it was us* who protected them for the last three thousand years."

"…Well, shit."

My thoughts exactly.

CHAPTER 54: FALL BACK

"If you leave my wrist unattended, I may never be able to use a sword again," I boldly addressed Captain Garvith in the makeshift mess hall at my first opportunity. Volker, agreeing to support my pleas, stood at my side, visibly uncomfortable, as he maintained the binding rope securing my hands behind my back.

"Nonsense, it's a clean break," he retorted as he finished the last of his rations. "But if it fuses wrong before we exchange you, we'll just break it again."

"Are you planning to negotiate with Chairo for my release while denying me proper aid?" I asked in sheer disbelief. "Holy Sage Relias won't let you get away with this!"

"Relias… *Relias*?" Garvith mused, feigning forgetfulness as he leaned back in his seat. "That name sounds so familiar… You mean that coward who begged for my help? The one who left you in my care as a child yet constantly questioned my disciplinary approach?" He paused to take a long swig from his rusty canteen. "What do you think he'll do, petition the Assembly to write another letter of condemnation? I'll have a full dozen if he dares!"

The more decorated knights erupted in laughter, though the younger recruits shifted uncomfortably at Garvith's awful attempt at humor.

After the tent fell silent, he continued, "You and I know the Holy City would do anything to secure your return. I want what's owed. I've dedicated decades to serving my country, defending it from the clutches of darkness and vanquishing demonic beasts. And all for what?"

He jumped off his stool and started to pace with an impressive intensity. "To be told I need to be more tolerant? To consider retirement?" His voice grew more fervent. "If anything, those who make the rules need to be reminded who paves the way for their luxury!"

To my surprise, Volker, who had kept watch over me, finally spoke up. "Captain Garvith, Sir," he began hesitantly. "It's just that Captain Lightbringer requested quarter, and you accepted. However, she cannot even eat properly of her own accord."

That wasn't exactly a problem because of the splint so much as the arms bound behind my back.

"Volker." Captain Garvith turned his piercing gaze on him, his lip curling to reveal a canine. "Did you grow a spine while I wasn't looking?"

"Yes, Sir." He saluted, though his legs trembled slightly.

"Very well then," the captain said in a strangely subdued voice before turning to the man on his right. "Lieutenant Balor, go fetch Mother Sorine."

Mother Sorine's weather-beaten features made it hard to tell her actual age. Lines crinkled around the corners of her eyes, but her hair was lustrous black without a hint of gray. She wore riding leathers, but the bright star and staff pendant hanging from her neck heralded her as a priestess.

Her only command was very brief: "Arm."

Volker untied me, and I presented my right arm as requested. After removing the splint, she took my forearm in one hand as she gripped and pulled my fingers with her other, eliciting an audible crack and a wave of nauseatingly sharp pain.

"Be healed," she said in an almost bored monotone, illuminating my limb with a glowing aura. It took a few minutes, but the pain ebbed and eventually subsided. I tested my wrist cautiously, noting it was back to how it had been, although I was privately disappointed that the old scarring leading up from it to my mid forearm was still present.

"Thank you." I inclined my head to Mother Sorine and Volker, intentionally turning my back on the captain as I did so.

"Volker," the captain called as he retook his seat at the head of the table. "No need to tie her back up since you hereby assume all responsibility should *my daughter* use her abilities against us. May the price of your newly found spine be something you can afford."

As we headed west, I dozed off in the saddle at the strangest times. The relentless hours of riding had left me with a general soreness that turned quite acute in my hips and upper legs. Our route was unfamiliar, regularly featuring small hostels between wooded areas. Here, horses were hastily exchanged for fresh ones, even as local intel was shared and gathered.

Despite my weird weariness, I listened for any mention of the Order of Silver or my companions. Given that the captain had not attempted to threaten me with their lives, I assumed their escape was successful. I didn't want to think about the other extreme possibility.

Every few hours or so, I would note the return of an increasingly oppressive heaviness in the air, and I would reflexively look around each time, trying to pinpoint the conjuring culprit. Whoever they were, they were subtle and precise. Even Volker, sitting right behind me, never seemed affected.

The elder knight who had actively engaged in my story had been keeping me under a watchful eye. "Are you all right, Captain Lightbringer?" he asked at one point, his voice full of concern.

"I think—" but the words would not come out. Spell. Dark magic. Curse. Animus. Sorcerer. Runes. Demon. Demonic. Devil. Voodoo. Juju! It was like they were all locked up and inaccessible. "I'm just tired," I finished with a sigh. *What other words was I banned from using? And where had Raedine gone? She didn't even say goodbye this time...*

During the first few days, I dared not to try and cast my inner vision, but after waiting and holding my breath for intel, I couldn't hold back any longer. Was I just banned from talking about the fact that something was trying to suppress me, or was it genuinely affecting my abilities? The answer was something I couldn't wait for any longer.

If things took a turn for the worse, I would need to know what I could and couldn't do.

It was much more challenging to focus now, and it took a few minutes before anything appeared before my closed eyes, but eventually, I could see it again.

Blue had merged into a long line retreating west, but Silver was following at a steady pace. How could they not know about them at this point, though? Could they not see each other's colors?

"Gah!" Volker suddenly cried as Lieutenant Balor rode up and smashed a gauntleted fist into the side of his helmet. Even I, sitting on the horse next to him, shook from the force of the impact. I whirled around just in time to see the initial trickle of blood leak from his nose.

The captain, who I swore had been far ahead, smirked and slid his horse to the other side of mine. "Tsk, tsk. Were you trying to pick out an escape route, perhaps? Do you plan to bring Volker with you? You won't be able to protect him otherwise." He laughed coarsely for a moment before again moving to the head of the column.

Using one of his own men as a card against me now? How low could this guy go?

Once again, I ignored the captain as best I could. "Are you alright?" I asked Volker, knowing the answer. "Let's go find Mother Sorine!"

"No," Volker said as he pulled out a cloth to staunch the blood. "She won't be allowed to help me, and I wouldn't want to put her in such a position."

"I'm sorry… I…" What excuse could I give? I had been warned, and yet I did something that got him hurt.

"We'll get through this if we work together, Holy Captain," he advised quietly, suppressing what I could only imagine was irritation with me. "Let's just do as we're told."

Later that afternoon, after winding around a series of forested hills, we arrived at a large garrison. The walls of the secluded fort were made of large stone blocks, and the entrance was guarded by thick wooden doors studded with rusty iron.

Within its confines, soldiers in variable qualities of chainmail and plate armor honed their combat skills, all of which looked patchworked, as if there was no official uniform and no one could decide what color blue to wear. Off to the left, a rickety stable was half-full of contrastingly well-trained warhorses, waiting patiently for their next foray into the field.

Would my horse get to rest here? How was she doing? What… was her name again?

Volker extended his hand, and I sluggishly dismounted with his assistance. After proceeding a few steps toward the interior hall, my left leg gave out, causing me to trip.

"Careful!" He grabbed me by the shoulder. "You're just tired, right?"

"Uh… no…"

"Captain Garvith!" the ever-watchful elder knight, whose name I still hadn't learned, shouted urgently from my other side. "Something's wrong with Captain Lightbringer!"

No… don't tell him!

"What do you mean, something is—"

I never heard the rest of Captain Garvith's declaration of disbelief as I was too busy succumbing to the darkness that drained the last remnants of my consciousness.

CHAPTER 55: RESCUING CAPTAIN LIGHTBRINGER

"Awake?" Mother Sorine's blunt and to-the-point voice questioned just moments after my eyes snapped open.

"Awake," I replied, feeling disoriented while lying flat on my back in a simple cot.

"Dizzy?"

"Very." I tried telling her about the dark magic I had noticed before but again found myself unable to utter a word about it.

There was a pause as if Mother Sorine was searching for the most concise response again. "You have too much animus. You need purging."

"Purging?" I mumbled. "Will it hurt?"

"No. But I've made numerous attempts already with limited success. I'm too drained to continue now," she said, rising slowly. "Rest more. Focus on soothing thoughts. I'll do the same."

Soothing thoughts? Easier said than done when you're a captive! Glancing around the sterile room, I couldn't help but groan in disgust. The uneven stone walls were adorned with Skreethi pelts, the only decorations in the otherwise empty chamber.

"Have them take those down!" I exclaimed in weak revulsion. "Those could have been my acquaintances."

"You're acquainted with mustelids?" Mother Sorine sneered over her shoulder. "No wonder you have so much animus…"

"They had nothing to do with this. It was—" My words caught in my throat as a sudden wave of nausea threatened to bring back my last meal.

"I'll instruct the knights to remove them," she said bluntly, sweeping out of the room.

I waited impatiently in bed, tucked under stiff covers, but no one was hurrying to carry out her orders. Indistinct murmurs of conversation drifted by intermittently, too muffled to discern.

"Captain Lightbringer?" a familiar voice later questioned from the other side of the stout wooden door. "May I come in?"

I sat up slowly to avoid embarrassment. "Yes," I answered Volker.

He opened the door carefully. "Mother Sorine said to take down the decorations in here…"

"I find them in the poorest of taste," I murmured. "I've met some nice Skreethi, and seeing their skin on display is very upsetting."

"Skreethi?"

"It's practically their philosophy," I explained, trying to sound whimsical. "They're quite intelligent."

"I've never heard anyone call them either of those things before." He made a wry face as he carefully removed the skins. "Vicious… vindictive… sure, but Skreethi? No, and certainly not intelligent…"

"They have a poor reputation, but they're not bad… just…" I stumbled a bit.

"Smelly?"

"That's an understatement. But that doesn't make them *bad*."

"Bad…" he said softly. "You probably don't even see me as bad, do you?"

"Bad? You've been nothing but kind to me this whole time," I replied. "I can't find any fault in your actions."

"Sorry…" He turned and picked up the pile of pelts, pausing as he did so. "For disturbing you. Rest well."

After he departed, I curled up in the starchy sheets of the bed, trying my best to conjure up some soothing thoughts. Playing with Chester now brought up a sharp pang of homesickness, so I quickly discarded that scene from my imagination. The idea of food was equally unwelcome; there was no need to induce additional nausea. I settled on a contrived vision of the future when I'd be reunited with my friends. However, as I tried to imagine their relief at finding me safe and sound, things started crumbling apart. I knew I had made a colossal blunder, and the thought of them *not* reacting negatively to that was strangely unsettling and ultimately unrealistic.

Nora's never going to let me forget about this. Pulling the blanket over my head, I pretended once again that this was all a bad dream, and when I woke up, I'd find myself laughing sheepishly about how weird one's thoughts could get.

***

The surrounding structure convulsed as a sudden earthquake struck, waking me with a jolt as it dislodged the plaster between the previously sturdy stone blocks. Panic rose into my throat as I clung wild-eyed to my cot, trying to determine if anything above was in range of falling on me. There was always the ceiling itself, so I stumbled into my boots, making my way unsteadily to the door as the shrill cries of terrified horses and knights filled the air.

The wooden door groaned on its hinges as I slowly but forcefully pushed it open. Volker's eyes, wild with fear, suddenly appeared in view as he lunged towards me. With a frantic grasp, he seized my arm and forcefully yanked me away from the doorway.

"What's going on? How long was I out for?" I asked in bewilderment, my chest tightening, but he ignored my questions. We ran, not toward the main entrance but back into what appeared to be a giant storage area. His gauntleted fingers dug painfully into my forearm, and I pulled back to escape his grip.

"That hurts!" I exclaimed angrily. "I'll run better if you don't cause extra injury!"

He muttered a curse under his breath, and an eerie, smoky lattice of runes materialized over the clothing covering my arms and legs. "Dark puppet!" he shouted, and in an instant, my limbs were no longer under my control.

I tried my best to resist. "You…! You're the one who—"

"Puppets don't talk," he snapped as he twisted his hand with uncharacteristically cruel resolve.

"Mmmfffm!" My voice was muffled by his sudden spell that robbed me of speech.

Against my will, I became an animated human shield, taking the lead in front of him as he had me test each corner before rounding it himself. The relentless tremors continued to wrack the building, and the discordant rumbling around us grew louder, eventually climaxing in a series of deafening explosions.

"A few Silvers I could handle easily… but that crazy wench!" he spat at one point during our perilous flight. "She's too powerful to take head on…"

Oh please, let that be the crazy wench I know and love!

The observant senior knight who had watched over us earlier stepped out from a side corridor. "Captain Lightbringer, Volker! This way! We've secured the exit ahead! Wait, what's wrong with her?"

Before the knight could manifest his aura, Private Volker struck him with a pulse of dark force, knocking him into the wall before dropping him into a noisy metal heap. "Thanks for the tip, *old codger, but I'm not splitting the reward*!"

Oh, I really know how to pick 'em, don't I?

As we made our way down the long hallway, the latest explosion's reverberation disappeared, displaced by the sharp, continuous clash of steel against steel in the distance.

"I thought he said the exit was secure?" Volker asked aloud, confused by the barricaded door before us. He gestured, but his repeated force blast only cracked it open slightly.

Then, an oh-so-familiar voice came through the door with a snide shout: "Here, let me help you with that!"

Could it really be—

An instant later, the entire rear wall of the building disintegrated into the finest grains of sand, taking the door with it. As the hazy air cleared before us, I coughed and saw two figures cast in silhouette. With her staff raised in a commanding gesture, the shorter figure undoubtedly belonged to Nora, who was panting heavily from her recent efforts. Yet, the other, tall and slender, appeared unfamiliar and did not seem to align with anyone I knew.

"If you want your champion back safe and sound, you better meet my demands!" Volker shouted before the dust fully cleared, jerking me back behind him. "First, you'll provide me with a fresh warhorse and full saddlebag of—" his demands cut off suddenly as Nora somehow set the garments under his mail plate ablaze with an imperious jab of her staff. Luckily, he panicked and threw himself on the ground, distracted by what I could only imagine was searing pain.

Meanwhile, a gold-glowing magic circle materialized under my feet, lighting the ground clockwise. As its two ends met, I felt a flowing surge of energy course through me, restoring my strength and granting me full control over my body once again.

"Rachel Emily Smith, get out of my sight this instant. Before I decide to punish you, too!" Nora screeched at me, gesturing to the right, her dark mage orb ablaze with an angry purple glow. I glanced with apprehension first at Nora, then at the somewhat smoldering Private Volker, and finally to the remarkably tall, handsome, blonde-haired man standing at her right-hand side.

Gawk later, Rachel!

"Y…yes ma'am…" I gulped and got out of the direct line of fire.

"Lady Nora," the priest standing by her side bowed deeply. "While I stand in profound admiration of your formidable powers, I humbly beseech you to *grant me* the privilege of tempering the sword of justice with the fires of compassion and mercy." His harmonious but somewhat windy speech contained a hint of barbed resolve as if he had been personally insulted by Volker himself.

Nora's stony face hardened even more as she turned to him. "You better not let him off with a warning," she declared with a hiss. "If he went this far, what's to stop him from doing it again?"

"I solemnly promise you, dear lady, that he will never find himself in such a situation to *act as such* again."

While still writhing on the ground, Volker managed to turn towards the duo. "You? Impossible!" he shrieked, scrambling away.

The young-looking priest focused on Volker, extending his hands outward as a radiant aura enveloped him. His robes began to billow with an ascending whirlwind of air as his long blonde hair flared outward from his shoulders. "Rejoice, Volker, for today, your Purpose has been fulfilled. Surrender your burdensome implements, and embrace a well-deserved retirement, free from toil until Her Supreme Holiness beckons you to cross her threshold."

He was as long-winded as he was handsome, but *Goddess* did he sound cool.

Now pinned in place by a gold magic circle under his feet, Volker screamed in fear as wisps of inky vapor emanated from his trembling form. They converged into the priest's outstretched palm, coalescing into a ponderous, swirling sphere of darkness. The priest's fingers slowly closed around the ethereal void, extinguishing it with his shining golden aura.

As I witnessed Volker's tortured tantrums upon losing his dark magic abilities, his froth-tinged lips contorted in madness. "Damn you, Relias, damn you!" Volker wailed in howling anguish as he frantically clawed at the unyielding stones beneath him, his fingertips stained with his blood. "I wish I had never sworn my loyalty to you!"

That's... him? The cover art didn't do him justice. But why... how... For a few moments, I forgot how to exhale.

"If only you had remained true to your oath and service, none of this would have transpired," Holy Sage Relias replied with a heavy sigh, his sorrowful expression causing my heart to pound. "Your greed led you astray, inflicting unwarranted pain upon the one I hold most dear."

CHAPTER 56: A HERO'S WORTH

Holy Sage Relias, First of Men, Herald of Euphridia, Guide of Humanity, approached us with a slow, confident stride. His golden sandals stirred up tiny dust clouds as his white robes billowed in a recurring gust of wind.

Volker, noticing his determined advance, scrambled to his feet and dashed off towards a distant tree line, swearing and stumbling incoherently. Letting him escape might not have been wise, but after all that transpired, he seemed even less of a threat than a fleeing coward. Relias's azure gaze followed the man momentarily, but a subtle shrug signaled he wasn't interested in pursuit either.

As Relias closed the distance between us, a sharp pang of guilt rose in my chest as if I had committed a grave wrong against him. *What is* he *doing here? He's supposed to be locked up in Chairo, and I should be rescuing* him! And I have no idea what Nora or the others told him about me…

"Raelynn…" He smiled, his face radiating pure joy. "Deep in my heart, I held onto the hope that someday we'd reunite!"

Oh no! They didn't tell him anything.

I glanced at Nora but quickly realized I wasn't in a position to ask for her immediate intervention. *That glare alone could turn me to stone…*

"I'm not… I'm not who you think I am!" I blurted in sudden confession, taking a reasonable three steps back. "There's been a misunderstanding!" I emphasized my statement by holding my hands out in front of me.

He paused mid-step, slowly lowering his outstretched hands. "Yes… yes, I can see that," he murmured, a crestfallen look settling over his aquiline features.

A lump formed in my throat, threatening to activate that awful cranial nerve responsible for tears of sorrow. "I'm so sorry; I know you were expecting her, but—"

"It's alright." He smiled wistfully, folding his hands together in front of him. "We can talk later when it's safe. I'm sure there's more to the situation than either of us fully realize."

Glancing between him and Nora, a complete contrast in adoration and irritation, I steadied myself. "Are the others all safe?"

"Yes!" Relias bobbed his head enthusiastically as if recalling his fateful reunion with them.

I missed that, too! *Gaaaah!*

Nora continued her chilly scowl. "*We're all accounted for, now.*"

At least I wasn't getting reprimanded in front of him…

I let out an ill-timed sigh of relief just as a loud rumble punctuated the air. The Orders of Silver and Blue spilled onto the fields farther in front of us from either side, charging forward with a screeching cacophony of steel and shouts. The first clash was the loudest, locking dozens of men into their final struggles.

"Isn't there some way we can stop all this?" I asked them both in desperation. "I'm okay now!"

"They were to be given the option to surrender, but it seems Captain Garvith refused." Relias shook his head sadly.

"But the others aren't responsible for all of this…" I frowned as I watched bodies on both sides fall limp to the ground. Some writhed and moaned after their descent, while others remained motionless. The deafening roar of battle increased, though many defiant shouts turned into screams of pain.

"Rae," Nora replied sternly as she folded her arms, holding back even harsher words. "*It's too late now.* Both forces are already fully engaged. You can't just say 'never mind' at this point!"

I cringed at the realization that this whole conflict was centered around me. *This is all my fault…*

"The most prudent course of action would be to safeguard ourselves and provide aid when possible," Relias replied, pointing to a sturdy warehouse off to the east. "I suggest we take refuge there."

As we made our way towards the sanctuary, I heard, perhaps felt, the twang of a crossbow bolt launching from the nearby bushes. "Get down!" I screamed at Relias even as I left him no choice, tackling him from the side with a strong-armed clothesline maneuver. Thankfully, the crossbow bolt missed, and only then did I realize I had landed next to him, just inches from his striking face. *There wasn't a single flaw to be found...*

Almost absently, I noted Nora retaliated on our behalf, unleashing a searing blast of Ignis upon the bushes that had attacked us. The magical fire engulfed the undergrowth and whoever hid in it, sending them off into the distance with a scream and a smoky trail lingering in their wake. Whoever it was, they were no official knight from either side.

"Uh, that was unintentional!" I gasped, realizing I had been gazing at him now for far too long.

"Saving my life... was unintentional?" Relias asked as he sat up, blinking twice before returning the look while rubbing his head.

"N-no, just... never mind..." I stammered, rising quickly. My hand trembled as I reached out to help him off the ground. "Sorry for knocking you down so hard... I guess I don't know my own strength..."

He rose to his feet with my help. "Feel free to execute a suplex maneuver on me whenever fate demands it," he quipped with a tiny grin, his cheeks taking on a rosy hue. He then released my grip to conjure a golden barrier, shielding us. "I should have established this protection sooner; I believe I was somewhat... preoccupied..." he trailed off with a sidelong glance. "My apologies..."

Waving off his unnecessary remorse, I shut my eyes again and surveyed the warehouse and its immediate vicinity using my amity. "No blues here," I confirmed before we advanced together, eventually reaching the warehouse door. Nora, wielding a set of lockpicks that likely once belonged to Vernie, swiftly disabled the lock. After taking a deep breath, I cautiously advanced.

"Hold it," Nora snapped, pushing me away before I could cross the threshold. "There could be others around like that archer, and you're not wearing any protection!" Her concern for my safety remained despite her evident frustration with me.

"Right…" I mumbled as she tossed a ball of light into the darkness. She glanced around furtively for a few moments before waving all clear. Entering carefully, I noted that the warehouse racks were strikingly bare, though here and there was a large wooden box or a barrel marked as ale. Tossed into one dusty side corner was… "My sword and shield! Oh, and my… *bo staff*…" It had been broken into several pieces and tossed in a nearby bin with what appeared to be large bits of kindling. *That was a precious gift, you bastards!* I picked through the pieces, but the blessing was long gone…

Where was my armor? I glanced around a bit before eyeing an extended workbench with several parcels, the last of which was unwrapped, exposing my chest plate. Stuffed inside the box was a lock of my hair and a verbose yet mocking ransom note. I picked it up and read.

> To the Illustrious Councilmen of the Holy Church of Euphridia,
>
> Be advised we have taken into our protective custody an individual of some repute, none other than your proclaimed hero, previously thought missing by those who call themselves the All-knowing Authority of the Church.
>
> This action was not taken lightly but with great deliberation, fueled by the necessity that we, as devoted servants of the Goddess and her followers, remain without resource or reward since the final campaigns waged upon the original demon king's forces over seven years ago. We continue without budget, without adequate equipment, and without representation in the Holy City. Yet, we are expected to defend and protect as we have since the formation of our Order over three thousand years ago. To rectify this administrative oversight and make things once again right, we demand no less than the immediate delivery of one hundred gold bars of

exceptional purity that meet international trade standards and weights sent forth to Fort Turri, where the bulk of our Order shall receive and authenticate due tribute.

Failure to meet our terms will inevitably harm the hero irrevocably—an outcome we hope to avoid at all costs. To help validate our claims, please find enclosed a piece of the Chosen One's missing armor and a lock of hair, which I am sure your holy priests can authenticate.

We trust this note has enlightened you with newly found wisdom and understanding of the situation at hand. The path forward lies up to you, and we await your decision. To hold your attention, we will continue to send you pieces of the Chosen One's ensemble. With all *due* respect,

Knight Captain Garvith, Holy Order of Blue

I crushed the ransom note in my left hand even as my right searched my hair in vain for the location where they had snipped the lock. "Money…" I grated my teeth. *They were just selling me!* They weren't looking to fix anything long-term through negotiations; they just wanted their cut! Even if they did cough up the cash, the Church certainly wasn't going to take their pleas for resources seriously in the future.

"I had been informed of their exorbitant demands previously…" Relias murmured after gently tugging the note from my hand to scan it. "However, my expectations were such that Councilman Procul would have successfully brokered a swift resolution with the Order by now…" He glanced at me with a rather bashful expression. "A hundred gold bars is not a bad deal, all things considered…"

The remark was probably meant to distract me from my irritation, but I wasn't in the mood for banter. "So they've been raising a stink for a while, I take it?" I snorted.

"Raising… a stink?" Relias looked lost. "Oh yes, the avaricious pursuit of the malodorous mustelids…" He scratched his cheek for a moment.

Av… avaricious?

He shook his head, still seemingly confused but unperturbed. "Nora spoke at length regarding that earlier. Worry not. I will issue a writ of condemnation for such acts as soon as possible."

Oof. Garvith got that one right about him…

"Thank you… but that's not what I meant." I sighed. "I mean… they've been causing a commotion about funding for quite some time," I clarified, realizing my own speech fell well short of his high-level vernacular.

See? I was not nearly as classy as Raelynn.

"Oh, then yes. Quite the odorous commotion, to say the least. Though I believe all of their recent alternative funding schemes are nothing but a ruse to garner sympathy," he replied as I began ripping open the parcels and equipping myself again with their contents. He watched me for a few moments in silence before questioning, "Raelynn?"

"Rachel," I swiftly corrected, belting my sword and sheath. *He's obviously in denial!*

"Rae," he whispered in concession. "You're not planning to venture forth, are you?"

I was preparing to defend us should it become necessary. But get in the middle of two armies fighting over budgetary funding and emotional saddle sores? No thanks.

Relias fidgeted with a parcel for a moment. "I believe it best to let Captain Corwin handle this," he finally advised.

"Corwin?" I asked in momentary confusion. "Who's he? Captain of the Silver?"

Relias nodded. "I have the utmost confidence in his military prowess and command of his knights. I am sure he will find a way to have the Blue capitulate without unnecessary bloodshed…" He looked at me then, curiosity burning in his eyes. "Perhaps we can distract ourselves with pleasant conversation while waiting for his all-clear?"

We had a lot to talk about. How did he know we were here? What was his relationship with Volker? How did he escape his penitential prison? The temporary peace the warehouse granted was not a long-term guarantee, however, even if he could use his powers to barricade us in safely. "Alright, but I don't want to be caught off—"

The warehouse door suddenly reverberated with urgent, frantic knocks. *It was like karma was waiting for me to say it!*

"It's one of the Blue," I confirmed with my inner vision as I instinctively reached for my sword.

"Captain Lightbringer! Please!" The panicked, somewhat wheezy voice belonged unmistakably to the older knight who had been assaulted by Volker earlier.

I grimaced with guilt. "Hold on, I know this one… he's in no condition to fight us." After double-checking that he was alone with a slow blink of my eyes, I sighed and put my hand on the door. "Don't try anything funny!" I warned before cautiously pulling it open.

He stumbled in, fighting through his unseen injuries, making it only a few steps before collapsing to the floor. "Captain Lightbringer, I beseech you. You must intervene! The captains are locked in a duel to the death, right in the heart of the battlefield!" His eyes, wide with urgency, sought mine, conveying the gravity of the situation.

I glanced back at my visibly shocked allies, feeling a heavy lump in my throat.

CHAPTER 57: STAND DOWN

Why me? Out of *all* those gathered here, why did this elder knight think I would be the voice of reason between a disgruntled soldier of fortune and a veritable stranger? "Sir…"

"Armand," he wheezed. "Though my name matters not. Please, you're the only one Captain Garvith might listen to!"

"I seriously doubt that!" I retorted anxiously.

"Corwin has resorted to single combat?" Relias frowned, crossing his arms. "His initial strategy was divisions from a distance, isolating the core from its ranks until they were compelled to capitulate." He locked his arms behind his back and began to pace. "The diversions were meant to provide Nora and I with an opportunity to execute our rescue mission, the outcome of which Corwin remains unaware. To shift tactics at this juncture implies a significant loss of control…"

"Wait!" I shouted in sudden realization. "Vernie, Tetora, and Aleph are with him too, aren't they?" There was no way they'd sit idly by, and Garvith had no problem targeting the others for collateral damage.

"While I have nothing but pure faith in them," Relias began, his voice tinged with concern, "they were indeed among the many in Captain Corwin's entourage."

Nora, Relias, and I exchanged glances, a mutual understanding passing between us as we moved toward the door. "Wait," I said. "What about him?" Armand perched himself against the wall, but pain was clear on his face.

"Just go…" He exhaled. "I'll be fine. I can tend to these wounds myself. I've taken far worse before."

I looked at Relias for some kind of confirmation. Relias observed him for a moment, then said, "His injuries are grave but not life-threatening. I suggest we consider triage and tend to the more urgent matter at hand. Many more may die while we linger here."

I looked uncertainly between the door and Armand, then reassured him, "We'll be back with help. I promise!"

With that, we sprinted to a nearby stable, where we promptly secured a trio of wild-eyed war horses. It only took a few moments to get them under control before riding off towards the sound of thundering clashes. I focused on my breathing, willing my amity to infuse me and my armor with the best it could offer. Relias's nimble fingers conjured a golden canopy over our heads as we rode. Some kind of protection spell, I assumed.

"Do you think Garvith called for reinforcements?" Nora shouted as our horses galloped across the field towards the convulsing armies.

"Perhaps," Relias answered. "However, Corwin is rather… passionate about his beliefs and has denounced Captain Garvith several times in recent seasons…"

"So, it was likely a personal loss of control then, not a strategic one…" Nora noted with a grunt. I knew what that was like, and Garvith was precisely the type to set off a proverbial powder keg.

"Most likely." Relias exhaled, shaking his head. "Corwin is young and stubborn. Life has not yet tamed him."

I referenced my inner vision to guide us and led the way towards a large group of Silver. We soon approached, with Relias bellowing, "Clear the way! Let us through!" After several startled looks, the entourage melted away to either side, revealing the two captains already in mid-duel. Our horses halted in unison, granting us the perfect dramatic dismount. A cursory glance across the battlefield revealed my other lost companions weren't immediately present.

Turning to Nora, I started to ask, "Where do you think—"

"Pay attention!" she barked, pointing at Relias.

"Cease this battle at once!" he proclaimed thunderously, conjuring a gold staff out of thin air as more eyes turned to him. While there were still a few skirmishes among the iron-clad crowd, most had stopped to stare in awe at the two legendary captains trading glowing blows with near-identical halberds. Captain Garvith, fully armored with a surcoat and cape of brilliant blue, showed no signs of stopping. The other captain, garbed in a black surcoat embellished with silver threads depicting Her Supreme Holiness's celestial star, grudgingly gave up ground.

"Euphridia's Herald beckons you to stop, old man!" Captain Corwin rebuked, his voice an octave higher than I imagined it would be. "Or have your wits left you entirely?"

"All know he no longer hears her voice nor speaks her will!" Garvith roared. "Only the truly ignorant would put faith in such a powerless incompetent!"

I glanced nervously at Relias, but he simply settled his staff on the ground before him, his face serene yet resolute. "Captain Corwin, do all that is necessary to swiftly conclude this conflict for those bound to witness its inevitable outcome."

Was Corwin *that* good?

With newly found determination, Captain Corwin's aura shifted from mere sparkles of glitter to that of holy lightning crackling along the edges of his form. He surged forward with inhuman speed, swinging the halberd faster than I could follow initially, streaking the air with a silver sheen.

Could I get my aura to do something like that?

Despite Corwin's swift, aggressive movements, Captain Garvith skillfully intercepted and disengaged each blow with his azure aura of flames, which flared anew as it unleashed a resounding boom with each successful counter. The deafening impact of their attacks drowned out all other sights and sounds, forcing the onlookers to watch helplessly.

Anxiously, I pulled my arms around myself. *He'll give up eventually, right? It might take a few blows, but he'll realize this isn't how he can get what he wants!* I briefly tore my gaze away from the two, looking at the other soldiers scattered before us. Captain Garvith… might have had a point about resources. The Order of Blue's equipment was severely lacking. Several of the soldiers' ensembles were ill-fitting and slapdash, with substandard patching. In contrast, the Order of Silver appeared as if each knight had been measured and fitted with the best a master blacksmith could offer.

A sharp cry from Captain Corwin caught my attention. Garvith's blazing blue halberd had penetrated his aura, catching him just above his navel. Corwin stumbled back even as he deflected a second blow before righting himself, the ground cracking slightly underneath his sabatons. Though his armor was dented from the assault, nothing was showing through. "Enough, old man!" he bellowed in pain. "This is your last chance for surrender!"

"Surrender?" Garvith slammed his halberd with both hands into Corwin's weapon to try and knock him back further. "To endure what little life I have left in derision and destitution? I'd sooner perish now, upholding my convictions!"

Why did I care so much about what would happen to this senile old fool? "Captain Garvith!" I found myself screaming. "Why must you always go to such extremes!?"

As was typical, he did not even acknowledge me. Not once had he ever listened to what I had to say. *Students can't teach the teacher. You are only a vessel to impart knowledge to. Don't question. Absorb, retain, demonstrate, and survive, all to do it again.*

Captain Garvith's flames began to flicker, almost imperceptibly at first, as his endurance evaporated. Corwin's calculated strikes slowed somewhat, now focusing on more vulnerable spots like Garvith's head, neck, and other briefly exposed gaps in his defenses. Garvith seemed unaware of his dwindling fire, still trying to hook Corwin in close for a lethal embrace. His efforts were eventually rewarded as he yanked his halberd back after lodging into the back of Corwin's left pauldron. Instead of resisting, however, Corwin discarded his own halberd, swiftly grabbing Garvith's polearm midshaft while drawing his short sword sidearm.

Captain Garvith's left underarm came exposed in the grapple—an opening Corwin seized with deadly precision. Both orders let out a collective gasp as the short sword disappeared halfway into his side. Captain Garvith stumbled back, momentarily glancing at the wound before falling. Even as he hit the ground, neither side of the conflict celebrated, the air suddenly heavy with a solemn silence. Corwin took a step back, his expression a mix of triumph and regret as he sheathed his blade.

Captain Garvith coughed, then gritted his teeth, even now steeling himself with resolve. He raised his arm weakly and beckoned to his adversary. "Remove my helmet, Captain Corwin, and set me upright."

Captain Corwin knelt, respectfully helping him into a kneeling position before pulling off his helm, exposing Garvith's sickly grey face as bright red blood gushed down through the openings of his chest plate. His eyes searched, unfocused, as he grabbed Corwin's hand. "Take my final lesson to heart, Brother. Ensure you're justly rewarded for all your loyal efforts." He closed his eyes then, turning his face directly toward me. "And you, Daughter. See now that self-sacrifice is truly worthless! This is my last lesson to you. Learn it well before you fall for it again yourself!" It was the *last thing* I ever expected to hear him say, further disrupting my confusion about what relationship we ever had.

I would have pushed Relias forward had he not already sprinted to the fallen knight, his hands glowing pure white.

"No," Captain Garvith croaked as he slumped to the side, drawing upon the last embers of his aura to repel Relias. "I refuse your aid. It is too little, too late, as always." It seemed like he let out a single laugh, although, in hindsight, it could have been his final death rattle as Knight Captain Garvith of the Holy Order of Blue.

The last thing I could do at that moment was cry. He would have *hated* that, showing such a weakness in public. Besides, many others had also died. If I shed a tear for him, I would have to do it for each of those who lost their lives that day.

"Captain Garvith's helmet, Captain Lightbringer." Captain Corwin presented it to me in a solemn ritual. Without any other choice, I took it with shaking hands.

"It's heavier than it looks," I murmured, not knowing what else to say.

"Forgive me, Captain Lightbringer." Relias knelt before me. "I was unable to save him."

"There's nothing to forgive," I said in a low voice, clutching the helmet to my chest, its broken blue and white plume cascading down my arm. *What point was he trying to make with this obvious suicide by cop? Get paid for your efforts? Don't sacrifice yourself? But he did just that only to teach me a lesson?*

"Please command your troops to stand down, Chosen One," Captain Corwin begged in a whisper. "I do not wish any more blood of my brothers to be shed."

I glanced at him in surprise, taking a moment to register his words. "These soldiers don't see me as…" But as I looked, every member of the Blue who remained standing had removed their helmet to lock their joyless, fearful eyes on me, waiting for my command. *Shouldn't they be looking to Lieutenant Balor? Where is he, anyway?*

With a tremulous inhale, I turned toward the largest group of Blue and shouted, "Order of Blue! *I, Raelynn Lightbringer, Knight Captain of the Holy Order of Gold, Chosen One of the Goddess, and Seventh Appointed Hero of Legend, hereby order you to stand down!*" I paused, fist clenched at my side. In a lower voice, I solemnly repeated the order. "…Stand down."

As I stood there, knees weak and heart heavy, I could see the soldiers begin to lower their weapons, the armor-clad bodies slowly returning to their neutral positions. Some wept openly, some remained stoic and silent, and a few even sat down on the battlefield, unable to process all that had happened.

Against my own will, I had just announced a questionable hero's return at the end of the battle, not only unable to prevent its inevitable tragic outcome, but serving as the catalyst that had ignited the bloody violence in the first place.

***

Here ends *A Hero Returned*, Book I of The Last Rae of Hope.
Please join us in Book II, entitled *Order of Gold*, where Rae and her
companions finally arrive in the Holy City of Chairo, where more
than just one adversary awaits them.

AFTERWORD

As I type this afterword for Book I of *The Last Rae of Hope*, I find myself reflecting on the journey that led to the creation of this story. What began as a series of scattered thoughts and absurd ambitions to challenge and maybe even dismantle some of the uncomfortable truths we face both in reality and in the realms of fantasy has since blossomed into the first part of a story that I hope has been both entertaining and a little thought-provoking.

This novel, which found its first steps on Royal Road in April 2023, was born from a desire to intertwine satire and storytelling in a way that shines a light on the flawed systems that both govern our lives and the fantastical worlds we escape to. Satire, by its nature, is meant to cause discomfort, to prod us into recognition of the nonsense that lies in what we consider normal processes, and ultimately push us toward the realization that we can, indeed, aspire to do better.

Throughout *The Last Rae of Hope*, I do try to keep a bit of comedy with the critique, aiming not just to entertain but to illuminate the often-unseen consequences of the systems we navigate daily. This story is meant to assert that while individuals *can and do* make mistakes (and goodness, have I made a lot of them even on my own), it is the systems in which we operate that often pave the way for these errors, guiding us unwittingly toward outcomes we neither desired nor intended. Sure, an *extreme outlier* here or there may wake up one morning, intentionally deciding to be the villain of the story, but far more often, we grab our pitchforks for a witch hunt that has no witch.

Writing this book is just the beginning of a journey of self-discovery, not only of the story's characters and their world but also of my own thoughts and beliefs about society, responsibility, and the power of understanding and directing change. It is my hope that as you follow the adventures, misadventures, and revelations within these pages and those volumes to come, you find moments of laughter, reflection, and perhaps even a spark of inspiration to question and challenge the systems you find yourself a part of.

At its heart, *The Last Rae of Hope* is a call to look beyond the surface, to see beyond individuals' blame and shame, and to consider the larger systems at play. It's an invitation to recognize that while we may not be able to overhaul these systems overnight, we can each play a part in initiating change just by asking one question, offering one challenge, or even laughing one uncomfortable laugh at a time.

I want to extend my deepest gratitude to all of you for embarking on this roundabout journey with me. Your engagement, thoughts, and reflections have been invaluable. The road ahead is long, and the systems we navigate are tediously complex, but together, we can continue to hope, challenge, and dream of a world made better by our collective, continuous efforts.

Thank you for your time, your mind, and your heart. Here's to the adventures that await us in the next book.

Follow us:

riverfolkbooks.com

Facebook /riverfolkp

Bluesky /riverfolkbooks.bsky.social

Instagram /riverfolkp

If you want to discuss our books with other readers and maybe even the author, join our discord server using the link on our website

www.ingramcontent.com/pod-product-compliance
Lightning Source LLC
Chambersburg PA
CBHW051133300726
48978CB00011B/264